Notes
from the Future

N. Amosoff

Translated from the Russian by GEORGE ST. GEORGE
(By special arrangement with the author.)

SIMON AND SCHUSTER ▪ NEW YORK

First U.S. printing

SBN 671-20547-1
Library of Congress Catalog Card Number: 77-107270
Designed by Edith Fowler
Manufactured in the United States of America
by H. Wolff Book Mfg. Co., Inc., New York

Part One

i
A Difficult Evening

Everything is clear. Leucosis. Leukemia. In my case this means a year, perhaps two. The world is naked and cruel. It seems to me that I have never seen it this way before. I thought I had understood everything, learned everything, and was ready. But I am not ready at all.

I come to the window. It is miserably damp outside. December, but without snow or frost. How strange the trees are—black, thin branches without a single leaf. Everything has been swept away by the wind. Nothing is left. Dead leaves are whirling in the wet sky. People are hurrying on under street lights. In black overcoats.

There is no point in my being in a hurry now. I must nurse every minute. No, every second. I must hold it in my hand and then release it. With regret. In the basket of time my supply has been drastically diminished. And not a second of it can be taken back. Once it's gone, it's gone.

Enough of high-sounding phrases. Throughout our lives we are play-acting a little. Even with ourselves.

There it is—the lab report, under the lamp. A mere scrap of paper with a death sentence on it. Leucocytes—hundreds of thousands. And the whole set of pathological forms in blood corpuscles.

It was a difficult moment for David today. One cannot help feeling sorry for him. It is good that I am working with dogs. Have been working.

"Your blood is not in good shape, Ivan. You'd better take care of yourself."

Neither of us had used the word—leucosis. I played the fool, and he probably thought, Thank God, he does not understand.

Liuba knows nothing yet. There will be reproaches. "Why didn't you go sooner? How many times have I asked you to!"

Everyone dies alone. Terminal loneliness. Not a bad definition.

It is good that I have no one. Almost no one. Of course, it will be hard on Liuba; but then she has her own family. Responsibilities. She must pretend, keep herself in check. When one suppresses one's emotions for a long time, they actually disappear. A law of physiology.

Well, at least now we need not resolve our problem. We have been putting it off. "Let's wait another year. . . . The children will grow up and understand it better. . . ." I had been afraid of the moment when we would have to face it.

Now it will not be necessary. We can go on like this to the end. A sick man . . . No one would blame me too much. And then we have been seeing each other so little of late. Probably my illness had something to do with it. But I used to wonder: Why? Is our love fading away? Have we got too used to it? After all these years?

Yes, everyone dies alone.

But why must it be me, of all people? There are so many others. I have so much to do yet. So much.

Probably my experiments with isotopes has helped this thing along. "Peaceful" atoms! Why haven't I let others mess around with them?

Stop! How would you feel if Yura got it?

I must insist on everyone's taking his blood test tomorrow.

Just like the old Gypsy song: "Coachman, don't whip the horses . . . I've nowhere to hurry, I've no one to love . . ."

Why do we know so little? Cancer, leukemia—these problems are facing us just as they were twenty years ago. Chemistry? Viruses? Radiation? It will be solved. Quite soon. I am sure of it. They are attacking it at the very core now—the mechanics of cell division. But all this is too late for me now.

There is no point in my reading up on leucosis. I must depend on David. A good doctor, a good friend. I found enough in the *Medical Encyclopedia.* "From one to two years . . ." The more you know about your condition, the more you feel it. Yesterday I felt nothing. Well, almost nothing. And today—here we are!— that dull pain under the ribs, sore gums, a bit of dizziness. Now I will be listening to my body.

They are experimenting with spinal-cord transplants. I must look up those articles . . .

And suppose I astonish everybody and get well? Then, one day, I will walk into the laboratory without that time bomb inside me ticking away the seconds . . .

Stop dreaming, my friend. Better get used to your new status. Death. An ugly word.

I am so sorry for myself. I wish Liuba would come in, comfort me a little. Stroke my head.

Should I call her at home? No. Not yet. Let's not have unnecessary dramatics.

What a strange feeling. As though I have been walking along a smooth path. And suddenly—an abyss. I thought that there was such and such town just ahead, such and such station, and suddenly nothing. Just a few meters of dusty road with a few miserable little flowers growing here and there. And no turning back.

And why turn back? What good was it? Don't be a fool. There has been much good in it. Very much.

Let's walk a bit. Seven paces—from the desk to the chest of drawers. There and back. There and back. There is no one I can leave my things to. No one? And what about the boys in the lab? They will have their own little library, their own furniture for a room to relax in.

Near the bookshelf there are my souvenirs under the glass. What to do with them? The little donkey from Istanbul. The Statue of Liberty from New York. The she-wolf nursing Romulus and Remus. The little gargoyle from Notre Dame. The memories: congresses, conventions, speeches, applause; the hum of receptions . . . All this will go with me.

Those cells in the spinal cord are multiplying rapidly. I can see them—splitting up, one after another, one after another, and plunging into the bloodstream. Flooding me.

I feel like screaming—"Help!"

How difficult it is to be alone.

Call Leonid perhaps? He knows nothing yet. We could talk. I could complain a little to him.

And then? What could he say besides the usual trite words? Words which he would hate to say. And what can he do? Get drunk perhaps?

No. It is best to talk to no one about this. Only to David. At least while there is still freedom of will.

There will be those last weeks, of course. I'll have to go into the hospital. That part I don't like at all. I know what it means—I have been both a patient and a doctor.

No. I'd better stay at home for as long as possible. But what about food and care? Of course, my friends and the laboratory girls will come to visit me. (Liuba will not be able to come very often even then.) They will have a lot of trouble with me, all of them.

No. It's best to go to the hospital after all. At least there you can close your eyes and say, "I am tired." Immediate relief in all the faces. Their duty is done. They can go.

The window again. The black, naked branches. The wind.

Loneliness.

I thought I was used to it, even liked it—no one to interfere with my life. But now this is sad.

This can't be true! It is impossible that there is no help, no way out! People never believe in death. And then a doctor just spreads his arms and says guiltily, "There's nothing to be done. Nothing."

A cup of coffee? The reflex—it is ten o'clock. Then I can work for three more hours. Work? What for? But let's have some coffee nevertheless.

My household is in first-class shape. The best coffee. The coffee mill is a mechanical marvel. The Hungarian coffee maker. An ideal contraption for a bachelor.

Perhaps all this is a dream? Twice in my life I dreamed that I had cancer. And then I woke up. "God, how wonderful!"

I am waiting until the water boils. Just waiting. It would have been better to drink some vodka, but unfortunately, I have never liked it. It would have come in handy now. A stiff drink and then to bed.

What a pleasant aroma. Coffee builds up optimism.

My friend, you are supposed to be a scientist. This is the important thing—to go on being a scientist. One is supposed to be able to sort everything out, to put each item into its proper compartment, study the correlation of things, work out systems and theories. And of course, a scientist must have courage, must keep a firm hold on himself.

Wait a moment! Wipe away your tears, blow your nose. You are not dying yet. Not quite yet.

Let's try to face the situation soberly. "In the face of inevitable death—" No, no phrases. It is better to sit down, take a piece of paper and a pencil, the way I have always done.

The given factors: myself and my illness. The optimum problem: to find the best way of living out the remaining span of life with the maximum of pleasure and minimum of suffering.

Let's mark it all down. I am a well-known professor of physiology. I am forty-seven years old. Had I completed my work, I would have made an important contribution to medical science.

I could have completed this work long ago and be an academician today, had I not spread myself around so much. Remember it? All the mistakes, all the wasted years. If I could only have those years now!

Too late to start whining. . . . Perhaps they will still discover something new . . . Stop!

And now, will there be any "contribution"? Yes. How sure are you?

Quite sure. Everything is really here: methods, techniques, the collective. My team. All those boys and girls. First-class workers—pleasant, solid.

Back to the theme. The maximum of pleasure. The sources: (a) creative work, accomplishment . . .

Any creative work? No, only that which benefits humanity. What? Are you ashamed of the fact that theoreticians give so little to working doctors? But then, they are also strange—they accept primitive interpretations, mistakes. No, don't judge them. It is more difficult for them; their patients die. Just remember your own past.

October, 1942. A young graduate physician at an army base hospital. The first month of practical work. Overlooks a gaseous gangrene. In the morning the chief surgeon amputates the hip. The patient dies. "Not good, Ivan. Not good at all." I will remember this for as long as I live. Why didn't he slap my face instead?

Back to work. So we want to benefit humanity. Now, how much of it is "love of humanity" and how much pride of accomplishment? I don't know. About fifty-fifty. Perhaps the latter predominates just a little.

The sources of pleasure: (b) books; the theater; good food; a hot bath . . .

Yes, all this, but not that much. All this is pleasant on Saturday when you are tired. But during the vacation—tedium. Nothing to do. No interests.

You are lying, my friend. Just wait till you are dying. "Just one cup of coffee more . . . just to look at the fire again . . . listen to the surf . . ."

I don't know. I'm not dying yet.

What else? Love?

Well, not so successful here. It just hasn't worked out with me. Unpleasant to remember. Only now do I have—Liuba.

My dear one. My only one. She is close to forty. Her children are already big, but to me she's just a little girl. She is always good—when she is sad and when she is gay. "She has the eyes of a gazelle." I haven't seen any gazelles in my life, but their eyes should be like hers. And the most important point: she is intelligent. Often I think that I know her mental "ceiling," and then, suddenly, she will come out with another brilliant flash. Had she been more ambitious and had more time, she could have been a professor. Without any doubt. And her character? Well, she has a quick temper; she flares up, then, the next day, a telephone call: "You know, I was wrong." And as a woman? Unfortunately I am not an expert. Not enough experience.

The most banal words suddenly shine and scintillate when I am thinking about her.

It is really too bad; she will have no one anymore. And then, her husband. I've never felt any jealousy toward him, but for her this is difficult.

"The source of pleasure . . ." No; wrong words. "The source of suffering," perhaps.

And still, my friend, you are lying, even in your present state.

You have been getting more than you have been giving. And you have been a bit of a coward. And an egotist. Do you remember how, a few years ago, everything could have been done? Paul was drinking and carrying on with other women; the children felt it, and they would have gone away with Liuba.

And you? You were a weakling. All those mumblings—"Not yet . . . let's wait a little." You were simply afraid to lose your freedom. It is as simple as that. A confirmed bachelor. You were afraid that someone would interfere with your thinking, would claim your attentions and care. It was so comfortable: love, plus intellectual discussions. A secret affair colors everything in romantic hues. The rest of the time you could browse among your books and formulas, dream up theories, argue with Leonid and others around a bachelor table.

In other words, you have been skimming the cream.

And for her it has been very difficult: work, the children, and the constant deceit.

Your defense—"She came to me on her own"—is not worth a damn. She fell in love. Had you been honest, you would have kept her with you. But then you did not want to get married, did not even love her.

Everything is clear. Let's go on.

Well, let's. "A scientist must always look the truth in the eye . . ."

Enough dreaming. Love must be excluded from your balance of "pleasure." Therefore the maximum of your pleasure must be derived from work. This is so elemental that one should have started with it, instead of going into old and useless memories—and getting one's face slapped.

However, occasional slaps are useful. They serve to destroy one's sense of importance.

What importance? So far you have produced no happiness for anyone. You have not fathered children, you have not raised them. Your science has benefited no one so far. Except perhaps your staff—some of them have written good dissertations.

Very well. Let's accept it. In any event there is only one goal now—to complete the work which has been started. To justify your existence.

Another cup of coffee, Ivan Nikolaevich? For optimism?

The coffee is cold. Warm it up? No, it is best to make a new pot.

It is obvious that I must work out a detailed plan of action. Making plans is my pet occupation. They make sense even when they are only partly fulfilled.

The problem: to create an electronic model simulating the actions of internal organs and their interdependence on one another during different pathological processes.

Let us dream a little, while the coffee is getting ready.

Let us say we have before us a "Department of Artificial Management of Morbid Disorders of the Human System"—a cybernetics center in a large hospital. The name is awkward, but one can use just the initials like DAMMDHS, or something like it. Not very euphonious. Not important. They will think of something. In a large room there stands the machine. Four panels of interchangeable signal boxes. On the wall—a gigantic structural scheme of the human system. The heart, the lungs, the liver, the kidneys, the brain, the endocrine glands. Many multicolored wires connecting these squares. Here is a thick red one—the system of gas exchanges, O_2 and CO_2. The yellow lines, hormones; the blue, nerve channels. I can see it all; the drawing is on my table, under the glass. In each square there is a control panel relating to the given problem—the possible functional disturbances in each organ. For the kidneys, the ability to separate water and salts, to filter or discharge sugar and albumines. They would take an analysis, turn on the proper controls and get an instant picture of the kidney action under various conditions involving the functions of the heart, liver, nerve and endocrine systems.

In my case, for instance, the analysis would be fed into the square marked "the blood-manufacturing organs." Then in response to the pressing of the proper buttons the machine would show when and how the spleen would be affected, then the heart, then the metabolism, and so on. Up to the moment of death. With exact time indications. Then one can repeat this over and over again using various medicaments and treatment routines. Of course the terminal result would be the same, but time differences could be important.

The creation of such a "modeling installation" is a very realistic proposition, but it requires an enormous amount of time and effort. So let's make a list of what must be done, what has been done, and what is being done. A very long list.

The direct purpose of my laboratory is to study characteristics of various organs. For instance, in what way is the pressure in arteries and veins affected by the volume of blood expelled by the heart during each contraction? The same applies to the liver and the kidneys. How are various organs affected by the malfunction of the endocrine glands and nerve system? And so on.

This work takes a great deal of time. So far we have not completed a single characteristics chart. If we go on like this, we obviously will get nowhere. We must have help. And we must make a much wider use of clinical experience.

Sad.

Should I put pressure on the Institute of Cybernetics to speed up the engineering processes?

Easy to say. Professor Sergievsky is a good man, but he has many problems besides our machine. I can hear him: "I'm sorry, Ivan Nikolaevich, but I can't spare any additional personnel for your project. Everyone's busy. But I'll try to prod the experimental factory handling your orders."

Well, thank God for small favors. Yura, for instance, always eggs me on: "Go and raise hell on the highest level!"

A good lad.

Just suppose I come to Sergievsky and say: "Boris Nikitich, I have leukemia. I have only one year to live, maybe a few months more. Please help. It is very important for me to see a completed mock-up of my machine, at least."

This is unpleasant to contemplate. It would put him in a difficult position. He will start to express his sympathy. It is awful to play on people's compassion—dishonest.

How many compassionate words do I have in store for me?

Just the same, if we keep after it, we may be able to assemble the mock-up. Not for all the diseases, no, but for the most common ones. It is just possible.

Then others will take over and carry on.

Others.

It is necessary to start selecting my successor and grooming him for the part. The main requirements: scientific initiative and good character; strong principles combined with tolerance. Of course it is important that he continue my work. "My teacher, Ivan Nikolaevich—" Wait, is that what you are after? It's funny, dig deep into yourself and you come up with manure. Are we all stuffed with it?

If my successor would just "continue in my footsteps"—he would be worthless. In a few years the laboratory would fall apart. True, our purpose—the modeling of physiological processes—is clear; but it could easily degenerate into juggling with formulas, and the human connection would be gone. Science for science's sake. A lot of mathematics and electronics, but clinically nothing would be accomplished at all.

I will map out an exact program for them for a few years to come. The detailed study of the functional characteristics of all organs. Then, the construction of the machine and the connection to a living system so that it can adjust itself to the organic interdependence processes. The machine's predictions must have a high degree of accuracy. The next step: the mechanical management of the body functions through return influences. For this they will need new methods, new medicinal agents, new routines, new technical equipment.

It is sad to leave this world of ideas! What could be better than thinking and searching? Is the end really so near? Then all those reams of scratch notes will turn into waste paper.

Of course they will. No one will preserve them in any memorial museum.

I have never considered myself vain, but now I do want to "leave something behind." Funny, I know with absolute certainty that I have nothing to look forward to but damp earth, but deep in the subconscious there is a persistent mad thought: It just can't be true!

Well, anyway, whom to nominate as my successor? Semyon is obviously unsuitable. Solid, honest, but not intelligent. This would upset him. He is sure that he is fully qualified. Hasn't he been my second in command for years?

This leaves only three: Vadim, Igor and George, whom I call Yura in the traditional Russian way. If only Liuba had been a physiologist! Oh, she would have "preserved my inheritance." A woman's devotion borders on fanaticism.

Vadim is young and talented, but intolerant. His explosions of temper would drive everyone away. And he has no respect for his late chief. Not a bit. I can hear him: "Our Papachen sure made a mess here . . ."

Igor is "perfect"—too perfect. Everyone's favorite. But perhaps it is not too good for a scientist to be so well liked. It may indicate a budding weakness, the lack of a strong "attack." As he grows older he will get fat and complacent.

Yura is too young. But then, he is an engineer and mathematician. This is more important than being a mere physiologist.

I can't decide now. Let's see what the reactions will be. Tomorrow I shall assemble them and say, "Well, children, here we are."

Yes, "Here we are and let's not go back to this any longer."

Let's clear the table . . . This is a very pleasant little apartment I have here . . .

Shall I smoke a cigarette? What's the use of denying myself any longer? Smoking was not the reason for my fatigue; I know this now. But, of course, cigarettes did not help either. I had noticed this even before there was any question of leukemia. But to start again, after suffering for three months? And, of course, I can't do it in front of the boys—I can't show them my weakness. But at home? While alone? A cheat.

I'd better hold off a bit.

I have drawn the plans, but where is the strength to carry them out? There is more to be done than thinking in one's room, or even experimenting in the lab. One has to fight for every little thing.

When I think about it, I become almost desperate.

Here they are, those notes. "Obtain the necessary technical

equipment . . . Assemble the supplementary systems . . . Verify data on electronic computers. . . ." So, again: "Boris Nikitich, we need programers. Allow us to use one of your M-20's for a while." Then it breaks, and I have to ask for a new one. Too bad we have no machine of our own. I have been pleading with our Director: "Let's buy one." "What for? We have no room for it anyway. Let's wait until we get a new building . . ." But I cannot wait now!

I will have to tell the Director about my illness. We must select my successor together. We must safeguard the future of our laboratory. My dear colleagues will start pulling it apart just as soon as I am gone. I must also insist on some additional room. Listen to all complaints and reproaches . . .

Isn't it simpler to just abandon all those plans, to live the remainder of my life quietly. Come to work, of course, for as long as there is strength. But without any excitement or pressure, read books in my spare time, travel stories, if there are no good novels. Now and then one can find some interesting stuff. Go to the theater, to concerts. Listen to celebrities, talk with intelligent people— No, they would not feel comfortable with me any longer.

Or, finally, go to some seashore resort. Perhaps even with Liuba?

Remember that happy month? Your little separate room? A miserable room without even a washbasin. The wallpaper with little pink flowers. We were happy there; we had forgotten that our love was "sinful," that people would condemn us for it.

We could never repeat it. We had to operate like thieves. Public opinion! And the most important thing—her children. The boy was beginning to put two and two together. Even then. The world is small. It is impossible to preserve a secret.

So even now, even before death, we cannot repeat it. And in my present condition, it would be pointless.

All right. Shall we surrender, then?

There is nothing to lose. Duty? Responsibility? It is all fiction. It all has been invented. There are several thousand cells in the cortex with high reaction frequency—the model of "duty." I know the mechanics of it so well. I know how this "model" has been developed through books and examples, how it has invaded the "pleasure centers" and gradually displaced their old tenants—food, love . . . And the end product was the Human Being.

They say that this process can even be mechanically duplicated, just as we are trying to duplicate the heart and kidney functions.

I am afraid I will not be able to live my life out lying on a sofa, under a reading lamp, doing nothing.

How then shall I live? How must I behave?

I am so cold and lucid now. True, my self-pity is whimpering somewhere, deep in the subconscious, and there is also a tiny admiring voice there: "I am so good." But otherwise, I am lucid.

My sins? I haven't had too many of them, and all of them rather small. I have been obeying the Commandments without much effort. Greed for pleasure has never played any important part in my makeup. I haven't stolen, haven't schemed. Adultery? Yes, I have been guilty of that, but never without love. Extenuating circumstances? Besides, I have usually been the suffering party—they left me. Said I was not interesting enough. Personally, I think I am not so bad. And Liuba, for instance, says . . .

I am no hero. I have accepted compromises. Of course, again there were mitigating circumstances—the price of courage was much too high; I have always loved thinking and working too much to risk losing the chance of doing it. Is this a proper defense?

There is much talk around nowadays about some "positive program"—some magic way of justifying all behavior, of differentiating between the truth and nontruth. Apparently the new science will supply all the answers. All qualificative meanings of good and evil, of human happiness will be reduced to a set of figures.

I won't live long enough. So I must be content with intuitive approaches.

What else? Go out in the square and cry some new truths? Or even during our professional union meeting? "Since I am dying anyway, I might as well state that Comrade N. is a fool, and that we must improve the return channels in the process of digesting information."

No, not for me. This would not make any difference to me now, but it would compromise my colleagues. "What sort of chief do they have? And anyway, isn't all their work utter nonsense?" No. Let's be frank. I am simply afraid of difficulties and complications. Of struggling.

Enough! Let's go to bed. It's midnight. By the time I read the newspapers, there will be time to go to sleep.

I open my bed. Sheets, blankets, pillow, pajamas. All the old familiar things, old familiar movements, but tonight they are colored by some new meaning. Eventually, of course, I'll get used to my new status.

The bathroom. Peeling paint. Let the next tenants worry about it. It is good enough for me.

My gums are really swollen. Or maybe I have never noticed them before? Perhaps they have always been this way?

It is so pleasant to stretch out under the blanket. Why not just forget this day—strike it out of time? No. The analysis is lying on the table, and the conversation with David has been etched out in the cortex.

So the session is resumed . . .

The feeling of pleasure is gone. There will be so much I shall have to go through in this bed.

Newspapers? I don't feel like reading.

I have been making plans. Funny—a doomed man making plans. I have avoided thinking about death my whole life. But now, in this bed, it is very real. I don't know yet how people die from leukemia. There was nothing about that in the *Encyclopedia*. But I have never seen a pleasant death.

There will be pain. I've always been afraid of pain. Anemia will progress. Shortness of breath. Gasping with an open mouth. Fear in the eyes. Sweat.

I am terrified thinking of the last days. My will power will collapse. The instinct for survival will grasp me and turn me into a rag. There will be a subtle change of my entire personality; I will become a miserable, sick man. I will talk only about my illness, my medicines, and everyone around will lie to me and hide the analyses. And I will believe all their lies like a child.

To lose oneself. This is the worst thing of all. The very worst.

No, I don't want it! To hell with it! If I must die, I'll die. But on my feet.

To stop the clock at the right moment. No one would object. A good thing. This also requires courage, of course, but nonetheless, this is a solution, my friend.

Suddenly I feel a sense of relief.

A noose? No. Not aesthetic and not interesting.

A gun? Where would I get one?

Poison. An obvious choice for a medical man. I must read up on it. I can even experiment a bit—on dogs. Science!

The best would be nitrogen oxide—the way it is used in surgery. But no. One must have an anesthetist and an additional strong narcotic.

Funny. I am acting like a child. Many others considered all this before, and then died in bed. However, there were a few who did dare . . .

I will dare. My situation is ideal: all alone, no relatives. The problem is to catch the right moment. No use being premature, but if you procrastinate too long, the doctors will grab you and you lose your freedom of action—

Wait a second! An idea!

Anabiosis. A scientist's sacrifice. (Sounds beautiful.) There have been experiments with hypothermy. True, unsuccessful ones, but there hasn't been proper technical equipment. No one even thought of an oxygen chamber. Now that we have advanced automation. Our machine. What an idea!

Also a suicide, of course. But what a brilliant one!

Wait, wait. There is even a bit of a chance . . . Deep hypothermy is used in surgery—or *has* been used. Piotr Stepanovich used it for heart surgery, dozens of times. True, he has discontinued it. He says it is too dangerous. But he was able to cool human bodies to 50, and even 45 degrees. And half the patients have survived! They were presented at the meeting of the Medical Society.

Many fantastic books have been written about anabiosis. Sheer nonsense, most of them. But the idea has a realistic basis. To fall asleep for, say, ten years. And then—not wake up. Well, in my situation this is not too bad either.

But the awakening is possible. To die from leukemia then? The problem of leukemia will be solved in some very near future. So one can sleep until it is solved.

A straw—I am grabbing at a straw.

So strange! I can see myself split into several persons: A scientist soberly studying a scientific problem. A scared little man who fears death, and is willing to risk anything. Another, even smaller man, who does not want to risk anything until the very last day, who will not accept his death until he's dead. And still another one, who sees glory, newspaper headlines, radio, television . . .

A fantastic sarcophagus rests in the center of a glass-enclosed pavilion. Machines, tubes, a control panel with winking lights. A pale majestic face under a plexiglass enclosure. It is not so important that I am not handsome. Everything has been changed.

The time to wake me up. A crowd of academicians from various countries. "Switch on the program of awakening."

Tremendous tension. Ten, twenty, thirty minutes . . . Oscilloscopes flash their curves. Figures dance upon an enormous screen. "The heart has resumed beating!" "He has opened his eyes!" And so on.

■ ■

No, seriously, this is quite possible. That is, to go to sleep instead of dying. Without *completely* dying.

And what about Liuba? Wouldn't it be terrible for her? Me lying there neither dead nor alive. For her my real death would be better. A marble slab in the cemetery where she could sit down and cry a little.

Also, they might not even permit it. They might say: "Die normally. What sort of nonsense is this? This way everyone would want to become immortal. All this costs the government a good deal of money."

No, I cannot sleep now. I'll get up and work. Try to remember things, put them down, organize them.

ii
The Morning After

The laboratory. It is 11 A.M. I have left late this morning; all night I was thinking about anabiosis. It has become a routine scientific problem. This is good. Whether it will work or not, it is bound to distract me.

I am walking across the yard. The building was put up before the war. Three stories. There was a time when it looked very imposing, but now it is uncomfortable and too small. Modern science demands more than mere walls. Laboratories are now built like factories—to fit technological requirements.

I am sorry that I won't live long enough to see the new building. It is difficult for us to work now. We are conducting experiments on the ground floor, "thinking" on the second, and building our equipment in the semibasement.

Someone once said that all organizations have their best days while occupying old buildings. The moment they move into palaces, decay sets in. This is what I tell my boys whenever they complain about their working conditions.

Would they have any good days without me?

I should be ashamed of myself.

In the hall there stands a ping-pong table. Some loafers are already playing—probably from the department of respiratory physiology. This is called "a physical-culture pause." Designed especially for drones.

What a dark corridor!

Here is our wing—three rooms on each side. All the doors are open. It is good to see that the work is going on full blast; people are hurrying to and fro. They skip their morning calisthenics, despite the regulations.

I feel like a guest today. I look at everything with different eyes.

"Good morning, Ivan Nikolaevich!"

The first greeting of the day—Aunt Glasha, our cleaning woman, carrying a pail.

The pail is full. This means good luck, according to an old Russian superstition. Pleasant.

The first operation theater: Semyon is conducting an experiment with a separated kidney.

"Good morning, Comrades!"

Everyone is smiling. Greetings. No matter what one says, it is pleasant to see smiles and warm looks. So far no one knows anything, of course.

Here he is, my second in command.

"Ivan Nikolaevich, we are studying the kidney characteristics under the influence of hypocsia."

"Very good."

But in fact, not very. Semyon cannot understand the new technical approach to experimentation: One must concentrate one's attention on the "intakes." I am following Yura's terminology; this is what he calls all outside influences upon the organism.

"Semyon, why is your temperature not stabilized? You have thirty degrees here."

"Our heat-exchange is out of order. So we have decided to do without."

"Too bad. A valuable experiment probably spoiled."

He is blinking his eyes. What can he say?

The picture: In the center, upon a pedestal, rests the kidney in a glass container. Two tubes are running from it to our heart-and-lung machine, called AIK. The machine is being operated by the machinist, Sima—she is turning the controls. A whole network of wires connects the entire operation with a battery of electronic gauges, standing in three rows. Two technicians are in charge, Misha Samokhin and Elena Gandja. They are very young, fresh from the Technicum.

"How many parameters are you controlling today?"

It seems to me that Semyon becomes confused. The engineer, Nikolai Goulyi who I know is running the whole thing, looks at him with a trace of pity. Steps into the breach—"We are constantly checking blood pressure coming in and out, and the O_2 and

CO_2 content. Besides we are watching the PO_2 in the kidney tissue. The biochemistry lab supplies the analyses every thirty minutes."

He rattles off the whole list of chemical terms—adrenalin, organic acids, alkaline reserve, aminoacids, the pH and certain ferments. And of course reports on the quantity and quality of the urine.

"But why didn't you stabilize the temperature?"

"The heat-exchange sprang a leak, and I—"

He becomes silent. He does not want to implicate his superior. Semyon cuts in: "I've ordered the experiment to go on. I did not want to waste the kidney which had been isolated already."

"Very well, carry on. But please study the kidney function under the cooling process."

This is important for me. My kidneys will be extremely cold. It is doubtful that they will function in cold temperature. However, this is not fatal; there is a special apparatus for that.

Everyone is doing his job. The atmosphere is one of quiet efficiency. It seems to me that they treat Semyon with indifference. And what about me? Well, I am a good superior. I never pick at minor errors. "I suggest . . ." and "Will you kindly do this or that . . ." I avoid giving orders. In some cases this undermines discipline. But they all appreciate my politeness.

"How is the new code-analysis machine performing?" This to Nikolai. (What do I know about him? Practically nothing.)

"Seems to be doing all right. Here are the records."

He indicates a paper roll covered with figures. Clear, steady eyes.

"It means that you will have some spare time which you have used on working out the curves? I'd like to assign you some additional tasks."

No particular enthusiasm on the faces. They are all working very hard, and they had hoped I would lighten their load. No, impossible. Dear comrades, you do not yet know how important time has become for me. (Or perhaps they just don't care? Perhaps Semyon has failed to charge them with proper enthusiasm?)

Nikolai: "First we must get some additional time on the machine. We still have some unfinished experiments."

"I'll do my best to get it for you. Nevertheless, you'll have to conduct three experiments next week instead of two. I will explain the program to you, Semyon. You too, Nikolai."

Semyon is good at isolating dogs' kidneys. A solid experimenter. But he has failed to master electronics.

Well, I can leave. I feel like saying something warm and encouraging, but this is not my style. It would be ridiculous.

I walk to another room. I know that here they are conducting an experiment to study the characteristics of the heart and blood system. New methods.

What a setup! Igor and Vadim are operating, and Yura is running the technical equipment. They don't even notice me.

"Good morning!"

"Good morning, Ivan Nikolaevich! You're just in time. We are trying to isolate the heart together with the lungs, to cut all the nerve channels, retaining the regulatory capacity of nerves governing the vessels and other organs."

"And?"

"And we can't separate it from the esophagus and the spinal column. Too many small vessels. Please help us."

This is Vadim. He is liberal with requests for help.

"All right. Let me change."

I did not expect to operate today, but now I am glad to do it.

In the next room, which serves as our storage place, I put on white pants and jacket. They are well pressed. Julia, our chief laboratory technician, can be credited with this.

I like to operate. True, this is a mere experiment, without any antiseptic requirements, but nonetheless I like utmost cleanliness.

I wash my hands, I put on the white robe and rubber gloves. Everything has stopped; they are waiting for me. Only, Yura and his two assistants are fussing with their equipment. Obviously something is not altogether in order, and time is pressing. Vadim is winking at me.

"The engineering department is letting us down." Gay, mischievous eyes.

"Never mind. Worry about your surgery."

The dog has been cut almost in two. The operation is difficult: we must separate the heart and the lungs from all other organs and connect the blood channels with the system of tubes to regulate the flow. At the same time the blood supply to the brain should not be interrupted even for a moment, and several measurement gauges must be inserted into the veins and arteries.

I learned surgery during the war. That was real surgery. Even though, to tell the truth, surgeons should not overestimate themselves—it is more difficult to operate on dogs. Take the pulmonary veins, for instance. They are so small that they can break at any time.

My movements are neat and precise. This is pleasant. I can see that the boys are admiring my skill—they are assisting me with eagerness. It is I who have taught them surgery. Are they grateful? Do you *want* gratitude?

"Yura, how many channels are you recording today?"

"We planned for ten, but two are out of order. We'll have to conduct the usual measurements there."

Vadim: "Shame on you, Yura. The Chief himself is operating, and you haven't adjusted your damned mechanics."

Vadim has a long nose and black eyebrows. Is he from the Caucasus? His family name is Pliashnik. A Ukrainian? From Odessa? All the nationalities are mixed up down there.

Well, the hardest part is over. The heart works well, it did not even react to the tube which we have inserted into the aorta.

"Julia, did you apply heparin?"

"Yes."

"It seems there's no bleeding anywhere."

This is important. We must tie up all the smallest vessels. The blood does not congeal, and the experiment lasts quite long.

"How much blood did you prepare?"

"We have only two liters. There are no more dog donors."

"That's bad."

"Ivan Nikolaevich, you know yourself how our vivarium works. We ourselves have to buy dogs."

"Or steal."

I am silent. It is not in my power to do anything with the vivarium.

But Yura cannot contain himself. "We should hit that Shvechik fellow during a party meeting."

"We've already hit him. But he must have some pull somewhere."

"They say he's been doing favors for Ivan Petrovich!"

"Vadim, don't talk like that. You don't know whether it's true or not." (I am defending the Director. I do not believe he could have done it. However, to hell with him. This is not important.) "We shouldn't spend our energy on petty things."

"No, Ivan Nikolaevich, one can't overlook principles even in petty matters. Once you start doing this, you don't know where to stop."

"You oversimplify everything, Vadim."

"Because it's simple—Shvechik is Shvechik. We all know him!"

"True, but can you say the same thing about Ivan Petrovich?"

Vadim is taken aback a little. "Well, given that Shvechik is a louse, everyone covering up for him is a louse as well! That's the law of formal logic, isn't it?"

"Perhaps. I must think about that."

I like his sharp directness. Igor is making signs to him to be quiet. A politician. After all, I am a superior.

We continue to work. Now it is mere routine—tying up all the smallest vessels. My head is free for outside thoughts.

"As I see it, Vadim, not all principles are necessarily good. Have you ever thought about that?"

"What do you mean?"

"I mean that everything must have its proportions. Some principles are not creative; they don't take into consideration other elements, other circumstances. Such principles drive one to quick conclusions and quick condemnations."

"You are probably right, Ivan Nikolaevich. But I'm afraid that such an attitude can lead to justification of people like Shvechik. The sense of proportion is fine, but it can turn into weakness and cowardice. By the time one considers and weighs all the factors, the crime is forgotten, and one needn't commit oneself at all."

This is meant directly for me. I could let myself become offended. But I don't feel like starting a quarrel.

"Yura, you're a cyberneticist. What's your opinion?"

Yura is in a difficult situation. He even blushes a little. His sympathies are with Vadim. They all consider me too mild and a bit of a coward.

"We technicians deal with simple equations which can be translated into figures. I don't know whether this is applicable to such detached spheres as ethics, politics and philosophy, but perhaps it is."

"A theft is a theft—whether one steals a kopeck or a million!"

Someone adds quietly: "But for some reason the punishment is different."

Now everyone is involved in the discussion and this interferes with work. We must finish with it.

" 'What is good and what is bad?' That's Mayakovsky. On the physiological plane everything that causes pleasure is good, everything that interferes with it is bad. This is the animal approach based on bare instincts. In humans, there are additional factors— ethics, morals, rules of behavior. They also differ because of classes, religions, different philosophies. From here we have different appraisals of human actions, different interpretations of good and evil. Society uses the criminal code as a measuring stick, but each individual has his own convictions often deformed by subjectivity depending in turn on 'animal programs'—love, hunger, vanity. The criteria of good and evil in society are only good so long as they insure its stability and promote its development. This is all. Let's finish this discussion. Otherwise our experiment will come to nothing."

While I have been delivering my oration, everyone has stopped working. Some out of curiosity, others out of respect for me.

"Yes, Ivan Nikolaevich, but we shall argue with you some other time!"

"Of course. Any time."

I must clear all those thoughts up with Leonid. It is surprising that abstract questions can interest a man to the last day of his life.

The surgical part of the experiment is completed. I am admiring my work. First class. The heart and the lungs are fully separated and are connected with the rest of the body through the aorta and the empty veins with the inserted tubes in them.

"Discontinue the anesthesia, Mila."

We are watching. In a few minutes the dog starts to move and opens his eyes. It means that he is alive and that his brain still governs his body outside of the heart.

"Let's start measuring and writing down. Is everything ready?"

"Yes."

"Where is the program?"

They hand me a long list with every phase of the experiment marked down. Seven general phases, with almost two hundred measurements. This should take about six hours. Providing that the dog doesn't die in the meantime.

A good, thorough program. It is Yura who has taught them to do this—rather like the testing of a machine.

"Igor, Vadim, Yura, please come to my office at two o'clock. There are a few things we have to discuss."

I change and go to my room.

I am a little sorry that our discussion had remained unfinished. Good and evil—who is interested anyway? Many of us live by momentum. We like to talk and argue now and then, but just as a brain exercise, that's all. All noble deeds are performed during working hours—from nine to five. The teacher teaches, the doctor cares for his patients, the functionary receives callers. And few bother about the problem of good and evil.

It seems to me that nobody suspects my condition as yet. I haven't noticed any curious looks. It is good to work in public; all thoughts of death fade away. Now they are crawling back. I want to drive them off. I cannot do it.

My private office is small but cozy, a mixture of old and modern.

The desk. Manuscripts, articles, dissertations. Science! My opinion about it is not too high. It has spread around, lost its form. Individual prospectors are digging around looking for specks of gold. There are no attempts to absorb everything in one sweep, from atom to society. Are encyclopedists hopelessly outdated? Perhaps even ridiculous?

Should I devote the remaining year of my life to the problem of good and evil? It is doubtful that I would come up with anything worthwhile. I had better concentrate on the problem at hand. Everything looks different in daytime. Death has receded, I do not even believe in it. The problem of anabiosis seems a detached scientific proposition; it is someone else who would be lying in that sarcophagus, not me.

Here are my notes, the fruit of my night's work. I don't think I should show it to the boys yet.

Then what am I going to tell them?

"I am ill. No sentiment, please." Ask them to redouble their efforts—I want to see the results. Not a word about my successor. Not yet. Nothing about the anabiosis plan either. Just give them some concrete assignments. I have them all written down.

That's all. No. Let's see their reactions first. Important for the selection of the successor. The one who would praise his "teacher"? No; the one who would continue the work. *Honestly?* Almost.

I am reading my scribblings:

NOTES ON ANABIOSIS

Theoretically one can imagine the possibility of conserving the human body as well as the bodies of all warm-blooded animals. It is a well-known fact that lower temperatures slow down all chemical reactions including metabolism. The tests on animals show that at 75° F. the organism performs at 25% of its normal intensity, and at 50° F. at 6%. In all probability these figures are applicable to humans, perhaps with minor corrections. At the point of freezing, metabolic action is all but arrested. Of course, conservation by deep freeze would be ideal. This works on lower organisms, even on some fish. But mammals do not survive it.

Why?

The human system consists of a wide variety of cells which have developed in the process of evolution. Some of them, the oldest, are no different from those of lower organisms. Others have appeared in later stages of mammal development. These are causing the trouble.

There are two forms of chemical processes composing life. One consists of nonspecific reactions—for instance, derivation of energy from simple oxidation. The other consists of such specific reactions as muscular contractions, nerve impulses and hormone formation, and these depend on specific conditions: sufficient oxygen supply and certain temperatures. However, the lack of such conditions does not necessarily kill individual cells. Once the normal conditions are restored, the cells resume their functions.

Therefore, each individual cell can be preserved by freezing provided that the most essential feeding and evacuation of wastes are properly organized. This has been proved on tissue cultures kept alive outside the system in artificially supported cell colonies.

Unfortunately, what can be done with individual cells cannot be done with the whole system. In the body the cells are fed by the blood, the composition constancy of which is assured by the activity of the internal organs and regulatory systems depending on the action of the cells composing them. During the process of freezing, these cells cease functioning first and the oxygen feeding of the body is interrupted while the necessity for oxygen is still comparatively high. If we take a dog and begin to freeze him, at 85° F. the breathing stops, and at 60° F. the heart ceases to function. Meanwhile the system still requires 15% of the normal oxygen supply, which it now does not get. Further freezing must be conducted under conditions of acute oxygen deficiency, which destroys some cells, notably and primarily such delicate cells as those of the cortex.

Modern technology permits overcoming this difficulty. There are machines which simulate blood circulation, respiration, the functions of the kidneys and even of the liver. Used together, these machines may artificially create the proper conditions for sufficient feeding and waste evacuation in all cells.

Then, during the entire period of anabiosis, no matter how prolonged, it is necessary to preserve the blood constants. Frozen cells endure fairly well the lack of oxygen and other feeding, since their requirements are very low, but not beyond a certain period. All metabolic action practically stops in the process of freezing. This means, first of all, a complete interruption of blood circulation for a certain period during freezing, and its gradual restoration during the period of thawing out. Here the artificial aids come into play. What is still unclear is how the cells would react to the crystallization of their fluids when they start turning into ice.

Therefore, theoretically, there exist conditions for obtaining and maintaining anabiosis through lowering of temperatures, but there is absolutely no certainty that such a frozen body can be kept under refrigeration like perishable products.

Those are the theoretical postulates for the application of anabiosis to the human body. Unfortunately, on the way to its practical success, there are many difficulties.

It is necessary to consider some of them.

Through the internal regulatory system—blood—the feeding and cleansing processes are maintained at a certain optimum level. Tissues are the consumers; and various organs, governed by regulatory systems, are the suppliers. Here a very delicate balance must be maintained. Let us look closer at the problem.

The interchange of gases. The tissues use oxygen and produce carbon dioxide. The quantity and correlation of gases are based on the intensity of metabolic processes and the interrelation of the consumed products—albumins, fats and carbohydrates. For the optimum function of the cells it is necessary to maintain the gas pressure in the tissues, and therefore, in capillaries within certain limits. Under the condition of anabiosis the gas-exchange processes can be maintained by the use of the "heart-lung machine" circulating the whole of the diluted blood. The action of the artificial heart and the interchange of gases in the oxygenerator (artificial lungs) should provide for the proportional pressures of oxygen and carbon dioxide in tissues. If whole blood is used, the action of the machine can be reduced in proportion to the lowered metabolic function—i.e., cut down 15 to 20 times at the temperature of, say, 42° F. However, whole blood may not be practical for circulation under low temperatures because of its high viscosity. Besides, it has been noted that during the slowing of the circulation the erythrocytes become connected and stick in the capillaries. Therefore, under lowered temperatures it may be advisable to dilute the blood with plasma, or even use pure plasma. True, this would necessitate the quantitative increase in circulation, but this represents no particular problem. The fact is that there still exists no ideal heart-lung machine which would preclude destruction of erythrocytes during prolonged use. But the use of pure plasma would eliminate this danger.

Lately there has appeared another possibility for supplying the system with oxygen through the use of a high-pressure oxygen chamber. Under sufficiently high pressure, up to 25% of necessary oxygen can be supplied directly through the skin. Under low temperatures, when the respiration is slowed, this percentage would greatly increase and may even be sufficient for the complete oxygenation. True, there is a danger that the outer tissues would be oversupplied with oxygen, while the inner tissues would not get a sufficient amount of it. Also, and this is the main point, this sort of oxygen feeding would not provide for the proper evacuation of carbon dioxide. Therefore, the main method of maintaining the gas exchanges in the system in anabiosis still remains the artificial-blood-circulation machine with the use of plasma. However, one must take into consideration the danger that slow circulation under a low pressure may produce dangerous "centralization" when blood would circulate through the large vessels without reaching the secondary network. Therefore, it is quite possible that proper circulation could be achieved by a series of quick spurts under higher pressure rather than an even, low-pressure action. Such pulsating rhythm of circulation may also serve the secondary purpose of mechanical massaging of tissues.

Probably in the second place of importance lies the hydrosaline balance of the system and its acid-alkaline regime. Water and salts enter the system through the digestive tract and are eliminated through the kidneys. It is unnecessary to describe the importance of maintaining the proper level here; it is obvious. This balance may be maintained by the mechanical kidney acting on the principle of simple dialysis. By changing the composition of fluids washing through the dialyzator it is possible to maintain the necessary level of salts, the pH and the general level of fluids in the system. One must not depend on the action of natural kidneys since the low pressure in the arterial system would depress their function. But some kidney function must be maintained nonetheless, so that the kidney channels would be periodically washed through with the urine. This is another argument for the "spurt action" of the blood-circulation machine which would create periodically the proper pressure. Besides this, the artificial kidney would eliminate urea—the terminal product of the nitrous albumin exchange. The blood-circulation machine would probably have to be switched on periodically, at intervals of four to six hours, or even less frequently.

For the maintenance of the energetic balance of the system and for building new structures to replace those destroyed in the organic metabolic processes, some food substances would be necessary—albumins, fats, carbohydrates, vitamins. Since one cannot count on the action of the digestive system, all these substances would have to be introduced directly into the bloodstream. Glucose has been introduced in this way for some time now, and the introduction of fat emulsions and aminoacids has been properly experimented with. The entire range of vitamins is also available in liquid form. Then one must take into consideration the fact that a large amount of nutritive values will be obtained by the system from the plasma, which would have to be revitalized daily. It contains some rare substances, hormones, animonacids and other factors, many of which are still unknown. The amount of necessary nutritive products would be minimal if one considers that metabolism would be reduced from 20 to 30 times its normal intensity.

Normally, a certain amount of toxic products forms in the system and is rendered harmless by the liver. Its functions under the anabiosis conditions might be greatly reduced. Therefore a periodic replacement of the entire amount of plasma may be required. Besides, during recent years, various types of artificial "liver" machines have been successfully tried out which neutralize high-molecular toxic nitrite products.

Therefore, it is theoretically conceivable that the anabiosis condition can be maintained by providing the cells with the necessary nutritive environment and the elimination of their decomposition residues.

There exists, however, a whole set of problems and technical details which require discussion and experimentation. It is even difficult to foresee all of them now. But let us mention a few.

The prophylaxis of cardiac hyperdistention. As I have mentioned before, the heart would stop when the temperature reaches 60° F. Rather, it would first start fibrillating and then would stop altogether. During the process of "thawing out," this would be reversed: the fibrillation would occur first; and then, when the body temperature reaches near-normal level, the proper rhythm would be resumed. In most cases, artificial defibrillation would have to be brought on with the application of high-tension electric shock. During the period of stoppage, the inert sections of the heart might become distended and packed with blood (or plasma) if the arterial valve is not sufficiently tight. It is impossible to start a heart in a state of hyperdistention. Prophylaxis in this case consists of draining the left ventricle, using a slender tube introduced through the right auricle and a special opening in the interventrical wall. This method of drainage for determining auricular pressure has been developed clinically.

To avoid the deformation of lung tissues, artificial respiration would probably have to be resorted to periodically. The best way of doing this is by the mechanical creation of an area of low pressure over the thorax.

In all probability the maintenance of asepsis in the intestinal region would present difficulties. Even though microorganisms develop poorly at low temperatures, they might become adjusted to this condition. Therefore a person slated for anabiosis must have his intenstines cleansed and as microbe-free as possible. This can be achieved through proper diet and the use of antibiotics.

During anabiosis a periodic cleansing of the oral cavity, the esophagus and the intestinal tract would be essential. This could be done by the use of double tubes as in colonic irrigation. True, certain portions of the intestinal tract cannot be reached in this way, but that may not be too important.

To avoid the irregularities of blood circulation it would be necessary to subject the entire body to periodic vibration massage, or do this by body sections. This is especially important for those skin surfaces which are subjected to constant pressure. Perhaps a special bed would have to be constructed providing for a constant wavelike vibration.

The most crucial period of the experiment will be bringing the subject back to "life." Gradually the metabolic action would be restored to normal level while the action of various organs would still be greatly depressed. It is also possible that a prolonged anabiosis condition would cause disarrangements in cell "coexistence," and a considerable period may be required to organize it again. During this period there might be various regulatory difficulties and irregularities in the functions of nerve and endocrine systems.

Therefore, supplementary artificial blood circulation might be necessary, as well as artificial respiration and the use of the artificial kidney for some time after "awakening." Naturally, the freezing and "thawing out" processes, as well as the postawakening period, would call for the use of light anesthetics.

Before subjecting a human being to prolonged anabiosis, some important exploratory work must be done in many different spheres. It is possible to indicate only a very few of them:

1. The anabiosis of tissue cultures to determine the influence of various temperatures and O_2 and CO_2 proportional pressures on life functions of various cells.

2. The anabiosis of isolated organs. The preservation of certain organs under low temperatures with artificial blood and fluid circulation and various proportional gas pressures. It is especially important to study the liver and kidney actions under these conditions.

3. The anabiosis of the entire system. The study of the proper composition of the circulatory fluid—blood and plasma—with various admixtures of erythrocytes and without them. The study of the influence of high pressures with various oxygen contents under different temperatures and during different time periods. The selection of the optimum regime of interchange of gases. The study of metabolic action under low temperatures with special attention to the interchange of carbohydrates, albumins and fats. The determination of the extent of decomposition, and the quantity and chemical structures of wastes.

4. The best methods of cooling and reheating. The influence of the period of anabiosis upon the mechanics of bringing the subject back to life.

5. A whole set of purely technical medical problems requiring study and solution. Among them, the best methods of draining the left ventricle, periodic ventilation of the lungs, intestinal irrigation, prolonged draining of the bladder, etcetera.

The solutions of almost all difficult problems in anabiosis are based in technology. The experiments are feasible only after creation of necessary technical conditions insuring the artificial control of chemical and physical conditions of the experiment. On the basis of conventional technical development of present-day laboratories it is impossible to undertake the terminal experimental anabiosis of advanced organisms or human beings. Therefore, the very first goal should be the designing and the construction of installations permitting the above-outlined preliminary exploratory work.

■ ■

I have finished.

Science fiction. Never before has it been as popular as today.

The prestige of the arts has diminished and that of science enormously increased. At least, so it appears to me. Many do not share my views. Very well, my opinion is my opinion. Fairy tales have had their day; this is the age of adventure and facts.

Liuba . . . No matter what I am thinking about, she is always at the back of my mind. I must tell her today. It would be worse if she happened to learn it on her own. Telephone her? Probably she can come and see me around six o'clock.

There is still some time left before two o'clock. I'd better go and see Ivan Petrovich. The Director must know. I wish I could avoid it. As a man he will be sorry for me, but as the Director he will start calculating: ". . . no longer a worker. Empty words about finishing his experiment, he's just deluding himself . . ."

I must go.

I am going.

iii
The Afternoon

The Director's office. The reception room. Bare branches are scratching at the windowpanes. The secretary, Zenaida Alexandrovna, a gray-haired marchioness. Pince-nez. Gives her a touch of elegance. (Turn of the century. Chekhov. The Moscow Art Theater. Stanislavsky. Now all that is left: the horn-rimmed glasses.)

I greet her politely. I respect her.

"Ivan Petrovich in?"

A double door with heavy padding. Only important people have doors like that. To keep secrets from seeping out. Why here? What secrets?

What an imposing figure, our Director! He doesn't greet people; he honors you with his greeting. In his voice, notes of metal. Or, sometimes, a sort of cooing, depending on the effect he wants.

It isn't easy to remain the Director of an important institute for twenty years. He rose on the crest of the "Pavlov wave," in the early Fifties, after a periodic crusade against "pseudoscientists." His own scientific achievements: zero. But his telephone is connected right.

Don't spread your bile, friend. He's not bad. Not malicious. He just has his own style: a scientist of a certain school.

Talk about the weather? Or just get down to brass tacks? What if he just liquidates the laboratory after I'm gone? He's quite capable of doing that.

"Ivan Petrovich, I must inform you about my illness. Yesterday they diagnosed leukemia."

His eyes become round. His age, cardiac disorders. Death is quite real to him.

"Are you sure? Have you seen hematologists?"

"Yes. David Portnoy. A friend of mine."

"And what did he say?"

"Nothing. He just showed me the figures."

He sits there, thinking. Has suddenly turned into an old man whose heart is weak. And he has a family, grandchildren.

Then he wakes up. Becomes once more the Director. Many people come to him with their troubles. They have to come.

"You must take care of yourself, Ivan Nikolaevich. Go to a hospital, to the Moscow Institute of Hematology. I could help."

(Of course. He has influence in many places.)

"Thank you, Ivan Petrovich. I can't go to a hospital. And there's really no need. David will treat me."

"It's unwise to neglect your health."

He probably hates saying these words. And I hate hearing them.

"Not at all. I'll do everything that is prescribed. But you know yourself the result will be the same."

A protesting gesture. He is protecting himself from a dying man's complaints. I'm beginning to boil over. Why? It's natural, I suppose. Everyone tries to avoid pain.

"Ivan Petrovich, I haven't come here for sympathy. The point is that I must finish my work and I need your help. You know that with the collaboration of the Cybernetics Institute we are working on an electronic installation to duplicate the human system in various pathological processes. This project has been approved at the All-Union level. There is promise that it may be adopted in clinical practice. Physicians need it."

The "practical application" is the sore spot of all theoretical institutions. And, of course, of their directors. He should rise to the bait.

He is reflecting. Or pretending to. "I understand. Science to a scientist is the most important thing in his life."

(For you, let's be frank, the main thing is to strike a pose, to satisfy your taste for power. But, no, he honestly thinks he is helping science. Every man considers himself good and important. Everyone? Really?)

"I need a room to start assembling the machine. I need an allowance for three additional science workers, mathematicians. Also some technicians, three or four. The personnel department tells me there are vacancies."

"They are being held in reserve for—"

"I need them just for one year. Then you can have them back."

Can he turn down a man in my condition? No. But he can promise and not fulfill, yes. That is one of his gambits.

"Very well, you may have them. For one year. But perhaps not immediately."

(There it starts!)

"I beg you to do this right away, Ivan Petrovich. You understand that 'not immediately' doesn't fit my situation. We already have candidates."

"All right, let them file applications."

"And the room?"

"There will be a room. But please don't overwork yourself. Your health is the important thing."

"Of course. I am very, very grateful to you. Good afternoon."

"Be well."

He realizes that the expression is unfortunate, gets up, walks with me to the door, embarrassed. And I am a hypocrite: ". . . very, very grateful . . ." It looks good—a scientist thinking only of science. In reality it is simpler—I just can't do anything else. To continue working is the only way for me. Not to be alone. Misery loves company. A very apt saying.

I am walking, thinking. Back to my office. Back to my armchair. Comfortable. Looking out the window. Gray sky, whirling snow-flakes.

There are many directors like ours. They've done nothing for science but are ordering scientists around. What line can he follow? What ideas? Every laboratory works as well as it knows how. The budgets and personnel are allocated on the principle of yielding to the maximum of pressure. The only criteria: number of works published and number of dissertations produced. Quality is secondary.

There is still another way of running these institutions by telephone—"Please, Ivan Petrovich, I'm sending you Comrade N. Get him set up somewhere, will you? Looks like a brilliant man, an innovator. They seem to think so. . . ." This means that some scoundrel has gone directly to the top and has sold himself to that level of leadership. Easier than passing before a panel of scientists. And our Ivan relishes the role of Protector of Talent. So Comrade N. is fixed up for a few years. Then, of course, it all blows up.

No use getting bitter, my friend. All this is coming to an end. Anyhow, you haven't done so badly yourself. Ivan gave you a laboratory and kept building up your team from year to year. Without telephone calls. Again, a protector, a man with advanced views. He likes to say on occasion, "We are experimenting in the field of cybernetics." We?

Forget him. All this means nothing to you now.

So I have gone through one ordeal. Now I'll have to face another. Then Liuba. I'm sorry for her. Why? Her double life will come to an end. She will be able to look her children straight in the eye.

How shall I tell her? I can see it: the corners of her mouth will droop; she will look old and plain. ("I don't want to grow old! I don't want you to stop loving me." Remember?) Darling, how can I stop loving you? Unto death . . .

"And death walks four paces behind . . ." There was a song like that during the war.

I must not think. I must hold myself together.

My conversation with the Director has left an aftertaste. I don't like him. His condescending manner has always irritated me. Of course, a member of all sorts of committees, academician. Envy.

Science needs freedom. The freedom of open discussion, that's our sustenance.

Could you now, in your condition, defend your ideas before a committee of scientists, convince them you need money for your machines, your engineers? Perhaps, yes. Of course, big brains are often conservative, but they can be convinced. By honest arguments. If one is given a chance.

Never mind. They are already burying the label pasters. Remember, when they used ready-made epithets? "Weissmanist-Morganist. . . . Anti-Pavlovist." They would just drop the label and then, the next day, they would take away one of the victim's laboratory girls, would ask him to surrender a valuable piece of equipment. And the director's face would be like stone. "The development of Soviet science requires readjustments."

And then, during the next meeting, the scientist would recant. A red face, trembling lips. One could see that he hated himself. But what else could he do? He wanted to work. He had to eat. And then, his wife, his children . . .

All this is behind us. I myself have not suffered. I was still a young man; I had nothing to lose. Still, I did not raise my voice in protest either. Perhaps, in my own company. Please note this, ladies and gentlemen of the jury.

Not pleasant to remember . . .

It is two o'clock. Where are they? The experiment is already at the stage where their personal attention is not necessary. Routine. However, anything can happen. The heart, for instance, may stop.

May stop. Mine surely will stop.

Now the whole Institute will talk about my illness. The hero of the day. Especially the laboratory people.

There will be various reactions.

Simple pity. From those who love me. Are there any? Yes. One can judge by their looks.

Others will be sorry to see a promising scientist, a guiding light, flicker out. Interesting work will be interrupted, dissertations may suffer.

Still others will merely wonder who will take my place.

Probably no one will say, "Serves him right." I don't seem to have enemies. Is that good or bad? Probably bad; it shows that I've avoided conflicts. Just a harmless scientist.

How will this affect my laboratory? We must preserve efficiency. No, we must increase it. Otherwise we won't fulfill the program. In time.

A knock at the door.

"Come in!"

Here they come, the three of them. Smiling, excited, young. All at once the room becomes crowded, but light and pleasant. Vadim has been trying to prove some point. I can see that there is an unfinished argument. They were probably having lunch. Our dining room is the usual arena for violent discussions.

"How's the experiment? How's the heart?"

"Strong as a bull! We've been changing pressure in the aorta from forty millimeters to two hundred, and the productivity graph is as straight as an arrow."

This is Vadim.

Now, Igor: "We've written down reams of figures."

Yura: "I think we'll have to make a few minor corrections on my model. We'll stay all night if necessary to study various degrees of pathology."

"Very good, Yura. Call in Semyon Ivanovich."

I must gather my thoughts. I pretend to study the manuscript. It is before me, "Notes on Anabiosis." I hear Vadim's whispering: "What's all this mystery? Is the Chief getting married?" Yes, married. "Till death do us part."

Thus passes one human life. Only yesterday, it seems, I was like them. Not as carefree and gay. I have always been proud, suffered from an inferiority complex, dressed more poorly than others. When I was their age, I was not handsome, did not know how to dance or flirt. "The bookworm"—that's what my mother called me.

Envy. They are young, gifted. And on the right track; physiology combined with mechanics and mathematics make for a brilliant scientific future. Science degrees, prizes, admiring looks from girls, conventions in Paris, Tokyo, Rio de Janeiro.

Life. Full to the brim. And not a worry in the world. Not a doubt, not a disturbing thought.

How long ago did I start worrying about life, about the duty of a scientist? Long enough. I had gone through the war.

And what about the boys? Is anything worrying them at all? They work very hard. I haven't noticed signs of careerism in any of them. They detest phrases—they are fed up to the ears with them.

"Sit down, Comrades."

A pause, the bewildered looks.

"I must tell you some news . . ." (What a stupid word, news.) "The fact is they have discovered leukemia in me. Many leucocytes. Enlarged spleen."

I take a look around me. Fright on all the faces. Then they drop their eyes. Pity is spreading now.

I must control myself. Put on a mask. Hide behind it.

"I have asked you to come here not to get your compassion, nor to resign. I have about a year at my disposal, perhaps a bit more. I want to use this time with maximum efficiency."

I am holding myself well. I can even visualize my face—calm, with set jaw. (And perhaps it is completely different—"a child trying to fight back its tears"?)

"This means that I must see the mock-up of our machine and make sure that it works."

I almost said, "To make sure it will help physicians to treat people." But I held this back.

"I have developed a plan for more intensive work and I want to discuss it with you."

I'm looking again. The second reactions. Semyon probably thinks that he will take over the laboratory very soon. Igor is worrying about his dissertation. Yura looks at his friends in bewilderment; he probably knows very little about leukemia. Vadim appears to be completely crushed, not even listening. In all probability they will not be able to discuss anything today. But I continue:

"Problem number one: the characteristics of the organs. Obviously we have no time to conduct all the proper experiments. Therefore, I suggest that we rely more on clinical experience."

I must talk on. On and on. Bury pity, self-pity, and bitterness under a flood of words. Even if they don't listen.

"Number two: we must speed up the mathematical digestion of the characteristics. It is not necessary to waste time trying to determine all interrelations. In any event we shall have to schematize everything, because many factors will remain undetermined. We need differential and algebraic equations showing the intensity of functions of various organs under the influence of irritants and under generalized pathological conditions. The director promises to give us mathematicians, but the role of physiologists and physicians will remain paramount. They must draw the approximate curves of interrelations."

(To achieve this we need an able biologist. Who among them? Probably Vadim. But even he may not be competent enough. We'll need outside help.)

"Number three. We must verify in sum the interrelationships of those organs for which we already have characteristics. For instance, the hydrodynamics of the circulatory system and its fluid balance. This is necessary before constructing the actual models of the organs."

Why am I trying to say all this? They are looking at me with absent eyes. And I feel now my own faith in the success of the whole thing melting away.

A pain between the ribs. My mouth is dry. Go and lie down? Fill out a hospitalization form? "Each man . . . must . . . do . . . his own dying." I have heard this somewhere.

Very well. (This to myself.) "Number four. The design and assembly of various groups of organs. We must use more extensively the results of already existing analogy machines. Since most of our characteristics will have to be amplified. This is all—for a while. I'll tell you later how to proceed further. Please think about this and give me your views."

Everyone is silent. What can they say? I put myself in their place. A pause. It is becoming awkward.

Then Semyon sighs and says haltingly: "Ivan Nikolaevich, first of all, you must think of your health."

Look at him—he is already anxious to take my place! But why do I think so? Are there any signs? No. Therefore, let me be calm.

"Of course I'll be treating myself, but without leaving work. And let's not discuss this further."

Vadim jumps up: "What do you mean, not discuss further? Who do you think you are to us—a man from the street? And are we mere puppets, computers, just to be switched on? And don't think that your decisions are always correct; we'll be working like hell on our own trying to improve your program for you!"

How noisy he is! Always so direct, even rude. But today this is pleasant. It is good to see that someone really cares. I haven't been pampered by affection since childhood. Really, how little human warmth there has been in my life!

Why do you force me to talk? Don't you see how difficult it is for me? How sorry I am for myself? And I don't want to die. I have just found my real work. But what can I do? I am a physician, even scientist . . . (Why "even"? Stupid.) "I know this is hopeless. But I cannot just go to bed and wait for death, taking treatments and pills. And another thing—I must pay my debts. I've been very conscious of this lately. My whole life has been *taking*, without giving anything back. No one has had the slightest benefit from my work. Now here's the first possibility of *doing* something. I must try to finish it. You are young, you are still not conscious of these things and you count too much on your future. You think that there's plenty of time to square away the accounts. But life passes very quickly and, after all, a moral debt is not just a word. It's something very tangible."

Silence. They feel the hopelessness of the situation. Many of them are seeing such utter hopelessness for the first time. I must end the meeting. I feel a strange embarrassment, as though I were guilty of something. And then those stilted words about moral debts! I go on:

"I am aware of everything. The laboratory is in danger. You may feel that all this is futile and become lax. The problems are tremendous, there are quantities of work, and you can't count on me. Or you may think that all my plans are the product of my despair and that I will give up in the end. I won't. I'll hang on until my dying day. Whoever doubts this should leave now. But those who stay must give me their word of honor that they will work harder this year than ever before. For our task—and for me."

To hint that they owe everything to me? No, no use. If they understand this, fine. If not, words won't help. Of course, no one will get up and leave now. But I must watch them later.

"Let's discuss the plan." It is Yura who says this, and in a strangely flat, businesslike tone.

Fine, let's. But deep inside me I feel that I would like to dwell a bit longer on emotions. I would like to have my poor head stroked a little. But no.

Yura continues: "Without considerable outside help we will not be able to finish our machine. None of you realize the complexity of the purely mechanical work involved. The Institute of Cybernetics could help, but even they can't handle this alone. We must raid other institutes, talk to directors. But even this won't be enough; we must find volunteer enthusiasts. There are many of them and I can ferret them out. But you, Ivan Nikolaevich, will have to speak to them. And, of course, to the directors."

Yes, Not by bread alone . . .

"I will do that. How much time do you need?"

"Three days for reconnaissance. But this is not all. We must know exactly what we want to model. After all, besides the heart, the kidneys and some nerve regulators, we have no characteristics. And even the scheme of organic interrelation is not yet fully worked out. When I came here three years ago, everything looked simple to me. Now, on the contrary, I see it is very difficult. There is no hope that we can obtain all the characteristics before—well, within one year. There's one thing left: the heuristic approach. We must take mere hypotheses and just model them."

He is speaking well and correctly. I must devote all my time to this too. No lectures, no articles. Just thinking.

"All right. Has anyone anything else to say?"

Vadim: "The nerve and endocrine systems will give us trouble. There are no ready methods of study. The nerve impulses cannot be caught; they travel along many as yet undetermined channels . . . and the hormones in the blood . . . To study them we need very complex chemistry."

"Vadim, we must work on the presumption that at the beginning of any pathological process, all regulatory systems are standard. Then I think their reactions would be more or less stereotyped. That's what some foreign researchers tell us. Then we must grasp a few knotty points and using them, visualize the scheme of the entire system. Semyon Ivanovich?"

"Yes?"

"What would you say?"

"My problem is modest—the characteristic of the kidneys. I think we will have this. Within a month or two."

"And this is all?"

"What else can I say? I don't know mathematics, and fantasy is not my sphere."

"You could take upon yourself the liver. We can't move without it. It plays a part in all pathological processes."

"I'll try to find something in the literature about the methods, but I'm afraid I won't get much. This seems to be a very complicated sphere."

Is he unable or unwilling? Unable. He is used to working along narrow channels—from "A" to "B." The boys watch him with hidden animosity. There will be a conflict here. Let's leave him for a while.

Now, what about Igor? This one can work with the best of them. At last: "Ivan Nikolaevich, may I say something?"

"By all means, Igor."

"I'm not going to touch the heart. Things are pretty good there. Yura, Tolia and I will work out the exact formula connecting the quantity, pressures, pH, and the oxygen contents. But only under limited pathology. The influence of the regulatory systems, the hormonal and nerve influences are still very obscure. Yura's electronic model is good enough as far as the characteristics go—"

"Igor, I know all that."

"Forgive me, I'm just unnerved. What I am trying to say is that we need a good doctor, an experienced physician practically familiar with pathological processes for which our machine is being built. Alexei Yurievich, the anesthesiologist, could be our man. You know him; he has come to watch some of our tests. But you must speak to his chief."

"Very well, I'm putting this down."

I will tell Alexei Yurievich everything, even though I can't scare him with death. He's used to it. However, he *is* interested in our work. A progressive physician. But very dry. It is hard to tell what he is living for.

"Forgive me, I want to add something. Why not let me go into clinical physiology? Temporarily. One can get much there for the characteristics of heart pathology."

"Very good, Igor. We'll arrange that."

Everyone has become settled and is discussing things in a businesslike way. Will they carry out their resolve? So far I have always had to push them. Now I have no more strength for that. Everything may fall to pieces. I must stimulate them.

"Listen, boys, do you realize that all the results of this work will benefit not me but everyone of you? That you're working for *yourselves?*"

The reaction. Vadim again: "You needn't talk this way. We

understand everything. And we don't sell ourselves for titles and degrees—even though we don't decline them."

A pause. Yura has blushed. Igor is looking at the window. Semyon's face does not express anything.

I have offended them. Saying noble words about morals, but overlooking simple human feelings. "Forgive me, boys."

Yura: "We're not ideal heroes, Ivan Nikolaevich, but we are trying to do our best."

I can't say anything to that. The best way is to pretend that nothing has happened. And anyway, it's time to end this.

"There's one more point, Comrades. In all our schemes, the tissues, their cell levels, are represented very poorly. But it is they who consume oxygen and glucose, and eliminate hydroacids and wastes. For the tissue characteristic we need good biochemistry, and you all know what our lab is. Semyon Ivanovich, could you go to the Biochemistry Institute and sound them out about collaboration? Do you know anyone there?"

"No, no one, but I'll get to know them. I'll go tomorrow. I don't know whether I'll be able to explain precisely what we need from them, but I'll try to interest them and then I'll bring them to you."

This is all. What else do I have to tell them? Yes, about general behavior.

"Our immediate agenda is exhausted, Comrades. I have noted everything. Just report to me from time to time. Don't hesitate to come to me at any time. When I feel weak I'll tell you myself. And, yes, another thing: It's unnecessary—and impossible—to make a secret of my illness. But idle conversation about it should be avoided. The most important thing is not to slacken our tempo. You may go now. I'll drop into Surgery later on and take a look."

I add this to avoid goodbyes. I feel that leave-taking would be awkward for them.

They get up and silently file out. One after another—tall, straight, young, healthy.

Thus starts the new era in the life of our laboratory. Now they will start thinking. I am not at all sure that all of them will retain their noble fervor. Human nature is complicated, the instincts are powerful, the subconscious drive for possession, for power, or simple laziness. Envy may arise, suspicion, greed. Are their defenses against these things strong enough?

Should I telephone Liuba before she has left for home? How unpleasant it is to organize those rendezvous—lies, lies, lies. They are an agony for her. Thank God, it will soon be all over.

I lift the receiver.

"Operator? Is the outside line free? Get me 53-67-20."

The connection.

"Let me speak with Liubov Borisovna, please."

I wait. What will I tell her? She will be surprised. She doesn't expect this call.

"Liubov Borisovna? This is I. Yes, me. I must speak to you. Tonight. No, nothing has happened, but this is important. I'll be home after five—as usual. Until then."

I can feel that she is disturbed. But I must see her tonight. I can't wait until next week. And I dread this encounter. I'll play my part of a courageous male who can face his doom. She will play her part, too—encouraging me. And then cry all the way home, wiping her tears, powdering her nose, carelessly, blindly. And then put on her usual frozen mask.

Everything inside me is turning numb. All those ghosts again—illness, hospital, suffering, death. And pity, awkwardness, insecurity.

What did the boys think about me? That their Chief is such a self-possessed scientist? When, in fact, he is a weak, frightened man who would like to hide his head under a pillow and moan, moan with anguish. All those plans are a mere attempt to escape from myself. Action always attracts action, and activity helps one to escape that hopeless loneliness. Science is an excellent thing. You think and think and forget that one unanswerable question: What for?

Too bad I have no family. No! It would have been so much worse. But this way, what does anyone else stand to lose? Objectively speaking, my death would simplify Liuba's life. The laboratory? Yes, they need me. For a time. It is useless to build illusions; somehow I've never noticed particular emotional affinities between teachers and pupils. They grow and go away. Just like children. I haven't experienced this yet, but I can hardly be an exception.

This is the right time for me to go—while they are still young and still attached to me.

A loss for science? That's what they will say at the cemetery. My contribution to it has been so infinitesimal that one can hardly see it.

It is a terrible thing—materialism. Nuclei, atoms, molecules. Cells, organs, organisms. The brain—just a modeling installation. Love, friendship, inspiration—mere programs of digesting information. One can model them on a computer. They have no particular quality. There is no God, no soul. Nothing, really. I am a mere minor element in a complex system—human society. I live, suffer and act in accordance with strict laws of the materialistic world. I can learn those laws, but never escape them. Rather, yes. Into death. Let it come. I love no one.

Easy, my friend. Bitterness will not help. Life is not, after all, a bad thing. The joy of discovery. Contact with a loved one. A cigarette. A talk with a friend. It is not important that all this is just a set of vibrations of the molecular and atomic arrangement of the nerve cells forming some "pleasure centers" in the brain. It is still good.

■ ▪

I am sitting, thinking. About anabiosis, and some other things.

It is late. I should go and look for Yura. It would be best if others did not see this. In the "collective," private conversations are frowned upon. I am taking my notes with me.

He is probably in the workshop. Shall I send someone for him? No. Better do it on my own.

Our laboratory is scattered all over the building. The result of our aggressive policy: as the work developed we fought for more and more rooms. Ivan Petrovich complained, whined, but usually gave way. Of course! "Cybernetical methods, progress . . ." A feather in his cap.

I am walking along endless shadowy corridors. People are ready to leave; doors are open, people are dressing. Snatches of conversation. On some doors there are still signs: "Experiment in progress. Do not enter."

After hours the building is almost empty. Science is performed during working hours. Idle conversation is included in working hours as well.

But all my boys are still here. True, they like to complain now and then about "overwork." "You are exploiting us"—half in jest, half seriously. Fine boys and girls.

At last I reach my destination. A dull pain in the pit of my stomach . . . subconsciously I am constantly "listening" to my body now. This is what will always happen from here on—pain here, pain there.

The three doors of our workshop. Yura must be in the first room: there stands the mock-up of the electronic heart model, his baby, his love.

Yes, here he is. He is sitting alone on a high stool before the oscillograph. The ray of light follows along the quick curves—the pattern of the pressure in the ventricle. He does not see me. His eyes are glued to the screen while his hand is turning a gauge. The amplitude and sharpness of the curves change. I know—he is trying out various "entries," pressure levels in the veins.

"Yura, I must talk to you."

"Huh?"

He is startled, and then he smiles broadly. His face can look very young; it is difficult to believe that he is twenty-seven. I could have had a son like him.

"This is a private talk. Shall we stay here or go into my office?"

"Up to you, Ivan Nikolaevich. This is a quiet place now. The boys have scattered around, and some of them are in the experiment room."

"Let's stay here, then."

I sit down close to the radiator. I am becoming sensitive to cold lately.

"May I smoke?"

"Of course, Yura! I'd be glad to smell your cigarette." A pause. Somehow I'm embarrassed to touch upon such a fantastic topic as anabiosis. "How is your dissertation coming along? You realize that now you must hurry, Yurochka?"

When we are alone I use the familiar form of addressing him, just as I do with Vadim and Igor. I love them; they are my pupils.

And even if I know that they will forget me, this is a cerebral knowledge; emotionally, I don't believe it.

"If I can detach myself from work for two weeks, I can finish it."

"Impossible, Yura! You may leave the lab, but not the organizational work. You must find a compromise; do what's most important, and then go home."

"Once you're here you get stuck."

"The dissertation must be ready in two months, at the latest. This is important to me as well. Has Dimitri Evgenievich read all the chapters?"

"Yes, and approved them."

I must come to the point. There is no other way.

"Yura, I have another important thing to discuss with you. I am a little embarrassed to speak about this; I may sound like a bit of a cheat. Don't make such a face; this is right. I want to cheat . . . death." (A cheap show-off!)

"What?"

"You see how startled you are? All people die, but I want to beat death."

How crudely I am expressing myself! Gangster-film talk. But where to find the words to explain my fear, my bewilderment, my confusion? He is looking at me with a mixture of alarm and disbelief; my prestige is sinking fast in his eyes.

"Yura, I don't want to die. No, don't think I'm a coward who would try to buy extra hours with pills and tablets. No. I want to gamble for the highest stakes."

Badly expressed again. I've never gambled in my life. Yura is confused, he seems to shrink from me. Or is this my imagination? Back to the theme:

"In short, I want to subject myself to anabiosis. How much do you know about it?"

"Not much. I have read some articles and novels. Nothing serious."

"Do you remember our experiments with hypothermy? Have you watched some of Piotr Stepanovich's operations?"

"Yes—or rather, I've *heard* about them. But those methods have not been successful, if I'm not mistaken."

"That is why this time we must conduct this at the highest technical level. And I need your help."

"I must think about it . . . Is there any serious literature about it?"

"Here are some rough notes which I jotted down last night. This is just to trigger your imagination. You read them and tomorrow we'll talk. Then I'll indicate some other sources."

I give him my notes. He takes them and begins to read. A pleasant eagerness, but not polite.

"You'll read them at home. And I ask you not to discuss this with anyone. Besides technical problems, there are ethical ones."

I am ashamed to talk about this. As though I were doing something not quite decent. Like trying to advance my own interests by dishonest means.

"Ivan Nikolaevich, I can't talk sensibly about all this yet . . . All that has happened today has stunned me. I am not Vadim; I can't grasp things like that. Please give me a day."

"But of course, Yurochka. And now I'd better go home . . ."

Probably my face looks pitiful because he reddens and starts to blink suspiciously. Or am I hypersensitive? Possibly.

"Could I do something for you? Come and see you tonight?"

"To comfort me? Thank you, my friend. This you will all have to do later. But not tonight. I'll tell you when. Good night, Yurochka."

He walks with me to the door first, then along the corridor to the stairs. It seems to me that he wants to say something nice but cannot muster the courage. Unfortunately.

On the way to the office I stop at Surgery.

The experiment is proceeding. The heart is working well and almost half of the program has been carried out. Lena and Alla are keeping records. Mila is attending to the anesthesia—squeezing the bag with regular movements. Polia is working with the blood containers which hang over the dog—changing the blood flow. Igor is sitting at the table, the graphs of the heart characteristics in his hand. He does not notice me.

"Well, how is it?"

He jumps up, embarrassed. Has been probably thinking about me. Now it seems to me that everyone is thinking about me.

"It's going well. Look at these curves. Interesting, aren't they?"

"Yes. And where's Vadim?"

"Gone home. A headache."

Also a reaction. Especially with him. He is the most expansive of them all. The girls obviously do not know anything yet. That is good. It is best to let them all get used to this gradually.

"Well, I'd better go, too. Tomorrow you'll show me the curves."

"Goodnight, Ivan Nikolaevich."

iv
And Another Night

I am home. I have had my dinner and I'm resting on the sofa. Food disgusts me. I must ask Agafia Semyonovna to cook something else. Borsht, borsht and cutlets. I hate them. But she doesn't know how to do anything else. Well, never mind. Restaurants and dining rooms are even worse. Waiting, ruining your nerves, listening to rude waiters.

A bachelor existence . . .

The dishes on the table are unwashed. Laziness. Liuba will come and wash them. She will grumble, but deep inside she likes doing it. It makes her feel as though she is at home here. I can see her wearing Agafia's apron. ("Why is it always so filthy?")

Liuba, Liubushka. Liubov. It must sound odd in any other language. *Liubov*—"love." In Russian it is tender.

Tonight we'll have no time for illusions of domesticity.

Let me dream. I am well. She has come to me. Forever. Has done the dishes. Is walking around the room, doing something, humming some sentimental tune. I am pretending to read a newspaper, but I'm watching her, admiring her. She no longer has to look at her watch—"Oh, it's already nine. I must go"—she is my wife. I am happy.

How many times have I dreamed this scene?

Now it's all over. Hopeless.

I will die alone.

But it could have been different.

I remember an apple orchard. An evening in June. A large surgery tent. A sound of a generator. An operation is in progress. The bright light of a portable lamp and dark shadows. Shadows dancing grotesquely across the tent flaps. Pavel Mikhailovich is operating. A stomach wound. A scout has stepped on a land mine. Vera is handing the clasps right into his hand, with clicks— one, two. Pink intestines move among white napkins and sheets.

Everything is going on normally. Audrey is holding the lamp, Kolia and I are standing by. I look at the intestines and at Vera. "Darling, darling . . ."

An explosion close by. Vera squats, holding her hands high—they have been sterilized. A reflex. The plane roars low overhead.

Pavel Mikhailovich, evenly: "Ivan, Kolia, down. No point in taking chances."

I walk to the flap, fling myself to the ground.

Burr-rrumph—boom!

The shadows jump. Vera's cry: "Ah-h-h!"

I jump up and see her sinking down, grasping at the sterilized sheets, pulling them down over herself.

"Pick her up. Volodia, Masha, do your job. Hurry up."

The man of iron.

That was the end of my first real love.

How slowly and with what difficulty had she died. Peritonitis. Enormous eyes on a gray face. "Why?" Restless hands. "Darling, I won't die, will I?" And in her voice I heard a reproach: "Went away . . . Lay down." Even now I am disgusted with myself. I did not shield her.

From then on I never took cover during bombardments.

Let us see how you will lie in that sarcophagus, my friend. You will probably tremble, bargain with yourself. "A month more. A week." And then die in bed, begging for a shot of morphine.

Almost six o'clock. It is quite dark outside. Soon she will be here. I must get up, go to the door, listen. It has been six years now, and still I am as nervous as though this is the first time. I thought I would never fall in love again. And here I am.

There were others, before Liuba. But it never grew into love. No, I was not promiscuous. They all were good women. Probably it was simpler—I could not measure up to them. Yes, that is true. Let us be honest. But then none of the partings was particularly difficult for me either.

Someone has walked down the stairway. I hope he will not run into her.

Am I sorry? No. No. With Vera it was almost a puppy love. It did not leave any lasting mark. With others it was different—

sometimes good, sometimes not. And only here there is real harmony.

A strange thing, love . . .

I can hear my heart thump. Why, really? No, no passion. Certainly not tonight. Why then? Intellectual communion? But Lenya, for instance, is more intelligent, more interesting. But my heart does not thump when I am with him.

She will come in, put her hands on my shoulders, rise on tiptoe and kiss me—quickly, sharply. That specific aroma of her breath . . . "Well, how is it?" And everything around will turn into light. Flowers.

I am a poet now.

There are centers in the brain. There are hormones. Patterns in the cortex. There is nothing else. Materialism.

But I'm living by this. It warms me up, illuminates my work, my science.

Why isn't she here? Has something held her up? There are so many obstacles.

We have been making plans . . . The children will grow up . . . No. Don't. It's best not to remember. She could never run the gantlet of her children's eyes. I—well, I haven't been too insistent either. Let's be honest: solitude has its points. Liuba is a very strong woman. It might be fatiguing.

A ring. "Coming!"

She runs in, breathless. I want to kiss her.

"Wait, let me catch my breath. I don't think anyone has seen me. . . . What happened?" An alarmed, inquiring look.

"Nothing special. Take off your coat. Give it to me."

She is fussing with her hair at the mirror. Specially bought for her. Her request.

We are sitting side by side on the divan. As usual. . . . No, not as usual. Already there is something invisible between us. I must overcome it.

I kiss her with special tenderness but she is alarmed, sensitive.

"Anyway, what *has* happened?"

I have planned to tell her later. After a while. But I know this would not work.

"All right . . . Let's sit here, in the chairs."

We move to the little table. What comfortable chairs! I have been preparing for this scene, but still I don't know how to start.

"Shall I put on some coffee?"

Sharply: "Go ahead. Tell me everything!" She is used to giving orders during surgery.

"Yesterday I went to see a doctor. David. Remember I told you about my spells of weakness, the unpleasant taste in the mouth? I just told him and he sent me to the laboratory—for a blood test. Then he started questioning me, listening to my heart, feeling my stomach—especially on the left side. I was watching him, but one can tell nothing looking at his fat, kind face. He told me to wait for the analysis. We sat around for maybe forty minutes, just talking. I was telling him about the machine. I got carried away, and then noticed that he was not listening. At this point they brought in the analysis—"

"Where is it?"

I take it from my notebook, give it to her.

How hard she can set her mouth! One can see how she contracts inside. Then her face sags, lips tremble, she drops her eyelids . . . But only for a second or two. Then she frowns, throws back her head, looks squarely at me.

"And so you've gone to pieces? Decided to die?"

I am taken aback. I was ready for tears, hysterics, anything. And suddenly, this attack.

"No, but this is leukemia . . . You know what that means. You're a doctor."

"First of all, I'm not sure that all this is correct. Then there are ways of treating this. Successfully."

But the corners of her lips are still trembling a little. My imagination? Yes, probably. She seems to be calm. Then perhaps all this is not really so final? David did not say anything definite. But the encyclopedia? An error? Doctors don't like patients to read medical literature. But I'm not just a patient. I am a professor, a medical man. And still . . . ?

Maybe she is just playing a part? Does not love me really, does not sympathize? I need sympathy so much, now.

I must play my part as well in front of her. I can't show fear. It is even better to control each other, not fall apart. There is still a second part of the conversation ahead—about anabiosis. Kiss her? On account? I bend over, kiss her.

"Come, let's sit together."

"No, darling. Please." She moves away a little. Does not accept me. Very well. I did this only to please her. But she feels everything. Soon all this will be over. Forever. No, I must not wind myself up. Let everything proceed along its normal course. I kneel before her, kiss her hands. Soft little palms, so strangely inert today.

I must tell her about my plans. She must not think that I have given up and that I only need compassion.

Once again I take my place in the armchair, facing her. "I have looked up my case in the encyclopedia and I know the prognosis. Don't try to mislead me. But I don't want to give up. I must finish my present work—at no matter what cost. I have worked out some plans . . ."

I tell her about today's events in detail. I need to talk. I must talk. Liuba looks straight at me with wide-open eyes, listening. Her mouth is set, she is all attention. But it seems to me that she does not hear me, does not even see me. Even though, usually, professional topics hold her attention; they are the best part of all our talks.

"I don't know whom to train as my successor. If I could combine Yura and Vadim . . . They are close friends—but for how long? You know, friendship is not a solid basis for collaboration. Mutual respect and a bit of distance are the best elements for effective common work . . ." How stiffly I'm expressing myself! Professor.

"And why do you want to solve all these problems now? Let it go as it's gone before. You're in too much of a hurry to bury yourself."

"You mean live while I'm alive and then let the devil take it? No, this is not my style. I have started something and I must protect it. At least in the beginning."

"You are vain. You professors are all the same."

"No, you're wrong. Absolutely. This is a matter of duty. You have your duty to your patients, I to my science. Yes, I know that duty and all that is self-delusion, but it's become a part of me, got into my blood. And I don't want to destroy it. I couldn't live without it. Not even these last few months."

She winces at the last words. She is right—I needn't keep rubbing it in.

"I look at you and I envy you." (She, envies me?) "No, not that—I envy your determination. You're possessed. This is why you've remained a bachelor. You've given yourself to science, created an idol, built a temple in which you officiate. You don't see anything else. It's easy to live that way."

Bitterness in the voice.

How can I talk to her about anabiosis after that? She would not understand, would never accept it. She is not "a possessed one." So I'd better hold it back—even though it is difficult; I would like to share everything with her. Completely.

"But you approve of my plans?"

"Of course."

A mechanical answer. Her thoughts are miles away. I can sense her logic. "Let him rave. It will be easier for him." No matter how she pretends my ideas are foreign to her. Too bad.

Then suddenly she says: "You know, Vanichka, I have been thinking about your machine." A pause. Then she continues. "There are doubts. Would it be able to reflect specific aspects of each pathological process? There is a difference between, for instance, the blood reaction to a perforated ulcer and to a stomach wound. And the blood biochemistry is even more unpredictable."

Her mouth forms words, but her face, her eyes are not here. And there is a mournful expression in them. She is not interested in any machine at the moment. And it is all-important to me.

"I understand. This is our weak point, certainly. But we simply can't model each organ down to the molecule. And molecules cause all the differentiations."

"But if you overlook those specifics you may fail your main purpose. How can you determine the seriousness and progress of each illness without them?"

"That I don't know yet. For this we must express deviations in the system on the quantitative basis, and determine what is caused by cells and what by organs. What is general and what is specific. But even the modeling of this 'general' would already help science."

All this is too complicated for her. Why continue? She is suffering.

I look at her. She is sitting there, her face between her palms, looking at the table from under her knit brows. Her words fall like stones.

"I walked here to you like a blind person . . . hoping that a car would run over me . . . Such despair . . . praying to God to let me die, or you, or *him*. Even the children. . . . I am a criminal, am I not?"

Then we talk about other things, jumping from subject to subject. She is complaining about her Kostia. The boy is growing up, maturing. And all around him, in books, in films, there is violence, struggle, strife. He is fascinated—and she is frightened.

"You know, with age this will pass. All boys go through these phases. The most important thing is that he's intelligent."

"Is that so important? There are many clever scoundrels. More than enough."

"The really intelligent ones are rarely scoundrels. Those are average ones usually."

"How can I be sure that he will be really intelligent? Or really talented?"

"Intelligence and talent are two different things. Talent is innate. Intelligence must be developed."

She gets up, walks into the kitchen. Looks around with unseeing eyes. "Shall I do the dishes?"

"No, I beg you. Just sit down and let me look at you."

All this is very sad. I can see that she is dying to go, but is sorry for me. She knows what loneliness means to me now.

"Well, darling, you'd better go. If you must, you must."

"Help me with my coat." She likes for me to take care of her, to notice her a little.

The coat with an expensive collar, bought by her husband. A doctor's pay does not provide for luxuries. The familiar aroma.

For a few moments she stands near the door, listening. Then turns, raises her little face. It looks almost normal. A smile. No, but the eyes are different, uneasy eyes.

"Kiss me. I'm going."

That is all. A slam of the door and the staccato clicking of her heels down the stairway. Then, silence. I am alone again.

Don't let yourself go, my friend. First, let's wash those dishes. Agafia will not come until the day after tomorrow. Can't let them stay this way. Even though I am a bachelor, I hate disorder.

As a dishwasher, I'm a flop. A jet of hot water, one, two, and they are dripping in a dish rack over the sink. Ten minutes. Then I must sit down and work, work, work. Think. There is not a minute to lose. I must visualize the characteristics of all the main organs. Give the mathematicians approximate curves. Then there will be formulas. Then machines, models.

But perhaps all this is not the main thing? Maybe I should spend my last months thinking about culture, philosophy, psychology? There are many unsolved questions. They are interesting. A scientist must periodically give old dogmas a good shake. As I see it, this is long overdue with us.

No, I have thought enough about all that. All I can do is raise questions and find no answers. A special investigation is needed here. However, I may still come back to it—in due time.

The main thing is the plan. I must leave something positive behind me. Very well, I'll be at it in a minute. I never knew vanity could be so compelling. A desire to present the world with yet another toy.

The dishes are done. All are sitting in the rack. Now back to my chair—and to my thoughts.

I am very comfortable. My feet on the radiator. They are cold. Illness? Old age? No.

I have not spoken to Liuba about the anabiosis idea. How can I prepare her for it?

I simply must do this—this anabiosis. Very interesting. When again would they risk such an experiment? Ethics will stand in the way. But Liuba will get used to it. In time.

What if I really wake up in twenty-five or fifty years, as in those novels about cosmic travelers? I must memorize—or even write down—all the questions facing the world today. It may be that I will wake up an idiot. That would be terrible. However, what is the difference? The idiot does not realize his condition. It is worse when it is halfway, when critical sense still remains.

Why should I worry about this now? The odds are so small that thinking about details is just stupid.

I must prepare for death. Real, final death.

Again, who can take over from me? Vadim? Yura? Yura will be able to give more, but Vadim also may absorb mathematics and mechanics in time. Everything is possible for an intelligent man. Thus, their chances should be equal. No, Yura's horizons are still wider. He combines practicality with fantasy. If only he had a few more years to master physiology.

Tomorrow I am seeing David again. What course of treatments will he prescribe for me? I hope not too bothersome.

Lenya may drop in tonight.

I just don't feel like starting work. I am tired. I have had so much trouble today, and no chance to rest after dinner. Liuba.

I must work. There is something inside me that urges me on. "Go ahead, go ahead . . ." I can't stop. This is frightening. Loneliness and senselessness will take hold of me, and then I will feel like howling—like a wolf.

Gorky has written a good phrase: "Had Jacob been a dog, Jacob would have howled from morning to night." It is the same with me. I feel like howling.

Ten o'clock . . . I'm sitting, honestly working, books all around me. I'm thinking about the scheme of controlling all life functions. The regulatory systems which I have designed (I!) are holding up well. However, all this is not enough: the blood system, the vegetative nerve system, the cortex. I must determine their "floors," their correlation with one another. This scheme must be introduced into our machine as a governing force over the organs.

Actually, this problem has been assigned to Vadim, but he will be obviously incapable of coping with it alone. I must be prepared to take it over. My head is still quite clear and productive.

Happy? Why not? I have this ability to arrange things logically, guessing correlations, developing hypotheses. From the reactions all around me I see that I am good at it. Whose reactions? Of my helpers? They are still immature. No, they are very demanding; it is difficult to gain their respect. And what about all the others? Ivan Petrovich would not have given me such a laboratory had he not trusted me. And all this without any protection or pull.

No, my friend Ivan. All this is not so. You know yourself that your abilities stop short of talent. You are a good combiner. You have taken together physiology, cybernetics, mathematics, technology, brought in a bunch of bright kids, and have created something interesting. But you have discovered nothing, and it is doubtful that you will ever make any real discovery. And all your ideas are still in the conversational stage. When and if they work out all the mathematical characteristics and construct a working machine—well, then it will be different.

True. But the characteristics and the machines will be here. I am certain of that. And this will be a new and important advance in physiology and medicine. Absolutely. Even though without any genius on my part.

The real stumbling blocks are the regulatory systems. There are all those books on endocrinology and yet it is still obscure how the glands affect one another. The assertions are contradictory. Why? Because no one has attempted to investigate the question on a quantitative basis—the way we are doing it. So we will have to work with approximations.

A telephone ring in the hall. Who can it be at this hour? I go out, lift the receiver.

"Yes?"

"Ivan Nikolaevich, this is I, Yura. Are you in bed?"

What a fool! It is not yet ten. However, this is just a polite gambit.

"What happened?"

"Nothing. I have read your notes and I'd like to speak to you."

I am thinking. Ask him to come tomorrow? He is interrupting my work. But his opinion is important: a realistic, technical approach, my life or death. Besides, the fear of the approaching night. Loneliness.

"Where are you?"

"At the lab. But it won't take me long."

"Come, then."

I will keep him here overnight. He can sleep here. We shall discuss various matters. I like these tête-à-têtes. A man opens up. Begins to search within himself, verifies his thoughts.

The kitchen. The refrigerator. The dirty dishes again . . . Never mind. What do I have to eat? He will arrive hungry. Youth. Do I feel myself old? I didn't—until yesterday; but now it is different. The end is near. It is hard to get used to it. But I must. Otherwise, I'd be in real trouble.

I have everything—sausage, cheese, butter, some canned peppers. Not enough bread. But there are crackers.

How quickly age changes a man. Today's youth is a different breed to me. Not at all the way we were when we were young. Or is this my imagination? We were poor. I remember myself coming out of the Technicum. I didn't have a jacket, just a worn-out sweater. It was a little embarrassing, but not too bad.

However, this is the normal reaction of an aging generation. "We were better." I must talk to Yura about it.

What will he say about the project? The purely technical problems might be insurmountable, might defeat us. The important thing is to concentrate on the cooling routine—I won't need "thawing out" for a while; they can work out the methods for that later on. And the real installations also later. Now just the temporary models. Then, while I am lying there, they will have to build permanent ones. Men, money—everything will be found.

Well, I'd better grind some coffee. Funny, in my mind I have worked everything out, but subconsciously I don't believe in it. As though I am playing some game.

Liuba must also be thinking about it. I can see her. She is busy but she is not really there. Wrinkles around the mouth. A child that has been hurt.

My whole life I have been training myself not to feel sorry for things I lose. Gone, gone. Forgotten. And now I must learn to face the final loss. To accept it. Yes, inevitable. I am incapable of supreme heroism—of bearing torture silently, or throwing myself upon a firing machine gun. But this I must go through with. I can see myself lying down on that table. Last goodbye's. The last look at the window—a piece of the sky. The anesthesiologist is giving me the nitrous oxide, "laughing gas." I am falling asleep pleasantly. This is all. They will say later, "The Chief was bearing up well."

I will go through with it.

I had better set the table, so that he will not refuse—sausage, cheese, butter. Dishes. Yes, napkins.

I am a little too old for this kind of experiment. Hypothermy has always worked better with puppies. Unfortunately there is no choice here. Perhaps to experiment on someone . . . ? Stop! Such a filthy thought—from the backroom of the subconscious, so deep that it can't even be set to words. Let us face it squarely. And say once and for all: no experimentation. Perish the thought. You will be the first one on this flight into eternity.

Words, just words . . .

A soft ring at the door.

Yura. Always polite.

He enters. Handsome, rosy-cheeked. Girls must be crazy about him.

"Getting colder outside?"

"Yes, feels like a winterset. Forgive me, Ivan Nikolaevich, for this intrusion so late at night, but—"

"Forget it, Yurochka. I'm very glad you called. I feel a bit lonely—" No, no hints. "Let's have a bite and discuss things."

"No, I've had my supper. I'm here for a minute—"

"Oh no. Now you're a guest and must obey your host."

He hesitates, for just as long as prescribed by etiquette. We sit down. I keep him company just to make it easy for him. He has been well brought up. A good old family.

"Take more. I know you're hungry. Don't try to fool me."

"Well, I am—I'm afraid I'll eat up all your supplies."

I fuss with the coffee maker. Put in more coffee—instead of

cognac. I don't think Yura drinks. But I have heard that he has a girl friend.

Perhaps now is the time to start the conversation. "Well, I'm dying to hear your opinion, Yura. Only, honestly, no gilding the lily."

"One moment . . . I'll take it point by point."

He walks into the entrance hall, brings in a folder. It has been lying there under the mirror.

"Ivan Nikolaevich, I'm not competent to discuss biology or physiology. I'll speak only about technical questions."

"Don't be modest. You have plunged into our science pretty deeply already." (Flattering him. Playing on his vanity. No. This is true.)

"Very well, let me start. I see three basic problems here: designing a program of advanced controls and building the machine, probably of analogous type. Then the measuring indicators. Then the activating mechanisms. The time for the creation of the entire complex is drastically short, and our means are limited."

"Not enough time?"

In other words, no hope. I can see that he is uneasy.

"No, I haven't said that. But we must discuss the maximum curtailment of anything not absolutely essential."

"Yura, I understand that all this is extremely difficult. But certain things could be simplified. First of all, let us concentrate only on the cooling process." (Putting me to death!) "Then, build all the mechanisms on a temporary mock-up basis. Third, not to get overinvolved in automatization. Use it only when the manual approach is impossible. I think that we must just start up this thing, and you will work out details later."

He is listening attentively, but looking aside.

I don't like it. Is it really impossible?

"Well, I wouldn't like to bet on it."

This is unpleasant. Is he backing out? Without him, there is no point in even trying. No time to find a new engineer and train him in our procedures. But, easy; speak quietly, and do not push.

"If you say 'impossible,' we'll abandon the whole idea. Especially because we have our main task—creating the machine."

"There's no need to offend me, Ivan Nikolaevich. When have I refused to collaborate? It is just that I can't as yet reconcile myself to the thought that this *has* to happen . . ."

He does not believe it. Neither do I. But this is a fact.

"Unfortunately, it will happen."

"And you actually feel that there are chances for success?"

This already is a little tactless—to express doubt and destroy the last straw. But I must overlook it. He does not mean it that way.

"All this is in my notes. Yes, there are chances. Just consider hibernation of mammals. Their body temperature is lowered to 45 degrees, but they have developed the mechanics for suspending animation and coming back to life. In all probability this ability is locked in the endocrine system and responds to outside factors. Some hormones come into play, the metabolism and the nerve system slow down. And then the process is reversed."

"I wish we had such hormones!"

"Well, my friend, they have been looking for them—so far unsuccessfully. This means that this is a difficult task. At any rate, cells are capable of surviving low temperatures. The main danger is the time element in our case. We must organize our anabiosis experiment on such a basis that all cell discharges are fully compensated."

This sounds very reasonable, even to myself. But it is important to make him believe in it—no, a wrong word—to *convince* him. He is a man of exact science.

"Don't you see what an interesting experiment this is?"

"If it were just an experiment!"

"We have no choice, Yura. If you want to know, I also have doubts. Hamsters, bears, bats are going through winters at the expense of their own energy sources, their depletion. But what about synthesis? A certain portion of albumin will be expended. Would it be possible to replenish it? This must be verified."

"Very well. Since this is inevitable, let's consider concrete points. Even though, I must admit, all this is very frightening."

"Naturally. This is no joke—sending a man into the future. And a person close to you at that. Right? However, I hope you have given this your thought and come up with some concrete ideas."

The coffee is ready. I pour it. The crackers.

"Drink it."

"Well, I have already spoken of the three main problems. We can't go inventing new measuring gauges; we'll have to use what we already have. For the program of the cooling process we might —just *might*—find or adapt some existing schemes. The same can apply to the maintenance of the stationary regime."

"We could utilize our machine."

A protesting gesture. "No, we can't rely on it that much. It is designed to model actual conditions, not to control them. But a few things we may borrow from it. The most difficult problem is the third—the maintenance. We need a faultless apparatus for artificial blood circulation, an excellent mechanical kidney. And the high-pressure chamber. Can't we eliminate it?"

The whole thing becomes increasingly complicated.

He picks up his coffee cup. His hands are not too clean—a practical mechanic.

"Unfortunately, I don't think so. At least not during the cooling and warming stages. It is quite possible that high pressure combined with low temperature will produce gratifying results. What if we find it possible to introduce the entire oxygen supply through the skin?"

"You yourself write that the supply would be disproportionate in the upper and lower tissue levels. And then how to evacuate carbonic acids? No, artificial blood circulation is unavoidable. I'm afraid that if we abandon hemoglobin we'll have to run the machine at a high production rate. And this would probably be beneficial for the tissues, this constant flushing out."

He has understood everything. This is pleasant. Yes, he should be left in charge, and no one else.

He continues to talk. But my thoughts are drifting away. To Liuba, and even further.

"Therefore, we must design several installations. First, the artificial-blood-circulation machine with the built-in controls for a constant level of oxygen and carbonic acids in the fluid outflow.

This will affect the design of the sarcophagus and its regulated level of pressure and gas composition. Along with it, the control of the body temperature—probably also at the point of the fluid outflow."

"No, we need additional measurements in the esophagus and colon. Surgeons do this. The gas pressure in the tissues must also be measured directly. Blood analyses are not enough."

He nods in agreement. "Minor points."

"The next system—the artificial kidney along with the pH, fluid-and-salt-balance controls. And don't forget the evacuation of the urea. I doubt that we can create automatic controls here since we have no indicators for this."

"Not important. These indications will change slowly and we can use regular analyses. When the operation becomes stabilized they will remain constant anyway. We need only a time-control mechanism to switch the machine on and off."

My life in the hands of a mechanism. What life? Can one call it that?

"Possibly. But to design these systems we would require quantitative characteristics of the body mechanics under given conditions. This means the consumption of oxygen per minute, production of carbo-acids, the expenditure of glucose and nitric products."

"It is highly improbable that we can obtain exact characteristics in time, Yura. Especially under different temperatures. But can't we design things with 'reserve'—to maintain the constancy of this or that parameter?"

"Of course. But we need some departure points just the same."

"One point—the normal metabolism at the cooling point. The second—approximately two or three percent lower at the anabiosis. In those limits we can organize controls."

"No, Ivan Nikolaevich. The designers must know the exact requirements, in figures and graphs. Tell me, are we going to build the . . . real installation directly, or a trial one for experimentation with dogs?"

He did not say, "directly for you." Did not want to hurt me, obviously.

I too decide to avoid direct implications.

"We must design everything for human beings, but it must be usable for dogs as well. Besides, we must preserve secrecy. Let them design an experimental installation. This is not a cosmic rocket or a hydrogen bomb. And we will use the already existing components—the blocks of organs, the blood-circulation machine, the artificial kidney."

"Why not do the opposite—make it public? Call it the Travel-into-the-Future Machine and bring in the newspaper reporters? It would be a worldwide sensation. And, at the same time, an appeal: come and help the shock construction group."

"And what would our superiors say?"

"Let them say anything they want! As soon as the papers come out with it, we'll have mobs of enthusiasts wanting to help us."

Really, what can they do to me? I can't be punished any longer. Or can I? They can stop me from working, deprive me of my last joy. Then, goodbye anabiosis, goodbye, my machine. (How attached a prisoner can become to his wheelbarrow!)

"No, Yura, that wouldn't work. Why brag in advance? The return journey is too problematical. Let's look for more modest ways."

"Right! Then let's sit down and start figuring out technical requirements. Tomorrow I'll visit some plants and sound them out on placing some orders. Can you work some more tonight?"

I am not in good shape, and I would like very much to stretch out with a newspaper or a book. It is eleven o'clock. But time is pressing.

"Let's, Yura. What do you propose concretely?"

"I'd like to go through your notes, to write our proposed regimes, parameters, figures. To draw the scheme of the installation itself. Then determine what can be used out of the existing stuff and what must be designed. To draft an approximate technical plan."

"Come into my office, please, sir."

We work for about an hour. Discuss the main points of the program. Discover that ideas and technical means to implement them are often miles apart. We need the characteristics of organs and systems under low temperatures and under transitory stages of cooling and reheating. Some thorny problems come up; there are no local means to resolve a number of the mechanical questions; we must consult Moscow. At the same time, we must consult physicians.

What for?

Illness. Death. We talk, we argue as though we were discussing an abstract scientific problem. But now and then there is a quick fleeting thought: this is for you. And there is a constant subconscious feeling that this is the end. This colors everything in a different light.

It is good that Yura has come tonight. I watch him; he is deep in some computation. Straight nose, willful mouth; eyes a little small and too deep-seated. I am sure that human faces can be read—intelligence, character, inner traits—only we don't know how to do it. Perhaps cybernetics will solve this problem.

"All right, Yura. Enough for tonight."

"Well, I must go."

"No! Over my dead body! I have a camp bed, sheets, everything. Your mother knows where you are?"

"Yes, I called her from the lab and told her I am with you and will be home late. But she will worry just the same."

(But I need you!) "Never mind. Don't tell me you never spend nights away from home?"

"The way you mean it, never."

At twenty-seven? However, I was the same myself. I will have to let him go.

"Well . . . if you must go . . ."

He understands. A quick, sad thought crosses his face. He hesitates. "I could try calling a friend . . . in our building."

He goes out into the hall. How soon will we have telephones in all apartments? Greed. It was not long ago that we had no apartments, and now we want a telephone in each.

He is dialing. How long will he have to wait? No, not long.

"Dima? . . . Did I wake you up? . . . Forgive me for calling so late, but can you walk up and see my mother? . . . No, nothing.

But I want her to know that I'm staying overnight at the Chief's. ... Of course, she's waiting up. ... Thank you."

"Of course" means she always waits up for him. No ground for envy here; my mother was the same. It is good that she hasn't lived to see this. Good that I have no one. Liuba? Well, it's not the same thing.

He comes back smiling. He loves his mother.

"Well, now all is well. You know, I'm the only son."

I know. I was an only son.

"Shall we go to bed or have some tea?"

"Anything you say. I'm not tired."

"To the kitchen, then. Tea or coffee? Or a little drink? We have vodka, cognac, wine." (Cognac for Lenya, wine for Liuba, infrequently.)

"Oh no! I don't drink!" Protestingly.

"You're a model son. You don't drink, don't smoke; you spend your nights at home."

I wanted to say, "don't sleep with girls," but thought better of it. A professor. And he a man from a good home.

He is silent. I set the table. For how many times tonight? Three. We sit down. The teapot is whistling.

"Listen, Yura. Can you tell me how youth lives nowadays? You know, somehow I have lost touch with the young ones—have lost you, as they say. This is strange: before the revolution professors used to arrange informal weekly meetings with their students; but here I am, working with young boys and girls, and I learn about them from the newspapers."

"Well, I am probably not a typical example. You see, Mother is waiting up for me."

"Still you are closer to the young people."

"There are different kinds. I don't know the rural youth, but I know students around here. My general impression is not too favorable. But I am not a pessimist either, as many are."

"Be more precise. You're a scientist."

He smiles, and instantly his face becomes childish, appealing.

"I'm not a scientist. I'm an engineer."

But deep inside, he likes my words.

"All right, don't depreciate yourself. Have you ever thought about life?"

He becomes serious, almost grim.

"Often. And I don't like many things about it. They often say, all youth is bad. But honestly speaking, why should they be good? All the time one hears that this is bad, that is rotten . . ."

He is warming up.

"And you would like to see everything running smoothly?"

"Of course—the dialectics of living!" Ah-hah, he's coming out of his shell. Irony! "This is a very useful thing for many—the dialectics of life. You failed, you fell down, you got scared; or even worse, you submitted; and here is a crutch for you—the dialectics of life. One can explain anything by it—anything at all."

"Do you believe in communism?"

He gets up, paces the kitchen, three steps this way, three back. Then he stops, facing me. "Why do you ask?"

Indeed, why? "My friend, I propose to travel into the future. Just suppose your automatic machines wake me up in fifty years. You see, the future is a very concrete thing to me." (As if he can tell what is going to happen in fifty years! Do I know myself? I will learn when I wake up. If . . .)

"Very well, I'll answer you. Yes. But the word 'believe' is wrong for me. Communism is not religion."

"Nobody has said that. It's science."

"They taught it to us at the Institute as though it were a religion. Quotes, quotes . . . And if it's science, I have the right to look for new proofs."

"What do you have in mind? Discussion? Would discussion help in such matters?"

I can see it: meetings, speeches, passions, loss of discipline; nothing but harm.

"Who talks about open discussion? Scientific subjects are not solved at meetings." He has read my thought! "There are institutes. They must study it from all angles."

"Study what? What do you want to learn?"

He shrugs his shoulders. "As in all science—the truth."

"A rather vague term."

"All right. We engineer-cyberneticists want to express every-thing in mathematical equations. Including ideals. We need cyber-netic sociology and economics. Some objective methods of study of human behavior, the efficiency of people's labor, the level of their spiritual comfort. The stability and prospects of the social system."

"Really? Even ideals—in figures? Well, perhaps. But don't you exaggerate the possibilities of cybernetics in this area? After all, this is the sphere of human relations. Is it possible to program them and find a single correct solution for each? How durable would it be?"

He does not answer at once. Not so self-assured as I thought.

"I don't know." Then, after a small pause: "Still, every solu-tion must rest on a scientific calculation."

"It would be interesting to know what philosophers think about it. Do you have friends among them?"

"No. So far this interests me in a formal way. Enough for me that I got into medicine. One can live as it is. But some day I'll look into it more closely."

Can one live without these questions at all? Yes, or no, it is not for me, now. I'm all alone. I have not fulfilled my duty. "He who bears a son plants a tree." I've neither son nor tree.

Wait! Let us see. Am I ready, as I am, to live under true com-munism?

Probably, yes. I am not attached to material things. I could do with less. I'm not greedy and I'm neither envious nor vain—or rather, just sufficiently.

"However, time to sleep." This is aloud, to Yura.

"Yes, of course. It's past one! Forgive me for babbling!"

"Don't be silly."

What kind of person is he really, Yura? Clever, but young. This means that his intelligence is not yet real. Too emotional and a bit limited. Wisdom comes with maturity. Even I have not yet achieved it. But strange, at any age man considers himself able to comprehend everything.

Yura, for instance, feels sure he can master any science, any subject. I, too, thought so once . . .

I make his bed. A folding cot, rubber mattress. Good, but the sheet keeps slipping and must be tucked under.

"Yura, there's a brand-new toothbrush in the bathroom. The red one."

A quilt instead of a blanket. A warm one.

"Go to bed. Do you want to read? I have newspapers."

"No, thank you. I go to sleep quickly."

Probably does not want to bother me. I too will turn off the light.

The evening wash-up. Teeth look all right, but gums are obviously swollen. Very obviously? Yes. Never mind. They will serve me for a while. I get into my bed.

"Good night. Don't get up early."

"Good night."

I turn off the light. I stretch under the blanket. Warm. It is pleasant to get into bed after a long and hard day.

On the ceiling, squares of light from the street lamps. Swinging. Must be windy. Another source of light, coming closer and closer, then going off. Someone must be driving with full headlights. There is no inspection at night.

To sleep . . .

But the brain resists.

■ ■

Another day is gone. "Swift as the waves are the days of our life . . ." An old student song. Not many days are left in mine? Each must be treasured. What for? What difference does it make? An affectation? No, not quite.

The waves . . . sea waves. It is pleasant to fall asleep lying on a beach. Listening to waves surge and recoil. Soothing. They have been going on for millions of years. I'll never see them again.

No, I still may go there in the spring. Sit on a rock. Think of eternity.

Yura has fallen asleep. Really very fast. Youth. Clear conscience, as they used to say. Probably.

No aches, no pains at the moment. It would be good to have Liuba in bed with me. It is good to feel the soft little sole of her foot on my leg. A memory from the past: the aroma of her hair.

I sigh . . . What a man—has never slept with a woman the whole night. "Oh, it's so late! . . . Oh, I must run!" Yesterday morning I still had some hope to sleep the whole night with her. It has melted away.

In the next reincarnation perhaps. Improbable. I am lost; will anabiosis work or not? Sometimes I think it's nonsense; then, reality. One thing I know: the odds for success are microscopic. All the logic of our plans is primitive. Many things we just don't know at all. We can't grasp the whole complexity of the problem.

What we need is experimentation with prolonged anabiosis. No time. The program of awakening will not be even properly touched.

And why experiment? Just suppose it would prove the impossibility of awakening? This way, at least, there is some illusion. No. Dishonest.

One must not sell oneself for a few extra chances to live. What interests me most in this? Is it the scientific experiment or my own fate?

I consider it and I can't decide.

Would the cells synthesize their structure or would they just disintegrate? If we lower the temperature to 35 or so, the metabolism would slow to three or four percent of its normal rate. Plus the glucose, which, however, must burn off. Just carbohydrate feeding is enough to preserve life for two months at least. Multiply this by thirty and you have five years. Then one can be brought back for a while for some intensive building up.

Maybe it is best to forget it.

No.

The picture: I am lying in the sarcophagus. If plasma is used for circulation my skin will be absolutely white. Brrrr. Unpleasant.

Sleep . . . Go to sleep, my friend.

There is still time.

I remember how they told us about the death of one foreign communist. His wife was supposed to have begged them not to cut his jacket. "It is the only one he has." All eyes in the room were moist. And only one man said, "Nonsense. Jackets are cheap in that country."

It was in the Crimea. The waves . . . Liuba, in a light dress walks toward me. Her walk is a little jumpy. She is laughing, stretching her arms toward me. Happy.

"Why are you late?"

A dream.

V
Another Day—Six Months Later

I am going back to work. Walking briskly—left, right, left, right. A beautiful day, warm, with a light breeze.

A quiet street. Chestnut against the sky. The last blooms twirl in the air like white and pink snowflakes.

Passersby. I'm looking at them, trying to guess their thoughts, their destinies.

A fat old woman in black is walking slowly, leaning on a stick, eyes half covered with heavy eyelids. A wise frozen mask—fatigue of life. "Gather me unto thyself, Lord . . ." Her shadow is also large and black.

A girl with a milk can with an attached cover runs skippingly along the sidewalk; loud banging fills the air. Her mother sent her to the milk shop. "Quick!" School is out. A whole happy summer is ahead. And a whole life.

A middle-aged man walks quickly, with an unhappy, angry face. An office worker. Late for work. He has quarreled with his wife. He is expecting a reprimand from his superiors for having failed to finish the accounts. "Damned life!" But take it easy, friend. Everything passes. Tonight your little three-year-old will climb upon your lap, wrap his short arms around your neck. Your face will contract into a mournful expression, then your moist eyes will open wide and will shine. "One must live."

Liuba has told me about those things. No warm child's arms have ever embraced me. "All your science is not worth one such embrace." She told me this. I don't know. Perhaps she is right.

The Institute. It looks more handsome in summer. Chestnuts. No one at the entrance; work has started. What a heavy door. My strength is all but gone. I haven't walked fast; but listen to my breathing! No, no need to listen. I have lost hold of myself during this month. The spleen is pulling at the left hip . . .

I am walking toward my office. After the street it is gloomy here, musty and dark. Some people from other laboratories greet me in passing. Hungry, scrutinizing eyes. "They said he had cancer . . . was on his last legs . . ." A sense of disappointment— no, this is not true; warm looks, compassion, sympathy. I must not give in to envy and irritation.

Our rooms . . . *Ours!* Even the heart starts beating a little faster. How much thought, love, energy have been put into this.

I look into Surgery. A pleasant, familiar scene—an experiment is being set up. Everyone is here? Polia, Kolia, Gulyi, Tolia, Vadim . . . Vadim is leaning over the table.

"Good morning, Comrades!"

Vadim rushes to me, grabs both my hands, shakes them, laughs.

"Three cheers for the Chief!"

No respect. Everyone is around me, touching me, smiling. A bit guiltily. How shall I behave? Healthy people are always self-conscious in the presence of illness.

"How are you? How do you feel? Haven't you left the hospital too soon?"

"No. I'm all right."

This is Vadim, of course. Valia has run into the corridor and to the next rooms. I hear her voice.

"Girls, girls! Ivan Nikolaevich is here!"

Such warmth. They are good children, all of them. They like me. Love, even.

"It's been dismal here without you! The Director has been torturing us. We're running three tests per week—from morning till night. And in between we're drawing and calculating."

To Vadim: "What are you drawing?"

"What? Characteristics, curves! We get tons of figures out of every experiment—thousands. The code machines are clicking like mad. Look—rolls and rolls!"

Yes, true. Rolls of figure-covered paper on the window sills.

"Very good, kids. Set up the experiment and then I must talk to the section leaders. Vadim, get them together in my office." (He winces—". . . no time.") "Don't worry, I won't keep you long."

I walk out amidst the hum of voices. Then there is silence. They probably whisper to one another, "How pale he is . . . how thin." Never mind. There is a lot of fight in me yet.

My office. I greet it mentally like an old friend. Everything in its proper place. The picture of Pavlov. The books on the shelves. Even flowers in a vase. How thoughtful.

A succession of emotions. The joy of the reunion. They love me. In the back of my mind, a thought: soon we shall part. This thought never leaves me now. The relapse has made me conscious of my condition.

They will not tell me anything new. Each day someone had come to the hospital and reported to me. Not everything, I'm afraid. They tried to spare me. Today I will check on everything myself. Compare it with the plan and make corrections. How much time do I still have? David tries to encourage me, but can I trust him? He is reproaching me for not following his orders, for working too much. He wants me to surrender to illness. Well, he has succeeded; the thought of my condition is always with me now. And I am losing my grip on life.

I know this very well. I am still controlling myself—but always on edge. This is bad.

I must hurry the departure; otherwise the sickness will tie me into knots. Dizziness again, nausea. I haven't eaten anything that could cause it. Have I taken all my medicines? David demands punctuality. Perhaps I should have stayed in bed a little longer? David—

To hell with David and his medicines! Today we have an important experiment. Or have I nothing at all left but pills? To breathe an extra day, eat and urinate? It would have been different if I could do other things. But this . . .

All is clear. I must control my thoughts, keep the sickness from getting the better of me. Go through treatments, but not overdo it. Living as such is not the supreme purpose. And I ask myself now and then: What for?

I must not give up.

■ ■

They enter all together. It means that they have met in advance and discussed the program for this meeting. It is good that they want to spare me; bad that they try to conceal things. Should I talk to them individually later on? Is that really necessary? There are enough unpleasant things as it is.

"Good morning, Ivan Nikolaevich!"

This is Semyon. A normal voice, but it seems to me that his manner has changed. No, to hell with suspicion!

Igor, as handsome as ever. Yura and Vadim are thoughtful, unfamiliar, new. Of course I have seen them recently, but the surroundings change things.

"Sit down, boys. I've asked you to come here to discuss some points. Of course I know the general situation—if you haven't been concealing things from me."

I look at them one after another. *Inquisitively.* A cliché. I can see that not everything is well here.

"Semyon Ivanovich, go ahead."

"Everything has been going all right. As you know, we have been given a room to assemble the sarcophagus in. We've been working hard. I think that we are on schedule. Of course, I don't know everything; they do not report to me."

He falls silent. So, they haven't been minding him. The crack is widening.

Vadim jumps up. Igor motions to him—"Don't!" A dull pain in the pit of the stomach. There it comes! I hate it.

"Don't try to shush me, Igor! The Chief is not a schoolgirl!"

Shall I stop him? I am a sick man. No, let him talk.

"No, everything was *not* going all right. Just as soon as you entered the hospital, the Director started cutting us off at every corner." (This about the Director! No, he won't make a career here.)

"And you, Semyon, you have been playing up to him! We all know it. Don't stop me—I'll tell everything anyway!"

"You're just hysterical, that's all."

How unpleasant all this is. The pain in the stomach, nausea. I am sick. I don't want to hear all this . . .

"All right, tell me. But without emotions."

"The Supply Department has stopped supplying us. 'We've no money. Your appetites are too big!'" He imitates Shvechik, and does it well. "And we need a lot of things, for the machine. They don't even talk to Yura; they consider him an outsider. And the room they gave us is only on a 'temporary basis'—I had to sign a receipt. They just don't need it now—that's why we got it. All that we've done has been done on enthusiasm and theft. How many articles have your boys smuggled out of the factories, Yura?"

Thievery. That is all we needed.

"Don't be disturbed, Ivan Nikolaevich. They give them to us— but we can't always take them out through the front office."

Well, this is not too bad. They have always been cutting us down. And then, our Institute has never really had enough money. What else? I am waiting.

"This is not all. That man started calling us in one by one. I don't know what he told Semyon—"

"Yes, you do! I told you!"

"—I don't know about Semyon, but he asked me point-blank what we intend to do when you die. 'What sort of new chief would you like to have? You need a strong one, one who could protect the laboratory program.' I got the impression that he wants to take it over himself."

What a scoundrel! But then, what can one expect from him? Perhaps Vadim has misunderstood it.

"Did he tell that to you?"

"No, but then I asked *him*. He just laughed. 'Wouldn't you like it?' You know his hypocritical soft chuckling . . ."

"And what did you tell him, Dimochka?" Hell, I should be more formal!

"I told him what I thought. I won't repeat it."

I can see Ivan Petrovich's face!

"But why would he *want* it?"

"What do you mean, why? He has milked Pavlov's theories dry, and now cybernetics is the new vogue. He feels that his chair is slipping from under him. And how can that fool live without the Olympian heights?"

"Vadim, I beg you, don't be rude. Nonetheless, he is our Director, and with his help we've arrived where we are now. Semyon Ivanovich, what would you say about it all?"

What can he say? He's probably made a deal to become his deputy at the lab!

A quarrel. Disgusting. I'm still here, but there is already a division of the inheritance starting. Vadim is too emotional; he may be exaggerating. Semyon? Not too dependable. But he controls his temper well.

"I don't know anything about all this. The Director just asked me about our work, about the fulfillment of the plan."

"That's all?"

"He asked me about you—what I think about the state of your health—whether you would be able to come back."

"That's normal. It's his duty to know. Igor, Yura, can you tell me anything? Please, Vadim! Keep still a minute! Don't turn this into a bazaar."

Those two have level heads. Yura speaks up:

"The attitude of the Institute toward us is not good, that's true. They giggle and hint that we are secretly working on some earth-shaking discovery—"

"That's not serious, Yura. Let's talk business."

"About what Vadim has told you? Yes, this is quite probable. We are dealing here with a crafty gentleman."

"I'm not interested in that either—not yet. I want to know the facts of any discrimination against our laboratory so that I can take it up with the Director."

Silence. What can they say? If they only knew how I hate going to that man. Then, Vadim again:

"I don't think you should go to him. We will apply our own pressure. 'The Chief has come back; he is raising hell.' Going there only upsets you."

"You started all this and now you're sorry for me?"

"I know how you dislike dealing with him. It hurts us to see it. After all . . ."

(". . . it won't be long now, we can bear it." No, he didn't mean it that way. I'm unjust.)

"What else, boys?"

I am looking around. The atmosphere is tense. Vadim is ashamed of his outburst against Semyon. Semyon sits there with a stony face, offended. And with good reason—even though he might very well sell out to the Director, or rather, submit. There is a difference: weakness is not dishonesty. And Igor has not opened his mouth. A saint.

Yura speaks up again. Obviously he is a driving force here. Naturally—technology is the main thing now. Machines.

"Unfortunately, there are more unpleasant things that we should have started with if it hadn't been for Vadim's emotionalism."

A pause. What else? I might as well have it all. This is not as happy a reunion as I thought it would be.

"The point is that we are losing prestige. The Institute of Cybernetics, Plants 22 and 13, learned that you were in a hospital and they are slowing down on our requisitions. The managers just avoid us, but the shop boys tell us that without you they don't trust us. And the former enthusiasts are cooling off as well."

So they have realized that I am on my way to my grave.

"How can we remedy this?"

"Well, you could call the managers—or, better still . . . No."

"Go ahead, Yura!"

"If you could give talks at the plants working for us . . ."

It seems I am still a force! True, my lectures always have been well received . . .

"I am ready. Only my appearance—wouldn't it frighten them off?"

"Never mind! You can shave just before each lecture. We will get a bright shirt for you, a light suit—"

"And a bit of makeup?"

"Science demands sacrifice!"

There is a thaw in the air. Everyone looks brighter. Even Semyon manages a smile. And Vadim seems to have forgotten everything. What a man! Very well, I'll deliver my lectures, put on a new suit —but about a bright shirt? A necktie will do. Enough is enough.

"Now we'd better discuss briefly the actual state of affairs. Even though you've kept me informed, I'd like to hear it once more, to see how we can overcome the drawbacks. Who will start? Vadim, as usual?"

"Very well. My sector is the structural schemes of the functional and regulatory systems. In general, they are ready."

"You think they are ready! The squares with arrows between

them. For the technical scheme I need more: the exact correlations."

"And where would I get them? Out of the thin air?"

"From literature. You doctors have written thousands of books, and it's still unclear how, for instance, the heart affects the gas exchange in the lungs!"

"Wait, don't quarrel," I tell them. "We knew from the beginning that some characteristics we'd have to get by intuition. This is the meaning of heuristic modeling. I want to know what has been done in this sphere."

Not much has been done. I can see it. A lack of fantasy. It is good that I have had time in the hospital to think about this.

"Listen, Ivan Nikolaevich! Igor and I have drawn the main scheme—the correlation of organs supplying the gas balance to the system. The heart, lungs, tissues. We've combined the mechanical energy, the changes of O_2 and CO_2 in the heart, lungs, vessels and tissues."

They have drawn? I told this to them long ago.

Yura: "Your characteristics are limited by a very narrow sphere of the physiological norm. A healthy heart, good lungs, sound vessels, normal metabolism. A scheme like that models the reaction of an average normal human being to physical loads. And even this, without allowances for emotions. That's all. But what about pathology? All the characteristics would change."

"Don't cry. A few of these things we have already given you. Besides, the clinical work is not yet completed."

"Stop arguing, boys. We'll discuss this matter later on. I have a few ideas about that."

Somehow one forgets one's illness working like this. As if nothing has happened.

"Semyon Ivanovich, your task was the second scheme the hydrosaline balance and the alkaline-acid balance. Where do we stand there?"

(Nowhere, I think.)

"Vadim, Yura and I have drawn up a general scheme. I can show it to you. The weak point is the tissues: our collaboration with the Institute of Biochemistry has not yet worked out. And we can't determine the exchange of fluids and salts between the tissues and the blood. And the nerve impulses are altogether obscure."

"Has the connection with the gas exchange been determined, at least?"

How subjective are all evaluations! Subconsciously, I am already trying to trip Semyon. Even though there is no proof of any disloyalty. He is doing his best.

"No, it hasn't. More precisely, we cannot as yet express it in figures."

"And why not conduct some perfusion experiments with an isolated part of the body—a leg, for instance?"

This idea has just occurred to me. What will be the reaction of my team?

Vadim: "The idea is good, even though it's not new. Also, it is difficult to implement. One would need a great deal of time to work out methods and conduct a conclusive number of experiments. And we don't have time."

He has hit the nail on the head—time; we have no time. I must always remember this. My illness.

"Then try to find in the existing literature some indications of the metabolic changes during various pathological processes. Do I have to tell you everything?"

Silence. They should not be offended. I am not attacking them. I am attacking the whole world. Including myself, and my illness. So I go on, in a milder tone: "The balance of gases and mechanical energy of blood must be tied to the fluid balance, the balance of the electrolytes and the pH. I think that during the next few days we must sit down and try to get some order into these schemes. I shall help you with characteristics. I have an intuition for those kinds of figures."

I am bragging. Shamelessly.

Yura: "Let me say again, the nerve and endocrine systems are our undoing. There is nothing in any book about them except mere abstractions. How are we going to overcome this?"

(If I only knew how!)

"In all probability, we must determine several levels of emotional condition and the connecting reactions of the hormone functions. Then introduce some corrective coefficients into the autonomous functions of the cells."

Yura glances at his wristwatch. Looks at me. Vadim gives this look a voice: "We must go, really. This is the first experiment and the program is extremely extensive. They would mix everything up. May we?"

"Of course, by all means. We'll finish this conversation later. So you don't think I should go to the Director? What do you say?"

"No, to hell with the Director! Let him come, if he wants. Come on, boys." This is Vadim—categoric as always. I like this, but it might be annoying.

They are gone. The door closes, but I can hear their voices outside.

I am tired. The body is complaining, but the brain compels me to work. No, I won't go to the Director. I can afford this, in view of my illness. Actually, I should have gone. The situation demands that I go around and grovel before that nonentity. This is an exaggeration, of course; he is just an average man. He probably thinks, This very important work needs firm guidance; Prokhoroff will die, and everything will go to pieces.

I'd better lie down for a minute. Weakness . . . It is good to stretch out. To loosen up the tendons. Every organ whispers: "Good . . . good."

I'd go to him and say, "I don't advise you to take over the laboratory. This would cause nothing but harm. Appoint Yura, I beg you." My lips would tremble. He would try to comfort me. "Yes, yes, don't worry about a thing." Then he'd do exactly what he wanted to do. He considers himself a very important person, an independent thinker—"Organizers are more important now than abstract scientists."

I won't go. The hell with it!

Liuba will come tonight. Also, Leonid.

Liuba is difficult. She is an experienced physician, she understands everything.

Well, I'd better go. Will the dog come back to life, or not? Not necessarily. The purpose of this experiment is to sharpen the technique, to test the equipment. Still, it would be good if he *would* wake up. A large dog, over sixty pounds. Poor thing, he doesn't realize . . .

How will they work without me? Is it possible that *he* may really take over? They would all leave—except Semyon and perhaps Igor. This would mean the end of our work, our laboratory. Humanity would not perish, of course, but it would be a pity. And then, what about supervising me in that sarcophagus? Impossible without Yura and Vadim. The machines would fail, physiological research would come to a stop.

Should I go to the Director and explain everything? Then the whole thing might collapse. He might stop all work, to secure permission at the top level first.

I have really hoodwinked them with my "installation for the artificial control of the most vital body functions"! How they flattered me when they approved my plan. The Director: "Physiology finds practical application. We will revive some clinical-death cases—during shock and heart seizure." True, we will. Rather, *they* will. Even the hypothermy will be needed—to put the pieces together first, then revive them. Like a fairy tale. The elixir of life. Many engineers took the bait, too—of course, cybernetics! A magic word. Creation of systems governing the human body. This is true —without cybernetics all this would have been impossible.

It is unfortunate if they have started to cool off at the factories. What can one do? They are overloaded—orders, norms, plans. At first, enthusiasm—"Let's help humanity . . . let's work to promote life!" Then, a gradual reaction—"And what about our own plan? We're behind. And they are reproaching us for wasting time on toys, on charity." One can understand them. The managers, especially. No allowance is made for *their* fantasies.

It is unpleasant to go and beg them again. "Please, help us, Sergei Pavlovich. We can't cope without your help." And he: "Very well, Professor, we must help medicine." A condescending chuckle. He is a producer, and who are we? He is earning money for the state ("the people"), showing a profit, and we are just drones.

Let us face it: he is right. Take our Institute—millions are spent, and the results? True, hundreds of articles have been written, books published, dissertations defended, and the net result? Zero. We contribute nothing, either to today's or tomorrow's science. Mediocrities with science degrees, starting with our Director.

To shut down the Institute? Yes! But, unfortunately, this is not up to me. However, there are a few other good people, a few other laboratories. That of Levchuk, for instance. Yes, but how many? But there are also other institutes. One must not exaggerate one's own importance . . .

Yes, I have to go to factory managers . . . and deliver a few talks —light some fires under them. The chances are not brilliant, one must not overestimate human nature, but something can be done. Some enthusiasts would emerge, like Yura, for instance—years ago.

A warm feeling inside. I love him. He must take over after me. Vadim is noisy; but without Yura he doesn't work out a single graph. And I myself have learned a lot from Yura. If he and Vadim could only function together! How can I keep them from arguing? Vadim is explosive, though kind. One must have patience with him. Only with my even temper . . . *Even?* Well, I am kind.

It is interesting to watch yourself from outside. What a scientist! New ideas, a good team. Then, kind and tactful. Dedicated to work. Or just a weakling? Has selected for himself the most pleasant function possible—thinking. Has built an ivory tower, and looks down on the world critically.

Very well. Since we have come down to the practical level, let us go and watch the experiment. Everything about me has long since been determined. A positive person with a rather limited coefficient. If I succeed with this anabiosis, well, then I can die peacefully. I will have squared my accounts. For some reason I feel they need squaring.

■ ■

I enter Surgery. One look, and I know that I have come just in time. They are starting anesthesia.

"A chair for Ivan Nikolaevich!"

Vadim's thoughtfulness.

"Go ahead, work in accordance with your program, and pay no attention to me."

I will not unnerve them with my interferences. Let us imagine that I am not here—that I am lying on that table instead of the dog.

I sit down near the window. Outside, a hot summer day. Clear and beautiful. Back to the room: three groups. In the middle, near me, the operating table with the heart-lung machine. Physiologists—Olga, Alla, Rita, Mila. Vadim is in charge here. On the right, half of the room is taken by the controls and regulators. Engineers—Gulyi, Tolia, Yura. Near the door, a table of biochemistry. Valia is taking the analyses. Igor. Near the window, another table—records. Lena and Piotr will keep the simplified lists of basic factors.

Each group has its own functions, its own head. Yura is in over-all command.

This is the first time that I see the entire installation all at once. They have assembled it while I have been away. The blood-circulation machine, the heat exchange . . . And the cooling and heating? Oh, those tubes running out through the door. They must have installed it in the next room. No space here.

The control installation is enormous. Well, there is no point in trying to understand it all. There is an expert engineer in charge. Yura.

"How many channels are you recording?"

"Sixteen, and periodically we'll be checking on about thirty additional indicators. Here is the list."

The list: the pressure in both auricles, aorta, the vascular tonus, the consumption of oxygen by the lungs, the heart-lung machine, the pH, the oxygen pressure in the tissues. One channel has six subchannels. The pressure of O_2 in the arterial and venous blood. The pressure of CO_2. The heart-lung machine productivity. Several temperature points. The electrocardiograph, of course, the electroencephalograph.

"Yura, have you put in the new depletion meter?"

"Yes, we have just adjusted it."

"Are the gas-pressure indicators dependable?"

"Not absolutely so, but we will double-check on the oxygenometer."

"No controls of the heart productivity? Why haven't you connected in with the ballistocardiograph?"

"Ivan Nikolaevich, we couldn't do everything! Not enough time."

This is Vadim. There is a note of irritation in his voice. "He is picking on us." He is wrong. They had to find time. He should keep quiet.

Pauline comes in. "We can judge it indirectly by the oxygen consumption of the lungs. We know the gas content at the entry and the exit points."

Entry. Exit. A new phraseology for physiologists. The work goes on. Mila smoothly introduces the tube into the dog's trachea, and starts squeezing the anesthesia bag. She is as good at this as any physician. But when it comes to the real thing, I'll ask Liuba to lend me her Vladimir.

Vadim and Pauline start opening the vessels on both hips for the heart-lung machine and control gauges. Will the venous outflow be sufficient from the upper part of the body?

"Listen, Vadim, we have spoken about the introduction of one tube into the neck vein. I don't see this."

"Two tubes will be sufficient—in the lower vein."

"No, they won't. Please do it as we have planned it."

He gives me an angry look. A little more and he'd argue. No, he would never be able to work with Yura. They begin to shave the dog's neck. Still obeying me.

Yura is fussing with his machines. Obviously there are some difficulties. It's not easy to control sixteen channels all at once. Igor is working with test tubes; he is responsible for biochemistry. Here is the list of analyses. Fuller than I thought.

"Yura, how did you manage all these analyses?"

"We've mobilized biochemists from other laboratories, even from the clinic."

"Good boy!"

"We're trying."

Semyon is doing nothing, he has been given no assignment. Too bad. I should have interfered. Too late, now. True, his artificial kidney is not working today. Not ready. Naturally.

Everyone is busy except me, the invalid. However, this is good. It proves that the team is functioning.

Yura has organized the experiment very well. Everything is planned in all details. And still he always complains that our system is unwieldy. Too many errors are being made. It is all right so long as we are working with dogs. Just the wasted labor—about twenty people are involved in each experiment. Physiologists have never tried anything so complicated before.

They are working smoothly. Even Vadim is controlling himself. The scene in my office must have had its effect. For how long? Such temper! How many times has he been rude to me? Then he would come and say "Forgive me, I couldn't control myself . . . But, then, you were also wrong . . ." And still, I like him. He is *real*. There are too many lukewarm ones nowadays. "Diplomats."

"Dima, have you learned to drain the right auricle yet?" I call him by his diminutive name on purpose; he likes it.

"And how! I worked at Surgery for a whole week. Now I can do it better than they do. They even offered to take me into their probing department. 'When you have quarreled with everybody in your place, come over and we'll give you a try.' "

The dog is completely pierced by tubes and probes from all sides. Will I too be lying there like that?

No, all this does not seem real to me. Me? On that table? Impossible! I don't think I'll ever be able to go through with it. Will I die in my own bed? A miserable coward!

How many people are working in this room alone? One, two . . . twelve.

Each has his own life, his own fate, own stimuli. Lena, for instance, our technician. She used to cry over every dog in the beginning. She wanted to quit. I had to argue with her—"experimentation benefits humanity." "Human beings can take care of themselves, but this—this is cruel." Even now she's not quite used to it. And Mila is so pale and thin. It is hard for our girls, the pay is not generous. It is all right for those living with their families, but some of them have come from villages and are on their own. Girls want to dress, to look well. Somehow one does not consider those things.

Almost all of them are studying. At night, or by correspondence. When the school year starts, they walk around like ghosts. Alla, for instance, had taken the exams six times before she was admitted. A vogue? A drive for material benefits? They are not large in medicine, in any case. A qualified factory specialist earns more. No, obviously this is something else—the thirst for real culture.

"Ivan Nikolaevich, we are ready to start cooling."

I get up. A momentary dizziness. A second or two. Then it is gone.

"Igor, are all the biochemical indications normal?"

"Yes. The alkaline reserve of the blood is a little down. We are using soda."

"Mila, increase respiration. Yura, is your department in order?"

"Well, we'll never have it perfect, but it's all right. We'll write down most of it."

"I'm not talking about records. Will the automatics function?"

"I don't know. They should work, but who knows? We're switching them on for the first time."

"Very well. Start."

This means that we start the surface cooling down to 45 degrees with the working heart, and then switch over to the extracorporal circulation.

The dog is covered with a long plexiglass cylinder. At one end, a hose connecting it with a refrigerator and a ventilator. Cold air is being pumped in. The dog's fur has been doused with cold water.

"Mila, deepen the narcosis and introduce neuroplegics. Do you have this in your program?"

This is Yura.

He will be giving orders like this during the *real* thing. If I have the courage to go through with it.

The refrigerator and ventilator are switched on. The plexiglass fogs up. From the vents come jets of cold air. I feel chilly. A conditioned reflex.

A wide roll of paper creeps into the recorder and sixteen styluses scratch the curves on it. Now and then the coding machine is switched on, translating them into figures.

The dog's body cools very slowly. The fur. With a human body this would be faster. Tolia is switching on the indicators, getting the temperature reading on various levels—97 . . . 96 . . . 95 . . . It should go one degree per minute, but here it goes slower.

The pulse is falling—100 . . . 96 . . . 84 . . . 79 . . . The blood pressure is a little down, the oxygen consumption has decreased from 150 to 100. The metabolism is weakening.

"Igor, just as soon as you get the adrenalin test, tell me. The adrenalin content reflects the body resistance to cooling. How is the vascular tonus?"

"Rising."

It means there is a spasm condition. We must open up the vessels.

"Polia, add pentamin into the dropper!"

All this should be automatized. Manual operations are undependable. We shall discuss this later. No time now.

"What is the heart productivity per minute, Vadim?"

"I'll figure it out."

"Why figure? It is about a liter and a half."

This is Yura. He's at home with figures.

"Not enough. Perhaps it is time to switch over to the machine." Unoxidized residues may be building up in the tissues."

"Temperature 86. Let's switch over."

The ventilator stops. The plexiglass is raised. The wave of cold air spreads through the room and melts away. Summer. It is hard to believe that the air temperature inside is down to 45.

"Misha, are you ready?"

Misha is a young technician, a "machinist"—scientifically, the "extracorporal blood-circulation-machine operator." He is supervised by Polia. "Switch on. Check the clamps."

A new sound: the hum of the motor. Increasing as the revolutions build up. Z-z-z-z . . . An unpleasant sound.

The glass cylinder goes down again. The ventilator starts to turn.

How will the machine and the heart work together? This machine does not include synchronization, it cannot produce an absolutely even blood flow. However, this would not help the function of the heart in any event. Its regularity is already disturbed.

Vadim and Yura are carefully studying the curves creeping across the oscillograph screen. "The machine output is fifteen hundred milliliters. The oxygen consumption is down to fifty."

"Yura, when does the automatic temperature regulation start to function?"

"We'll switch it on now."

He is fussing with a whole battery of gauges on the main control panel. This is his pride—the single-panel control of the whole system.

The machine is working in accordance with the cooling regime. The speed of the circulation depends on it.

"Fibrillation!"

"Switch the pump to the pulsating rhythm."

We think that this pulsation is important for the system.

"The automatics perform well. Look at the temperature line."

"Stop bragging. Don't count your chickens before they hatch."

"I'm not counting chickens."

"The hell you aren't. You engineers are all the same."

This, of course, is Vadim.

The physiologists probably envy Yura. And they are a little jealous. It annoys them when I praise Yura in their presence.

A well-designed experiment. Clear and precise. Only biochemistry is lagging behind. When it is switched over to electronics, then everything will be fine. Igor walks in. He appears to be worried.

"Change the oxygenation regime, Comrades; the pH of the blood is seven point four. Add carbonic acid so that the hemoglobin can separate the oxygen."

It is quite possible that the ferments break up under low temperatures. So far this is a very obscure area. And there is no time to study it.

Yura is changing the gauges regulating the flow of gases into the oxygenator.

The venous blood temperature—63. It is just as red as the arterial. The oxygen consumption is down eighty percent.

"Ivan Nikolaevich, it is time to dilute the blood. There is a danger of the erythrocytes sticking together."

"Yes, yes, very important! The viscosity of blood rises; the brain capillaries may become clogged. No time to lose."

"Yura, can we stop the machine?"

It is stopped. The lines are unclasped. Half of the blood in the oxygenerator is replaced with plasma.

Vadim: "Start her up! Put the blood into the refrigerator. We'll need it later."

I sit down again. It has been an hour since the beginning of the experiment. I am a little tired, just from watching the activity.

The noisiest group is the physiologists'. Vadim. Pauline is always arguing with him. Of course, they are on familiar terms.

"Polia, look, stupid! Your flange is leaking."

"You yourself tightened it up. Men! . . . Come, Lena, help me!"

The engineers are quieter. This oscillograph is an imposing contraption—sixteen channels running like one. Something must be the matter . . . They are calling in Yura.

"The electrocardiograph condenser has quit on us!"

"Not important: you can't see anything during the fibrillation, anyway. Take it out and give it to Alexei; he'll fix it by the time we're switched to heating."

This means he has thought of setting up a repair group. Good.

What is Igor looking at in that test tube?

"What's the matter, Igor?"

"I'm looking at the last blood sample, fresh from the centrifuge. It seems there are signs of hemolysis . . . But not serious. They are analyzing it now."

This is the quietest group. You can hardly hear them. Of course, they are merely taking the samples and sending them out to be analyzed. They have already written down a whole sheet of figures.

Hemolysis is a very dangerous thing. In this respect we just cannot bring our heart-lung machine to perfection. Chemistry is letting us down—there are no proper materials for the tubes. But they are working on the problem now.

Never mind, at this point it is not too bad. We have cut the whole blood down to one half and soon will switch to plasma altogether. And we will cut down the circulation rate. Yes, but what about heating up? Then the machine will have to work much longer—and with whole blood.

"Listen, Vadim. How much donor blood is there in reserve?"

"Three liters. Why?"

"It won't be enough. During the heating process we'll have to change the blood. Hemolysis will exceed the tolerable level. Can we get some more? Do we have dogs?"

"Yes, but they have not been checked as to blood-type compatibility."

"It's not too late. Get busy!"

Silence. He is thinking.

"Just as soon as we change the blood, I'll send Polia."

It means I will not have to convince them, or order. I have never learned to order people around.

"The temperature is already down to forty-three!"

I must check all the indicators. I go over to Lena's table. "Let's look at this together, Lena. Igor, give me your list."

Lena is a good girl. Why don't I have a single woman among my senior personnel? Well, too late to worry about that now.

"Look, Ivan Nikolaevich, all indications are first class: the pH, the oxygen pressure in blood and in tissues. This is the main thing."

"Potassium is low. We must add some. And the oxygen pressure in the venous blood is too high."

"I'll add some air to the gas mixture."

"Yura, the gas regulation must be automatized. Without fail."

"It's not very easy to do. The oxygen supply must be changed along with that of the carbon dioxide and the air. And then all this must be correlated with the chamber pressure. Some complicated computations will be necessary."

"I don't understand. You can regulate the oxygen supply according to its pressure in the venous blood, and the carbon dioxide, to the pH and its pressure. Two independent control points."

"I'll explain to you later. We may think up something—if we don't shoot for any fast and precise results."

Again I don't quite understand something.

The temperature is going down very slowly now. Yura has switched over to a different automatic regime.

Forty-two degrees . . . forty-one . . .

"We must change the blood. We'll conduct the further cooling with plasma."

Everyone goes to his place. There is no time for conversaticn. I am the least busy of all. I am sitting and watching. Everything has been arranged very well. A big feather in Yura's cap. I have never read in any foreign sources about such a complicated experiment.

The machine is stopped. Only the ventilator keeps on humming. Polia is emptying the oxygenerator and pouring in plasma with glucose. No hurry here; at this temperature, the circulation can be interrupted for an hour. But, of course, it is best to avoid this.

Finished. The motor is switched on again.

Two or three degrees more and we will switch to the stationary anabiosis regime. The dog will depart for a trip into the future. No, he won't come back. The awakening is extremely improbable. It would have been wonderful, of course; but that is not the purpose of this experiment.

It is noon. I should be taking my pills. Well, I can wait a little longer. Soon I'll be able to rest. We will keep the low temperature on for two hours. My chance to stretch out.

In which way is the state of this dog different from death? Practically there is no difference. The electric brain function is absent. The encephalograph shows a straight line. The heart is motionless. And still some molecules are drowsily moving in the cells, exchanging electrons, discharging energy.

My rendezvous with Liuba tonight should be really canceled. I will get tired. No. I can't telephone . . . conspiracy. Humiliating. Soon, the end. Tonight I will tell her about my plans. Poor girl. However, if the results of the experiment are disappointing, it is best not to tell her anything. Often I grow impatient—"Let's get all this over with"—but then, ten minutes later, "Why hurry?"

Some day they will invent dreams. Dying will become pleasant. Maybe all life is like that. "Glory to the madman who will submerge humanity into a golden dream." Who said that? I don't remember. Not important. So many things have become unimportant to me of late.

The tension is decreasing. Now the dog can survive most of the technical errors. All the sophisticated processes are suspended. All that is left are the most primitive chemical reactions—as in our most distant biological ancestors.

The plexiglass is pleasantly cold—for a hot day. The dog's tongue is not blue. A sure sign of the oxygen sufficiency in tissues.

Poor thing! . . . Where did he live? How? A mixed breed—a bit of a shepherd. Since he got into the pound, his life must have been difficult. "A dog's life."

I can watch them all without thinking . . . Are they all friendly to each other? Sex interest? Love? I don't talk about this side of life with them. Vadim is looking at Rita meaningfully. She is looking back at him. And I have seen Yura twice with the same girl with a birdlike face. Probably she is mad about Gumilev.

"Yura, have you read Gumilev?"

"Who is he?"

(Ask your girl!)

"A poet. He wrote, 'I wish I could run away . . . hide like a thief . . .' "

"No. Never heard of him."

He blushes. And others exchange ironic glances. How would he know? Gumilev has not been published for many years. Also, if you read ten pages of his poems, you'd get tired. So few thoughts. Only Liuba can read him night after night. When there are too many "ideas" it irritates her.

"Well, how's the temperature?"

"In the outflow, about thirty-five. When it goes through the machine, almost thirty-two. Yura, check the tissues!"

I am waiting. Yura is checking various indicators.

"In the esophagus thirty-four; in the large intestine almost thirty-five; in the brain thirty-three. In the sarcophagus just thirty-two."

The *sarcophagus*. What a name!

"Very good. Igor, have you taken the samples?"

"Yes. But we won't have the analyses for about fifteen minutes."

"Fine! We won't wait. I don't suppose we can lower the temperature any further. Let's stop here. Now, as we have decided, let us test out two programs: intermittent blood circulation with high productivity, and a steady flow at a low-quantity level. One hour for each variant. What do you say, Comrades? Yura?"

"Let's start with the second one. Three hundred cubes per minute—what do you think?"

Vadim: "And I think that the machine productivity should be increased gradually. For instance, a hundred cubes each ten minutes. Then we will get a correlation graph."

Vadim says this just to contradict Yura, because I asked Yura's opinion first. However, what he proposes is logical.

"At ten-minute intervals we won't get the balance, and we won't be able to verify the stationary regime."

Yura also has a point there.

"Do as Yura said—three hundred per minute—and then we'll see. Another possibility: five minutes, eight hundred millimeters, then a ten-minute break. Any objections? That's it, then. I'll go and work in my office a while."

I am walking along the corridor. Head high, trim step. Must pretend. Finally, the door.

I am tired . . . I've lost much of my vitality. Two hours in a chair, a few emotions, and I'm done for . . . To stretch out. To close the eyes . . .

Slight dizziness . . . Music. No thought at all.

The dizzy spell is over. I can open my eyes. The ceiling with a crack on it. The hanging lamp. Some dust on it. Pavlov's portrait. The corner of the table. If one could only die like this . . . Dizziness . . . Ringing in the ears. Abyss.

But it does not happen this way. Other memories.

The night in the hospital. Dry, swollen tongue. Fever. Labored respiration. Loud voices of nurses in the corridor. Some Kolia, it appears, is drinking and running around with women. "He's a bastard." To call the doctor, complain? No. To hell with them! Soon they will sprawl in their chairs and go to sleep. I am tactful. There are two of us in the room. My roommate is having a high-blood-pressure crisis. Headaches. He's turning, sighing. We keep silent.

But the nurses are still talking, damn them!

The whole world is disgusting. Dry, self-satisfied doctors. Stupid, bothersome patients. Illiterate nurses with crudely made-up eyes.

They say that somewhere there are laboratories where dedicated scientists perform miracles, that somewhere composers compose beautiful heroic music, that there is love . . .

A pack of lies! There is only short breath, thirst, swollen tongue. The spleen like a large stone, rolling in your stomach every time you turn.

I don't want to live. Stupid ravings of a half-wit; models, anabiosis. What for? God, let me breathe a little, and then take me away. Not to paradise, not to hell. Into nothing.

But God did not take me. The doctors were good, the nurses, kind, dedicated girls. Later I brought them flowers and a cake.

And now I feel just fine. Breathing is easy. Pleasant fatigue makes my body light and languid. And my thoughts slide smoothly and effortlessly from subject to subject . . .

The experiment is going well. The dog went to sleep without any pathological changes in the blood composition. It means that harmful residues had not accumulated in the cells. This is an important prerequiste for the awakening. And the left ventricle has not become blood-packed. I had been afraid of that. It would have given us no end of trouble.

The most difficult stage is still ahead—the awakening.

We will gradually build up temperature, still using plasma. Then, as the oxygen content in the venous blood starts to decrease, we will add some whole blood . . . I am afraid that the heart will contract insufficiently in the beginning, and our heart-lung machine is not well adjusted for the parallel use . . . True, the whole process of awakening is not too important now. They can perfect it while I sleep. There will be enough time.

There is still much to be done . . . To be started and finished. Not enough time, not enough strength. All I feel like doing is lying down like this, listening to the red bell-ringing . . .

"Red bell-ringing . . ." That's what they called Easter bell-ringing in old Russia. In our neighborhood church they kept ringing bells for a whole week. As a little boy I used to climb the belfry and look around open-mouthed; the world was suddenly so big!

All this was so long ago . . . Mama. Mamachka—"my little mother." I don't think I had ever called her this while she was alive. Sentimentality was not in vogue then.

Any illness affects one's psyche terribly. Why "terribly"? Why such exaggerated expressions? A sick man looks at everything through the prism of his suffering. Indifferent things become unpleasant, unpleasant ones disgusting. And good things are just not noticed. All people irritate one. Envy, Egotism. "Doctors and nurses must be attentive and kind. They are paid for that."

No, I must not allow myself to disintegrate. I must watch myself constantly. To create a control technique—just as in mechanics . . .

A knock at the door. I must sit up! I don't want them to see me lying down.

"Come in! Ah, you . . ." Yura and Vadim. Yura: "We have brought you some coffee . . ."

Yes, and a plate covered with some gauze.

"Thank you. Sit down. How is it going?"

I am contemplating the coffee with pleasure. It is just what I needed.

"Nothing has happened as yet. It's been forty minutes since we switched to the stationary regime."

"The analyses?"

"The oxygen pressure in the plasma outflow is down to forty millimeters of the mercury column. The temperature in the large intestine, thirty-four."

"And the metabolism? Have you figured it out?"

"Of course! What do you think Yura has been doing? About three percent of the normal. Right, Yura?"

"Yes, but still, plasma hardly supplies all the necessary oxygen."

"When we have pressure in the chamber, it will be sufficient. A good deal of oxygen will penetrate through the skin."

I think so—I *want* to think so.

"It may hurt the upper tissue levels. They would have an oversupply of it."

"Under low temperatures this is not dangerous."

(We must still verify this. Will we have enough time?)

"The urine? I have missed this completely."

"Not a drop. As soon as we switched to the stationary regime with low productivity, the system dried up. An artificial kidney is absolutely essential."

"Well, that was expected. Now, boys, don't you think that all organs may become 'rust-bound' from long disuse?"

They are silent. Afraid to express their candid views. Well, it would be up to my body to answer this question.

"Well, we must admit that we just don't know. It is important to preserve the complex molecular structures to ensure specific cell functions—heart contraction, urine secretion."

(Thanks! As if I didn't know this.)

"It would be well to conduct a few additional experiments in this area." This is Yura, pensively.

I don't know. Perhaps it's best to work on hope.

"We won't run any experiments. There's no time for that."

I remember the hospital. Gasping for breath. No. Let them verify this later. If the results are negative, they can just switch off the heart-lung machine. It is best not to touch these over-all problems, but to concentrate on details.

"Better tell me what we must add and improve in our present procedure!"

They brighten up.

"Oh, many things!"

Yura's face shows his excitement. A creator.

"First of all, soon we will have a membrane pump with electromagnetic connections which will ensure the synchronized work with the heart. Then, we will develop an automatic control of the extracorporal blood circulation depending on the gas pressure in veins and arteries at any given time. It will work on two programs: the steady and the intermittent."

I know all this, but it is pleasant to hear. I envy Yura; he still feels that he can achieve anything he sets his heart on.

"Good. But what are the prospects of improving the machine itself, so that it doesn't ruin the blood?"

"For the new machine we'll get the very best plastic materials, all surfaces polished with microscopic precision—they will be as smooth as the natural vessel walls."

"All very well. However, the difference between today's experiment and the real anabiosis is still enormous."

We won't have time. They too think so, but they don't want to say it. Vadim is frowning.

Yura: "Not that enormous. They are finishing the pressure chamber for the sarcophagus at the aviation factory. I saw it the day before yesterday—a fine cylinder of thick plexiglass; it can stand pressure up to five atmospheres. The chamber conditioner will also be finished, giving any desired degree of pressure and humidity. The new heart-lung machine—"

"And the mechanical kidney?"

"Semyon Ivanovich is handling it."

A conflict is ripening here. This is why Semyon has been walking around today as though he were an outsider. A bad man? No, but he does not "pull" and does not realize it.

"All he's good for is going around factories, prodding them—"

Vadim cuts in: "No, he's all right. We are watching this. The kidney is being built. Since it is not much different from the standard model, we'll have it in time."

Wait a minute—*what* time? I have not set any time limit. Did they speak to David? This is unpleasant. Why? It is logical. They must be informed in order to plan properly.

The coffee is delicious. The fog in my head is lifting completely.

"Who made this wonderful coffee?"

"Oh, you don't know? We have a powerful coffee-making machine now. Kolia built it in the shop. We are all coffee addicts now. They come to us from all over the building!"

"And what do they say around the Institute about our anabiosis?"

"Nothing—they don't know what we're up to. They think we're developing a new technique for modeling body functions."

"That's why we can't conduct too many protracted experiments. We'd give ourselves away."

When they are together, Vadim usually speaks for both. Yura is taciturn by nature, and it is not easy to warm him up. They are friends.

"Do you two quarrel often?"

"Every day."

"Why? Tell me, Yura."

"You know him—he's impossible. All his opinions are subjective, actions illogical. A highly emotional individual." How stiffly he is expressing himself. "However, we make peace quickly."

"It's I who makes peace. He can keep a grudge for days."

I am glad to have them here. But they should really go back. It is always like this: when you feel like relaxing, no time; and when there is time, there is no desire to see anyone.

"Shouldn't you go back now?"

"Why are you chasing us out? We've been here only ten minutes. What do you think, Yura?"

"Don't worry, Ivan Nikolaevich. We'll be switching to a new regime in fifteen minutes. Until then, they can run it."

"So you're depending on them?"

Vadim: "Only to a certain extent. You know what people are nowadays. The moment the experiment runs overtime, there's grumbling. 'We can do better in a factory.' It is mostly Yura's people who say that. We physiologists are stuck—there's no place for us to go."

"Stop it, Vadim. My boys are working all right; nobody quits. It's not easy to work with you either. One thing today, then you get a brainstorm, and everything's got to be changed. Or you disappear altogether, and they are walking around, doing nothing. You're a difficult one to work with."

They are both dedicated. But differently.

"Tell me, Vadim, what motivates you in life?"

"Nothing. I'm just living. I derive pleasure from work. I like discovering what you call 'programs' of cells, organs, organisms."

"What for?"

"Just for the sake of discovery. Of course, it would be good if physicians could use those things to cure people, but that's secondary."

Yura: "You've no ideals, Vadim."

"And then I don't go after utopias as you do, but I have my principles. I work honestly—to the limit of my ability. And I don't let people tread on my toes. Including idiots like our Director."

"And you think you'll stand up against life like this?"

"I hope so. I know what you think, Ivan Nikolaevich—'life will smooth his rough edges.' Not mine. I'm sure."

Have I stood up? No. I have always been *timid*—not to use a stronger word. But in the long run I have not been plowed under either.

"And I'm not so sure. I know you youngsters—ideals, principles, but the moment you hit deep water you begin to conform. Of course—family, apartment, furniture, refrigerator. Then, a car, and then the professorship and a country house. Then it's difficult to go to the top and raise hell. I've been through it all, my friend."

I am looking at them and laughing inside. Vadim is taken aback. Yura is looking at him with an air of superiority.

"Don't make a face, Vadim. What the professor said is true. The danger of surrendering to life is very real. Vanity, a lust for possession—these are instincts, and these instincts are durable. Therefore, the system must develop safeguards. How many professors do we have in our Institute who contribute nothing to science, but draw salaries—and large ones at that?"

"It's easy for you; you're single. Even though your Tatiana will probably live on poetry when you marry her. It was funny the way the professor tripped you with—what's his name?—Gumilev! Such an intellectual, and you haven't even heard the name! Tatiana will roar with laughter when I tell her about this!"

Yura reddens. He has this remarkable faculty of blushing. His skin is very white. He glances at his watch.

"You know, we'd better go. It's about time to switch over the machine. You'll excuse us, Ivan Nikolaevich? And don't worry, we'll call you if something goes wrong."

"Of course. Too bad you must leave now, but we'll discuss these problems some other time. Why not come to my place some evening?"

"Of course. With pleasure! May I bring Lida?"

"By all means. Tatiana, too."

They are gone.

Lida is Vadim's wife. He is trying to involve her in science—a subconscious desire to find more common interests. And Tatiana must be Yura's girl friend. Her nose is too long and she's much too thin. Appearances are important in life—and not only to women. I know this from my own experience. All this is in the past, however. But Yura is still unconscious of this. Strange—he is down to earth otherwise. He knows how to handle things—what to tell the Director, and when it is best to keep his tongue. Vadim does not know this. But it is intelligence with Yura, not craft. I don't like craftiness in people.

The boys still don't have real aims in life, but they will develop them. Yura, at least, thinks much and deeply. He should go into philosophy and psychology more, rather than physiology. But he's already going into those spheres as well. He has changed a great deal during the last few months; he has matured.

My stomach begins to ache—every day, now. The spleen is beginning to adhere to the intestines: perisplenitis. Also, small infiltrates in the intestinal walls . . .

They have forgotten the plate. Good coffee and a buttered roll. Someone's lunch. Vadim's? His wife must have given it to him. I don't believe he is strong. It is mostly pretense. He says, "I know everything!" And he knows nothing beyond his science. His home life is not too happy. A large family, and a difficult, nagging mother-in-law. Later, he can move into my place. Temporarily. I will give him written authorization. After all, technically I will not be dead. They can't take my apartment away from me.

Wait a minute, a thought! I can maneuver Yura to take my place very easily. An official request to the Director, with a copy to the Presidium of the Academy. "I request that Comrade Y. N. Sitnik be placed in charge of the laboratory in my absence. He is the only person who can ensure the proper functioning, development and maintenance of the anabiosis experiment"—my body. I can even say, "urgently request." I may mention that he is the main designer of the whole thing. And not "in charge," but "as director."

This is wonderful! This request, properly publicized, will bind everybody. *Everybody.* But Yura must defend his dissertation first. This will establish his scientific qualifications to run "the laboratory of the modeling of vital functions of the human system." Of course Ivan Petrovich will try to cut him down, but

Yura is a tough nut to crack. He is an excellent organizer; he has organized everything for this experiment.

How can I make sure of their collaboration with Vadim—even though only for a few years longer? I will talk to Vadim frankly. "Vadim, I am leaving Yura in full charge. He can do it better than you. He knows how to handle the Director. I ask you not to leave the laboratory. Try to control your temper." He will promise, of course. A tender scene—"For you, yes. You are my teacher."

This, of course, is no guarantee. It will last until the first serious outburst. Igor? That one will stay. He is working on his doctor's dissertation and he must finish it. Without my guidance? Again, no problem. It is almost finished, and anyone would sponsor him. Even Ivan Petrovich, our Director.

The direction of our laboratory has been firmly set: modeling of physiological and pathological processes. Development of the artificial controls of body functions, using these installations. No problems there.

Finally, the anabiosis. What can be done with it? Its practical application is unclear. For cosmic travel? This would work only if it were used for very prolonged flights lasting years. Otherwise, the installation would be too heavy. But it can be made much lighter —sixty–seventy pounds. There is enough cold in outer space. The weight problem is paramount. The psychological factor is also very important: cosmonauts would have to stay together for years within a cramped cabin, and this might lead to all sorts of conflicts. But this way they would go to sleep—no food or anything— and then be automatically awakened at the proper time.

It is interesting. Will *I* wake up? Miracles do happen. So many fairy-tale fantasies have come true.

Anabiosis for medicine? I don't know. Probably it could be applied in some cases. Microbes and viruses might be destroyed by cold. But, then, most of them are very tough. If the sickness has already caused damage to cells, cold will not help.

But then, using it, one can do any kind of surgery. For instance, complicated transplants. Yet even here one should not exaggerate. Such transplants usually fail not because of surgical techniques, but because of the incompatibility of tissues. It is doubtful that anabiosis can help here. Very doubtful. Probably not.

The flight into the future? But why would anyone want to travel there? Curiosity? One would probably find oneself completely out of one's depth awakening in ten or a hundred years.

Let us wait. After all, I can back out at the last moment. No. It would be too late then. Too embarrassing.

The miracles of science will make all men happy.

Nonsense. Happiness is only the agitation of certain pleasure centers in the brain; for various reasons, but never lasting. One adapts oneself to this condition, it ceases to excite one and becomes a memory. Memory records it and puts it away. To be happy, one must be unhappy first—one must suffer. Not necessarily badly or for long periods. One can find an optimum regime for this. Short stretches of periodic unhappiness—to set off the happy stretches. Future cyberneticists will work it all out.

I shall have a chance to see it all for myself.

Nonsense! It won't be so soon. My molecules will not last that long, they will fall apart. And then I doubt whether artificial happiness will appeal to me.

Shall I go to the experiment room? Soon we will try to revive the dog. No, not yet. And what if he just gets up and walks? I don't even know his name.

We will probably have to have a long postoperative stretch. The boys will have to sit here nights.

No use guessing. It may never come to this.

I have good boys here . . . I could have had sons like this. If not for that bombing raid in 1943. But probably it would not have worked anyway. I can't blame the women in my life or the circumstances; only myself. I'm an emotional failure.

Yura is an intellectual. In the best sense of that word, without wrong connotations. Intellectualism does not presuppose insensibility.

I am resting . . . Thinking a little. I can feel every organ inside my body; each is connected to my brain by some sort of commutator. The heart—thump-thump-thump. Then, irregularly—thump-thump. Thump. Thump! The lungs. I can feel the air

coming in, stretching the alveoli . . . Something stands in its way
—irritates—I want to cough. Must control it. This is important: to
control coughing, just like all feelings, all emotions. The stomach
. . . The intestines—grumbling a little. And the spleen is enlarged,
it is crowding everything on the left side . . . An angry giant, fat
and dull. No pains at the moment. Almost a bliss.

> *Friends of today will go away tomorrow*
> *Some into happiness, others to sorrow.*

Why "sorrow"? A stupid idea.
I am falling asleep.

vi
Yura

Someone knocks at the door. I sit up. My surgical gown is wrinkled. Embarrassing.

"Come in!"

This is Elena—Lena.

"Yura wants you to come. We are ready to start the awakening procedure."

"Coming."

I have had a nice little sleep. I look at the watch: forty minutes.

I am walking to Surgery. My organs have not as yet awakened. I don't feel them. How wonderful. It won't last long.

Everything is so peaceful here. As though I have never left.

The hum of the ventilator under the glass cylinder. The grumbling of the heart-lung-machine motor. Yura stands at his control panel, ready to start officiating.

"Ivan Nikolaevich, we are ready!"

"Good luck, then. Is your automatic machinery working well?"

"First rate! So far everything's proceeding normally."

"And the electrocardiograph?"

"Has been fixed."

We have an hour for this procedure. I don't know whether we have drawn the heating curve correctly. First stage, ten degrees; the second, twenty-two; then up to normal. Twenty minutes for each stage. Perhaps not enough? Never mind, we have worked out a careful program not to heat the blood too quickly, and to keep the temperature as even as possible in all parts of the body. The procedure provides for corrections, if necessary. We shall see.

"Well, let's start, Kolia. Switch on the program!"

Some day they will do the same thing with me. "Switch on the awakening program!" And I will rise from the dead. What for? The pleasure of investigation and discovery? The joy of achievement, work? Would there be enough of that for me in the future? The thing that frightens me most is loneliness. *Then.*

Let's forget this for a while. I must watch.

The new program so far has involved only the increased tempo of the heart-lung machine—the motor is revolving faster. Also, the air under the plexiglass jacket is becoming warmer. We can't find a proper name for it. The cylinder? Geometrically inaccurate. Tub? Too crude. Not important. The air is whistling through escape vents and I can feel it on my knees.

"Igor, please take the analyses as often as possible. It is important to watch the dynamics, and correct things, if necessary."

I should not interfere, really. Everything has been written down —both the frequency of analyses and the reaction to each new set of figures. But I must do something. I still can't get used to the new system in which each participant is given his part written down like music in an orchestra. Physiologists are used to the "instant" guidance—the chief has a plan in his head and issues orders like a general on a battlefield.

I look at the graphs. It is interesting to see how the automatic controls would handle the heating program. I must not disturb the team, though.

A wide ribbon is moving steadily. In the process of recording, its speed may be increased or decreased. The most interesting point at the moment is the temperature curve. It is highest in the esophagus. There it has already reached 45 degrees. In the large intestine still around 40. But then the reserve adjustment comes into play and the difference is narrowed to two degrees. The automatic controls work well so far.

"Pauline, what's the productivity of the machine?"

"Two and a half liters."

Vadim appears on the scene. He has missed the salient moment. Begins to raise his voice—why hasn't he been called in? Well, he should have thought about this himself. Polia cuts him down to size. "Imagine, it all works without you, Dima!"

Yura is all over his controls. "Aligning the zeroes," he calls this. It is important for the pressure curves. What is the situation in the left ventricle?

The esophagus temperature is up to 50. In the large intestine 47. It means that the heart temperature is even higher; the whole mass of blood is passing there and the blood temperature is already up to 64. Some definite electric activity might already occur. Let us see the screen. No, nothing definite yet—either a small fibrillation, or just mechanical agitation.

"Ivan Nikolaevich, it is time to add some whole blood. The oxygen pressure in the outflow is very low—only twenty millimeters."

This is Igor. This is what the double-check controls mean. If one person misses something, another picks it up.

"Go ahead, Vadim. You're the captain here."

"All hands on deck! Masha, stop the machine. Rita, remove six hundred cubes of plasma. Polia, the same amount of whole blood into the oxygenerator!"

"Wait, wait a minute. We have some diluted blood—it must be used before we switch to the whole."

"Right! What's the hemoglobin content there?"

"We haven't measured."

"Why? I told you!"

"You told us nothing, and we didn't think of it."

"Stop arguing! Change a liter of the fluid."

"Yes, sir! Right, sir!"

This is Yura who commands. Vadim salutes him ironically, but one can detect a note of annoyance in his voice. Up to now, physiologists have run all such tests; now it is the engineers' turn. Never mind. Vadim is intelligent enough to understand.

The machine is stopped. They are pouring out plasma, pouring in the blood. They are too slow, they must hurry! Keep still. There are too many bosses as it is.

"Start it up!"

The motor starts revolving. The interruption has lasted for two minutes. At this temperature this means nothing. No danger at all.

The dog's tongue has become pink. Now it is blood and not merely plasma which is circulating through his body.

The esophagus temperature—55. There is no apparent electric activity in the heart or the brain. This is strange. I am beginning to grow uneasy. Is it possible that oxygen deficiency has been allowed to develop and has been overlooked? Perhaps, whole blood should have been used earlier. Damn!

"Please, measure the hemoglobin level, Vadim. Yura, I think we should add some more blood—the whole this time."

Yura: "Let's wait until the temperature rises to 65. There is no ground for anxiety. Look at those readings of the oxygen and carbon-dioxide pressure in the tissues!"

Yes, this is reasonable. These new indicators are very good, and new to me. I don't quite trust them yet, but I agree. I must trust Yura at this stage.

The air temperature in the cylinder is nearing 80. But the warmth penetration through the skin is very slow. We must use more heat.

Is it possible that the dog will not be awakened? This question is on everyone's mind now. Nonsense, he must awaken. That is, the brain should come to (should?), but I am not so sure about the heart. Even if we succeed in starting it up, how would it perform?

In point of fact, this is not so terribly important. Before my turn comes, they will have perfected the parallel blood circulation —the heart and the machine working simultaneously. Besides, the pressure chamber should help. The calculation is very simple: at the pressure of two atmospheres each cube of blood carries the double amount of oxygen. Therefore, the heart productivity can be cut in half. So even if the dog dies, this would not affect my chances.

However, I wish the dog would come to. It would give all of them a tremendous morale lift. They have spent so much time and effort.

"Look, the temperature is already 65, and in the large intestine only 48. Yura, your automatics are letting us down." Vadim, of course.

"Don't worry—it will level off. You see, the rise rate is already slowing down! Just change the blood! Quick, don't go to sleep!"

Too abrupt, too domineering. This is not right. Yura should not throw out orders like that. However, Vadim has swallowed it.

Now there is a burst of activity around the machine. They must take out a liter of the diluted blood and replace it with whole blood. I must not interfere; this is Vadim's sector. I can even sit down for a while, my legs are numb. It is past three now. I sit down. Weakness. The mouth is dry. A strange feeling in the stomach as though something were pulling it from one side.

For the first experiment everything is going fine. So many machines, and all are working. Amazing. Yura has done a fine training job on his team. I almost forgot—tomorrow I should call the members of the committee, the people who will attack his dissertation. Ask their opinions, prepare them. Anything may happen! My presence would have been very important; they would not have liked to pick on me. Enemies. I'm such an inoffensive man, and still some of them dislike me. Many people can't stand criticism, even of the most academic kind. I'm exaggerating, of course —"enemies" is a strong word. Semyonoff and Aaron Grigorievich honestly disagree with all cybernetics. "The qualitative differences in pathological processes can't be expressed by formulas and electronic lamps." "He and his pupils are working themselves into a blind corner." It is impossible to convince them. For them, the multiplication table is the highest level of mathematics.

No, let's be just. Generally, they are decent people. They will not pick on Yura unreasonably. Aaron loves music, plays the violoncello. An intellectual of the old school.

Our Director has not even bothered to attend the experiment. Apparently he couldn't care less. This hurts a little, nonetheless. However, we'll live through it. I'd better go and take a look. I have rested a little.

"Look, Ivan Nikolaevich! You can see fibrillation!"

Yes, true. The amplitude is still very shallow, but there it is. The temperature is only 76. In the heart, of course, it is higher. Must be nearing 85.

The brain has started to work as well. Good waves on the encephalograph. It means the brain is fully alive. Good. This is the way it should be.

The air within the cylinder is quite warm. Automatic controls are working—two minutes per one degree. Our main problem is supplying oxygen to the tissues, the evacuation of carbon dioxide, and the maintenance of the nitric-acid balance. The machine productivity remains at two and a half liters. We can't increase it—the width of the veins is small, the blood outflow is difficult. Nothing can be done about that. But this is sufficient.

"Mila, increase the respiration gradually so that the alveoli can straighten out."

The temperature, 86.

The electroencephalograph shows deep waves as during normal sleep. The dog must awaken any moment now. We are all watching him.

The first breathing spasms—this means that the brain begins to really function. However, this must be stopped; it interferes with artificial respiration. Vadim is on the job.

"Introduce the relaxants. Directly into the oxygenerator."

This is done. The whole body is completely inert now.

The heating-up process has been going on now for an hour. Soon we must start worrying about the hemolysis; our machine begins to ruin blood when working uninterruptedly for long stretches. How about the urine? Just a little bit, on the very bottom. For some reason the artificial blood circulation inhibits the kidney function. Surgeons have noticed this also. Some reflexes are affected.

It is quiet in the room. Each person is attending to his proper task. Conversations are conducted in low whispers.

The most important moment is nearing—the starting of the heart. The cardiogram is showing a large-wave fibrillation. I can imagine the heart surface twitching. Why can't it just start contracting? No, it doesn't want to.

Defibrillation through the pectoral wall is more difficult than with an open heart, but still it is usually successful.

"Get the defibrillator ready. Wet the gauze on the electrodes well. And shave the fur around the heart—close. Why haven't you done this before? Vadim, this is your department."

"We haven't forgotten. Just a superstition—if everything is prepared for the end of the experiment, the dog dies before it. Come on, girls, start shaving. Quick!"

"Superstition"! The scientists!

We are waiting. The temperature is 96. It is even higher within the heart. Time to act.

"Vadim, go ahead."

He puts on rubber gloves. A rubber mat under his feet. The electrodes, wrapped in wet napkins, are pressed against the dog's body. Kolia is charging the condenser of the defibrillator. We shall use 5,000 volts.

"Switch off all systems."

"All is ready, Yura?"

Vadim is consulting the "superior." This is good.

"Go ahead. Contact!"

A small click. It is all over. Yura is in full charge. "Switch on all systems. Tolia, switch the cardiogram over to the large oscillograph!"

We are watching the screen. No. Nothing.

"Fibrillation is continuing. Vadim, we must repeat it. Yura, what's the safe charge maximum?"

"Seven thousand volts. Kolia, set it up."

The whole procedure is repeated. This is just like a novel about astronauts—"Contact! All systems go." The tension in the room is mounting; this may not work, after all.

"I'm switching it on. Contact!"

A loud click. The dog's body quivers. This is quite a shock.

"Switch on all systems!"

"Hurray! It's going!"

The heart is contracting. The rare and weak beats. Now they must be built up. This is wonderful. So far.

"Introduce five-hundredths cube of actrenalin! Directly into the machine! Mila, good respiration! Deep!"

The heart action is improving. One, two, three . . . twelve in ten seconds. The heart must be given a chance to handle an increased load.

"Cut the machine productivity to one liter. Gradually—take two minutes."

Now we are watching the arterial pressure curve. Yura has switched it over to a large screen.

The pressure is low. The curve is barely reaching the 70-milli-meter line. The diastolic is high—60. This is caused by the machine. The pump is delivering its steady one liter per minute. If only parallel blood circulation were perfected! We could have run the machine indefinitely—until the heart built up its full strength. But this has not been worked out. And this way, the machine might do more harm than good.

"Comrades, suppose we switch off the machine altogether?"

I am addressing the whole "collective." They do not answer. We have had no experience with this.

"Igor, will you please arrange the measurement of heart productivity every five minutes? This is extremely important. Is this possible?"

"We will try."

"Then let's stop the machine. Ready, Pauline? Stop it . . . now!"

The machine is stopped. The pressure begins to fall off—more and more. It stops at fifty. This is low. But the contractions seem to be good. Let us continue.

"Get me the capacity per minute, Igor."

"Let's wait a moment, until the regime sets in." This is Yura. He is right. We can wait for five minutes while they are changing the blood in the oxygenator. Then we can pump in some fresh blood—if this is necessary.

So far this is a success. The heart-lung machine is turned off, but the dog is alive. I am very happy. However, this may be premature; the dog was not yet awakened. Surgeons tell us that brain complications represent the main danger. The most minute brain vessels may become clogged by erythrocytes—and then, edema. But we used only plasma during the low-temperature stage, so this danger should not be present in our case. We shall see.

It is four o'clock. Not really very late, but I am tired. I wish I could go and lie down. But this is impossible. I may still be needed here.

To cancel my rendezvous tonight? "Liuba, I must tell you something." "What?" "I have decided to subject myself to anabiosis." "What? What!" I can see her face—bewilderment, alarm. The expression "subject myself" may be a wrong one. But what else? "Freeze myself?" "Put myself into cold storage?" Like a side of beef. No, absurd.

"Well?"

"Nothing new. The pressure fluctuates between 70 and 80. The venous is up to 165. They are trying to determine productivity per minute now."

It seems that we have succeeded. Of course, the pressure may still collapse. There are grave disturbances in the whole system— in its regulatory spheres, especially. Our "terra incognita."

Come on, dog, wake up. Come on!

No. Not yet. And the experiment has lasted only three hours. And after twenty years? Impossible. I am a scientist, a realist, and suddenly, such fantasies!

But what do I have to lose? The respect of my colleagues? Of course, they would say: "What a fool, to fall for such nonsense. Just a bad physiologist." But to die in a hospital—pneumonia, bleeding, anemia . . . Horrible! I don't want it. Why grasp at illusions? To gain a few extra months?

"Ivan Nikolaevich! Boys! Look! He's waking up! Look, look!"

This is Mila. She is working the respiration bag and therefore is watching the animal's face.

We are all around the table. True, the eyes are open, the look is intelligent. Bewilderment—"What's happened to me?"

"What's his name? Call him by name!"

"Druzhok! Druzhok!" *

He is trying to move his head.

The dog has awakened, awakened! After two hours at the temperature of 34 degrees!

"Let's remove the breathing tube. It's bothering the poor thing!" This is our softhearted Lena.

Yura protests (now as a physiologist!): "No, not yet. The respiration is still ineffective. On the contrary. I think we should give him some light narcotic—the nitric acid, perhaps. Let him stay quiet until the organs resume their normal rhythm. And it would be easier to take measurements; otherwise he'll kick and struggle."

* "Little friend! Little friend!"

"Can I take the heart-lung machine out? We must flush the tubes before the blood dries in them!" This is Alla, worried.

"Yes, of course. Vadim, order the tubes to be taken out of the arteries and veins. The measurement catheters must be left in, naturally."

Vadim is attending to this himself. He likes working with his hands.

I am once again examining the ribbon with the curves. All is in order. The encephalograph indicates sleep—wide, infrequent waves. The blood pressure 85. This is sufficient. The heart is racing —a hundred-forty beats per minute. We should try to slow it down. There are medicines for that.

There is a hum of voices—the general release of emotions. Discharge of tension. Let us listen to them. Vadim and Pauline are over the dog, discussing soberly the defects of the experiment— "It would have been better to let the machine work a little longer . . . To try the intermittent regime—perhaps some long interruptions could be permitted." Lena and Piotr are filling in the graphs, taking the figures from the ribbon; gossiping about someone— ". . . disappeared and came back for the grand finale." Probably about Semyon.

Igor and Rita are doing nothing—just blabbing and laughing. Yes, about water skiing. "He crashed into a wave . . . I thought he'd never surface again." An exchange of eloquent looks. Igor is quite a male predator. That's all right. Only Yura is working silently with his pocket slide rule, marking something in his notebook. He has a lot of figures to organize and digest.

I envy them. I would like to join one of the groups, talk and laugh with them. I can't do it. I don't know how, and I have no ready words. Never could do it, and have been suffering my whole life because of that. Never mind. We'll live through it.

I would like to go home, but at the same time I feel like staying here and watching the dog for a while—for an hour or so. Afraid to miss something.

But I don't want to hang around here either. Go to my office and speak to Yura? He can leave now; the poor dog is very well attended as it is.

"Yura, let's go to my office and discuss some technical points."

This, so that others would not become offended. "Can you leave now?"

"Why not? The recording is practically finished."

We are walking together. Each thinking his own thoughts.

"Yura, I must speak to you about a very serious matter . . ."

"What is it?"

"I want to leave you as my successor here."

"Me? Who would agree to that?" ("Who would?" In other words, he himself is willing.) "Besides, I wouldn't be able to handle it." (Ah, he has caught on—modesty, the best ornament of ability.)

"You will. Let's forget false modesty."

I am thinking: a real scientist should not refuse any challenge, even if it is a little over his head. It gives one a stimulus to improve.

We enter my office. Suppose I lie down? Yura is a close friend. I hope I am not mistaken in that. It has happened to me in the past.

"Forgive me if I lie down? I'm a little tired. Sit down in that armchair."

The illusion of spiritual proximity. And perhaps to him I am just a superior? He sits down silently, looking at me. A good warm look.

"You know that I'm not doing this out of sentiment." (That, also.) "It would be a pity if our work fell apart, and I think you'd be able to hold it together. I'd like to hear what you would do if you were left in charge of the laboratory?"

I am putting him on the spot. Never mind, if he has real ideas in his head, he'll be able to face this.

"You mean, now? Without any preparation?"

"Don't be coy. Haven't you thought about this?"

"Yes, but I have never systematized it in my head. I won't be able to develop this logically."

"The best you can."

"Then permit me to start from a little distance . . ."

"Go ahead."

"First, we need general principles. Learning is modeling, the brain is a tremendous modeling installation. Remember, we talked about that?"

Yes, I remember. Models out of nerve cells. The multilevel principle of modeling: models of sounds, words, phrases, chapters, books. The supplementary models reflecting qualities . . . He is not going to tell me all about this again?

"The human being has well-developed stimulating programs by which he translates his cortex models into action—words, pictures, objects. Those are extracerebral models."

"And Creation? Inspiration?"

"There is a model for creation—it is really building complex models out of primitive ones. Combinations assuming independent qualities."

"And so?"

"During the last twenty years engineering science has achieved an enormous advance—electronics. Now there is the possibility of building mechanical installations to create very complex models, and not merely statistical, like books or charts, but acting. This is a tremendous step forward. A whole collective of scientists can create a computer which will be more intelligent than any of them individually."

"This does not yet exist. And many doubt this possibility."

"The possibility is here, and it will become a reality. Of course, a computer is no miracle, and it is difficult to compose programs modeling complicated systems. But this is supported by various supplementary mechanical possibilities, you know it. Besides, other machines are being designed with the quantitative principle of digesting information—rather, like a brain."

"Nothing realistic has been produced yet."

"But every three years the speed and memory potential of the computers are doubled. So it will be produced."

"All right, perhaps. But let's keep closer to physiology."

"For me, physiology is interesting primarily in connection with the application to it of the general principle of science construction. If you permit, I'll make an attempt to formulate something in this direction. There are many of your thoughts in this, as well."

("Principles." A mere boy, and already "general principles"!)

"Go ahead."

"Each given science is the model of some part of the world, of some system or a group of systems connected by common structure or function. For instance, cytology is studying the cell, and sociology, society. In all cases some models are created reflecting the specifics of structure or function of the respective system. The precision of any science depends on the degree of similarity between the model and the original."

(This is unquestionable.)

"One can recognize several stages in the development of any science. First, investigation through physical senses even though armed with telescopes or microscopes. As a result, some approximate models are created in the cortex reflecting the general information about the system. Then, they are reflected physically—into descriptions, pictures, diagrams. Those are qualitative models, hypotheses. The second stage is the quantitative investigation. The purpose here is to reduce to figures the hypotheses and their correlations within the system under study. The third stage: creation of working models reflecting the hypotheses about the structures and functions of the system with its qualitative interrelations. I see this as complex electronic installations or universal electronic computers. Our proposed model of the inner sphere of the human body is a prototype of such an installation."

(Thanks for remembering it!)

"The fourth stage: the creation of controlling machines or programs. They must be able to transform any given system from one state into any other desired state. This is the optimum control. Of course some complex self-regulating systems such as the human body can be rather loosely controlled, because they have the faculty of self-correction, but only to a certain extent. Hence, the fatal medical errors. Those are the main principles, Ivan Nikolaevich. Do you agree? Of course, there is nothing very new in all this . . . I think this is applicable to any science; they all need mathematical expression and working models."

"All this is true, Yura. And your principles are also correct. But there is a big 'but.' As I understand it, each model can only more or less reproduce the original. In many cases, rather less than more.

The degree of perfection here depends on the limitations of mathematics, methods of investigation, the mechanical means. If a system is very complex, as the human brain is, for instance, and there are no sure methods of investigation, the model would be very primitive. And then it would not serve any useful purpose. This is why I have taken as my object the inner organic structure of the body, without even its cell level. Here, I think, the problem is not too complex, and can be solved by the existing methods of modeling."

I am not altogether honest here. "I have taken"—when, in fact, we have selected it together. And there are more of Yura's ideas here than mine.

"But, Ivan Nikolaevich, technology is progressing! What is impossible to model today, will be possible tomorrow. We must prepare for this. Working models always will be better than the static. The brain model will not be created very soon—I grant you this—because it is an area very difficult to investigate, and is composed of very many elements. But I believe that human social relations, for instance, already can be approached on a cybernetic basis."

Oh, so that's what you are aiming at, my friend? In your place, I might have done the same.

"Yes, but then, at first, it is necessary to model man's behavior only on the 'camera obscura' principle—without exaggerated attempts to reflect the concrete nerve network governing it. The psychological model, so to say, rather than the physiological."

I agree. And many people are already working on this.

"Look, Yura, if you are attracted by such distant horizons, would mere physiology satisfy you? Must I knock myself out trying to set you up as my successor? Perhaps this work needs someone with simpler thinking?"

(He will abandon physiology for sociology and who then would supervise and maintain my anabiosis?)

"Of course, psychology and sociology attract me. I don't deny this; but physiology is the basis of psyche. I am still young. I can afford to dream a little. You yourself have often said that medicine is a lightweight affair, that it will never affect human destiny."

Yes, I have said this. And I believe it. But it is too late for me to jump into any other sphere. And when I could, I lacked the courage or faith in myself. I did not trust my intellect. But he trusts it. At his age I was quite a fool. No, no fool; but I did not have a proper education. Also, the approach to science was different then. "The qualitative differences" stood (like stone walls) between different science disciplines.

"And how do you evaluate the present position of physiology in relation to your—what do you call them?—stages?"

"Physiology is still in the first stage, or just approaching the second. A bunch of unconnected hypotheses. Quantitative modeling is still in its infancy."

"And medicine?"

"Medicine operates in the same way—by touch and by primitive controls. The same applies to society, incidentally. Both spheres are saved only by their self-regulating faculties."

"Clear. But let's come back to earth. What do you propose to do in your—in our laboratory?"

I am looking at him. He is excited. It is the first time that he is speaking like a full-fledged scientist.

"The same things we are doing now. Conduct physiological experiments, record them, translate into figures as many factors as possible. Out of these figures we will derive differential and algebraic equations—the characteristics of organs and systems. Then we will run them through mathematical computers. After verifying the results, we will create special electronic models of various organs, combine them into groups and, finally, into a model of the human system. Just what we are doing now. But the main direction will be aimed at the regulatory endocrine and nerve systems—to get closer to the cortex."

"And that is all?"

"No, that is not all, even though, frankly, there's enough work here for a lifetime. What we are creating now—I mean, our machine—is the first primitive prototype. You know it yourself."

(Of course, I know it. We are just scratching the surface, but even that is remarkable. But must he tell this to me? He's depreciating my work, the little upstart!)

"For the solution of even the most general involved problems we would need a hundred laboratories like ours."

"Even more!"

"I'm glad you agree with me. Therefore I'm thinking of something else. We must bring clinical experience into our work—the study of actual cases. Along with that we must rely much more on heuristic modeling—thinking up hypotheses, making educated guesses, trying them out in clinic, evaluating results, making corrections. You yourself have spoken about this, but so far we have taken just a few faltering steps in this direction."

(Thanks for remembering me at all! Could it be that within a year after my death, he will start saying, "my theories, my ideas"? But then, what *should* he say? "My late teacher's ideas?" Life goes on, and there's no way of stopping it.)

However, back to the matter at hand.

"To do what you suggest, we would need a whole flock of good physicians working with us. Or we must move the whole laboratory into a clinic. In principle, you are right. To change physiology, we need thousands of laboratories and several lifetimes. Does it mean that we should abandon our present experiment, primitive as it is? Perhaps I'm speaking as a hidebound physiologist, but I don't think that the clinical approach would solve all our problems."

"Why not? I spoke to physicians at the Clinic Town when I was visiting you in the hospital. There are many enthusiasts among them. Can't you see how this would work? We would supply them with precise instrumental data, and they with clinical observation to correct our findings!"

"Our Director would never permit you to do this. He's a firm believer in so-called pure physiology."

"That's why we should perhaps get out of here and move over to the Institute of Cybernetics. They are interested in practical application of their theories, and we will supply them with this opportunity."

"What? *What!* The Institute of Cybernetics? Have you already spoken to Professor Sergievsky there? Then it appears that I have been trying to promote you when you have already promoted yourself!"

"No—without you, I would not speak to anyone. But I have scouted around there a little. They are responsive to the idea. Please don't misunderstand me, Ivan Nikolaevich, I didn't mean to abandon you, or sell out—no—but after Vadim spoke to our Director, I felt sick to the stomach. The laboratory means a lot to me, and I didn't want to see it destroyed. I meant to speak to you first, but you know how sick you were then. Now that you've recovered—" (Recovered!) "—we must decide everything together."

"Together." I feel a little better. He is right; our work must not perish just because one man dies—even if he is their "teacher." Teacher? I must not be offended. There is nothing personal in all this. But it is a little sad—Yura has caught up with me, passed me, and is drawing ahead. Sad. The dialectics of life—and death?

"What is there to decide, Yura? Your idea is very good. But how to arrange this big switch? Of course, both our Institute and the Institute of Cybernetics are under the same Academy . . . But would Sergievsky, Boris Nikitich, accept us? They probably would . . . But where would they find room for us? They are building something at the Clinic Town—have you looked into that?"

"Yes, I have." (He has covered everything!) "They will put the Department of Reanimation there—and there is no space there for us. But they can easily build another building for us. That wouldn't take long."

"Reanimation, you say? That is very good. Many people can be saved this way—people brought in with shock, bleeding, heart attacks. And our sarcophagus would come in very handy, too . . . Yes, this is a very good idea . . . Have you spoken to anyone about it—concretely?"

"Only to Vadim here. And to some physicians at the hospital where you stayed—"

"And not a word to me!"

"Do you think we'd do anything without you? We were just waiting until you were a little stronger!"

"So that you could hit me over the head with it? 'Sorry, Professor, but we've got another setup all arranged—more interesting than yours.'"

"Why do you say that? We would have come to you and said,

dear Ivan Nikolaevich, we have a suggestion for you—to move over, bag and baggage, to the Institute of Cybernetics. There are such and such reasons for it. First, this would advance your work. Secondly, you know how they push us around here. Of course, this is just a suggestion, subject to your approval."

"All right, all right, I believe you." (I really do, but there's still an unpleasant aftertaste in my mind.) "So, let's move over to Boris Nikitich—that is, if he will take us. It is true that our work is closer to mechanics and mathematics than to pure physiology."

So it seems that my brilliant plan of maneuvering Yura into succession will not after all benefit anyone. It is good that I have not spoken to anyone about it; otherwise I would be in a ridiculous position now. Being ridiculous is the worst thing.

Now, back to reality: "It's all very well, Yura, but I can't move anywhere in my present state. I wouldn't survive the struggle and the excitement. So please wait until I'm dead. It won't be long now."

Dead? Yes, dead.

"Incidentally, how do you propose to solve the problem of my anabiosis experiment? The sarcophagus would require constant servicing—and improvement. It will be a full-time job for all of you.

"I know. We'll do everything. This anabiosis experiment will help us more than anything else." (How shrewdly he has calculated everything, and how frankly he speaks about it!) "If we sell this right, they will give us everything we ask for—all the facilities."

("Sell?" Sell me in that sarcophagus?)

I wince. He notices it.

"Ivan Nikolaevich, are you shocked by this conversation? Do you think perhaps that we don't value you sufficiently?"

I am silent. All I need now is to burst into tears. Sentiment.

"Then you're very mistaken. We love you very much. And we never forget what you have done for us. And we will never claim any of your ideas. Everything I have told you is really yours. We only want to continue your work."

He is flattering me—"selling" himself to me.

I keep still.

"But proper organization is necessary to do all this. Remember, you said once that noble ends can only be achieved by noble means. I have not forgotten this. We'll never surrender our basic principles and ideas; we won't lie, scheme, crawl on our bellies before anyone. But neither will we waste ourselves fighting windmills." (What does he mean by this?) "We will pursue our goal, but avoid hidden reefs on which our work may founder. What's the use of winning a skirmish and losing the war? Work, achievement—those will be our weapons, not words."

I am becoming a little sick. And I am going to let him know it.

"Yura, what I have heard from you today frightens me. Such rationalism, such calculation, bordering on cynicism. Perhaps I have misunderstood you. You see, I'm not yet free of sentimentality. When you say that my anabiosis will help you 'sell' your scheme, it disturbs me. Tell me, what's back of this all? What stimuli are moving you?"

"They are noble, even sentimental, if you wish. Service to humanity. This will never become outdated. But in order to be efficient, it must be properly organized, like everything else. We will not succumb to personal vanity—this is the greatest hidden danger, and we must avoid it. We must do our work intelligently rather than spectacularly—without noisy conflicts and loud phrases, step by step. Use the existing means at our disposal to create new means, to achieve first and speak about it later."

I just don't know. I don't know what to think. This is just not the Yura I thought I knew.

"You have changed a great deal during the last few months, Yura."

"I have been thinking a lot since our last conversation . . . I have a rule now: every morning I think for an hour—just think. About something important: cybernetics, psychology, philosophy . . . I've been making some notes too. It is very interesting . . . At first everything is hazy, but then it starts to clear up, to come into focus. I think this makes one grow inside . . ."

"Oh well . . . Let's go back and see what's going on . . . And then, I must go home . . . You've certainly given me a good shock . . . Everything inside me has started to ache all of a sudden . . ."

How complicated everything in this world is, how logical, and how cruel. I had my work, my laboratory, my team, and now I have outlived my usefulness, and everything is slowly slipping from under my feet.

I had love too. No, that had never been secure—"You're my Mona Lisa, which can be always stolen from me." I will see her tonight . . . Yes, I must be going home. I must rest.

We are walking along the deserted corridors. Everyone's gone. The working day is over. Only our wing is seething with furious activity.

What a change! The dog is lying on his side, breathing by himself: the respiration tube has been removed. I catch a quick exchange of inquisitive glances between Vadim and Yura—two conspirators. They are not as simple as I thought.

I come to the table.

"Is he conscious?"

"Absolutely. *Druzhok! Druzhok!*"

The dog opens his eyes, full of pain. "What else do you want from me?" A lazy wave of the tail. "Leave me alone."

"Give me the stethoscope."

I press it against the dog's chest where the fur has been shaved off. Listen. Good, clear tones.

"Show me the table and graphs."

Everything is in order. The arterial and venous pressure, the pulse, the respiration. However, in the blood there is a slight surplus of unoxidized products. The oxygen content of the venous blood is a little low. The general metabolism is also down. Apparently there is some endocrinal insufficiency. The hormones have not yet been checked . . . Not enough urine, but its analysis is good.

"Now he needs care and control, children. Watch the gas balance, the fluid, saline, and nitric acid equilibrium. Watch the pressure, conduct periodic tests of the exhaled air, use the electrocardiograph. The dog needs narcotics; otherwise he will tear out all control gauges. But not too much—it may affect respiration. Vadim, you'll have to stay here overnight. Keep a biochemist with you, a technician to keep records, and the necessary chemical lab personnel. Everything must be checked hour by hour. You will telephone me later on, at home."

I am looking around. Everyone is tired. The first excitement has worn off. Now there is a reaction.

"Well, you've done yourselves proud today. The experiment has been extremely complicated, and it's gone off well—even better than well. Excellent performance. Now most of you can leave, I suppose—eh, Yura?"

"Let everyone finish his notes; otherwise he will forget it by tomorrow. Then, of course, home."

"We should go to a restaurant after what's happened today! To the Poplavok, on the river!"

This is Tolia. They say he loves his drink. However, this really calls for a celebration.

"Not a bad idea. Too bad I can't join you."

I wouldn't have gone anyway. Restaurants are not for me.

"Well, good night, everybody! Igor, have you let your people go? Thanked them?"

"Oh yes. Definitely. In the name of science."

"Call me, Vadim—in any case. All right? Good night."

I have not even looked at Yura. I don't feel like speaking to him.

I go to my office.

I am still in charge of the laboratory, but they are no longer my team. It seems that dying is really a good idea for me. The Moor has performed his task . . .

No, don't be a sentimental schoolgirl, my friend. Life goes on along its normal course. They will all be sorry to see you go, some will even cry. And you must be happy that you have someone like Yura who can take hold of your work, and carry on, probably much more efficiently than you.

No, I don't believe it. My horizons are wider, I am more intelligent. All the ideas he is playing around with are really mine.

Not true. They are in the air. And Yura has been helping me catch and formulate them. And he understands them more concretely, as an engineer and a mathematician, and not as a dreamer like me. No use moping around. Let's go home.

vii
Liuba

Evening is approaching. Long, black shadows. The last ones before sunset.

I am sitting in an armchair, on the balcony, waiting for Liuba. I have had my dinner, and a nap. I am looking at the street below, almost without any thoughts. Life goes on, as it will be going on without me.

The experiment has gone well. I am happy. But, at the same time, a little sad. I am trying to understand why. Because this means that I will have to start packing soon. Had the experiment failed, I could have refused the anabiosis—"What for? One cannot awaken." I could have deluded myself, into living a few extra months. But now it is impossible. The odds for "awakening" have improved. Since the first experiment has gone so well, even without a high-pressure chamber, the whole thing has become quite feasible. Why don't I rejoice? I now have a realistic hope for a long life.

But do I need a long life? Especially in the future, where I would be a total stranger? Suppose I do awaken. What would I do? Look around? Travel? Interesting. And then I'm a scientist. I may start giving talks to large crowds. "There was a terrible war . . . I was a doctor working in a military hospital . . ."

"Alms, alms . . . in the name of Christ . . ."

Liuba is due here at any minute. It would have been better if she hadn't been able to come. To be left alone, to depart alone. She will start nagging me—"Live! You must live!"

What does she need me for? What could be more absurd than our being together now? I am a dying man, an invalid. She, a strong healthy woman. And she has a husband. In the past it was painful for me to imagine them together. Now, it seems immaterial. Let them be together. This is what depressed hormones do to one. Physiology.

She has offered: "Let me abandon everything, come to you,

stay here to the end." Just a pose, perhaps? She knew I would not agree—under any circumstances.

Forgive me, my darling, perhaps you would have done it.

Is it really possible that she would? And what would she have done later on? What about the children? No, certain things just can't be done. No mother should be capable of doing that. I myself would have stopped respecting her. So, then, she wouldn't have done it, anyway. It was a wild sacrificial impulse.

When she is not here, the distance between us grows. "You have your family, children. I, nothing but my work and my 'children'— Yura, Vadim, Igor, Pauline . . ." My pupils.

It is very important to feel that one is needed, no matter by whom. To feel that one is indispensable. This is why I feel depressed tonight.

The "children" have grown up. It seems that they don't need me any longer. Yura has a clear program in his work. Authority, prestige. They call him by his first name, but they all listen to him, obey him.

I have no envy. I am honestly glad that he'll go further than I, and faster. All I want is a little human warmth. "You are our teacher . . ." It is true; I have put into them a part of my soul. Have led them by the hand through the labyrinths of science, showed them the ropes. Corrected their mistakes. Set up experiments for them. Vadim, for instance, came fresh from the university; he knew nothing about our work.

Time to get ready for a long voyage . . .

She is late . . . She'll come, stay an hour, and then cry, "I must run!" How will I tell her about my decision? Or will I—weakling that I am—postpone it again? No, tonight is the night. Especially after a successful experiment. I will tell her everything. Poor darling, what a new load for her.

I don't think that the boys really believe I will dare to go through with it. And I myself am not so sure at all. No, I must.

I remember: The ward. A blue night light over the door. The uncomfortable, unpleasant silence. A hot pillow. I am gasping for air. The humming in the ears . . . "Come, death, I don't want to live . . ."

Quick, approaching, clicking footsteps. She? *She!* She runs, like a little girl, lithe, thin. Swinging her purse. Such a funny, charming walk. She skips along, her head high. This way she thinks she looks taller and more imposing. An experienced, learned doctor, if you please.

I see her and all my mental detachment melts away at once. I need you, my darling, need you desperately. Yura is drifting away, Vadim too, probably. I can't be left all alone, understand me! Yes, there is still Leonid. But he is so coldly rational, and I want a little tenderness. Only you . . .

I'll run out to meet her. No—the flowers—here on the table! She loves them. First gladioli . . .

The heels are clicking up the steps. My heart is clicking too. The door is already open. I'm waiting.

"Good evening, Ivan dear! Let me kiss you!" Her hands on my shoulders. An unusually long kiss. The aroma of her hair.

I am holding her tight. A thin dress. I can feel all of her. My beloved, my desired. My only one.

We are having coffee. Liuba has set the table. She likes doing things here. "This is my home." True. No one had ever been here before you. Strong, lovely legs, not yet properly tanned.

"All right, tell me all about your experiment."

I tell her briefly, skipping details. She is listening attentively. (We should have tried the intermittent-circulation regime. Well, next time.)

After I finish, she remains silent for a moment or two.

"I don't think this can be used clinically very often . . . Not in surgery anyway. If a patient has a shock, has wounds, then you can't decrease the clotting power of his blood by using artificial circulation—"

"You are wrong! When the parallel circulation is fully perfected, then you can use it for all patients with cardiac weakness. You know yourself how many of those there are. And when we combine this with the pressure chamber, artificial kidney, and prolonged narcosis, it will be a real revolution in reanimation. Some doctor you are—not seeing such an elementary thing!"

She is still pretty narrow. A pity.

"But you don't have all that yet, Ivan. It is true that oxygen deficiency is the main cause of death . . . But all this sounds so complicated. You say that twenty people were working today? Do you need a team like this? Our Health Department will die before they give you anything like that. Do you realize what a unit like this would need for round-the-clock service? A hundred people!"

"Do you think it will always be like this? Everything will be simplified. First, automation. Then, the unnecessary analyses will be eliminated; we're still working by touch. Probably ten people per shift will still be needed. Plus, of course, the equipment and proper space. But, then, consider the effect! In a city like ours we'll be able to save a hundred people each year.

"Heart cases, too?"

"Of course!"

"Then our bosses will be interested. They are scared stiff of heart attacks. Write an exposition!"

"Don't laugh. I won't write any exposition, but Yura too says that this idea must be 'sold,' as he calls it."

"He's right. Publicity is paramount in a thing like this. One must catch public imagination."

Now she begins telling me about her department. Small facts, almost gossip. I do not really listen. I'm just looking at her, thinking.

Why does she love me? My scientific ideas do not interest her all that much. She is a practical physician, not by accident, but by dedication. She weighs science against sentiment—will it benefit her patients? She knows her business, reads a good deal, but does not react to theories. Too bad, of course. She should, with her brain.

"You know, Lou, with our installation we may be able to develop anabiosis. Does the word ring a bell with you, doctor?"

"You must think I'm an ignoramus!"

She does not yet suspect what I'm driving at. "His usual fantasies." She is busy with the flowers, arranging a bouquet.

"You know I've read that in Japan flower arrangement is a special art . . . I wish I could learn it. Have you bought these for me?"

"Yes, of course. Now what would you say if I'd try anabiosis on myself?"

For a moment this does not penetrate. Then, an explosion:

"*What!* How long are you going to torture me? Do you think it's easy for me to sit here, blab about flowers and your damned machine, and see how day by day you're getting—"

She dashes to and fro like an infuriated tigress. Red spots on her face, pressed lips.

I keep still. Let her unload herself and calm down a little.

"Do you think it's easy for me—this love, your illness? Look!"

She pulls the dress tightly around her waist. Yes, she has lost quite a bit of weight.

"Hero, indeed! He tries anabiosis on himself! I need you alive. Understand? *Alive!*"

She hasn't understood, of course. She thinks I want to conduct an ordinary, routine experiment. Freeze myself, then thaw out. I must break the truth to her gently. No, let her dash about a little. She is always wonderful—angry, happy, laughing or crying. I don't know how to explain it. Sincerity? Directness? No, I simply love her.

She stops near the window, drumming with her fingers on the glass, her back to me.

"Have you calmed down?" I attempt to embrace her shoulders. She doesn't respond. I turn her around. "Look at me . . . Look!"

Her eyebrows are knit, eyes misty. Still distant, but already melting. I know those eyes. My darling.

"For me death is inevitable anyway, Lou. And soon. Remember how you came to me in the hospital?"

I remember: lips pressed together painfully, despair in her eyes— "Help . . . Someone. Help!"

No, let us not remember. I feel better now, and I don't want to think about that nightmare.

"Lou, you're a doctor. You know the truth, better than I do. Let's sit together—let's talk quietly."

She surrenders, sits down on the divan, next to me. I hold her hands in mine, soft little hands with clipped nails. I love her. Yes, and also play in love, just a little. I must convince her.

"Do you know how frightful it is to die of asphyxiation? It would be all right if death came some other way—a hemorrhage, for instance. Then one would just sink into unconsciousness. And just suppose, a brain hemorrhage? Then you're lying paralyzed, speechless . . . mumbling something with a twisted face . . . No longer a human being. You've seen enough of this in your life . . ."

She drops her eyes. Thinking, "Oh God, what for?"

"You have, of course, seen my case history and spoken to David. New relapses are inevitable—no matter how careful I am. It is a matter of time—a *short* time. I don't plan to be simply cooled and thawed out. I want to remain in anabiosis for a long time, for years. Until they find a way to cope with leucoses. How long do you think it'll be?"

She answers mechanically: "I don't know. David says they may find something soon—a year, maybe."

"You see? So I would be lying there asleep for a year, two, even three. Then they would wake me up and cure me. You see how cleverly I want to cheat death?"

She is thinking. "And what about me?"

She is giving ground. I must keep up the pressure. "I understand this is hard on you. But you must also think of me. This is my only chance, if only a small chance."

There is no chance, of course. Another way of suicide. No, there *is* a chance—a microscopic one. Shall I talk to her about the scientific side of it? No, that won't work on her.

"Just imagine the sensation! A professor comes back to life after three years!"

She snatches her hand out of mine. "To hell with sensation! I need you!"

This doesn't work. She's too emotional. Or is it a lack of imagination? Well, whatever it is . . .

"All right, there won't be any sensation. I will just wake up quietly, like this dog today."

"And you actually think that this . . . this awakening is possible?"

"Of course, very possible!" (If I only believed that!) "I wouldn't say there's an absolute guarantee, but in my condition even a thirty percent chance is a gift. After all, all I have is another half year . . ." (Let us not be too specific. I hope for a year.)

"No, I just can't imagine all this . . . You mean, you—like this dog? And soon?"

Has she surrendered?

"No, not very soon. We still have to build a pressure chamber, a new heart-lung machine, new kidney, new automatic controls. Also we must run many complicated experiments. A lot to do yet. More than I'd like to do."

A sad little smile. "My friend, you are a dreamer . . ."

Meaning, "All people die normally, but you are putting up a fight." No, I should not try to guess her thoughts. I've been mistaken so many times before. She's simpler and more decent.

"Then you agree?"

"You're not fooling me, Ivan dear. I know that you've decided everything already—without me. I know how much weight I carry with you. Remember that time I wanted to divorce Pavel?"

I remember very well. "But perhaps it would have been even harder on you now if you had, Lou? To have a dying husband on your hands . . . And nothing but loneliness ahead . . ."

She strokes my hand. "Don't measure me by your standards . . . You don't know how terrible it is for me . . . at a distance. Can you imagine what it was like for me at home when you lay in that hospital near death?"

I try to put myself in her place. Suppose it was Liuba who was gasping for air in a hospital. Her husband, her son Kostia were with her. And I had no right even to see her. All I could do was walk outside . . . Forgive me, darling.

"Let's drop this. I am not yet ready to die. Tell me how your children have finished their school year?"

She is smiling to her own inner thoughts. "Wonderful! Dola has won the first prize. And Kostia has only one second-best mark. He and his father are getting ready for the summer hike. Three of them—one of his friends is going with them. I am so worried. Suppose something happens to them? You know what a coward I am. Now I expect some new blow all the time."

Yes, it's difficult for her. Worse than for me.

"You know, I'm trying to be firm with the children, to install principles in them, honesty. And, at any time, I expect a rebuke, especially from Kostia—you know his temper—'And what about you, Mother? Do you call what you're doing honesty?' What would I say then? Just imagine . . . You know, they are talking about us already in town . . ."

Yes, what is my jealousy, my loneliness, compared to that? "It'll all come to an end, Lou. Soon."

"How cruel you are, *really!* Or are you just insensitive?"

"Lou, darling, of course I'm not as sensitive as you. I have learned to face reality, harsh as it may be. I know that everything is forgotten in time. You have two children. They will help you to bear the loss of your—the man you love."

She does not like the word *lover.* She says that it doesn't express love, just bed. Probably true.

It is a sad meeting we are having today. To bear death is not easy, but this thing—the sarcophagus—is even harder. I only hope she doesn't do anything emotional . . . Psychosis? Suicide? I don't know, but I must try to take her thoughts away from it all.

"And how's Dola?"

"She's reading a lot—novels. Some people say she's overdoing it, but I don't feel like interfering with it. She remains a normal girl—she embroiders, even still plays with dolls. Her girl friends like her. What do you think?"

"I don't know . . . What is she reading, for instance?"

"She's just finished *Don Quixote.* Before that, *Ivanhoe, The Two Captains*—everything of that kind . . ."

"Well, books like that can't hurt her. They print a lot of trash nowadays, but nothing harmful—not in this country, anyway. True, I'm not up on it. I have lost the taste for literature. And then, I have no time, of course."

"And I'm reading all the time. Even trash. I just can't live without books."

She gets up, paces up and down. Comes to the desk, runs her fingers over it. Shows it to me, smiling—dust.

It is growing darker. Nine o'clock. The boys haven't telephoned yet. Everything must be in order there.

"It's a difficult thing, Ivan—bringing up children."

"Yes, I know. I'm interested in this, too—but from another angle: how will future society develop? Only today I've had a talk with my boys . . ."

I tell her about my talk with Yura. She sits down, listens silently. The twilight has changed her face, made it softer. Her eyes have sunk in, become dark. She speaks in a low voice:

"Once it was all much simpler—religion, God. 'Our Father which art in heaven . . .' 'Honor your mother' . . . And, if that fails, a belt. Of course this is not for us any more."

"And what *is* for us?"

"First of all, work. Not an idle hour. And, of course, ideals. At first, simple ones—official, so to say—but then one must broaden them to the all-human level—service to people, humanity. And also one must struggle against moral laxity . . ."

It is slightly unpleasant for me to listen to her. She is repeating someone else's words, probably her husband's. They sound more like theses than views.

"And do you think that's easy? Ideals, especially. It's a large order."

"Why? Young people are just as susceptible to good examples as they always have been. But one must find those examples—and then sell them to the youngsters."

Irritation. "*Sell*, again! Selling seems to be on everyone's mind today."

"Forgive me. Maybe that's an unfortunate expression. But selling something is not cheating. It all depends on what one is selling."

The phone rings in the hall. Vadim. Has the dog died? Then, a normal end for me. It would be better for Liuba. And for me?

"Excuse me!"

It is dark in the hall. I am groping for the receiver.

"Yes?"

"This is Vadim. Here is the latest report: *Druzhok* has fully awakened, he even had a little milk. We are watching, and writing down all the data. The blood pressure is a little down, about 80. Apparently some cardiac weakness, because the venous pressure is above normal, and there are slight rasping sounds in the lungs. The urine runs well. We are trying to regulate everything, but still there are symptoms of some oxygen deficiency."

"Give me all the readings."

He asks someone for the list. I am waiting. Liuba is standing next to me. She hasn't switched on the light, but I can feel the warmth of her body close to mine. But my mind is not on her now. Vadim is citing figure after figure. Things are not brilliant, but it's by no means a catastrophe either.

"Please, don't transfuse too much fluid."

Liuba whispers into my ear: "Only albumin preparations. Strophantin. Oxygen. They shouldn't give him anything to drink."

An experienced physician. I repeat all this to Vadim.

"Did you get it all?"

"Yes, yes. But I still want to tell you something . . ."

I can hear him talk to someone—"Valia, leave me alone a moment; take a walk"—then: "Yura has told me about your conversation. Forgive him, he's just an idiot. You must have thought we had formed a conspiracy against you—behind your back. I can imagine how hurt you must have been!"

"A little, yes."

"Well, all this is not so at all. We love and respect you. And we would have never—do you hear, never—let you down. We wouldn't dream of any reorganization without you. This was just a tentative plan subject to your approval. Don't you like it? You know we can't work with this scoundrel here. You won't hold this against us, will you?"

"Is Yura with you?"

"No. But he's asked me to talk to you. He's ashamed." (True, or not?)

"All right, don't soft-soap me. Intellectual giants! Goodbye until tomorrow."

"And you're not mad at us? We're not so bad, you know. Good night."

He hangs up. I can see his excited face. "We are not so bad." I know this.

"They are pretty good boys, Lou!"

"Something has happened between you?"

"Yes. I had no time to tell you."

I just didn't want to tell her. But now it is different. I feel better about it all.

"All right, tell me. And then I really must run. It's already dark outside."

She must run, as always. She comes, brings in a little light with her, and then she's gone. Perhaps this is why our love has endured.

She refuses to sit down. "No, no; no time! I'm listening."

I tell her very briefly about my plan for my "will" (she winces), about my conversation with Yura, about the way I was hurt by it.

"You know, Ivan, I think your boys have the right idea. If you work in a clinic, you at least will do something useful." (Her opinion, as always, is categoric. Where did she get this self-assurance? Is this professional? It's a little offensive—"We doctors are helping people; and you?") "No, no, don't argue! I have practiced for eighteen years and so far we haven't had any help from you physiologists. Chemists have contributed, so have bacteriologists. And you? Ah-ha, you have nothing to say!"

I am irked a little. Even though she is right. No, not quite right.

"Wait, wait! Where would anesthesiology, reanimation, artificial blood circulation be without physiology? Tell me!"

"I will. There are different kinds of physiology—pure and practical. The pure, that's you; no help at all. The practical, is doctors who examine patients and, well, experiment with them. They have been responsible for reanimation, artificial circulation, kidney —everything. This is the physiology I understand."

"But all your clinical physiology is based on our theories!"

"Maybe it was once, but now you are just fooling around with dogs, while we are treating people. Here is an example: one of your physiologists, I forgot his name, is studying the circulatory changes in rabbits after the removal of one lung. I talked to him. Why kill rabbits, I said; come to our hospital, study our post-operative lung cases. You can run the same tests, the same experiments. No, he said, it is not the same thing. And he couldn't explain why. And he's writing a doctor's dissertation, too! Can you imagine?"

I know the man. A classical "pure" physiologist.

"So you think that physiology should be abandoned as science?"

"No, not entirely. There may be some special theoretical questions which need study." (Thank you!) "But the majority of those loafers should be sent into hospitals—to work with doctors."

I know myself all our weak points—but still, when someone attacks us, it's very annoying. In fact, she doesn't even understand the real purpose of our work. And many doctors feel the way she does.

"Then, according to you, one can study the cell construction, the brain structure, in a hospital?"

"Not in a hospital, but near it. So that they can see whom they're working for. Anyway, you won't change my mind for me. So you'd better move over to Clinic Town and impregnate us with your theories!"

Of course, one can't argue her out of any preconceived notion. "Impregnate us." What a word! I'd better keep quiet.

"Ivan, even though you've asked me not to inquire about your health, still, tell me, how do you feel?"

"Well, as you can see, I've lived through another day."

"All right, I'm going!"

I am sorry to let her go. If she could only stay here once the whole night! She understands. My face probably betrays me.

"No, darling, impossible. Just impossible. All right, kiss me!"

I kiss her, many times. Her cheeks, eyes, lips. I embrace her body, tenderly. No passion. Just tenderness.

"Let me go, or I won't go at all."

I release her. I have no right to keep her.

She is gone. The door closes, and her heels click down the stairway. Then silence.

I walk out onto the balcony. The slight little figure melts into the darkness. She doesn't even look back. All her thoughts now are there.

And I am alone. Once again. It is so dismal when she leaves. I can still see her here, my darling. She has run her little finger over the desk, showed me the dust, with a smile. When she argues, her eyes sparkle, her face becomes cold. Then suddenly she smiles— dimples on her cheeks. Like a child. And still another Liuba: white arms under her head, half-closed eyes. Moist lips. It's best not to remember. I don't want to remember. It is enough to sense her presence here. To feel the faint aroma of her body.

She has gone. Had I insisted, she would have stayed. Suffering inside. But who needs her with suffering? It's even worse than being without her.

Loneliness is now slowly surrounding me from all sides. I feel a strange urge—and it's not the first time—to crawl under the desk. To sit there between two solid posts, to barricade myself in with the armchair, to become inaccessible. Everyone is looking for me, and I'm sitting there like a little mouse. Death comes, looks around, walks away. Love too. Friendship. All the irritations and obligations. And then, I fall asleep there . . .

Am I going insane? Not a bad solution. No, not *that*. I remember the psychiatry classes we had when I was a student. Dante's inferno. Naked bodies, unnatural poses. And eyes! Some insane, others full of indescribable anguish. No.

Back to work! Vadim has given me his new schemes of regulatory systems. Should I look them over?

To lie down and read? There is a new novel. No, I have already started it. Official optimism just irritates me these days.

Yura . . . I thought I knew him so well, no mysteries. And suddenly he is a stranger. A grown-up man—knowing very well what he wants to do. Perhaps nursing some grandiose dream deep inside. And perhaps just a dedicated idealist-fanatic of a new modern kind. A cyberneticist. I should go with him to Sergievsky and talk him into taking our laboratory into his Institute.

I am glad that Vadim has called me. It's so terrible to find yourself mistaken about people. Pupils' disloyalty. The lover's betrayal. The friend's hypocrisy. One just can't live with those things . . .

And what if I telephoned Leonid? Ask him to come over? It's only nine-thirty. I'd like to talk to him . . . I saw him last week, in a hospital. There were people around. We could not communicate, really.

Actually I should look over Vadim's schemes. Several chapters of his dissertation, and one of Igor's . . . I am tired of dissertations. Even though ours are often interesting. The characteristics of the heart, the scheme of the regulatory systems. They will defend them without me. Two or three more years, and they will be standing firmly on their own feet in their new laboratory—if they don't quarrel meanwhile. Vadim, it seems, has finally accepted Yura's authority. A good boy . . . Bad manners, too rough, no tact. I'll leave him my apartment. That will be my last good deed. I must admit I'm a little sorry to let anyone in. My books, my things, will be disarranged, some of them ruined, some lost. Objects are like living things; they have been living with me, and suddenly they will be deserted by their master, like stray dogs.

Shall I telephone? Ask him for an hour or two? If he is not already drunk. Why should I wear myself out with those dissertations? I have earned my rest today. The experiment has been an unqualified success . . . After Liuba's visits I can never get back to work, anyway.

I am going to the hall.

"Marina Vasilievna? Is Leonid in?"

She says, yes—and almost sober. Reading something. She will call him.

"Lenya, can you drop in to visit your ailing friend? . . . Yes, a little bit." (This, about the cognac.) "Don't let Marina worry, I won't give you much. Come on, I'll tell you all about the experiment! A realistic hope to see the future. All right, I'm waiting. My best to Vitaly."

Here we are. I have fallen from grace. The evening is ruined. The real problem is that time is irreplaceable. What one doesn't accomplish today, will remain unaccomplished.

viii
Leonid

What is this? Liuba has forgotten her flowers on the table! She was arranging them (as in Japan) and then forgot all about them. Should I put the poor things in water? Sentiment? But why? They are thirsty. The border of life lies in plants. Complicated structures with their own programs providing for growth, development, propagation and death. No, death is caused by the malfunction of these programs. Aging is the accumulation of foreign residues. Between the cells, in the cells, every second throughout life there accumulate some "nonstandard" atoms, molecules. They obstruct, clog, stand in the way. The machine works more slowly, more laboriously, until some important part like the heart quits altogether. Death.

Aging is unavoidable. Of course, theoretically it is possible to design a machine to watch over the body, more complicated and durable than any yet designed. It would check on various functions, safeguard organs from accumulation of harmful residues, eliminate most of them. In some areas this would work, and the average span of life could be greatly increased. But this machine— the model—would also accumulate its own foreign residues, and would also age . . . And so on, *ad infinitum*. The immortality of biological systems is impossible to achieve. Even theoretically impossible.

And what of whole species? Do they disappear only through violent destruction in the process of competition with others, like American buffaloes? In all probability, yes. But also "obstacles" may accumulate in the genetic apparatus of the whole species, lowering their adaptability to outward factors. They then perish, unless some beneficial mutation interferes, corrects and reverses this process.

And social systems? This is even more complicated. I should discuss this with Leonid. All my aches and pains seem to have disappeared—replaced by these thoughts. One can even forget death. The human brain is a powerful instrument.

Leonid will be here any minute now. He doesn't live far away. Marina is probably not too happy about my invitation. He was already at home—safe from temptation. It must be difficult for her. Alcoholism is a destroyer of families. No, he is devoted to his family. He always had been indifferent to women. Then he surprised us all by getting married. I am not too sure that his life at home is all harmony. Perhaps this is why he drinks? We never discuss these things—the masculine taboo. We never mention Liuba, either. He knows all about her, but we avoid mentioning her.

I think that subconsciously Liuba must desire my death. Writers and psychologists are very naïve; they look at man on a single plane. As though he were driven by a single force, single urge. In fact, each human being is a maze of contradictions. One moment it's one thing, the next moment another, or even several contradictory urges together. Or does this happen only with me? You can't get into other people's heads. No, it must be universal.

She was already prepared for my death. It is like a fire—suddenly everything is consumed by the flame, terror, despair. Then, smoking ashes. Apathy. Then one begins to collect the remaining pieces, brings them together into some new place, finds some new purpose to go on with. She has enough to live for. Her children. Her work. She has started talking about writing a dissertation. "Am I more stupid than others?" And whenever I mentioned this to her before, she always protested: "What do I need it for? There are too many scientists as it is!"

The children. "We've talked about everything. Pavel is a reasonable man." Yes, a handsome male at that, not like myself. Perhaps just a little too fat. A matter of taste. Some women— No, let's not be vulgar.

How love has degenerated! Before, people would fall in love and forget everything. They would break church commandments, social obstacles, abandon children, their work, their positions in life. And now? Divorce is easy. But, no. I have my science, she has her children, their intellectual upbringing. Besides we both have our work. It leaves only so much time for love. From here to there.

There is no danger to the family in the new society. There won't be any "free love." This is good. Passions should not be turned loose. It might hurt one's intellect and the society one lives in.

Now she must be stunned again. She has to reconstruct all her thinking. Apparently I will not die (good!), but also she will not be free of deceit. However, she will be freer—no more secret rendezvous; only this sarcophagus, like a silent reproach. And also, a small fear: what if he wakes up and claims his rights again? A complicated problem. Either way I am a loser.

Let's pace the room. Seven steps this way, seven back. Those old prints on the walls should go. I'm tired of them. Why? Maybe I shouldn't leave my apartment to anyone . . . They may give one to Vadim at the Institute of Cybernetics. This is not just an apartment. I'll be a hero—going into the future as though into the cosmos. A correction: the cosmonauts are young and healthy. And Vadim wouldn't get any apartment. They have enough living space for their family. In our housing regulations there is no provision for giving a man a place to escape from his mother-in-law. And that lady would make his life miserable, more and more as time goes on: the more they age, the more impossible they become.

So, the apartment goes to Vadim—with all my personal things in it. Fool—what do I want all those stupid things for? The little bust of Tolstoi, the clay cylinder for pencils. (Tolstoi was given to me by my mother.)

Now I understand why they used to bury men with all their personal belongings. People did not believe in death. And they still don't believe in it. However, I know with an absolute certainty that there will be nothing there. Why isn't he coming? I could have done some work . . . But doing nothing is also a pleasure. I didn't realize this when I was young. Every free minute, a book. And now I can just walk about, or lie down and think—on any subject whatsoever. It's the thought of the future that drives people on. And I have no future.

A ring. Here he is. We embrace. No one would have believed this. Leonid, such a hard-bitten cynic, and this sentimentality.

"Hello there . . . Come in! Sit down, there!"

"All right . . . Now, give me an ashtray. And take this out!"

(This about the flowers. He does not like flowers. Or is he just pretending?) "This vase is top-heavy; it'll fall over and douse me with water."

I am bringing the ashtray for him. The biggest I have. Otherwise he'd scatter the ashes all over the place.

"And you still don't smoke, Ivan? A will of iron. Well, how's your health?"

This irritates me, "How? How?"

"Oh, go on . . . Why do you ask those things?"

"What do you mean, why? A big part of my life will go out with you. We've known each other for almost thirty years. Do you realize that?"

"Yes, and I realize something else: you're sober tonight. How come?"

He grins. He looks like a Mongol—cheekbones, eyes. The face of a sardonic Genghis Khan. Does he take anything seriously? But he likes philosophizing; he would rather talk than eat. Just give him a theme. If not, he'll find one himself. Here it is:

"You know what I was doing tonight when you called? Reading Hemingway. Wonderful. And do you know why? There are social notes in every line. We have been conditioned, without knowing it, to evaluate everything from a social angle. Have you noticed it?"

Not everything Leonid says coincides with my own ideas, but what of it? We can certainly sort things out for ourselves, and most of his thoughts are provocative.

"And what do you propose? Publish everything without any discrimination?"

"Everything must be organized intelligently."

"Then you are for some sort of limited regimentation?"

"For an *intelligent* one. And also, for more trust."

(I will now catch him!)

"All right, my friend. Is it possible to determine the limits of regimentation, and if so, how? We all know that some rules are necessary for running any society. There are certain limits of morbid deviation beyond which some regulatory correction must come into play—just as in a human body. But how does one determine these tolerable limits?"

"Do you want to know what's tolerable in freedom or, for instance, in pornography?"

"I'm serious, Leonid."

"All right, so am I. There are all sets of significations which may be classed as socially indispensable. They have certain positive qualities that set them aside from all others. They also have degrees within them—there can be too much of a good thing. I think that the necessary degrees can be determined by public-opinion sampling. This is a form of social study which seems to be largely neglected with us."

"Wait, wait! If one follows the quantitative mass opinion, one can fall into all sorts of traps. Just suppose we run a public poll—'Do you like the unlimited sex in films?'—and get, let's say, a sixty percent affirmative vote. What then?"

"Your argument doesn't impress me one bit! One must use brains to interpret any results correctly. And not everything should be put to a vote, and not everyone should be asked. In some matters, only specialists should be polled. In others, the general public."

"This is a very complicated matter . . . There must be some basic principle for solving such a problem. Obviously it is senseless to ask people's opinion about highly technical matters about which they have no knowledge at all. But it is also dangerous to make decisions singlehanded. So what's the answer?"

"A scientific study conducted in the atmosphere of open discussion. This is the only sure criterion for finding a correct solution."

"Is it? Scientists are also very often subjective. In some errors in our scientific past, they played a very conspicuous part."

"To avoid this, the quantitative approach, as you call it, is necessary. Figures. In your laboratory you are working on mathematical modeling, which excludes subjectivity. The computer is accurate, but it has no opinion; it delivers facts. Well, the same principle should be applied to all branches of science."

(Yura has said the same things many times. Cybernetics. I am inclined to agree with him.)

"But don't you think, Lenya, that for mathematical evaluation of information, this information must be based on something more solid than a majority opinion—on some absolutely objective and uncontestable mathematical facts, on an iron set of broad general principles?"

He looks around. Lost for an answer?

"Look, Ivan. You're feeding me theories. Where the hell is the brandy? You know what acute dehydration of tissues can do to a human body."

"I thought that with all this intellectual masturbation, you would have forgotten about it."

"The devil I have! The brain requires nourishment! You're a physiologist."

An alcoholic. Marina tells me that he drinks every day. There must be a reason for it. Ask him? No, he doesn't like that kind of confidence.

"Very well, but I'm warning you: don't count on much."

"Bring on what you've got. And then we'll search the premises for more."

"Search all you want. I just don't buy much."

He will never find it. I've hidden it behind the books.

I am setting up a small table in the front room. Leonid doesn't like drinking in the kitchen—"Am I a guest or not?"

I am watching him. He is sitting there blowing smoke rings. They are slowly drifting outside through the open balcony door.

He looks very well—a picture of health. A strange man—something is missing somewhere. A brilliant brain going to pot. Alcohol. Nicotine. Idle talk.

We sit down. I pour myself a small drink too—just to keep him company, and to prevent him from drinking it all. I don't want his brain to get numbed; nothing is duller than drunks trying to be brilliant. There is sliced lemon, cheese, sausage. But he is indifferent to food.

"To the success of your experiments, Ivan!"

We drink. That is, *he* drinks—tosses it off. I barely touch mine. This is a good time to ask.

"Tell me, Leonid. Why do you drink?"

"Are you going to preach temperance?"

"No, but I just would like to know. I don't ask this very often."

"Good for you. All right. Everyone has his weakness. You're a science drunk, and I prefer brandy. It's hard to tell who's happier. Pour me another one. Since the supply is small, one must create a shock concentration."

I fill his glass. Has his system adapted itself to alcohol? I have never seen him really drunk. Not in the conventional sense of this word.

"You didn't answer my question. I'm a physiologist, remember. This is not idle curiosity."

"You can be difficult, you know . . . However, I have nothing to hide. First, I don't consider myself an alcoholic. Do I ever drink in the morning? No. Has anyone seen me drunk at work? No. Have I ever behaved improperly in any public place? Again, no. Do I do my work and fulfill my social obligations? Yes. True, I'm avoiding the more demanding ones; but who doesn't? So I'm a normal human being. But I admit, toward evening I feel like lifting myself a little above the general grayness of life, to use a poetic expression. I do anticipate the first evening drink. This is true."

He falls silent. I am waiting. I know he will talk more.

He lights another cigarette. Which one tonight—second or third?

"Boredom gets me toward the night. I could never find any overwhelming interest in life, to delude myself into really believing that I'm doing something important or interesting—like you, for instance. And at my age I have no hopes of finding it. No passionate interests at home, either. Marina is a good woman— no question about that—but too correct, too one-dimensional. Let's not discuss that. Vitaly has grown up, and somehow I have missed it. I've never had any contact with him. He's been developing on his own."

"You are to blame for this."

"Do I blame anyone else? Everyone blames me, and I accept it. But that doesn't change the situation. Now, take my work. Something hasn't worked out there either. Hygiene is a noble science, but for some reason it doesn't inspire me. I'm a good specialist, a fair lecturer. The old man likes me very much. I'm doing his work and I have no ambitions to replace him in his chair. So what else does he want?"

A little pause. Then:

"Alcohol is a medicine—an antidepressant. You take a drink, and suddenly there's more optimism. And even more self-assurance and self-respect. 'I am still capable of thinking up interesting things.' And now and then, you begin to really do it—to think creatively, to make plans. Then you go to bed full of them. And in the morning . . . Well, you start waiting for the evening. And no particular problems. It's a good medicine."

You listen to him and it sounds like a happy solution, for him at least. But he's lying, of course. Look at his eyes: dull anguish, tedium.

"Another glass, friend. The last one."

Yes, the last. The little bottle is all but empty. No more. He can be cured only by some severe shock—a grave illness, for instance. The instinct for self-preservation usually does the trick. However, in his case, I'm not so sure.

"So, Ivan, you say we need some basic principles? Let me outline to you some of my thoughts. This is the latest—something I've been mentally working on. The goal: a rational society intelligently designed to bring happiness to all. Don't misunderstand me; I don't mean universal bliss—that is impossible. We've spoken about all this—the brain centers of pleasure and how they get adapted and stop reacting to it. Therefore, we can only aim for comparative happiness. Let's consider the basic components of animal pleasure—food, sex, rest, ambition. Now, the more complex reflexes—freedom, curiosity, drive to achieve one's goal. Do you think such reflexes exist, Professor?"

"They say so—the general-direction reflex. Even Pavlov admitted it."

"Ah, if Pavlov did, then everything's in order. Besides these animal sources of happiness, there are higher ones. Society, the pleasure of communion with people—preferably with brandy." (Oh, stop clowning!) "Creative work. Art. Noble acts—self-abnegation. Perhaps some others—I can't remember offhand. You don't meet them very often."

"That's untrue!"

"Very well, untrue. The important point is that there are different sources. And contradictory ones. One may derive happiness at other people's expense. So psychologists—together with you physiologists—must work out a precise, average 'balance of happiness'—find various levels for various types of people. Do you think this can be done? Do you physiologists have any methods of objective evaluation of various stages of happiness and unhappiness in various people?"

"Well, at least theoretically this must be possible. All brain changes are reflected in functions of various internal organs. It is very complicated, but probably the necessary methods and technical means can be developed in time."

"Good. Let's consider another situation. By overstimulating the brain pleasure centers, each instinct can be turned into a vice. The taste for food can turn into gluttony, the normal sex urge into debauchery, the instinct for self-preservation to egotism and cowardice. But by the same token, the positive traits can also be developed. Love of children can develop into general kindness, the direction reflex can lead to brilliant accomplishment; curiosity, to wonderful new discoveries."

Leonid is really at his best when he has had just enough to drink. Fantasy, eloquence, lucidity, charm.

"This brings us to still another problem: educability in children and, of course, in adults. To what extent is it possible to curb harmful instincts and develop the socially beneficial ones? I don't know of any serious research work in this sphere, and without it, there is no basis. Only the Utopians claim that every man is potentially an angel. The potential power of education must be enormous, but it must be scientifically studied and reduced to formulas. Without this, all thought about a better future is like building without a foundation. Do you know of any scientific works in this sphere?"

"I? No. I've never been specifically interested in this subject."

"Of course—a professor! Covering his little sector from here to there."

"And you encyclopedists are like a glass of water spilled on a concrete floor—you spread around penetrating nothing."

"You know, I envy the scientists of, say, three thousand years ago. They could absorb the entire volume of knowledge in one lifetime. Now it's impossible—you need thousands of brains, or one of your damned computers. If they had only given me a special institute, I could have done some exhaustive research for my project on happiness. But who's interested?"

There is vanity in him, deep inside. Is he trying to suppress it with alcohol?

"I am interested. Go ahead."

"If you're interested, fine. So first we establish the components of happiness, and then start organizing them into a system, to insure its optimum distribution among the largest possible number of human beings. I see three main directions: work and material well-being, education, and finally, the government."

"Careful! Doesn't this smell of disloyalty?"

"Not a bit. Science has progressed a great deal, and it must help the government to achieve its goals. Can I go on?"

"By all means. Don't pay attention to my remarks. I'm no specialist in these areas."

"Fine. Now let's start with work. No, with education. Here again we need basic principles. One of them—the minimum of force; this doesn't mean the nonresistance to evil, but the minimum of constraint and maximum of guidance. Number two—the respect for other people's freedom. Number three—the development of the urge to work; urge, not compulsion; this is possible. Number four—respect for family, sexual morality. Number five— curbing of vanity; not its complete destruction, but limiting it to healthy proportions. And last—control of the instinct for accumulation, greed."

I remain silent. Let him preach.

"I know that all this is difficult; but, without the proper solution of the problem of education, there are no hopes at all for any better society."

A theoretician. A typical one. He hasn't brought up his own son properly, but he knows all the answers. Liuba, for instance, is not strong on theories, but she knows exactly how to deal with her children. However, she has also mentioned some principles. Today is my day for principles!

"Work must become an obligation. This is done correctly with us. Now the amount of work to be performed, the length of time one must devote to it. An excess of leisure may be dangerous. Demoralizing. This also needs special study. Now the quality of work. It is important to ingrain in people a compulsion to work honestly. Here again we need a scientific approach—in the matter of proper compensation."

"You don't sound very clear on this point."

"I am not, I admit. I'm sure that monetary stimulation alone is dangerous. The proper encouragement, proper work education might be the answer, not simply pandering to the greed instinct. But bare enthusiasm is also as insufficient as bare greed."

"This is obvious. Some quantitative criteria for stimulation is needed."

"Correct! There's still another point: we must establish scientifically the beneficial level of material well-being beyond which we merely encourage greed, the optimum material requirements for physical happiness: an adequate attractive living space; good wholesome food; sufficient and comfortable clothing. Why would anyone want more, once this is absolutely assured? We must educate people in a new attitude toward possessions. They must never be allowed to become an end in themselves."

"Perhaps before starting to limit people we should first reach the level of abundance when such limitations will become necessary?"

"You're a hopeless stick-in-the-mud! Of course we must strive for abundance—absolutely!—but we must also work out the basic principles in advance. Now."

"Well, I don't think that any propaganda for limitations is needed yet."

"All right, let's leave it. Now the third point—government. This is a cardinal point; it must organize and administer all others and assure the over-all stability of the society. This may be achieved on the basis of return connections—self-regulation and constant self-improvement must be built into the very structure of administration. These problems, incidentally, can also be solved on a scientific basis."

I am watching him. He shows absolutely no signs of any alcoholic stimulation—perhaps a little more sparkle in the eyes than usual, more color in the cheeks. His system must have become completely adjusted; to him, drinking is like smoking. But all that he has said so far is nothing but generalities. I have no quarrel with any of his theories as such, but what about their realization? Has he any answers there?

He picks up his almost-empty glass.

"I'm draining the last drop. The fuel is gone, so the machine will soon grind to a halt. You wanted to tell me about your experiment."

You're lying, my friend. You want to hear my reaction to your theories. All right.

"All that you have just said is interesting; I agree with most of it. Of course it's necessary to have a scientific approach to work, education, government, everything. Only, so far there is no such science. Psychology, sociology, they are still in the stage of accumulating information and hypotheses. I think that without cybernetics, without mathematical modeling in depth, they will not provide us with any practical methods."

"Correct, Professor! We've long since agreed to that. Facts. Figures. Mathematics. But unfortunately, this concept does not penetrate many allegedly advanced minds—this cybernetic approach to what is known as human problems. But some advance is being made, nonetheless. Have you noticed that the cybernetic ideas are beginning to shake scientists out of their rut, to pull them from generalities into tangibilities? I'm speaking about ideas —not machines which are still in the nonsense stage."

"You know, Leonid, you have a hell of a nerve to delve into very specific areas, about which you haven't the slightest idea!"

"A prerogative of a dilettante, Professor. And a privilege. We amateurs take it upon ourselves to deal with any subject. Specialists laugh at us, revile us; but we are often proved right in the end. Besides, I allow myself such loose talk only with a glass in hand—and only with friends. There's no harm in it."

Maybe not, but I am getting a little tired of his talking. Also, I am thirsty. And, of course, I want to tell him about the experiment. Subconsciously, this is why I have invited him tonight.

"Let's have some coffee, Lenya—now that we've solved all the problems of the future so brilliantly."

A sudden thought: I actually might be able to see some of this future. Not a distant future; but the world develops so quickly, I might find myself in completely unfamiliar surroundings. Not really; people have changed little during my lifetime. They have changed, of course—for the better. And the world itself may soon be destroyed altogether. We can only hope that common sense and science will prevent this final disaster. Yes, they will measure happiness, they will find a formula for its equitable distribution. It would be wonderful to see all that: the structure of the new society, of government; to see the part science will play in all this; to see the new man . . .

It would be better, of course, simply to be healthy instead; but that, alas, is impossible. I can only hope to see the future, since my present is all but gone. (I am thinking all this while setting up the coffee maker.) Then I rejoin Leonid.

"Coffee will be ready in a flash."

"Coffee is no good for me, friend. Can you make me some tea?"

Back to the kitchen. Shall I offer him some wine? No more brandy—that's definite. No. Let him have some tea. Marina would be annoyed with me if he comes home drunk. What does he find in alcohol? To me, it's just bitter-tasting bilge. Before I get drunk, I get sick and I vomit. The natural-defense reflex. It's interesting what he would say about my experiment, about its prospects. He knows a great deal—if not in depth than on a broad level.

He either has no pity for me, or he is a good actor. This indifference even hurts a little. But then I'm a hypocrite: I beg everyone not to show compassion, and when they don't I'm offended —"Nobody loves me."

My coffee is ready. I'll wait for his tea and serve the two together. I'll give him some cookies. And I'm not going to go into any glowing details about the experiment. I'll present it modestly. I wonder how the dog is doing there?

The water is boiling. A powerful thing, gas. When I was a child, getting a samovar ready was a chore—kindling, coals, bellows. But then it was so pleasant to have it purring on the table. (I'm now just repeating someone's words.) Well, everything's ready. Let's put an extra spoonful in; strong tea clears the head.

He is sitting at the desk, reading.

"Tea is served, sir."

"It's interesting what they say here about genetics. I thought they'd forgotten their old sins, but here they go again. Have you seen it?"

"No, I haven't had time. I'll read it in bed."

"Right . . . Now, about your experiment. I'm dying to hear."

"I can't report anything terribly new to you. The usual hypothermy as used in surgery, but with a much lower temperature. We had it at two degrees above freezing in the esophagus for two hours."

I am playing it down.

"Oh? This is pretty good, isn't it? And what sort of metabolism rate did you get?"

"Something like two percent of the normal. They are still figuring it out."

"You mean, one day of hypothermy for fifty days of normal life?"

"Approximately, yes. However, as yet we haven't figured out many other factors. Nonetheless I can brag a little: the dog awakened normally and is still alive. Everything's done according to the highest standards."

"What do you mean by that?"

"I mean, the regulation of the inner area. All indications stayed within the tolerable limits."

"Tell me more, from start to finish. This is very interesting."

I'm telling him now, not in all details, but with enough to keep his attention. This is the second time today, like an automaton. At the same time, I'm watching his reaction.

He is listening silently, intently. Alcohol doesn't seem to affect his power of concentration. What sort of man is he? We've been close friends for almost thirty years, and I still don't really know him. A philosophic drift of mind. Even in the Institute he was given to endless discussions. He's never been particularly close to anyone; he's indifferent to people in general. No warmth at home —his wife and son on one side, and he on the other. He jokes on every serious subject. Or is he just pretending? I've never watched him in any difficult situations, but I know that he fought well in the war. Several decorations.

I am describing now the moment of the actual awakening—the tremendous mounting tension in the room—and thinking: He's indifferent to me as well. I've never seen him showing any genuine concern. But then, who am I to condemn anyone for lack of warmth? What about myself? Shall I tell him about Yura?

"Lenya, what would you think if we transferred our laboratory over to the Institute of Cybernetics? There is a project like that . . ."

I outline to him Yura's plan, painting it in attractive colors. Not a word of my getting offended or hurt. Dangerous—he would make fun of it.

"Your boys seem to be on their toes. Of course, they'll be better off there. This Yura sounds like a man to run this thing as it really should be run."

(He has written me off. This is the first time he has betrayed himself.) I am now telling him more about it all, "selling" Yura to him for all it's worth.

I can imagine Liuba at home now trying to adjust herself to the thought of my sleeping in that sarcophagus. All for nothing, probably. There's no assurance at all that I won't back out at the last moment. It would have been much better if something had happened to me—no more problems for anyone.

"Ivan, by the way, you haven't abandoned your anabiosis spectacular yet?"

(I shouldn't have told him about it!)

"No. Why should I abandon it?"

"I don't know . . . It sounds a bit like a trashy novel, you know."

"You know, friend, there are different points of view. Try to place yourself in my position, weigh everything, and then talk."

"I've tried. Of course, you have thought up a marvelous trick; but doesn't it look a little too melodramatic, like any suicide?"

"I don't give a damn how it looks. And my conscience is clear; I'm not hurting anyone." (Not quite. Liuba. Not you. You won't miss me all that much.) "And besides, since when have you become so concerned about appearances?"

"All right, all right. You're right of course. One gets used to certain conventions—without thinking about them. Really, whose business is it how you handle your own exit? The condemnation of suicide originally came from religion. And what is it with us? A citizen's duty? Maybe. It wouldn't be right if everyone started abandoning his obligations and walking out on life any time he wanted."

"Obligations! And what about your drinking? Aren't you trying to walk out on life every time you drink?"

"Very well, I surrender! Now, tell me—what exactly are the odds for awakening?"

"You know how I felt in that hospital, Leonid. I was sure I was dying. I had no fear, but when you're choking, it's horrible. Of course, had they told me that I'd die peacefully and without warning, I wouldn't have tried to avoid it. Why struggle and make so much noise? You know, I don't like 'spectaculars,' as you call them."

"Yes, but still, what are the odds?"

"I think that there are some chances for success. True, we have little proof. We must build a pressure chamber first, construct a new blood-circulation machine, and then conduct some conclusive tests."

He is thinking. And I am silent. I am interested in hearing his opinion. His intuition is often remarkable.

"I am sure that in the future this problem will be resolved. But now? I am afraid that physical factors are still inadequate. Chemistry must help—some new inhibitors for slowing-down life processes. I've heard that they are looking for some special hormones in hibernating animals. Have they found them yet?"

"I don't think so. It would have leaked out into the press. We are watching it."

"Well . . . Anyway, don't be in too much of a hurry. You can still last a while, with proper treatment. They tell me you're working much too hard."

"Are you going to ask me to be careful, to take care of myself? You're just repeating worn-out clichés, without thinking."

He becomes sad. Probably the alcohol is wearing off.

"Yes . . . Probably you're right. You've resolved your problem nonetheless . . . It would be fine to have a little drink now. You're a man without imagination, Ivan, not to have a little extra drop at home."

No, he's not going to get it. I don't feel like giving it to him. No.

"Have you thought about what you'd do in your next reincarnation? According to your plan, you'll be in cold storage for twenty or thirty years."

"Why do you think so?"

"Because to conquer leukemia one must decipher the mechanics of cell division. On the atomic level, and even lower. And what point is there in awakening too soon?"

A cynic. Or is he pretending again?

"No point. Twenty or fifty years—what is the difference? On the other hand, I could still find some people I know now—my pupils, for instance."

"A questionable pleasure. They will be smarter than you by then. No, really, have you thought of what you'll do when you wake up?"

"Are you trying to depress me on purpose tonight? Yes, I have. And I'm not too thrilled. I'll be lonely, of course. But then I'm not spoiled by too much attention as it is. Maybe people in the future will be easier to get along with. What do you think: is the world improving or not?"

"A difficult question. However, I think it is. My father told me that people were much cruder in his day. They beat their wives, wrote obscene words on fences—"

"Well, we ourselves were amused by some of that. Remember when we were coming from the Far East, after the war? How we went into station lavatories to read those slogans? True folk poetry you called it . . ."

"What a wonderful time that was, Ivan! Heh? Dreams: the world, fine people, science. And it's all come down to brandy.

However, you still have a chance to shake the world with your anabiosis!"

"Are you sorry that you haven't shaken it?"

"It's funny, now and then those ambitious thoughts appear in my head. Then, I catch myself and say, Idiot, what do you need that for? Put everything in its right prospective and live happily ever after. No, I'm not sorry."

"I hope that when I wake up people will be kinder than now and will find some place for me. I don't think that everyone will be a genius then and I the only fool. I don't think this anabiosis thing will last very long. And biology changes very slowly."

"Incidentally, the time element will be out of your hands once you freeze yourself."

"But why would they drag it out longer than necessary? Scientists will be curious to see whether I wake up or not. To evaluate the experiment."

A small pause.

I don't detain him. It is late and I am tired. I've had enough of pseudo-intellectual conversations for one day. And again, aches and pains everywhere . . . I can feel every organ.

"Good night, Ivan. Don't push yourself too hard. No point in being in a hurry."

"Yes, I know. I'll try. There's a lot to do though."

He is walking down the steps. Heavy steps—as if he were drunk. But he's not. . . . Should I go to bed? Or call the Institute? The switchboard is closed; the phone is in the corridor, they won't hear it. But anyway . . . I'm dialing the number. I will let it ring ten times. Long grumbling rings.

Nobody answers. Nine . . . Ten . . .

"Hello? This is Professor Prokhoroff. Who's this? Valia? Call Vadim or Yura."

She says, "Right away."

"Good evening, Ivan Nikolaevich. Don't ask—the dog's dead."

So what is left now of all my plans? Idiots, we have tried to outsmart nature . . . Miserable worms.

Let him tell me.

"Tell me everything. And why didn't you call me?"

"We didn't want to upset you. There was nothing to be done anyway. You would have learned in the morning. He died an hour ago. The indications were slowly growing worse, but remained satisfactory. The pressure eighty, the pulse a hundred and twenty seven—at the last reading. The dog was fully conscious, even though the venous blood saturation was low and there was some shortness of breath. Then suddenly short convulsions and death. The heart stopped. We did all we could—massage, defibrillation, adrenaline, until the pupils of his eyes decontracted. For about thirty minutes. Unsuccessfully."

"All right. Thanks."

I hang up. I don't feel like talking; nothing can be added to the final fact. And, anyway, what's the difference? All this stupid excitement. You want to sleep? Go to bed.

Medicine? Yes, Luminal, to fall asleep.

I am making my bed. I don't want to think about anything.

Such a long day . . . And such an end.

Let's not think . . . Brush the teeth . . . A tablet.

Fresh air from the balcony. Why look? Into bed and into oblivion.

ix
The Last Day

Today is my last full day. Tomorrow, at this time, I will be already in the state of anabiosis. I would like to postpone it, but it's impossible; my condition is deteriorating catastrophically. I have difficulty in walking, the percentage of hemoglobin is down to thirty-five. I am not going to list all the symptoms to prove the proximity of the end; this is unnecessary for everyone.

Everything has been decided.

During the last two days I have reread my notes. They now sound to me naïve, even ridiculous. At first all I wanted was to exercise my mind, to lessen my anguish. Then apparently I became involved. The style of the notes shows literary pretensions, and some events are described not altogether accurately—some continuous conversations, for instance, that were, in fact, broken by time intervals. It means that in my subconscious there was a desire to describe everything so that future readers would side with me. Something along the heroic-deed-of-a-scientist line. But, essentially, it is all true.

Enough of this. Time is very short. I will give these notes to Liuba. Let her keep them.

■ ■

I must once again explain the reasons for my decision—candidly, without any embellishment, so that there is no misunderstanding later on.

I am tired of being sick and I dread the suffering before the end. I have gone through three grave relapses, and I cannot face another one. In what I am going to do, there will be no particular pain.

It will be an interesting experiment. The sense of scientific "interest" has become embedded in my nature. Of course, I do not compare myself to true heroes who submitted themselves to dangerous experiments, often resulting in death. I have nothing to lose. I am a sick, doomed man. But the interest is still there.

I am curious to wake up and look at the world after several years.

The experiment can benefit humanity. I am not exaggerating its importance, but it will contribute something to science.

A man's action is rarely based on a single motivation. Usually there are several motivations, even though some may not even be obvious to the man himself. I don't know how to list mine in proper order. The important point is that I have very few things connecting me to this world. I love Liuba, but lately I have withdrawn from her. I am looking at everything and everybody, including myself, in a coldly detached manner. Had I felt some overwhelming attachment to anyone, I probably would have continued to live until the natural conclusion.

■　■

I feel guilty about Liuba because this experiment will cause her additional pain. However, I just can't act otherwise.

■　■

There is some hope that the experiment will prove successful and I will awaken. The odds are quite low. There are many areas that are still very obscure, and we have had no time to penetrate them. I evaluate the chance for success at about ten percent. Obviously, this is a purely arbitrary figure.

Unfortunately, the technical preparations for the experiment are not completed, and this greatly increases the risk involved. We should have several more months, but we don't have them. Not a single experiment with dogs has been successful. Out of five cases, three awakened, but later perished for various reasons. A rather prolonged parallel blood circulation is necessary, and we have had no time to develop it. Unfortunately, we also had no chance to verify the pressure-chamber action; the last two dogs that we tried to awaken in the chamber died because of casual errors in handling the equipment.

I am not unduly alarmed by this; my pupils will have sufficient time to perfect the awakening technique. One thing is obvious: the whole operation must be made fully automatic, because the risk involved in manual handling of equipment is inordinately and unnecessarily high.

Enough of this. There is no point in dwelling now on science or technical problems. Time is too short. The boys will be here soon, and we must discuss a great many things. Besides, I have been greatly weakened by my illness and by the preparations for the experiment.

■ ■

I would like to sum up my life, but I feel that I will be unable to produce any meaningful document.

The main interest of my life had been science. I don't know how this affects others, but for me the greatest satisfaction has been searching and discovering. Even now I remember with pleasure an overwhelming sense of well-being after every successful discovery. It is possible that this involvement in work has been caused by the fact that other sides of my life have never developed satisfactorily.

In his time, Pavlov wrote an inspired message to young scientists. The first word of it was "Dare." I can't remember the rest.

It is interesting that I still have a desire to urge youth to go into science. "In the face of death, I urge you . . ." I have always had a predisposition for rhetoric.

■ ■

In all probability the urge to create is the strongest innate human trait.

But one must guard against becoming involved in the first thing that comes one's way, lest one become sidetracked into some meaningless illusion. All accomplishment brings gratification; the very process of accomplishment is extremely pleasant, but scientists must always examine their motives and their goals and constantly ask themselves What for and Why? And now the responsibility resting on scientists is overwhelming.

I have thought a great deal about the directions of science and have discussed this matter with my colleagues. All directions are important, but some more so than others, in view of the fact that the world is facing a real danger of self-destruction. Psychology and sociology must be studied closely, because they are the keys to successful handling of man and of society.

It is necessary to develop such principles of human behavior that would represent the least danger of violating other people's freedom. I am not preaching universal love, even though it would have solved all problems; unfortunately, it is inconsistent with human nature. At any rate, violence should never be glorified. Probably, by special analytical processes, it is possible to find the quantitative expression of morals and ethics. And to build them into computers. It is the scientist's duty to think about these subjects, because the average man lives only in terms of a single day and just watches the sky—dreading to see the falling bombs.

Scientists have created this danger, and it is their duty to find a way out of it.

In these last days I have developed an overwhelming urge to teach people how to live. I know that this is futile and ridiculous. I myself have lived my life badly and incorrectly. I have wanted to give my advice to people, but all I could produce were the usual banal commandments. Their preachment by religions of the world has produced little positive result. Probably the very organization of human society has been at fault. And now this fault has placed the very life of this planet in jeopardy. It is much too late to look for those responsible for it.

But one thing is certain: the world must look for the factors that draw people together, rather than for those which disunite them.

I must finish my notes. Even though I dread doing it—it is like driving the last nail into my own coffin.

■ ■

I have reread what I have just written, and I feel ashamed of myself: the pompous style, preaching.

The prophet.

Will not do this again.

Actually, the best thing in life is to finish something.

Generally speaking, I am ready.

P.S. I am attaching herewith a copy of my letter to our Academy:

DEAR COLLEAGUES:

Taking into consideration the absolute hopelessness of my physical condition, I have decided to subject myself to prolonged anabiosis with the help of the equipment designed, developed and constructed in our laboratory. I did not apply for the permission to conduct this experiment, because I was afraid that it would not be granted in time for me to avail myself of it. All my collaborators in this work have been sworn to secrecy by me during the preparatory period. They cannot be held responsible, because they have only followed my explicit orders. Therefore, I am herewith assuming the entire responsibility.

I hope that this experiment will prove to be beneficial to science.

Prolonged anabiosis may be useful for long cosmic flights. It is also possible that it will have therapeutic value in some serious cases. At this point it is difficult to foresee all the potentialities of this method.

Unfortunately, we have been forced to begin the experiment with technically insufficient and imperfect installations. Further postponement is impossible, due to the rapid progress of my illness. Therefore, I request that further work be planned along the following directions:

A. Complete automation of all controls;

B. Creation and approbation of the programs and technical equipment for the automatic induction of anabiosis and the maintenance of optimum conditions required by the system in the course of the process.

I suggest that the responsibility for the above task be assigned to the principal constructor of the present installation, Yuri N. Sitnik.

The servicing of the installation requires a certain personnel since the automation is still incomplete and uncertain. Therefore, I request that the necessary staff be assigned to this work out of the personnel of the laboratory which is responsible for the conduct of this experiment.

The general direction of the laboratory toward the creation of the mechanical installation modeling functions and interrelations of the internal organs is, in my opinion, an extremely promising endeavor with considerable clinical prospects. I request that Yuri N. Sitnik be charged with the general direction of this work with Vadim P. Pliashnik acting as his first assistant. I also request that the question of the transfer of the laboratory to the Institute of Cybernetics and its removal to Clinic Town be resolved at the earliest possible time.

I request that I be maintained in the state of anabiosis until such time that effective methods of dealing with leukemia are fully perfected. Of course, the Academy may discontinue the experiment at any time at its discretion; but in that event I expressly request that no attempt for my awakening be undertaken.

I request that my apartment be assigned to Vadim P. Pliashnik and my library to the laboratory on a temporary basis.

PROFESSOR I. N. PROKHOROFF

X
The Terrible Sunday

I have read his notes and I feel that I simply *must* describe that last day. This is difficult for me, because I have never written anything in my life, except a few articles, letters and case histories. But I will try. I will write, correct, copy, and never show it to anyone. Whatever it will be. But I hope that he will awaken and read this.

I am frightened. This fear has been with me for several days now, since that Sunday when they operated on him. The man is alive, but he is also dead. It is hard to understand and to accept.

I go to work. I take care of my children, I talk to my husband. He probably understands something, because he knows that I took part in the operation, but he says nothing. I do not really care. It is hard to reconcile myself to the thought that he is now lying there in that sarcophagus. Today I dropped in to see him as I do every day. He is absolutely white. I never knew that human skin was so white, that only the blood gave it color.

Some newspapermen were there. Every day they come from all over the world. Vadim answers their questions. He is tired of this. He now distributes mimeographed sheets, describing everything, but they are not satisfied. They want to know all about Ivan, his work, his private life. I listen and I think, I know more than anybody. Ivan Nikolaevich Prokhoroff has become a celebrity. He would probably have liked it. He was vainer than I thought; I understood this when I read his notes.

I am writing small meaningless things, not interesting to anyone. But perhaps he will be interested to read about the public reaction to his experiment. I don't know.

I am writing these small things because I'm afraid to touch the main theme, even though there was nothing frightening about it; everything went according to plan. I am a doctor, I have seen enough operations, hemorrhages, deaths. I have watched operations with the use of hypothermy, even assisted in some. I felt a cold skin under my fingers. But that lasted for an hour or so, then patients came back to life. Not always. There were some cases I don't want to remember.

Probably it is so frightening to me because this time it is a man who was close to me. It is difficult for me to write, "whom I loved." This word doesn't seem to fit him any longer. Everything is very complicated. I don't know what will happen from now on.

For the last week before the operation I went to see him every evening. I would stay for an hour or two, speak to him, prepare him for the operation. The whole thing was secret; only two doctors knew about it—I and Volodia, the anesthesiologist from my hospital, whom he had not alerted until the night before. Vadim and I went to his house at night. He agreed. We didn't tell David about our plans, and he was very angry with me and with Ivan.

The preparations were rather complicated; we had worked them out together with him. It was necessary to have the intestinal tract empty, and possibly sterile. In abdominal surgery there are methods for this, and I know them—diet, antibiotics, laxatives, enema, blood and plasma transfusions. All this lasted for five days. In the end he was very weak; he could hardly move at all.

These meetings were difficult for me. I'm ashamed to admit it, but sometimes I thought, I wish it were sooner. And then I tortured myself for being so callous. I am healthy, I have Kostia and Dola, and I still have unlimited life ahead of me. And he was like a man condemned to death who knows the execution date. No, not quite. His illness had worn him out—pains, relapses, treatments— he began to hate medicine. He kept his irritation inside him and was tender with me—a special kind of tenderness, timid, distant, guilty.

He was very tactful—he had always been afraid of hurting people; but also he did not permit people to hurt him. He always kept his distance—"I don't touch you, but don't touch me either." He did not dance, swim, ice-skate or ride a bicycle. And his experiences with women had not been happy. I understood it from some of his remarks. One can feel it.

Well, those meetings. The room which I knew so well for years (for years—just imagine!) had been changing before my eyes. It had always been clean, but his desk had usually been piled high with papers and things. And now everything was becoming transparent. All the papers had disappeared. The desk was naked. Russian peasant women have an expression, "putting oneself in order," meaning, getting ready to die. He had arranged all the books on the shelves. Later he gave me his notes and my letters. I have locked all this in a drawer in my hospital office. There was no place for them at home—the children could find them. He told me that most of his other notes and things he had given away as waste paper; children from the neighborhood school had carried them away. The rest he locked in the lower drawer of his desk. He told me that he had a good chance of waking up, but I didn't believe him. I felt that he was deceiving me, that this was almost suicide. Besides, during the last year I have read a lot about anabiosis—so much, that now I could write a dissertation about it.

And still he succeeded in giving me hope. One dog had been in anabiosis for four days and came to. True, he died later from abdominal bleeding—they just overlooked it; he could have been saved. Ivan was very upset. Errors. Physiologists just don't know how to take care of patients.

Generally he was wrong when he thought that I would have preferred him to die normally. I had such thoughts, but very rarely. To me he was dead one way or another. And I don't want him to wake up while I'm still alive. I will be old, ugly, stupid. I expect nothing for myself in life any longer, but still I don't want to grow old. Kostia says that "Mama is still young," but during the last year I found many gray hairs on my head.

■ ■

I have reread what I have written, and I am ashamed. As though I wanted to write about myself! Ivan had often told me about "several planes" of thinking. He told me many clever things, and I have become more intelligent. In some areas I know more than he—in literature, for instance, and all the arts. (I don't know which tense to use writing about him.) He had no time to read during the last few years. Science, only science.

How will I fill this void? I still catch myself thinking, I must ask Ivan about it. . . . I must tell Ivan. It is very painful.

I can't reproduce our conversations during the last meetings; after all, the program for the experiment had already been set. One must have a professional memory, or writing talent, to invent. Ivan did a good job; perhaps he could have been a writer. Even his style seems to be quite modern. However, I don't think he is quoting all my words correctly. I don't remember saying some of them. But I might have forgotten.

We had one good evening together—about three hours. Pavel and the children went to the theater, and I told them I had a headache. (Thank God, I don't have to lie any more!)

I brought some magazines with new poems and some tape recordings. (This is Kostia's love now.) I read some poems. Some were good.

Then he read some Esenin and Mayakovsky to me. It appeared that he knew some of their poems by heart—I hadn't expected it. Then we had coffee and listened to the tape recorder. There is a charming song, "The country of Delphinia and the city of Kangaroo." On the same tape there were some modern American tunes. He winced and said, "Turn it off." He doesn't like them. But I dance very well to them. Sometimes Kostia and I dance at home. It is funny how he tries to lead me.

As always, we spoke about the children. I just can't keep away from them. Ivan is also interested in the "problem of youth," but scientifically, while to me this is my flesh and blood. We argued a little about his "boys." I did not like Vadim—until the last day; I thought he was overbearing and self-assured. How easy it is to be mistaken! Young people often used tough manners as a kind of protective armor. Vadim has proved to be kind and sensitive. Yura is much drier. I don't understand him.

I remember my thoughts when I was leaving. "How heartless of me, leaving him like this! Shall I stay?" And then another thought, "And the children? How to explain? How to meet their eyes?" And then my leaving was probably better for him too. Perhaps he felt easier being alone. Then he didn't have to play a part . . . He was—well, I can't find a word. He could have gone through any torture not to appear pitiful or ridiculous.

Anyway, I left. Whether it was right or wrong. He never tried to stop me.

Writing this will be a good therapy for me for a while. It will occupy me, stop me from thinking. I am writing in the hospital. I have my own little office—a full-fledged section director.

But now I must go home. To my children.

■ ■

I didn't write yesterday, I had no time. I spent the whole evening with a critical cholecystitis case, second operation, a fat old man. He had had a collapse of respiration, almost died. A high-pressure chamber would have come in handy here. Yura told me during the operation (we had to talk about something!) that in six months our Clinic Town will have one. We'll see.

I had been *there* twice today. I have now become used to all of them. Good boys and girls, especially this Pauline. True, she has a sharp tongue and always keeps after Vadim; probably he has given her some reasons. It is funny to watch all those youngsters from the vantage point of my forty years.

Everything is going on normally. Yura told me that the heart-lung-machine motor is not overheating any more; he has found and fixed something. I did not understand. The temperature is steady at 34 degrees, and the chamber pressure is about two atmospheres. The indicators show that there is no oxygen deficiency, on the contrary, there is too much oxygen in the upper tissue levels. This worries Yura a little; he will lower the pressure.

Ivan shows no change—white and serious-looking. The beard has not grown yet; they say they will shave him once a month, or even less frequently. Once every half hour he receives one deep breath automatically. This is well designed; it would have been unpleasant to see the tubes running from the mouth. The kidney has been connected only four times so far; the discharges are accumulating very slowly.

I am afraid that there will be difficulties with plasma—until they move over to our clinic. The station refused them plasma today; it was good that I have accumulated reserves in my place. I will have to make a scene. I'll ask Piotr Stepanovich to help me; they are afraid of him. (He was also offended that I didn't tell him anything in advance.) He does not understand the danger of "information leaks" (another of Yura's terms). I was upset when I was "promoted" out of the clinic, but now I am glad. Here no one asks any "science" from me, just the care of the patients.

■ ■

After that evening with the poetry and tape recorder, I can't think of anything pleasant. Ivan Nikolaevich was taciturn, distant. We could not find any subjects to talk about. The preoperative procedures were annoying him. It was difficult for him to do certain things on his own, and he wouldn't let me help.

To be frank, those meetings were unpleasant for me. Sometimes he would remember something out of the past, "Remember how we climbed the mountains that summer? I was pulling you up by the hand!" He would smile happily, but the smile would fade at once, his face would darken, he would say, "And now I'm lying here like a log of wood." And I felt so cold suddenly. He probably felt it, because he would say, "It's difficult for you to be with me, Lou? You know I can't help being angry at the whole world." And he would ask me not to be offended, kiss my hands, very lightly, with dry lips. And I would cry all the way home. Dola —such a tender, sensitive girl—noticed it all. "What's the matter with you, Mama?" (I don't remember what I answered.)

That was during the last three days. The boys would come to him, offer to stay with him overnight, but he refused. Leonid also came to see him every day. Ivan said that he appeared to be more drunk than usual. A very strange man, judging by Ivan's stories about him. I think that he is having trouble with his wife, but Ivan denies this. But then, how would he know? In general, Leonid evokes antipathy in me. On Sunday, he came to bid Ivan goodbye, waited until he went asleep, and then ran away without saying a word to anyone. I thought he was sober, but I had other things on my mind then.

Every evening there were tears. I could have stayed longer with Ivan . . . I did not tell Pavel where I was going, just "I must go out for a little while." He did not ask. This is also a very difficult matter—but why write about it here?

■ ■

The last evening, Ivan was terribly weak; through the preceding two days he had had nothing to eat by mouth—only coffee, tea and a little broth. He had always been thin, but now his stomach sank back almost to the spinal column; only his spleen protruded like a hard stone. I had a strange feeling examining him—so close once, and now just another patient. He was embarrassed, and I had tears in my eyes. I never knew that I could cry so easily.

Ivan was lying on the divan, in pajamas, covered with a blanket —like a real patient. Of course, real. The little table was pushed close to the divan—newspapers, magazines. When I came he was writing something on a cardboard file, resting it on his bent knee. I was startled to see how sharp his knee was, under the blanket.

I kissed him as always, "Sit down a minute, I'm finishing my will." I did not sit down, because I knew that he did not like to be watched when he wrote. He had told me before that he could not work in my presence. I asked him whether he had had tea, and went into the kitchen. I was hungry, but there was absolutely nothing in the refrigerator. I could not understand what had happened to all the things that had been there the night before. I started to make the coffee, but he called me, "Lou!" I liked when he called me this way. That wasn't always.

When I came in he was smiling. I remember I thought that his smile had become even warmer than usual.

"Well, all my earthly obligations have been discharged." (I am already starting to write dialogues—like a real writer!)

Then he read to me his "will" and asked me what I thought about it. I said I liked it, even though I thought it was too dry. But then, I don't understand the official style—writing hospital reports is always an ordeal for me. But my section is always in perfect order—both my superiors and patients say that.

Coffee was ready. I removed the newspapers and set it up on the little table. Ivan was sorry he had nothing to offer me. He laughed. "I threw it all down the garbage chute. I was afraid I'd weaken." He wanted to have his coffee strong, but I said, no. I was afraid it would keep him awake.

Our "last supper" was brief. I had some very strong, sweet coffee and it curbed my hunger. We spoke pleasantly—Ivan was holding up very well. He kept looking at me, touching my hand, and seemed to be relaxed. "This is just like going for a trip. I'm tired of the old town, but tomorrow I'll get into a train, into a private compartment, go to sleep and wake up in another town." Those are not his exact words, just the sense of them. And then he added with a little laugh, "And if there's a wreck at night, I won't wake up at all."

He said that leaving me was the hardest thing for him—he just wanted to say something nice to me. He had always been kind and gentle with me. Even when he was ill, he would tell me: "Thank you for your warmth. If it were not for you, I would have died without ever being thawed out."

During that last evening I didn't feel like talking about the operation, but he kept coming back to it. He was worrying that some last-minute information leak would prevent it. This was not very likely. Only seven people were going to take part in it: Yura, Vadim, Pauline, Igor, I, Volodia the anesthetician, and a laboratory technician, Valia. Of course the whole laboratory knew that a very important hypothermy experiment was slated "for Monday," but no one guessed what it was. The equipment had been tested, medicine stocked, linen and instruments sterilized. Even some dogs had been selected. Three liters of plasma and blood-replacements for the machine had been prepared by me, in my hospital. I had been accumulating it from the station little by little for the whole week.

The entire planning had been done during special conferences. The "closed ones" when only Yura and Vadim were present, and the "open" ones to which Pauline, Igor and I were invited as well. It was strange to me to come to his apartment as a stranger and talk business. Volodia and Valia did not know anything until the last evening.

The question of securing an official permit had been dicussed for days. Vadim insisted on it, "Wouldn't they understand?"— meaning the Academy leadership. But finally it was decided to keep it secret. Ivan was afraid that "consultations" might take months, that no one would want to take the responsibility in such an unusual affair. And after all, what could they do, faced with the accomplished fact? It had been done on the express request of the "victim."

■ ■

The first reaction, on Monday morning, was interesting. The Director called in Semyon, Yura and Vadim. At first he just shouted at them, then rolled his eyes to the ceiling mournfully. "How could you agree to participate in such a crime? You killed a man—a brilliant scientist!" Then again: "You will be prosecuted to the full extent of the law! I won't let you get away with it! I'm not going to jail on your account!" He sent them away and started telephoning. But Yura would not wait, took the copy of "the will" and went up "to the top" himself. It was necessary to present it all in the proper light. Everything turned out well—and on the same day the news was given to the press. The Director was receiving reporters in his office, posing for photographs. Listening to him one would think that he was the author of the whole project. But Yura did not sleep either. He took them into the laboratory and here the Director could not answer one question intelligently. Yura was in command—"selling" it, as he calls it. Everyone felt ill at ease; but Yura, the new, uncrowned "chief," insisted that this was necessary. Maybe, but I felt unhappy listening to him talk so impersonally about the "subject"—meaning Ivan.

■ ■

But back to that last evening: We chatted lightly, about this and that, about the children. We even discussed the last film, which I think he didn't see—only read the reviews. I don't remember everything. I only know that we both tried to appear and sound cheerful and calm, in front of each other. This happens when people meet before a long parting. My mother told me how she felt sending Father off to the war.

At last, at ten, Ivan told me that he was tired, and that I must go home. My emotions were complicated. I remember looking at him and thinking, These are the last minutes, and they are slipping away; remember them. And also, It's good that I can leave. And at the same time, feeling shame, because I knew I should have stayed, and feeling that he did not want me to stay.

He got out of bed and, swaying a little, went to his desk (empty and naked), and brought out a folder from it.

"I've been writing a little during this year . . . Take and keep this. If I wake up, I'd like to see it . . . Don't show it to anyone, until you decide yourself what to do with it. I've made the last entry today. And I beg you: don't read them tonight. That would be unpleasant for me. And here are your letters."

He tried to sound casual and almost succeeded. And I too was trying to hold myself together the best I knew how.

Then he offered to give me anything I wanted. I didn't know what to choose . . . The old dishonest thought; how would I explain? Then I selected a few old photographs. They are here now, in my drawer. I look at them every day and try to imagine how he was growing up, what he was thinking . . .

I also took a small bust of Tolstoi that I could put into my purse. That was all.

I kissed him and ran. I heard him say, "Forgive me, Lou." The door closed, I ran down the stairs, and in my head: "This is the end . . . end . . . end." I cried all the way home and the whole night. I saw him brushing his teeth, taking sleeping pills (I had brought them), going to bed, even reading a newspaper—a force of habit. And again, How could I leave him alone? It was a bad night for me.

I can't write any more today. I'm too upset. Also, time to go home, to my darlings. What would I have done now without them? I can hear Dola's chirping, "Mama's home! Mama's home!" And Kostia, in a low basso, trying to be grown up, "At last, Ma!" But then he forgets and kisses me, as he has done since he was a baby . . . I must go and see some of my serious cases. Actually, I don't want to, and it is not part of my duty, but I can't leave the hospital without it. Why?

■ ■

Here I come to the most important part—that terrible Sunday and the operation. I can't call it anything else—an experiment, a test? How can words like that describe what has been done here with a living man?

I must get my courage together and describe everything in detail.

The operation was set for nine o'clock in the morning. (This is probably the best word, and the one I'm used to.) I fell asleep toward morning and was up on my feet at seven. I had to do my customary work—get breakfast for the children, clean up. The usual Sunday morning conversations. "Kostia, get up!" "Dola, enough of reading!" "Pavel, here's a clean shirt for you . . ." Why am I writing all this?

I left at eight-thirty, telling them I had to be at the hospital, and would not come back before dinner. Pavel did not say anything, but gave me an angry look. Obviously he suspected the reasons for my evening absences. He knew about Ivan's grave illness; they knew each other, and I had casually told Pavel that Ivan was sick.

I walked quickly, imagining how Vadim had already come to fetch Ivan in a taxi, and how Ivan had met him after having shaved and having had his coffee. All this was a part of the plan. He must have made his bed—he liked order—and Vadim must be speaking to him with an artificial lightness, something like "Let's go, Chief!" Some casual phrase to cover up pain and bewilderment. I could not visualize Ivan's face, or imagine his words. Probably something insignificant, like "Was it easy to find a taxi?" I could see him putting on his overcoat (it is now hanging in his empty office and no one knows what to do with it). A rather old overcoat—he had been wearing it ever since I first met him. "I am used to it, and who am I—a dandy?"

Later Vadim told me that it was almost like this. He put on his coat, then came back to the room to take a last look. Then he said to Vadim, "Live here happily, I won't be back very soon." And probably thought, If ever. Then he said, "Let's sit down for luck"—an old Russian custom before any long journey. They sat down. Vadim said that it was just like any usual departure; instinctively he looked around for a suitcase.

It was a dull morning. The streets were almost deserted and there was a very thin snow in the air. I thought, It's March and still no sign of spring; still, it's dry—I could have worn my Sunday shoes. And then, What for? For Ivan? So that he could remember me like this in his next—other life? He had never noticed what I was wearing anyway.

When I came in, Ivan and Vadim had not yet arrived—Vadim

had had trouble finding a taxi. True, all the others were already there, and I felt ashamed—I could have come earlier.

Everyone was busy. Yura was fussing around his automatic control panel—I already knew what it was. Pauline was filling the oxygenerator with plasma. Volodia was connecting the hose to the oxygen cylinder for anesthesia. Igor was in the next room with his girl assistant.

I knew everything already; they had invited me for the last few experiments. I will not describe the setup—I'm not technically qualified. Besides, its description will appear in all the magazines; they have taken photographs, et cetera.

The room was cramped and not too clean. Yura says that the Academy will put up a special building where there will be a hall for the sarcophagus and all the machines. But when will that be? I know how the Academy builds—unless there is pressure from the top. This is possible—sensational reports already call this "the pride of Soviet science." It's unpleasant for me to hear this—as though Ivan was an inanimate object! But Yura doesn't object. "This benefits science." I only wish he wouldn't use some of this publicity to benefit himself.

The sarcophagus stood in the center—a large cylinder made partly of plexiglass. Both sides were open. Before it, there was the table on rollers where they would give Ivan the anesthesia and connect up all the tubes, catheters and probes. Then this whole table would be rolled into the pressure chamber, which would be hermetically closed.

All this looked imposing, but unfriendly. Besides the chamber everything looked ugly and rather crudely made. Yura said it was "a temporary mock-up"; later they would change it. But somehow it all reminded me of a fence around a grave.

My assignment during the operation was quite simple. I think that Ivan had involved me into this on purpose so that I could be close to him during the last minutes. But perhaps not—a physician could come in handy in case of any complication. I had to assist Volodia to insert the catheters into the heart. Pauline alone might not be able to cope, so I was to act as a sort of surgery nurse to her.

No one felt like talking. I washed my hands and started to prepare sterilized sheets, napkins, tubes and heart probes. It was easy; everything was already in sterilized containers.

They came when I had finished. All that I had to do was to dilute heparin.

Pauline looked out of the window and said, "They have brought him." My heart fell; my last hopes were gone. I thought that there could be some trouble with the equipment or something to postpone it, but now it was final. But why "brought"? As if he were unable to move by himself.

Yura abandoned everything and went out to meet them. I also wanted to go, but I was already sterile. Was it possible that we'd have no chance to exchange a few last words? No, impossible; he needed encouragement. So I covered everything with a sterilized sheet—there were spare gowns and gloves—and went.

I was walking along the empty corridors; it was Sunday and the building was deserted, and in my mind there was a stupid little rhythm, "corridors, halls, toys and rag dolls . . ." Why? I don't know.

Ivan was lying on the divan in his office—very pale, his nose blue and long. I looked at him and thought, How terrible he looks. He sat up when he saw me coming in. "Good morning, Doctor," and I understood. I had to be official and distant. Only the tone of voice and looks—that was all that we had left.

"Maybe we'd better postpone it, Ivan Nikolaevich?"

I hoped he'd say, "Yes, let's." There were no other thoughts, only pity squeezed my heart like a vice.

"No, why, Liubor Borisovna? It's today or never."

I knew it. His pride. He probably thought, If I go home they will think I'm a coward.

(Now, that I have read his notes, I understand him better.)

I took his hand—as a doctor I had to feel his pulse. The pulse was fast, about a hundred and twenty. The preoperative excitement; it is typical. My calming pills had not worked. I asked him if he had slept, and he said yes. Only here I noticed the others standing around. Vadim's chin was trembling and his eyes misty.

This was the first time I thought kindly of him. Yura was completely calm. A log, I thought.

"What are you doing here? Go and do your work. You know the old saying: Long goodbyes—extra tears!"

Ivan said this with irritation. Apparently his self-control was all but exhausted.

Yura spoke for everybody. "We are ready."

I was ready too. We must now bare the blood vessels for the machine, give him morphine and start anesthesia. There were no excuses for any delays, and perhaps it was better this way.

"All right, morphine. Yura, please ask Volodia to come here to administer the injection."

I said this—I remember clearly. Then I felt uneasy, as though I had taken the initiative upon myself. I probably looked guilty, because he took my hand and thanked me.

"Yes, Liuba, it's time to start."

After this Yura and Dima walked out.

I thought: Here are the last minutes I have with him. What shall I do?

I wanted to embrace him, to kiss his lips, eyes, forehead, to cry . . . but I just stood there. I knew that any emotional display would be unbearable for him.

"My dear . . . be brave. We will meet again."

Here I couldn't hold myself back, I embraced and kissed him. I knew I'd burst into tears.

"Goodbye . . ."

I ran out. I couldn't bear it. I didn't hear what he answered; I only remember his look—pitiful, helpless.

So I didn't use my minutes. (I still can't forgive myself.) I spent them crying in the lavatory. Then I washed, wiped my tears and went down to Surgery. This is all—the end, I thought. How will I live without him?

But I'm living. Going to work, cooking dinners. Yesterday I did some laundry. I'm operating. And studying English with Dola. Only my soul is still frozen.

What a strange thing, love.

■ ■

I will now continue. When I entered Surgery I looked calm. I could now move about like an automaton and even speak to people about various things; I don't remember about what, exactly.

When I came back to the room, Ivan and Volodia had not yet come in. It means that Volodia will bring him in. And what if he falls down on the stairway? Usually they use a wheelchair.

I started to wash my hands. As always, this calmed me down; I was entering the familiar reflex sphere. We washed hands together, Vadim and I, in a small room next to Surgery. We were silent, each thinking his own thoughts. I was afraid that Ivan's heart might stop before the proper time, or his left ventricle might become distended—if the valves of the aorta were not holding well. What then? To cut through the pleura and massage the heart at the same time, quickly warming him up, forgetting about the anabiosis? That would be terrible for him—it's better to die in anesthesia than suffer, dying slowly from the leukemia. I was thinking soberly. I'm a doctor and am accustomed to evaluating those things. But still we would have to go through all that—our medical ethics required it, to the very end.

Vadim told me that he was frightened. Suppose he wouldn't be able to open the vessels? His hands were shaking. I told him not to worry; I could do it if necessary. All he had to do was to insert a catheter through the intraventrical wall into the left auricle. I told him about my fears, which was wrong; he was completely unnerved anyway. I don't remember what he told me, but I understood that he loved Ivan. That was pleasant.

We washed up and started putting on the sterilized gowns. From a surgical point of view, the operation was nothing—opening two veins and one artery. We had decided not to drain the vein on the neck; the cooling of the oxygen chamber would not require high heart-lung-machine productivity.

For some reason they were not coming and Pauline went out to investigate. But she returned immediately. "Here they come!"

They came. Ivan was very pale and walked slowly. They were helping him. He smiled a painful little smile. "Good morning . . ," (He had not seen Igor, Valia and Pauline yet.) He was wearing pajamas. I recognized them. Even some scenes from the past flashed through my head ...

"Well, Ivan Nikolaevich, lie down and we'll start."

Such cruel words: "lie down . . . start." They are unavoidable; we all say them, but they assume a special, sinister meaning when we say it before dangerous surgery. Now it was even more frightening—as though they were said before an execution. Yura said it, and I felt resentment—as though he were in a hurry.

"Let's say our goodbyes while I'm on my feet. Let me kiss all of you."

Yura came to him first. Ivan told him in a whisper, "I rely on you." (Later, we sat together and remembered every word, every gesture.)

To Pauline: "Get married. It's no good being alone."

To Igor: "Keep together, please, don't quarrel!"

To Volodia: "Forgive me for dragging you into this." Volodia mumbled something like "Not at all" and turned toward the wall. I looked around at all of them. Probably people had such faces in old times after Confession and Communion: everyone was looking inside himself.

To Valia he said simply, "Keep well."

Vadim and I were in sterilized gowns so he kissed our foreheads, carefully, so as not to contaminate us.

To Vadim he said, "Control yourself dealing with people. But in science, on the contrary, be bold. I've been too timid. This is why I've accomplished so little."

He just whispered to me, "Courage, Lou." So soft that even I could hardly hear it. But to me nothing mattered any longer.

"And now . . . Help me, boys."

He started to climb the table, Volodia was helping him. It looked awkward and pitiful. It was apparent that his body didn't obey him very well. I tried to imagine his thoughts. Probably the strongest was "to run away!" But he kept himself well in hand, and nothing betrayed his anguish. Perhaps only an expression of bewilderment on his face. I also behaved well—the surgical mask covered my face anyway, up to my eyes. I hadn't used eye makeup now for a week.

He sat up on the table and took off the pajama top; he was all skin and bones.

He lay down and closed his eyes. (I panicked for a second—tears?) There was no sound now. Apparently he was mustering up all his courage. His face gradually relaxed; he opened his eyes and smiled. He was once again Professor Prokhoroff and, for me, Ivan.

He looked around, smiled half-tragically, half-ironically.

"Well, goodbye. See you in ten years."

He pushed his arm to Pauline for the intravenous injection. She pierced his vein at once. I even thought, "Good girl!" She drew some of the blood into the tube. Pauline looked at me, as though I were her superior, and I just nodded. Ivan was looking at the ceiling with an expression of complete indifference—as though he wasn't here at all.

In a few seconds his eyes closed. He fell asleep and everyone drew a sigh of relief—the difficult scene of parting was over. Now everyone merely had to perform his task. But still there was silence.

I am tired. I have been writing the whole evening—have filled the whole notebook. He's no longer here, so this is just for the sake of record. So why hurry?

■ ■

I haven't written for a week. The main things are already described, and I've lost interest. The last time I wrote was like burying him again. But I must finish.

Today is Friday—almost two weeks since the operation. I go to see him every day—as widows do in the beginning. Then they stop coming, and I will stop too, probably. Such is life. I protest inside, try to keep his image with me, but can't; other things are beginning to draw my attention away.

I will continue.

■ ■

After he had fallen asleep, his respiration almost stopped—the effect of the relaxants. Vadim quickly inserted a tube into the trachea, connected the apparatus and started to work the respiration bag as it is always done in surgery.

They removed his pajama trousers and drawers and he was left naked and lonely. I am used to such sights, and I didn't react to this nakedness. It evoked no memories at all; this was just a patient. But the general impression was strange—a naked man in the laboratory crammed with machines and all sorts of equipment. We looked like a gang of criminal doctors assembled to conduct some illegal experiment. Later, others told me they felt the same way, and that is why they all hesitated until Yura said, "Go ahead."

Then Pauline shaved off hair in the groin region, and we daubed iodine over the area. The incisions had to be small, because we had no right to expect quick healing under the anabiosis conditions. We started to open the vessels. Vadim proved incapable; his hands trembled, and I had to take over. It was simple; there were practically no fatty tissues under the skin, and the veins and arteries lay close to the surface. We tied off all the smallest vessels until the incisions were completely dry. We waited a few minutes and inserted heparin—to stop the blood from clotting. According to the plan we had now to connect the heart-lung machine—to be ready for a possible heart stoppage in the course of the probe insertion into the left auricle. We did this, and then Vadim started to insert the probe through the vein. This is a difficult procedure and Vadim was in such a state that I was afraid he would not be able to do it. I don't know what we would have done then, because I have no knowledge of this technique. We would have had to start the anabiosis without this control. However, all went well, and in about ten minutes the probe reached the left auricle. Vadim wiped off his forehead with the sleeve of his gown—his sterility reflexes are not too strong. After this we connected the blood-circulation machine. The experiments on dogs had proved what indicators are indispensable (the "volume of information"), and we did not insert anything not absolutely necessary. We did not even open the artery; we decided to judge the pressure through the pulse. The oxygen pressure in the chamber ensures good oxygenation of the tissues. However, it was important to have the clear picture of the venous-blood saturation, and therefore another slender probe had been inserted into the right auricle.

Over the chest and abdominal area they placed an artificial-respiration inner chamber made of wire and plastic. Periodically the air pressure is lowered in it, and some oxygen is drawn into the lungs.

So everything was finished and we now rolled the table into the oxygen chamber. Yura supervised all this, and soon Ivan was inside with all sets of tubes and hoses running out through special airtight openings, and connected with the blood-circulation machine and also with a very complicated apparatus registering all the information and regulating automatic controls. (I forget its name.)

Volodia inserted a small wire tongue depressor into Ivan's mouth and closed it. From here on, the artificial respiration took over.

My assignment was finished, and Yura asked me to keep the log of the experiment (operation!). All the others were busy: Pauline handled the heart-lung machine, Vadim and Yura watched the registering and conditioning equipment, Volodia was handling the anesthesia, and Igor and Valia ran the biochemical analyses. Even though the procedure had been considerably simplified since the first experiments with dogs, we were still shorthanded.

■ ■

Here are some of my notes:

11:00   The chamber closed, cooling process started, conditioner and ventilator switched on.
11:20   The esophagus temperature 86° F. The circulation machine switched on for parallel work, capacity 1 1/m.
11:25   The chamber pressure beginning to rise.
11:40   The pressure, 2 atmospheres, temp. 79° F., heart contractions 56 per minute. Fibrillation expected. Danger of left ventricle becoming packed.
11:52   Fibrillation. Pressure in left ventricle unchanged!
12:00   Temperature 62° F. Chamber pressure lowered to allow the blood change.
12:24   Heart-lung machine stopped to change blood.
12:40   The machine switched on again, productivity 2.5 1/m. Temperature 55° F. The chamber pressure increased.
13:00   The temperature 42° F. The machine productivity decreased to 1.5 1/m. The pressure, 2 atmospheres.
13:50   Temperature in large intestine, 35° F. The cooling process completed. They are beginning to work off the stationary regime.

■ ■

Again, a pause. The last time they interrupted me. Today is Tuesday, April 11. Sixteen days have passed since the operation. The first furor, thank God, has passed. There is less enthusiasm, too. In the beginning there were five people per shift—volunteers from the laboratory and the Cybernetics Institute (engineers and technicians to watch the machines). Now there are arguments about whose turn it is. Sometimes Yura has to fill in himself.

What a stupid thing a woman's heart is; it seems to me now that everyone has forgotten Ivan and that his pupils are trying to usurp his glory. I often catch myself thinking, "I alone want nothing, and have nothing left." But, after all, I'm not Ivan's wife, and I had no rights to him, and even less to his laboratory. All their mechanical innovations there are like insults to my comparative ignorance.

But forcing myself into objectivity, I must admit that there is nothing for which I can reproach Yura. After all, it was stupid to expect that things in the laboratory would remain unchanged. Some people there are dissatisfied with Yura, but when I look closer, I discover that he simply demands more discipline. Ivan Nikolaevich had never been strict, and many people took advantage of that. Semyon too was too soft. He has moved now into the Director's department, but behaves well. Even Vadim has to admit it. "He doesn't get in our way, even though he could."

Now, everything is directed toward the improvement of the installation which has been christened "ANA-I." An idiotic name, I think, but I didn't protest. I have read this and thought, "What right have I to express my opinion?" Ivan had been preaching objectivity to me, but had failed; I am too much of a woman. Of course, some of his lessons bore fruit; I often try to look at myself impersonally, but rarely with success. I started to learn objectivity too late in life.

Of course, the installation must be greatly improved, so that one person can control it. Fortunately, Yura is a fanatical worker, and his girl is not the going-out type; they spend evenings at home so that Yura can always be on hand in case of emergency. (Ivan has said they read poetry together. But how could he know?)

They have already started to call Ivan "Sleeping Beauty," and this offends me to tears.

Newspapers have helped a great deal, according to Vadim. Yura is using them as much as possible—pressing directors, superiors and enthusiasts. Enthusiasm needs fresh fuel all the time, and where to get it? Yura delivers lectures and talks, but he is a far cry from Ivan Nikolaevich. Strange, now everything in Ivan seems perfect to me, yet how I used to argue with him! Are there any psychological laws about this? I don't know.

I must write on. I'm already tired of it, and I can see that I'm no writer. But I feel that I have taken upon myself an obligation: to write this for Ivan. Therefore, I must.

The selection of the proper "regime" has proved to be a difficult task. Even though the temperature has remained constant, some changes have been taking place in the system. "The stationary regime" (all these terms are strange to me) was reached only after a week.

The main problem was finding the proper pressure level and determining the intervals for the heart-lung machine to work, so that the contents of O_2 and CO_2 in the tissues remained within tolerable limits.

During this period we had a lot of free time, and we talked to each other to keep from brooding. Yura was busy with his machines (the motor pump had started to overheat), Igor was running the analyses, but Vadim, Pauline, Volodia and I had nothing to do.

We sat around the pumping machine and talked. It was strange —here he lay, and we instinctively lowered our voices. It was like sitting around a dead body just before burial. I remembered how it was when my mother died.

No, this was even more difficult. Somehow we could not get rid of the feeling of guilt—as if we were accessories to a crime. Pauline said this first, and we all agreed. We discussed why we felt this way. The initiative was his, but perhaps we could have talked him out of it, or even refused to participate. But I knew I couldn't; that would have been treason.

Yura had told Vadim, long ago, that "he was intrigued by the scientific idea." Only on the very day of the operation did the thought of crime occur to him, but it was already too late.

Pauline said, "I could never refuse once he had asked me." I felt the same way.

Then she asked me how long he would have lived without "this"? I said, maybe half a year, maybe a month. The worst thing was that his system had started to reject blood transfusions. As a surgeon, I believe in blood more than in medicines. Two or three times a month, fresh blood transfusions had saved him from anemia. I must have transfused twenty liters into him during his illness.

Then I also asked, point-blank, whether they believed that he could be brought back to life?

Vadim started to mumble, "You know . . . you see . . ." but then, "No, I don't." Pauline jumped at him—"Then how could you . . . how dared you?" I was also taken aback, and he explained it something like this: If we should start awakening him now, he would wake up, but in several years the molecular structure of the now inert cells might change completely.

Yura, who must have heard it, came to him and said sharply, "How the hell do you know that? Have we run any conclusive tests? The anabiosis in animals is a fact, the failures with dogs can be all explained by the imperfection of methods. The cells and organs died because there was no proper technical means of preserving them. Ivan Nikolaevich proposed a revolutionary technique —the plasma and oxygen chamber. And we will create proper technical equipment with perfect mechanical controls, and then we may well solve the problem."

I remember well the gist of his speech, and I was grateful to him. Vadim sat there silently, like a schoolboy. Then Yura told us again, sharply (like a real superior), to stop fussing around with our own emotions. "The Chief showed real heroism for the sake of science; and we all must be worthy of his trust!"

He gave us quite a dressing down, and we all felt better. Even Vadim didn't try to contradict him. I have been noticing that he treats Yura with more and more respect—more respect than he showed Ivan, with whom he often argued. But Vadim is a very good man.

Yura treats me with deference, as though I were his superior here, and this embarrasses me. Of course he knows everything—probably Ivan told him. I feel it. But why is he hurrying so much with the reorganization of the laboratory and taking it over to the Cybernetics Institute? Couldn't he run the whole thing for a while as it was before, without introducing all this new strictness? Is he simply a careerist? I don't know. I don't believe so.

After giving us hell, Yura went out—probably to the workshop. We did not feel like talking. I sat near the window and looked outside. It was snowing and it was gray outside—the weather fitting my mood. Now my thoughts went the other way: If the awakening is possible, then we would have committed a crime in refusing to cooperate. I became mixed up.

I remember how hopeless life seemed to me at that moment. Even the children—Kostia is already hanging on the telephone talking to girls. True, so far he is telling me everything—or is he? How could I know? Dola is still mine, but she adores her father, and I don't know whom she would have chosen. My husband? Patching up our relationship is out of the question—at least that was what I thought then . . . With Ivan I would always have been happy—that I know. What else? Surgery? But what kind of surgeon am I? A section head in a city hospital. Hernias, appendices, minor abdominal surgery, now and then lungs. I am good at it, but patients prefer to go to the clinic. There are old men surgeons whom everyone respects, but I've never heard of an old woman surgeon. Maybe because women entered this field only after the war and have had no time yet to grow old? Well, I will soon start growing fat and little by little turn into an ugly old woman, unattractive to anyone but my grandchildren. And all that I will remember will be these few bright years. And even in them there has been more pain than happiness.

And will he lie there all these years? Or am I destined to meet with him again—when my life is all but over? No, God, no! I feel such fear when I even think about it. I a miserable old woman, and he as he was before his illness—not handsome by any means, but thin, straight, and always dynamic.

Those were my thoughts then. They recur now too, especially

when there's a difficult day at the hospital, or when I go to the laboratory to see *him*.

I have become calmer. Life goes on—everyone has his part in it. Not everyone is destined to be a professor, inventor, artist—someone must do the ordinary work. To find satisfaction in it; otherwise it's impossible to live. My children are growing; it is important to see to it that they grow into good human beings. I am a doctor; I must try to be a good one, to see that my patients have all the care I can give them, to heal their bodies, also their souls. I am writing in clichés; I have no talent for selecting original and beautiful words.

Have I made a mistake in my life?

There lived a woman . . . No, first a girl. She was a good daughter, good student, good comrade . . . In the difficult war years she worked in a factory—still a gangling adolescent, and not because she was poor. She dreamed of being a doctor, she studied at the medical school and graduated, worked three years in a village, and then came back to her mother in the city. Honestly, she should have stayed there longer but it was too boring and lonely; she wanted interesting work, surgery, she wanted to go to theaters. But most of all, she wanted to meet someone whom she could love—forever. Somehow she had missed all that before.

She was in luck: the surgical clinic of a famous surgeon. Pavel, tall, handsome, an engineer and a ladies' man, fine dancer, beautiful talker. Not a bad man. Love, marriage, and soon Kostia. It was difficult; surgery is a demanding work and here is a family, a husband and a child. There are two kinds of clinical medicine—that of the patients and that of science. The patients—with their pains and joys which become one's own. And work, work, work—often hard and thankless. Science in clinic is also work—no brilliant discoveries; they come later, perhaps. Somehow I liked the first kind of medicine, and never developed a taste for science, not the kind practiced in clinic. My chief scolded me, but he liked me. I can't complain. I did a good deal of surgery and cared well for my patients. I'm proud of it. I read the new medical literature, even spent some of my salary for translations. Pavel did not protest; he just smiled ironically. I spent some nights at the hospital, as every good doctor should. But I did not write a dissertation as all my classmates did and did not advance up the scientific ladder. So they transferred me from the clinic to a hospital. Our Piotr Stepanovich was not like Ivan; he could be rough with his people. "If you don't want to advance, get out of here—go to the hospital; there's a nice soft place for you, bedpans, enemas, hernias." I was sorry to leave the clinic; I had given it eight years, but I had to accept my "promotion" to a hospital as section chief.

Why do I write all this? I'm trying to find that "mistake." Well, for years I had nothing to reproach myself about. I loved my husband for several years, but then he first . . . Well, perhaps that was only gossip. And even if it was true, part of the responsibility was mine—I didn't give him the time and attention that he needed and wanted. He earned a good salary, worked well, though without any particular spark. He asked me to change my job. I refused. That was the start of a cold period between us, and we had bitter arguments. Love had died. All I had left were the children and work, work and the children. And books. But I had little time for that either—housework, washing, cooking—we had no help at home.

And then? For a while all went well; I could look anyone straight in the eye. I had made mistakes (in medicine it is impossible to avoid them), but they were honest ones. My conscience was clear; none of them was the result of neglect or laziness. Even when I left the village . . . I knew there was a young doctor to replace me.

And later? I don't know . . . Probably I should have been stricter with myself. Even when he was in the hospital (a fractured skull; he was run over by a car) I should not have spent all that time talking to him about books, science, the future . . . I shouldn't have listened to all those hints about loneliness—all men are crafty when they like a woman—but I listened and talked myself. It was cozy; he had a private room.

This was the first mistake—to fall in love. Suddenly I found a man, intelligent, lonely, a little sad, unorganized in life. It was not difficult when dreams have died and the soul is covered with ashes.

What did I have? The children and work, and life with a man whom I could not love. And I was still young, and sorry for myself. Also Pavel behaved much worse then.

Was it a mistake to fall in love? Perhaps the mistake was not to have acted, not to have left Pavel. The children were still young, they would not have condemned me. I should not have agreed to lie, to deceive. But then he was not very insistent either . . . On the contrary—"Think about it, weigh everything . . ." How difficult it is to sort all those things out now, in retrospect. Gradually everything was changing; we met rarely, the children were growing up and Pavel was becoming more and more attached to them. This served as a bond between us . . . And today it would have been even more difficult for me had I left Pavel then.

I've been writing, writing—and I don't seem to be able to finish. Still, my feeling of guilt has never left me. I've been lying many years—I who have always prided myself on honesty! And up to the very end I had hopes of putting it right some day. "The children will grow up"—and then, "No, too late!" I could not leave him; it was beyond my strength. I saw all his shortcomings and overlooked them all. Love? Nonetheless it's good that there is such a word in the world, a word which defies logic. Even now when I have nothing left but cold logic, I would still repeat it: good.

■ ■

I am living . . . keeping busy, like a squirrel in a cage with a wheel. There's always a lot to do if one looks for it. Only at night, before falling asleep, all those shadows of the past surround me; all that has ended so dramatically.

It's three weeks now. Not a long time, even ridiculous to count— "three weeks . . . now twenty years more." He had tied all of us to himself; maybe later we will stop counting days, but now we are counting each one of them.

Nothing dramatic has happened—not counting the mechanical breakdowns of the heart-lung machine and the conditioner. Some were serious—they had to pack the chamber with ice—but still they have succeeded in keeping the temperature at a constant level.

The metabolism has lowered to one percent—a hundred years

for one! They switch in the kidney very rarely—once every three or four days. They could even have decreased this, but they are very careful to keep the waste level down. They are training the permanent maintenance staff—one engineer and one laboratory-chemist for each shift. Yura has prepared a lengthy instruction chart; he's good at that. Ivan was the same in science. It was only his private life that he did not know how to organize.

The question of the albumin disintegration still remains unsolved. Now they are designing a new construction which will permit checking his weight precisely. The nitrate balance seems to hold up, but it is hard to determine with absolute precision; they are running constant analyses. I don't understand all this very well. Igor is in charge of the department.

Vadim moved into the apartment—without even waiting for the end of the month. His mother-in-law was making his life impossible. He came to me and asked whether this would be all right? I told him to move. We had a house-warming party, speeches, memories. Leonid was there; he drank, but didn't get drunk. He and I were in the same boat—the others were young, their lives ahead of them, but Leonid and I had lost big parts of our lives with Ivan. However, I tried to appear gay.

The boys are full of plans. Everything is progressing well, I think. Yura is integrating more and more engineers and mathematicians into the laboratory and is gradually discarding physiologists. There's some grumbling, but generally he is earning everyone's respect. Only old hidebound professors still address him as "young man."

However, if he stumbles, there will be many who will give him a push. But this is improbable. I still have no particular liking for him, but I must give him his due—Ivan's fate is in secure hands.

At home everything is also normal. It's a large order—to regain self-respect, not to let the sense of guilt destroy you. I am sorry for Ivan, sorry for our love, but I still catch myself thinking, Would I have gone through all this again? No, never!

I am surprised at myself. Am I so dry and insensitive? And what right have I to blame the boys for not showing more respect for their late "Chief."

That sarcophagus room has become cold and impersonal. There

are twelve-hour shifts, accurate records. It reminds me of the time when, years ago, Pavel took me to the control room of a large power station. (He wanted to impress me with his position, his importance.) There, too, engineers were watching their control panels and writing down figures. It is the same here. They even wanted to cover the plexiglass with a sheet, but Yura said, no. Something might go wrong inside and be overlooked. But it would have been better not to see that white face.

It's so strange—there lies a man, neither dead nor alive. And still one retains some obligations toward him. Why?

In the laboratory (it is now called a department) they have mapped out an extensive program of anabiosis research. They are building a brand-new installation which they will assemble in the new building, in Clinic Town. They'll use it for experiments on dogs—working out a new "awakening program." And if the first tests are successful, there will be no dearth of human volunteers. That's human nature—something compels people to court danger.

And if they are unsuccessful, what then? But Yura is very confident, and Vadim is now inclined to agree with him. They are sure that they can duplicate all Ivan's experiments—and gradually lengthen the period of anabiosis.

This experiment (I too call it that now) will probably give a big impetus to science dealing with physiological body functions. Many foreign scientists are coming here all the time to look at the "miracle." So I believe that this experiment will be successful.

I only fear for *him*. What will he be when he awakens? I would never have agreed to this; I would have preferred normal life. Too bad that medicine does not develop some way of letting people die peacefully. There's so much suffering before one reaches the quiet haven.

Today I'm finishing these notes. I don't see any sense in keeping them; everything is minutely recorded in the official log, with more details and on a more scientific basis.

And my own emotions, my unhappy days at work and at home (somehow there are more of those than of happy moments) would hardly interest anyone. A small life of a very average woman doctor who, through mere chance, has been involved in the heroic decision of a scientist. But was it heroic? Others say, yes. But I know him better than anyone, and I have read his notes.

But let's not quibble; let them have their hero.

Part Two

April 20, 1991

I am home, damn it all. *Home!*

Home? All this modern magnificence—steel, chromium, glass? Yes, but all my personal things are old—and *mine*.

My last memories? An empty desk. A flower in a vase. Sad. All this was on the *other* side. Gone.

But *they* were thoughtful. They left me my old desk. And the flower vase. All I need now is Liuba. But she won't come.

Yura has become so dry and solid, even though he is still young for an academician. He said, "Liuba is dead, Leonid is dead." All the others have scattered—Africa, Asia, Antarctica. Sad. This is like coming into a bright new world as a total stranger.

In the kitchen, instead of the usual gas range, there is a shiny contraption. I have tried working it—unsuccessfully. Electronics? Some atomic nonsense? (I must not forget to ask.)

And also, this gadget. One can contact anyone, even in Patagonia, and see a face on a small screen. The whole thing fits into a pocket. Fantastic! Only I have no one to contact.

They are all extremely nice. Those girls at the hospital and rest home were so polite. There are more pretty ones among them and their figures have become better. Proper diet? Sports? Somatology? Cosmetics? Strange that I notice these things again.

Why am I writing all this?

I don't know. For self-expression or for publication? Hard to sort those things out within oneself. I know that I have never had a single point of interest. Like an alpinist, I have always sought several points of support—three or at least two things I could do at the same time. Now all I can do is to write this.

My old notes have been published. There they are—a book on my desk. Why did Liuba release them? Or did they find them after her death? It is unpleasant—like being naked. But my eyes appreciate it. "Such a handsome book, and it is *mine*." Too bad I wasn't around when it first came out. They tell me it created quite a stir.

Now they might reprint it. There was a lot of noise about my "resurrection."

Anna has brought a bunch of magazines to me. Shall I read them? The picture reproduction at least is excellent. Electronics? I must start getting acquainted with the new world.

I don't think the world has changed a great deal. Twenty-two years is a short time. The thought momentum is still slowed down by the "gravity drag"; thoughts have their own speed limit. But technology, of course, is completely new.

I already have a circle of new acquaintances—mostly from the "awakening team." Anna, for instance. A fine-looking, pleasant woman.

And what about the old friends? Only Yura.

He said: "We already know everything about leucosis. We can control it. As well as the aging process in anabiosis. Physically you will pick up just where you left off." Yura. Yuri Nikolaevich Sitnik. An academician of international stature. To be perfectly frank, I envy him a bit. Even though he is my "disciple." An empty word. Science has gone ahead enormously since my "departure."

What place will I have in it now? Will I be able to catch up?

Alarming. It is best not to dwell upon it now. First I must get my bearings.

They are trying to help me. Ziama—Zinovy Yakovlevich—is the best. Such sad eyes, mussed-up hair, stooped posture. He resembles a Bohemian musician. He is a psychologist. His task is to check on me, to find out how "normal" I am. Frankly, I don't know whether I am or not. And neither does he, I suspect. Only time will tell.

What is Anna's position on the team? A public-relations woman? I haven't seen any other correspondents. I must be careful about her. Let me read her report. What a handsome magazine—*The Whole World.*

Enough scribbling. Let us do some reading for a change.

■ ■

. . . the news of Professor Prokhoroff's awakening has made the front pages throughout the world. He seems to be out of danger now, but still remains incommunicado under the supervision of Professor Sitnik's team. I would like to give a brief eyewitness account of the actual process of bringing him back to life—without technical details. They have been sufficiently covered in science magazines.

At 8 A.M. they switched the camera on and we had the first glimpse of Prokhoroff. The face of a corpse, completely colorless. The chamber is a plexiglass cylinder five meters wide and eight meters long. There are only a few people inside—Academician Sitnik, his assistants, Inessa Palmen and Ilya Stepanoff, and three specially trained technicians. There is a hermetically closed door leading into the chamber. This is Academician Sitnik's realm.

The operation table with the patient has a transparent enclosure over it. The pressure in the chamber is now normal, but the enclosure ensures the stabilized temperature of 10° C. The process of awakening has been going on now for nine days. The temperature has been rising gradually from zero to the present mark. The new electronic artificial-blood-circulation machine (first developed at Novosibirsk) has been flushing out the circulatory system with plasma and a whole number of ferments. Yesterday the level of metabolism rose to the level of the temperature—the requisite for awakening.

The process itself has been thoroughly worked out. There is a set of mechanisms taking care of all bodily functions. It is governed by the central electronic computer, based on an exact model of the organism with the action program operating on the principle of return connections. The mechanical aids cease operating just as soon as the various organs start functioning. Any malfunction is practically excluded. The entire system has been thoroughly tested on animals, and during space flights. It will probably be used for the first manned flight to Pluto.

At 8:30 A.M. the enclosure was removed and they started to open the blood vessels on the left hip and the neck. Special conductors must be inserted into the veins to stimulate the action of the blood-circulation machine. Some very fine catheters must be also inserted into the mouths of coronary, kidney and brain arteries to inject a number of specific stimulants.

Doctor Ilya Stepanoff is setting up some complicated-looking machine around the patient's head. They explain to me that with its help electric probes will be introduced into the patient's brain to determine the normal function of the most important cerebral centers, stimulating them.

I am questioning the physiologists watching the operation outside the chamber.

"Can it happen that the cortex functions prove to be badly affected?"

"Yes, of course. This has often happened before."

"And then?"

"If biocurrents from the cortex prove to be insufficient to justify the operation, the restoration of the functions of inner organs will be arrested."

In simple words, they will not revive the heart, and real death will quickly follow.

At 9:45 A.M. they started to raise the pressure within the chamber. Another gauge on the panel came to life. The tempo of heating is very slow—one degree every three to four minutes. Everything is completely automatized. Hundreds of probes measure the temperature in various parts of the body and send their findings back to the central Computer regulating the physiology and chemistry of the organism.

At 10:12 A.M. the temperature reached the 20-degree mark. They started to replace a part of the plasma with whole blood. Both the brain and the heart are still "silent"—the oscillographs show even lines. The artificial respiration is switched on—one can see the chest rising and falling. At least a semblance of life is already here.

Around 11 A.M. we noticed some alarming activity within the chamber. The heart had failed to react to the temperature of 25 degrees. The scientists were discussing what to do. To arrest the temperature rise, or to use stimulation, and if so, what kind—chemical or electronic?

Millions of people are watching this on millions of screens in their homes. Why? Suppose the whole thing fails? Very well, at least the world would know that everything possible has been done. Science requires honesty, and it must not be afraid of criticism.

Suddenly I hear: "The brain activity is matching the temperature level."

I look. Both the brain and heart oscillographs show good, though still disorganized, waves. The scientists are now checking the functions of every separate organ.

The point of anxiety is now the lungs. There is a danger of the alveolae walls having been enlarged too much for the easy flow of the oxygen. A girl technician is placing the defibrillation electrodes, while the others add some special components to the oxygen inflow.

"Contact!"

This is Sitnik. He presses a button on the instrument panel. No reaction.

"I'm increasing the tension to five thousand volts. Contact."

The heart starts beating. There they are—strong, even spasms. Prokhoroff was awakened on the twentieth of February, at 1311 hours!

He woke up, but this does not yet mean that he can live. The process of the restoration of bodily functions lasted the whole day and throughout the night. While the blood-circulation machine was still working, they woke him up—or, rather, checked on his ability to "fulfill the elementary instructions." He was trying to fulfill them; he moved his fingers and his toes and opened and closed his eyes. Then they placed him under sedation, and started to check on every single organ—the kidneys, the liver, the adrenal glands, etc. The main problem remained the heart productivity.

Only toward six o'clock in the morning was the heart action sufficiently stabilized to permit the lowering of the chamber pressure to the normal level. The artificial respiration was kept on for two more days, while the systems of electrodes stimulated the respiratory muscles, which have become greatly weakened. . . .

And so, Prokhoroff has come to life. In all probability he will live. But how? No relatives, close friends or associates. Science has advanced tremendously during his "vacation." What will he do? Will he be happy in his new life? This is not merely his problem, but an important scientific question.

■ ■

The end of Anna's report. She worries about my happiness. Too bad her report is so skimpy on technical details. But then this technology is probably already well known. And then, "No relatives or close friends . . ." This is correct, and very depressing. "Science has advanced tremendously." This is frightening. The director of the Physiology Institute told me yesterday that I had been assigned to his staff. What can I do there? So far I have no idea.

Tonight I will call on the Sitniks. His wife is called Tatiana Alexandrovna. The same Tatiana who was his fiancée when I "fell asleep" twenty years ago.

I'll ask him point-blank: Will my memory be affected, and how sure is he that my leukemia has been cured? No, not about leukemia. That would prove my anxiety. He has already told me that "all microbes and viruses are fully under control." It is logical if the albumin structure has been fully deciphered.

But the memory . . . Some minuscule cerebral systems might have been affected. I have tried to remember some formulas. The algebraic ones, yes; but some analytical ones still escape me. And how can I be sure whether I knew them to start with? Oh well. There is time to learn.

I am now a young optimist. Young? How old am I anyway—forty-five or sixty-seven? But my reaction to Anna is interesting. In fact one can even call her beautiful. She's quick, impulsive, sharp. Only her mouth is a bit too large.

Will all my instincts be restored in time? And if so, when? So far I am conscious of appetite and curiosity. And now and then, of anxiety.

Loneliness. Here I feel a contradiction: my sense of well-being is good. It comes from somewhere inside me—from the stomach, just as after a fine meal. But once I start thinking, there is an instant thought: What for? I am all alone. No, let's dismiss it. My health seems to be good. And all the rest will come in time.

April 22

The pocket magnetophone is terrific. I have just listened to the tape. True, the ending is lost—apparently I pressed a wrong button. It is difficult to operate it in the pocket, by touch. I feel slightly ashamed of having used it without warning Yura and Tatiana Alexandrovna that they were "on the air," so to speak. But then, I can't fully rely on my memory yet, and I must start learning everything anew. I must have some mechanical aids.

Anna dismissed my misgivings about it. "True, there is a little unpleasantness now and then when one is caught lying. But generally this is necessary with oceans of information piling upon us from all sides. A person's brain can't cope with it." Perhaps. But I'm still not used to it.

About lying, Ziama once told me: "People have become generally much more honest. There are statistics about that. (Everything is reduced to figures nowadays!) Fear has been almost eliminated, and dependence of man upon man has been drastically reduced. And economic insecurity as such has disappeared completely. The state provides for all basic needs of all people; all really important elements have been eliminated from the worry department."

Not bad. If I am able to work at all, that is all I really need. I was never interested in excess personal acquisitions.

I spent a pleasant evening with the Sitniks. The fish pie was delicious. We drank some wine. Warm waves started to spread from the stomach; the world became kind, warm, beautiful, like a sunny morning in autumn on a river bank when clusters of red ashberry begin to appear out of the morning fog.

Yuri Nikolaevich is a bit dry. Nothing but information. (Without the magnetophone I would have been lost!) He tried to fill me in about scientific progress while we sat together in his study before tea. The most interesting development is the structural models of complicated biological systems—cells, organisms, brains, society. This is just my line—or, rather, was my line in my previous existence. Pleasant. "My contribution." However, Yura did not mention me once. They have really progressed far beyond my wildest expectations, even though the artificial brain is still insufficiently developed. "The Japanese have something quite advanced in this sense." (I must check on that.) All the rest—cosmos, physics, chemistry, et cetera—was really expected. Medicine is a specific sphere. I am collecting and organizing information, sorting it out in my head.

Of course, we spoke about the people we had known—friends, associates.

Liuba had died of cancer fairly soon after my "departure." She had become friendly with Tatiana Alexandrovna (then simply "Tania"). Strange, to me Liuba is still alive; it seems I can still feel her skin on my palms. But to them she has been dead for over ten years. Gradually I too am becoming accustomed to the idea. Sad. I wish I could have her with me forever.

I have difficulty remembering events directly preceding my anabiosis. More distant memories are much sharper. Yura thinks this is normal. "The memory models" work this way.

Leonid too has died. They know no particulars; they didn't really know him. I will not go to Marina. She is not interesting, and she had never really known her husband. Vadim is in a hospital—something mental. He always had that touch of emotional instability. Too bad; he was the finest person of them all. Yura said it was some serious family trouble. Tatiana gave him a strange look. Was he a part of it all, or is this my imagination?

I know I will never be able to catch up with Yura. But that I always knew. He's brilliant.

He touched upon many other topics—all the changes in things and people. I am searching the answer to a cardinal question: Has human nature changed? So far I have no clear indication.

April 26

If things with the library are difficult, the television is a real breakthrough for me. I'm using it one hundred percent. When Yura listed all the latest accomplishments of science, he missed communications. This, to me, is the most important one. Perhaps even more important than all the others.

The pocket videophone is quite common. One can speak to and see people—provided the distance is not too great.

Cities and towns are now tied together by millimeter waves, space communication satellites and lasers have erased time and space. Instant automatic translation has practically eliminated all linguistic barriers even though semantics are still rather poor.

So far I'm concentrating on entertainment programs from all over the world. (The scientific ones are still too difficult for me.) The thematic contents remain basically the same—love, jealousy, friendship, villainies; fatal misunderstandings arising from subjectivity and mental limitations. But there is a new theme: Man and Machine. I have seen a shattering film about the tragedy of a robot. But not everything about it was clear to me; there are many specifics I'm not yet familiar with.

Documentary coverage has become really universal. It is difficult to see how cameramen can cover it all so quickly and so precisely.

I am trying to penetrate the inner world of modern man via television. But also to familiarize myself with the outer material changes. Have people become much happier than before? They have undoubtedly become less emotional and more self-assured. And this is not merely because of material abundance. They have become accustomed to prosperity, good health, freedom. They take them for granted. But to me these attitude changes are striking.

The whole universe is boiling over behind my little screen.

Five billion human beings are working, eating, watching the world through their own television receivers, sleeping. They are connected into families by love and the force of habit, into states and communes by political systems. Each one is living in his own microscopic world of thought forms, trying to push something new into the World of Things. It is this material world which seems to be all-important and vital to them.

But this is a mere outward impression—boxes filled with electronics, mechanics, hydraulics, atomic power. It is not the main thing. The World of Information, the World of Models—this is the true God of the Universe. Computer centers filled with machines composed of millions and billions of microscopic elements. The communication networks tie up buildings, machines, people and good old libraries. The mechanical memory (on disks, rolls, microrecordings and even some more complicated systems) knows all about man and his machines, and how to govern them. There are models of the universe as well—from the minutest subatomic particles to galactic systems.

Who is ruling this World of Models? People? But the human brain is capable of absorbing only a microscopic part of the information that is rushing in from every direction. True, each man brings in his little contribution into the beehive of science, builds up and enriches it. But it already lives without human help. Computer centers create their own information, their own models. Yes, but who is creating these centers?

No, enough! I want to remain alone in this room, my new luxurious study, beyond which there is nothing but the silent sky. I am protected from all these worlds by a brittle enclosure—from people, things, models. I can switch off my television, my telephone, electricity, and gas and water outlets. I am alone in my own world, the world of images, emotions and memories. I don't see all those mad automobiles and supersonic airplanes . . . Perhaps they don't really exist—all those insane computer centers?

I am surrounded by sounds and smells from the Land of Childhood. Smells are the strongest, the most ancient of all impressions. I can sense the smell of fresh pine logs which carpenters are sawing in our neighbor's yard. A log is resting on two sawhorses, and two men are cutting it with a long saw—rhythmic, powerful swipes and sounds: "zh-zh-zh . . . sh-sh-sh . . ." The smell of horse sweat and manure. The squeaking of a cart . . . I, a little boy, am walking beside the horse, holding the reins . . . I am proud—I am "driving" . . . The horse walks lazily, swinging its tail to shoo off big horseflies . . . My uncle Piotr is walking beside me, and from time to time, the breeze brings to my nose the smell of his cheap raw tobacco . . .

Illusions. Gone forever. Forgotten.

The world is going on. I wake up, and I don't know what to do with myself. All stimuli are weakened. To earn a living? But now this is unnecessary; my needs are so limited that they are provided for automatically—food, warmth, sleep. Is it worthwhile to live just in order to eat?

Propagation? No desire, and no one would collaborate with me.

There is curiosity, yes. To see, feel, explore, find. To experience joy with every new discovery. But so much has been found without me . . . All I have to do is to press the button connecting me with the library, give a number, and instantly an exact model will be given to me. And if there is no ready answer, it means that it is so deep that one needs to dig through miles of rough ground to get to it, and one can't do this alone. One needs staffs of experts, hundreds of computers . . . And where to find those people? They are all strangers. All are busy working, living, making love. Would they abandon all this and follow me? No. "We don't believe in your ideas."

To create happiness for others? But how? All I ever knew how to do was thinking and tinkering in laboratories.

There is also Vanity. To push oneself forward, to seek praise and appreciation. Yes, this is quite a stimulus when there is a loved one. But for myself? Too primitive, too infantile. It does not excite me.

Such hard, naked thoughts! Just like black branches of chestnut trees against the bright white snow of a park in March. But wouldn't there be leaves? Will spring never come? Will birds not come nestling in those branches?

One can also write—self-expression. To extract strains of cobwebs from one's own soul and turn them into a lace of memories—and then walk back and admire the pattern. But one must know how to create beautiful images. To choose scintillating words and to place them into harmonious patterns. And all my words are either white or black. Or gray. No talent. Such tedium . . . I almost feel like opening the balcony door, walking out and shouting, "Please, people, tell me what I should do!"

No. I don't like noise and dramatic displays. And what can they tell me? "What is the matter with you?"

Really, what?

Melancholy. Would I like again to postpone the end with anabiosis?

But this is remarkable. In my "first" life I didn't want to die. But now, after my "second coming," I would accept death with equanimity. But still I don't want to hurry it. It isn't a thing with which one has the right to tinker. Otherwise, there was no sense of my awakening. No. There are things I must do, accomplish . . . To perpetuate myself! This eternal, purely masculine stimulation is returning to me.

■ ■

The main trouble is this: the language of science has changed completely. Mechanical modeling has become a part of life. In my time the basic code of information and modeling (which is the same thing) was human language, with pictures for humanistics and biology, with figures and formulas for the exact disciplines. Now this is different. The basic code is mechanical models. Structures composed of geometrical figures, and devilishly complicated ones. Each square blossoms forth into a system, and often, more than once. There are floors, hierarchic superstructures.

Then come the characteristics of all these figures—how the "entrance" values change into "exit" ones. In some cases this is a graph with a formula attached to it, but in most there is a whole forest of differential equations. And if you dig deeper, there come programs—how all these schemes and their characteristics must be converted into mechanics, how these machines must be brought to life and productive action. I could never cope with the old programs, and the new ones defeat me completely. It is not too bad when the algorithms of the model are described, but in new works they rarely do it.

This is the basis of my quarrel with the libraries.

Fortunately, human beings have not yet lost the faculty of communicating with words. And then there is science for children—popularization. I am learning things.

May 5

Ziama is very amusing. No, a wrong word. *Amazing* is a better one. It is hard to find the exact term. He is slight, skeletal. Not handsome at all; his nose is too long and the eyes too bulging. Always pensive. Semitically fatalistic. A figure from the Bible.

He is studying me constantly, and I feel a bit uneasy about it. I told him of my misgivings concerning my ability to catch up with modern science. He said, "Never mind."

He is reading old books—books that I did not read even in my "previous" life—Plato, Horatio, the Koran, Hindu philosophy. "Eternal values . . . The joy of penetration . . ."

He has told me about the artificial brain. It must be a person—with personal feelings. It can't be accomplished on a purely mechanical level. There exists a scheme of emotions, and it must be used.

The criterion of the optimal society, according to Ziama: the maximum of happiness (from each according to his ability, to each according to his needs?), stability and progress.

The chemical "map" of the brain has been almost deciphered—not of the cortex, but of the brain itself—the centers of emotions—fear, anger, pleasure. The origins of conscience and will are still obscure. They know the chemistry of the basic instincts—sex, hunger, fear. They can be controlled with the help of drugs.

"Another principle of regulation is electronics."

(Electronics again! I have had too much of this as it is!)

"Complicated procedures are conducted only in science centers under mechanical control."

(Machines again!)

There are successes in the sphere of control of the human psyche, but not as startling as newspapermen claim. The human being resists. His brain is working itself free of any external influence. There are complications. There are too many various elements involved, the channels are obscure and flexible. Impossible to think of everything.

But with the help of machines?

Ziama says, "We can't ensure the general, or long-range happiness of a person, if misfortunes dog him, unless we excise the affected part of the brain, with a resultant personality loss."

(No, thank you!)

The origin of pleasure is unique and does not depend on outward circumstances. The level of the "pleasure center" agitation can be measured. I knew it before, but the measurement phase is new; it is achieved through the analysis of hormones and ferments in the blood. And also, electronically. But happiness is still the legendary Blue Bird, and adaptation is its worst enemy. A person becomes used to happiness and it ceases to satisfy him.

Yes, but at the same time, adaptation is a salvation in some cases. You are shattered, destroyed, the whole world seems to be hostile, but then you rest in your room for a day or two, and suddenly your attitude changes, and you feel like going out and doing battle with life again. It seems that some "activity reflex" takes over and orders you to go out and work. Undoubtedly. The very process of doing something—even without considering the end result of this action—is more pleasant and constructive than sitting down and trying to fathom "the meaning of life."

The "psyche control" is not new, but they have been doing much work on it while I was away. Besides education, much can be achieved with the help of chemistry regulating the brain. And again, electronics! So far, however, all those methods are used in clinics dealing with sick people. Terrible.

(Ziama says, "One can get used to it.")

There is the Psychology Service, a network of institutes and treatment stations, all connected with the Calculus Center. Besides treating patients, the Service produces the summary information about the level of the "emotional comfort" of the entire population.

Ziama has interested me in his psychology. It seems that now it is an exact science. No, I'm not going to delve into it, but it certainly gives one a glimpse into the future. And also, "know thyself."

But is that necessary? In their time psychoanalysts were helping in this sphere. One had to find one's "point," switch it from the subconscious into the conscious, and get relief.

But what if one has no "point"? Or is that impossible?

I don't know which is better—to know the mechanics of psychology, to pinpoint the cause of your dissatisfaction—or simply to live your life as best you know how.

Also I have questioned Ziama about thought-reading. He said, "Not yet sufficiently developed." Emotions yes, but actual thoughts only if a person silently mouths the words. Then biocurrents from his throat muscles can be electronically registered. Not very accurately. The Japanese are doing some close work on this, not yet successfully.

Good. That would be too much . . . Just suppose someone could read my thoughts about Anna. Well, why not? Here everything is quite clear. She's a fine woman. A friend? No, that's a profound word. This is when someone walks around—a distinct ego, but is connected with you with an invisible umbilical cord. I had only one real friend—Leonid. This sort of relationship is probably impossible with a woman; sex interferences would affect information. However, I don't know much about her anyway. A soft, ironic attitude toward herself and toward others. Somehow one can't question her about herself. She says, "The most exciting thing in nature is science. It is endless. One can't absorb it all. However, perhaps it is possible to describe the main points? Just the principal heights? This is why I'm a journalist and not a scientist."

What is that—bravura? She is very high-strung. Strong passions. This is why, probably, she has never become a scientist. No real objectivity.

I went to the theater with her. Saw *Antigone*. A famous Greek actress was playing the part—a small woman with electric tension, ringing like a taut guitar string, or rather like a cable strung over an abyss with a small car moving across it during a snowstorm. Every generation creates its own "Antigone" and hands over to her all its unsolvable conflicts between duty and passion. Duty emerges victorious. But at what price! And so far as I was concerned, that evening, passion was getting the upper hand. Am I getting back into that magic circle of desire once again?

When one does not know how to live, one seeks advice. I have questioned Anna about it.

"I'm just living, and I'm happy. I like the people I'm writing about. I like helping people . . . I'm happy with my banal part of a crusading journalist praising good and castigating evil."

"And are you sure you know which is which?"

"I'm trying to learn."

■ ■

I visited the anabiosis laboratory the other day. Now I'm trying to sort out my impressions.

First of all, Yura conducted me into our old Institute building. I asked him whether we shouldn't see the Director. "What for?" he asked. Doesn't he like him?

We walked along the dark corridor where we had our old rooms. I wanted to see them.

"There's nothing left here. Some sort of technical departments."

"Still I'd like to see."

Our laboratory rooms, the operating room where our first sarcophagus stood, are all rebuilt. The "holy places" have not been preserved. I caught myself feeling disappointed about it, even though I knew that it was nonsense.

"All experimental sections are in brand-new buildings, specially designed. Our technology requires a tremendous amount of bulky technical equipment."

Yes, of course, "our technology." It requires this and it requires that. Still I worked in cramped little rooms. In my time there was a so-called Parkinson's Law: "the best scientific work is always done in back-room holes."

Let us see what they have accomplished in their chromium-and-glass palaces. The "Anabiosis Center." Not a large building, but high—eight floors. The usual ultramodern construction. The only notable feature is the absence of windows on one side of the second floor. That is where the chambers are located. The en-

trance hall with the coat room and the usual bulletin board—
"Organized excursions to Japan, India and Sweden . . . the water-
ski club . . . tickets to concerts and music festivals . . . The
Komsomol meeting . . . Has anyone found the book of . . ." (Have
they gone by, these twenty-two years?)

Yura took me all over the building.

"This building was put up ten years after your experiment. I
must admit that your gamble helped us a lot. We had a worldwide
publicity—'The Russians have discovered immortality.' You know
the way journalists are."

Yes, I know. I know it now. Anna has a very sober approach
to your work, Comrade Scientist . . .

"Wasn't that a bit foolhardy, Yura? After all, the chances were
very much against my waking up."

Several times I caught myself with unjust and even bitter
thoughts. Envy? I don't think I had it before. The fear that I
won't be able to catch up and will have to live in the past?
Perhaps.

The Computer Center is on the first floor.

"Remember how we begged Ivan Petrovich to buy a machine
for us and he kept putting us off? He didn't last long, poor man.
A heart attack."

I was not particularly interested in the computers. They are
obviously above my head.

The main installations—the chambers—are on the second floor.
This was the place where I woke up.

"How many people on your staff?"

"Two hundred and seventy. Six departments."

I was watching Yura playing his part of "the Chief"—a con-
summate performance, in the best film tradition. (I was comparing him to myself. Was I like that? No, I've no talent for
histrionics.)

"Would you like to hear something about our work, Ivan
Nikolaevich? Our tour would be more profitable."

"By all means." I couldn't tell him that I was afraid I wouldn't
understand.

Yura pressed some buttons on a wall panel speaking to the department heads. "If you have time . . ."

I watched the attitudes of the men and women coming in. Some curious, others tense, still others with a show of nonchalance. But Yura remained the same—even, reserved, slightly superior.

Inessa Palmen. A very pleasant, handsome woman—if I still understand these things. She took both my hands in hers and smiled; she was obviously glad to see me alive and well. She spoke to Yura with studied courtesy, but looked past him. And I noticed those little wrinkles around her eyes. Sadness? Obviously there is some special relationship here, but this is none of my business . . . Can any woman ever be wholly devoted to science?

Then we had a thorough technical discussion. A few things about their work I already knew, I had been questioning them individually, but now I had a full picture of the tremendous growth of my "baby." (How strong is vanity in every man!)

Their accomplishments are impressive. I was working with low temperature combined with artificial blood circulation and high pressure, without knowing precisely what was happening with cells. Now they are governing life processes with chemistry and electrodes, slowing them down practically to zero level. This is a completely different approach. They have models of the human system, very large and complicated ones. They know the technology of extracting precise information from various parts of the organism and influencing their functions by artificial means. Their automation is almost complete and their equipment truly fantastic.

(Still, it seems to me that we, working in our cramped, drafty room, had more imagination, more daring, more pioneering spirit, so to speak. We had to improvise every inch of the way. We gambled and took tremendous risks. And, after all, the very principle of anabiosis was discovered before all this electronic hysteria!)

Yura: "Our work here is confined to the improvement of models, to the study of inner processes under low temperatures, to slowing life functions to the absolute minimum—and then, reversing this process."

(Of course. And what does he think I was doing?)

They are searching for new ways of influencing these processes, of replacing organic chemistry with the synthetic. Nature has not used the best methods in many departments.

I am not strong on biochemistry. I have always been a physiologist on the organ and organism levels. Therefore, it was difficult for me to follow some of their descriptions filled with brand-new terms which I have never even heard before. No, I did not pretend that I understood everything. Now and then I would interrupt them—"Stop. You have lost me here."

(Strange, this did not reflect upon their respect for me. On the contrary, they seemed to appreciate my candor.)

And all the while I was watching them on the human level, trying to read their individual attitudes. Yura obviously dominates them, but they seem to resist—a little. I was comparing him to myself—no, he does not imitate me. He has his own style. Inessa, of course, is not indifferent to her Chief. But Yura seems to be unaffected. Indifference or good control? He has real talent. The whole thing is in his head—to the last detail. Still he is human . . .

"Tell me frankly—after all I'm not a journalist—do you really have the organism models on the molecular level?"

They are laughing.

"No, not yet. Only rough mock-ups. Many small details are still absolutely obscure. The precision of influence factors is about eighty percent, at the most. Even in the cases of healthy animals."

Yura: "Islands of information connected by causeways of hypotheses."

But Inessa does not agree to such a definition. Like every woman scientist, she thinks in absolute values. But still she is obviously brilliant.

We spent about an hour in discussion, and then went around the building.

The most interesting are the anabiosis department installations. There are five chambers for human subjects.

Before we entered the room, special vacuum cleaners removed every speck of dust from our bodies. We put on special clothing and shoes. The rules are inflexible and extremely strict. The air vents were open; the pressure is increased only at the beginning and the end of anabiosis.

Three chambers were occupied. In one was a young man, a volunteer from the Institute, who was placed in "cold storage" for five years, especially for cosmic-flight training with simulated complete weightlessness. For him there is a special, fully automatic installation with its own governing computer. All preparations—inhibitors, stimulators, hormones, nourishment formulas are in special containers for the entire five-year period.

"He's been here for two years. All goes well so far."

"Yes, but we had to interfere and make corrections twice. In the cosmos, he might already have perished." This is Inessa.

Yura is slightly irked. "Nonsense, Inessa. All corrections were minor."

I cut in: "And are you sure that he will not perish here?"

"Absolutely. We have precise information about every part of the body. All is proceeding according to program."

This particular chamber is very cramped—rather like a submarine. I know that mine was much roomier. Under a transparent magnetized enclosure a young man is lying on an operating table. His face is completely white, with a brush of red beard. He looks exactly like one of the corpses on which we worked when I was a student. His entire body is covered with a system of tubes and electric wires. Some of them are familiar to me, but not many.

"How is he going to free himself from all these things, there, in a rocket? He might mix things up."

"No, Ivan Nikolaevich, everything is arranged. Until the automatic controls bring him into full consciousness—and test all his reactions—he won't be able to do anything. This installation has been tested and retested with short-term anabiosis experiments."

The technicians seem to be tired of repeating these explanations over and over again. Undoubtedly they have had to conduct many public demonstrations before.

"The second chamber is a stationary one. It is the standard size —much bigger than the first one. We have a woman patient here, a schizophrenic."

"Really? What for?"

"Psychiatrists have talked us into this experiment. We don't have much faith in it."

We did not enter the third chamber, just looked in with the help of closed-circuit television. A heavy-set man, of perhaps forty, clean-shaven, and also snow-white.

"This is a deep-freeze chamber; the temperature inside is —180°. No circulation at all. This is a long-range experiment."

"And do you expect him to wake up?"

"We hope so. Some experiments on animals were successful, but not all. This man is a murderer, a bandit. He was condemned to death for some multiple murders. An incorrigible criminal. We petitioned the court, and they agreed."

"And what about him?"

"He also agreed."

Is this humane? I don't know. Without sentiment—why not? This is no worse than natural death.

Two other chambers were empty.

"They are being refitted. This one was yours."

I looked in. Some electricians were working. It brought no memories at all. I knew that this was my third "bedroom." (The second one was at the reanimation center. Yura and Vadim moved me there after their quarrel with the Director.)

On the next floor they showed me their machine shops.

"We design and build many things on our own. You know how difficult it is to push outside orders." (Yes, I know. I remember my wandering from factory to factory.)

They showed me the drawings of the future installations, including those for long-distance, interplanetary flights. Very interesting.

We moved to Inessa's floor next. She is studying biochemistry in connection with anabiosis. The same chambers and installations, only in miniature—for animals. Saw one test monkey. Small, thin, with a pitiful expression on its wrinkled face. Many laboratory rooms. Modern chemistry with a lot of physics thrown in. Not in my range. But Inessa was explaining everything with enthusiasm, even her cheeks became flushed.

Still higher—the anabiosis physiology floor. An experiment was under way there, and therefore Professor Klimiff did not meet us. We looked in through the glass door.

This sight brought back a host of memories to me . . . The operating table, hanging lamps, anesthetic apparatus. Green sterile robes. Tense figures bent over the table. A large panel on the wall, with functional action figures jumping in the slits. One woman raised her head, looked in our direction and I recognized her—Lena Perova!

And she recognized me. Her eyes over the mask smiled at me. She waved her hand and went back to her work. Good girl!

Yura: "That's right. She's a science candidate now."

I remembered the little laboratory assistant who cried when we operated on animals, and who had a passionate desire to learn.

"How is she doing?"

"Fair. A very good worker—accurate when carrying out instructions. Those are also needed."

Yura's office is on the top floor. "It is quieter this way." A large bay window with a magnificent view of the park and the river shore with a swimming beach, bright umbrellas and weeping willows. And in the winter, probably an endless white wonderland.

The office itself is large, modern, completely functional. Even somewhat cold and bare. But the furniture, though also very modern, is very comfortable.

Yura politely dismissed everyone except Inessa. He did not sit behind his imposing desk with telephones and telescreens, but walked to the window and stood there looking out, tall, angular, but still quietly dominating. After a second or two, he invited me to sit down.

"Let's have some coffee, Ivan Nikolaevich, eh? Inessa Lvovna, perhaps you'd be kind enough to get it for us?"

Inessa—the mistress here?—walked to the wall closet and opened it. There was an automatic coffee-maker there, cups and dishes, and a small refrigerator.

We spoke about anabiosis. I wanted to speak about the past, about my loneliness, about time and those iron fetters which deprive us of happiness and love . . . But instead I asked all the correct questions.

The practical application of anabiosis is still very limited, but they have faith in its future. Especially for space flights.

No, it is still rarely used in therapeutic treatments—only for very complicated surgery with multiple organ transplants. But there is hope that low temperatures will help to unlock the mysteries of the genes.

And in capitalistic countries?

In the few that are still left, good scientific research work often becomes subordinated to "business." There are firms which promise "resurrection" but merely freeze dead bodies and keep them in cold storage. It is simply a form of burial—an expensive form. Churches tried to raise objections, but legally this practice can't be stopped—and it's flourishing. And on the scientific level? Just about the same—real scientists do not condone the "cold storage" practice. Incidentally it is known as the "Prokhoroff method."

Yura thought that was funny. But, deep inside, I caught myself thinking, Well, at least *there* my name is not forgotten.

■ ■

All this conversation has made me look at myself objectively. A dreary person, superficial and given to envy and vanity. Why should a man like me be given a second chance to live? How is he going to repay this privilege?

I'm not feeling well. The world is enormous, terribly complicated, and quite incomprehensibe to me in my present state. I am just a stupid little bolt which accidentally has fallen out of the machine and is now lying on the ground, useless and forgotten. The machine works very well without it.

I am trying to work it all out. "To create a model, study it and find a solution." Here is my diagnosis about my case: "Poisoned by overwork, plus a hormone deficiency." Of course, it is all more complicated, there are many other factors as well. For instance, "the complex of inadequacy."

The treatment? More work. I must select a problem for myself and then catch up with science to be able to search and discover once again.

Seems correct and simple. But where would I get the necessary strength? And then, what for? Any effort is justified if there is some lofty goal. "To make people happy." That would be good.

But how? I'm no fool, I know that this is clearly beyond my reach. The world of information has grown so enormously that my little brain can absorb only a microscopic part of it—even if I live for two hundred years longer. Therefore, all I can do is work on some very small problem. "The influence of A on B." I must scale down my ambition. To grow stupider. To be happy with crumbs.

This is quite possible. Medicine can build up one's optimism, heighten one's instincts, make one almost happy. It had been done, experimentally.

Ziama has told me: "At first the patient becomes bewildered with this sense of euphoria. But then he becomes accustomed to it, finds satisfaction in his limited world. And if there's a good wife and children, he might lose his dependence on drugs and live happily ever after."

No, not for me. I want to thrash about on my own for a while.

This is quite a scientific problem—governing the human psyche by chemical means. Even in my time (I often use this term thinking about myself) there was quite a controversy about it. "Drugs will destroy man." But no, man is basically indestructible; he can even overcome the brain drugs.

Of course, this is dangerous, and in our country, they tell me, this is strictly controlled by scientists. But what about other places? Couldn't this be used for military purposes? But then I noticed that the specter of war has generally receded; war is becoming morally impossible, like cannibalism or slavery. Humanity is growing out of its barbarous infancy.

Strange, I have written a few pages, and I feel better; I am even ready to tackle philosophy, of all things.

■ ■

Undated

Anna and I are in Moscow. A trip to widen my scientific horizons. Eventually I must go abroad as well. All my friends think it is essential.

I feel completely well and have even stopped "listening" to my body. The past is receding further and further away. New interests are taking over. I want to see what has been done in biology and medicine with reference to modeling. My old subject. And, generally, I am now "pro-life."

We walked along some Moscow streets—what a fantastic amount of building has been done during the last twenty years! But still the builders, whoever they are, had good taste to leave some things untouched—have found a way of combining them harmoniously with modern architecture. It is warm, the leaves on the trees are virgin green, as though covered with lacquer. On the boulevards one can smell the spring . . .

Memories . . .

Another summer—a year before the war. . . . I am a student, living on a government grant. I have come to Moscow. Trolley-buses, trucks, cars, Metro stations. What wonderful pastry they sell here. I am standing on the upper balcony in the Bolshoi, listening to Davidova sing *Carmen*. A perfect sense of peace. And yet, Norway, Belgium, Holland and Denmark are gone, and France is passing through her agony. Extermination camps are in operation, and fear hangs over Europe.

Could it be that things are just as misleading now? I have asked Anna.

"No. The world is secure today. Everyone knows everything. There are no secrets."

I knew the Hotel Rossiya before. Once it was the largest hotel here. (Now there is one twice as large.) A tremendous white quadrangle with small churches and boyars' mansions all around it

—built practically anew or restored in all their pristine splendor. But inside the hotel everything has changed; everything is automatic, modern, comfortable, brand-new, functional and yet tasteful.

Our rooms are not adjoining, but close to each other. In Paris, in many hotels, there were often doors between rooms. (Why have I remembered that?)

Yes, information . . . You touch the button in your room and the whole wall lights up—a visual news report from all over the world, day or night. The whole universe is at your finger tips.

And still. Still I don't share Anna's boundless optimism. Science is wonderful, but treacherous. What if some fanatic is composing a gas, or growing a microbe culture brought in from other planets which can paralyze life? No use worrying about those things. Anna is probably right.

We had dinner at the Aragvi. The old name, a brand-new place, but Caucasian food is just as good as ever, and the service almost automatic. (They say that most cooking is done now by electronic infra-red cookers.) We had some red wine. There was a good orchestra, and youngsters were dancing. The cosmos trot. Acrobatic, but graceful. People were dressed with taste—especially the girls; and so many of them were real beauties. (Genetics? Or just prosperity and security?)

Anna sat there, pensive. Somehow there was a touch of sadness about it all. The new world. Not mine. I thought about the past . . . somehow it always seems better than it was. Once, after the theater, I sat like this with Liuba, in this very place. A black lace dress, setting off the whiteness of her shoulders and neck . . . Narrow shoulders, touchingly girlish . . .

Enough. Mere illusions. Life was quite drab. And I had never liked restaurants . . .

"Why are you so sad, Anna?"

"I? Not at all."

"Can't you tell me something about yourself? Just a little. You know everything about me, and I nothing about you. This is unfair."

"You shouldn't have asked. You're not really interested, and my story is not a happy one. Why should you listen to sad stories? But then, this might be a little 'window' for you into the modern world, unfamiliar to you."

"Very well. Tell me."

"Only five years ago I was happy. Very. Unbelievably so. I had found my profession and my place in it. Everything was new, challenging. But, as you know, to a woman this is not the main thing. And so it came to me—love. I got married. He was—what shall I call it?—a sort of modern knight. He was an engineer-physicist at the Cosmic Institute. You know what happiness means. No, you don't; I have read your notes. But I knew it. At the very thought that he would go into the cosmos, my heart stopped beating. Funny—and sad, because this will never be repeated. Within a year we had a son. We couldn't have been happier. But then, they barred Evgenyi from cosmic flights. They found something in his psychology and his genes . . ."

She fell silent. I didn't know what to say. They barred him from the cosmos? So what? Many people are happy right here on our terra firma.

"A year passed, then six months more. A happy family. He got an offer to work at the Cosmic Station. I talked him out of it. 'Wait a little, perhaps you will fly yet . . .' Now I know that was a mistake. And then it happened . . ."

(I started to guess. I knew that she had no children now.)

"It was all my fault. I didn't watch properly. When our Kolia was two years old, he fell from the fifth floor balcony. He had climbed onto a chair and over the railing. I was doing something inside when the neighbors brought him in."

"But medicine?"

"Yes, medicine . . . They brought him back to life, with your chambers, artificial circulation, reanimation . . . I wish they hadn't."

(My God, the cortex!)

"He didn't come to. It lasted for three weeks. You can't imagine this nightmare. Operation in the chamber, artificial circulation, cooling off. Within a day his heart action was fully restored. Five more days of hypothermy. They were hopeful. Then they stopped the cooling. He was breathing, but wouldn't open his eyes. They said, edema of the brain—it might right itself. I was sitting near him day and night, watching . . . Did he smile? No, it was a mere muscular spasm. And before my eyes passed pictures, scenes, sharp as hallucinations—the first time he took my breast, embraced me, pressed his moist mouth to my neck, smiled, laughed; his first steps, first word . . . And there he was lying—alive and not alive, my boy . . ."

A brief pause. Music. Sound of dancing feet.

"What I did there in the kitchen? I don't remember. It was like a film . . . I felt that it had to be stopped there and played all over again."

"And your husband?"

"Husband? He was also there, but we didn't speak to each other. Some wall stood between us. Each lived his own pain, separately."

(Thank God, that music stopped!)

"Then they put me to sleep. When I woke up, he was dead. They killed him. No, of course, I'm talking nonsense; don't listen to me. They just let him die when they knew that his brain was dead. They made very sure—by instruments. But it still seems to me that they were in too much of a hurry. I still see his face. It seemed that he would start waking up . . ."

"You're unjust, Anna. The instrumental test is infallible."

"I know. I know everything. After the funeral, Evgenyi and I came home. Only he was not the same man. We drank some tea, spoke about something insignificant. I took pills and fell asleep. But I didn't sleep long. I woke up and I heard him walking in his room, but I was afraid to go in, afraid he would ask 'What else do you want?' Do you think that's all? No. Had he simply left me, it wouldn't have been so bad. After all, it was my fault, and he had the right to punish me. But not that way . . ."

(She fell silent again. And I thought about myself. My whole life I have been dry, have never really suffered. Probably never really loved, either. Liuba had probably suffered, but not like this one. Anna was speaking again—probably wanted to talk herself out, to unburden herself. That damned music again!)

"He became sick. Not really *sick* sick, but dependent on drugs—neuro-tranquilizers. They have developed many new ones. They don't sell them, but there are ways of getting them. At first he slept a great deal. He acted strange, but I thought it was a normal reaction after what had happened. I didn't want to interfere; I felt guilty. But then he started talking to himself. I would hear him running around his room, laughing, 'Kolia, Kolia!' I would come in, but he wouldn't even notice me. He would swing his arms up and down, laughing, the way he used to play with Kolia. I would throw my arms around him, but he would continue—'Look, Kolia, Mama is here!' Horrible."

(Those damned drugs. I must discuss this with Ziama.)

"I begged him to stop taking those things. 'Why?' he would say. 'Anyway, psychologists have written me off as far as the cosmos is concerned.' Finally I mustered my courage and told him that I would bear him another child. It wasn't easy to say, but I thought it would help. But he just laughed . . ."

"Why didn't you go to the doctors, Anna? Ziama says that now they can control those things."

"My fault again. I was hoping that it would pass. In the mornings he was quite rational. But then they started noticing something at the Institute, pulled tests on him, and sent him to a hospital. And that was that."

"And now?"

"He's there, very sick. They say that something is wrong with his brain. They are treating him, but I don't think there's any hope. Either they don't know what's the matter with him or they wouldn't tell me. They had introduced some electrodes into his brain, stimulating some centers and slowing down others; but that's all for nothing. He has changed a great deal . . ."

Another pause. I was silent too. What could I say anyway? I was very upset, but she became quite calm.

"I visit him every month, in that town of theirs. He is working there as an electrical mechanic—occupational therapy. They have everything there—theaters, shops, recreation rooms. But we have nothing to talk about. He tells me about his work, about films he has seen. Never asks me about myself. But still I feel that he is waiting for my visits, that he's glad to see me . . ."

A pause.

"Everything has changed in me as well. My former clarity is gone. I'm seeing everything in a distorted light."

"I understand. Everything. Forgive me for my blunt advice, but you must start everything all over again."

"That's easy to say . . ."

■ ■

Next morning I got up very early. Anna . . . My head was full of her. Something deep inside me was telling me, "Don't come close." But there was that terrible urge. Somehow everything about her was a promise—the promise of something unusual—light and happy; a sort of holiday. With all that awful tragedy inside her.

And why does she spend her time with me? She must certainly know who I am, that I have nothing, no anchors in this life at all, that I must also start from scratch. Just like her. Maybe that's why.

At breakfast she told me, "Don't think about what I told you yesterday."

Stupid advice. Just like mine to her. I was thinking of nothing else while we drove to the Biosynthesis Institute.

This very name was a shock to me—"Don't tell me that biosynthesis is here?"

"Of course. Even in your time, I think, they had already deciphered the nature of the living cell."

The Institute is located in a new satellite town. This is a new place, the foliage is still young and the buildings ultamodern. But with a good balance between concrete, stainless steel and glass.

Anna knew the local geography, and she took me straightway to the second-floor office of the Director. No one attempted to stop us downstairs and ask whether we had an appointment. All lifts were automatic.

The standard-looking pretty secretary smiled at Anna—she obviously knew her—and I too was favored with a smile. A friendly girl, or was it a standard way of greeting all visitors here? And did this friendliness reflect the personality of her boss?

She opened the door and ushered us in.

"Please, sit down. I'll try to locate the Academician Isakoff for you."

A very large office, but cold and rather bare. A small modern desk with telephones and screens, and modern chairs along the walls. A small table at one side. A large screen on a wall, now dark.

We waited for over five minutes. I was getting annoyed. "Why did we come here in the first place?" But Anna seemed to be at ease. She brought out her notebook and started writing something, paying no attention to me. A typical "newspaper woman"—with wrinkles on her forehead and around her mouth. Concentration. She was different yesterday.

Suddenly the door flew open, and a youngish-looking very tall and thin man walked in. A very high forehead, smooth as a football field, fine intelligent face and sparkles of humor in gray eyes. Instantly I felt warmth flowing across the room. This is how modern scientists should look and act.

"Hullo, Anna! I haven't seen you in centuries. Why? Professor Prokhoroff? I'm delighted to meet you."

He indicated a place for me in a chair near his desk and shouted through the open door: "Marusia! Can you conjure up some coffee for us, sweetheart? Strong!"

Then he checked himself and looked at me appraisingly. "I'm sorry. Would you rather have tea?"

(Once upon a time coffee was an exotic drink in tea-drinking Russia. Many scientists feel as though I had been "asleep" for a hundred years; science had gone so far ahead meanwhile.)

"No, coffee would be fine."

Anna's face brightened up. She must have also caught this little byplay, and she obviously liked this man. And so did I.

"How did you find Moscow? Changed a lot?"

"Changed, yes. But then you people think that you have done miracles while I was gone. Your office, for instance—just like the one I had, only bigger. And no double door. In my time all directors had double doors!"

He laughed. "Ha-ha-ha! The staff architect offered to install them —even insisted—"

"And you resisted?"

He winked at me. "So far, yes. But it's a tough fight."

They brought in the coffee. Quite strong and good, but the cups —modern plastic. Anna picked hers up at once.

"Your cups are ugly. You should see Danilin's. Genuine old porcelain. And the brandy carafe is a work of art."

"I'm green with envy, Annichka. Every time I visit someone I think, That's just what I've got to have. But then I forget. Too many other things to do, damn it."

This small talk continued for about half an hour. But then Anna maneuvered him into serious channels—something we had come here for.

What I heard then was illuminating.

During "my time" this science was in its infancy. But now they had already learned to synthesize albumin. Not all of it, but quite a few ferments had been created, and some other cell structures. (It is here that the large screen on the wall came into play. It proved to be an enormous structural scheme of a pneumococcus, a sort of animated drawing.)

Yes, they had already created schemes of single microbe cells. It had not been easy to separate many thousands of complicated molecules and then put them together—and not haphazardly, but in a strict order to ensure the proper atomic cohesions. A cell in itself is a whole city with its streets and canals, factories, power and chemical plants, warehouses with supplies, a communication network and, most important, a brain center sending orders governing this whole complex, its life, growth and propagation.

My host said, "This is why we can't yet create a multicellular entity in a test tube. The models of the primary cell are so devilishly complex that the human brain can't even imagine them, much less, construct them.

"Then, there's no hope?"

"There is always hope. But here is where computers must come in. Our mathematicians are only approaching these problems now. We have a math department here, but we're nowhere near any practical solution. You'd better see Patzker. Believe me, it would be worth your while."

Our coffee got cold, and the conversation wilted. The Academician could talk on and on, but he quickly realized that biochemistry and biophysics were not my sphere, and that I could hardly follow him. These twenty years which I have "skipped" stood as a barrier between us. Besides, he was a busy man. His Marusia looked in several times and reminded him of his appointments. Finally she was quite firm:

"Lidin is here, waiting, and growing nervous. He is chewing on his pencil."

My host looked at me with comical distress. "From the Ministry. Forgive me. One of my colleagues will show you around."

We took our leave of him. His "colleague" was a rosy-cheeked young man who obviously used no razor yet. He was modest and extremely efficient.

It is difficult to appreciate things you know nothing about, and which can't even be seen. What we saw were centrifugal machines, electronic microscopes, lasers with microbeams. Isotope installations. Rooms with structural designs covering entire walls. And, of course, innumerable computers.

And people—all young, efficient, self-assured. For them I was an uninitiated, a relic of the past. True, an interesting relic, a curious museum piece. Good enough to talk to for a few moments, to stun with some fantastic integral equation or some incomprehensible structural chemical formula. I took all this good-naturedly. Youth. Knowledge and intelligence were obviously there, but wisdom? It is a completely different thing. While talking to them I was trying to guess their future. This one will get stuck here. This one will not last here long; he's already getting bored. And this one will go a very long way, a true budding scientist . . .

I also watched Anna. (I am observing her all the time; in my mind, I'm never away from her.) I was noting her every gesture, every word, every smile. I tried to imagine her as she was some years ago—a young, gay, happy, beautiful girl who liked to flirt and impress people with her intelligence. I also tried to read her attitudes toward the young men around her. She doesn't understand this one . . . She thinks this one is a bore . . . She likes this one . . . Jealousy, I was trying to catch that eternally feminine "come hither" in her looks and smiles. And now and then, I thought I detected it.

All men certainly treated her in a very pronounced masculine manner. This was also true of the Academician. I thought, How well they match each other. What a wonderful couple they would make.

It was both disturbing and sad. Still, I had better get used to it.

May 24

Biologists interest me. Probably biology is something one can get passionately involved in.

On the way from the Institute and during dinner I spoke to Anna about this. She was sympathetic, but noncommittal. (Probably thought that I was just daydreaming, or trying to impress her. Which was partly true.)

We ate supper in the hotel restaurant, and I thought, what now? Her attraction for me was growing constantly, I wanted to come close to her, to feel her body against mine. To touch her. To make love to her. (What a stupid expression.) In my imagination I pictured, in all censorable detail, how this would be. It was pleasant to feel that I was a man once again. (But a disturbing thought: "Am I?")

She got up first. "Shall we go for a walk, or up to my place?"

(There it is! Everything is proceeding according to the classical scenario!)

"I'm a little tired tonight. Let's go up to your place."

We went up to her room. Somehow hotel rooms always suggest frivolity.

"Forgive me. I want to change."

She selected a simple house dress (a fashionable one—very long and with a slit on the side) and went into the bathroom. And I thought: Oh women! Nothing changes them.

In a few minutes she was back, looking stunning. "Sit right there, Ivan Nikolaevich, in that armchair. And I'll sit here, on the divan. And stop thinking about me . . . Yes, yes, I mean it."

I got up and walked toward her. But she stepped back.

"No! I don't want it. If you can't control yourself, go to your room."

What to do? Disregard it, throw my arms around her? In novels this usually works—"In her subconscious she was longing for his caress . . ." No, to hell with novels. And with the subconscious. Extinguish it. Crush it. Be noble.

"Really, Anna . . . You're insulting me."

(It was almost exactly like this *then*—with Liuba. Only the words were different. Then, I was a masterful male. But I was no longer the young man I was then; it would be ridiculous to repeat the pattern.)

I sat down, and she relaxed.

"This is better. Now, tell me, are you serious about your interest in theoretical science? Judging by your notes, you have always been a typical physiologist-experimenter whose hands always went ahead of any theory."

This was becoming annoying.

"This is not true. I was always interested in theories. But in my time theoretical biology was an empty concept."

"And why do you think it may interest you now? Why not go back to your proper work?"

Proper work! This wasn't at all what I wanted to discuss coming up here. Science again! To hell with science! It has ruined my "first" life, and now it is ruining my "second." Once you are "typed" you can't get out of it—you're a "scientist," and you are supposed to be absent-minded and not altogether human.

I'm afraid I was rather abrupt with Anna. I told her it was not up to her to judge what I must or mustn't do. I was no genius, and I didn't expect to accomplish anything new in my "proper work"—I didn't even understand half of what Yura was telling me about it. And it didn't interest me any longer. Anabiosis was the focal point, but now it was accomplished, and it was not my style to tinker with technical details. When I first tackled the problem it was a virgin one—"modeling the inner structure of the human body." Now it was old hat. A problem for technicians.

I did not even try to contain myself and told her about my bitterness about some of "my former pupils" grabbing credit for my work while, in fact, I was a pioneer there.

Anna seemed undisturbed by my outburst.

"Do you want me to write an article and reestablish your priority?"

This hit me as mockery. All my romantic aspirations were now completely gone. Anna was a stupid lightheaded female with pseudo-scientific ambitions who had the colossal nerve to appoint herself as my guardian.

"Forgive me, I'm really tired. I think I'd better go to bed."

I wasn't tired at all, and it was quite early.

I went for a walk along the Moskva river—the same embankment where I walked fifty years before. The city was glittering around me with millions of lights, and the Kremlin cupolas shone against a pale summer sky. Then it grew dark. The hum of traffic; snatches of music; black water under bridges.

Gradually I calmed down. Walking is good therapy. It eliminates adrenalin in the system.

What was the matter with me? I have always known exactly what I wanted, could analyze everything and make my own decisions. And now . . . lost and bewildered. Was this because of that woman in the slit dress? Hormones. Or just loneliness in this strange, cruel world? But why call it cruel? It wasn't cruel at all. It was trying to bring up new generations of adjusted and happy people—without contradictions and complexes. Perhaps it was I who was simply out of tune with it. A rank outsider tortured by his "inadequacy complex."

Anna. She was the key to everything.

But I was no good for her. Even if we could disregard our age difference, I could offer her absolutely nothing besides utter confusion, emotional homelessness.

Why was everything so damned complicated?

The walk did me good. I slept well—and even without the "sleep automat," that ridiculous-looking plastic mask which is standard equipment in all hotels nowadays.

May 26

She came in in the morning just as if nothing had happened. A firm handshake, a bright morning smile.

"Are we going to keep on quarreling, Professor?"

I was ashamed of my childish behavior of the previous night.

"Forgive me, Anna. You must understand my situation. I know that I have fallen far behind the present level of science. Still I want to tackle some real problem, and not become a mere scientific filing clerk."

"Spoken like a real man! Are we going to eat here or in the restaurant?"

"Here."

Automation. Three buttons, three different breakfast menus. In a few minutes, a bell and a small door in the wall springs open. Two trays.

Lucullus probably would not have approved of this mechanical feeding, but scientifically all the necessary vitamins and minerals are here, even though portions are rather small. However, one can repeat the whole operation if one is still hungry. (Overeating is the latest medical bugaboo. And for those suffering from obesity there is an electronic process removing excess calories from all foods.)

We spoke about Academician Isakoff. Anna told me that he had left his wife and was considered a stormy petrel of science. Has been conducting a running fight with the Science Ministries and the Academy. With that mild manner of his? I felt an instant sympathy for him. I used to be a rebel, but I didn't know how to control my temper. (How come Anna knows so much about him, and particularly about his private life?)

Then Anna became serious.

"I've been thinking, Ivan Nikolaevich. Instead of going around and seeing all those celebrities who are too busy to give any attention to you, why don't you let me fill you in about all the latest in science?"

Probably my face registered my doubt; she went on:

"I mean it. I have had a good modern all-around education, and for the last ten years I have been writing about science—and not once have I been caught in any serious blunder. You'd save yourself a good deal of time."

I liked the proposition. I liked it very much. This was an obvious short cut for me. I have never felt easy with all those luminaries, and library research was a tedious and time-consuming affair. And, of course, this presupposed our being together.

(Who knows, perhaps this is not as hopeless as I thought last night. Often, they say, a sharp conflict brings people together quicker than anything else.)

I saw that Anna was studying me, and I felt uneasy under her steady gaze. "Why are you looking at me that way?"

I knew the answer, of course. She was reading my thoughts and evaluating my attitude—was I serious about it all or just trying to find a way of getting closer to her as a woman? This morning she was in no mood for any romantic nonsense. She was a different woman from the one who told me her heartbreaking story and sought my sympathy over a plate of electronically cooked shish-kebab.

That was a temporary weakness. This morning she was a strong, clear-minded woman, devoted to her work. What was her work? She was now collecting material for her monumental article on "Artificial Intelligence." She had told me about it—something very complicated, almost like science fiction.

We had a good, long, constructive session. She told me about all the latest findings and theories, and I was impressed more and more with her erudition, her clarity of thought, her economy in formulating complicated theories. (A journalistic proclivity.)

Once or twice, while talking to me, she leaned over and I could feel the roundness of her breast against my arm. But when I attempted the same maneuver, she broke away, laughing, and offered me a white tablet to "calm me down."

"I've been taking them now and then, ever since I became a

bachelor girl. I'm not made of wood, you know, and I'm not good at having affairs."

A tablet against love! I was flabbergasted.

Anna told me that it was quite effective; a man or a woman became sexually inert for a while. It was useful where there was a separation of sexes, or when a person had to concentrate on some important task requiring complete dedication.

This was already the twenty-first century—a chemical way of creating well-being. One could get a prescription only from psychologists, and they were very careful about prescribing it. It could affect families and create a number of other serious problems.

"I think you really need one." (Laughingly.)

I refused, of course, also laughingly. There was something degrading about the very idea. Or was I hopelessly old-fashioned?

But then perhaps I needed it? It was obvious to me that my masculine urges had not only survived anabiosis, but might have been actually heightened by it. (Interesting; it should be studied.) But a tablet? No. If worse came to worst, there were many women in the world, and I had become "interesting" to some of them—a man who had come from the dead. Curiosity and sex are strongly interrelated; I have been noticing some appraising glances in my direction.

To give it a try? No. That was just a momentary thought. Not a serious one, of course. Thoughts like that often occur to all normal men. But I knew that Anna's "presence" in me left no room for anyone else.

And Anna wanted to work, and to put me to work as well. If I wanted to keep her near me I had to find my new place in this strange world.

■ ■

The labor problem in the new society is a complicated one. There's not enough interesting, creative work for all who are able and willing to perform it, and there is a good deal of work that must be done even if it is not glamorous or interesting. And then, there are also incorrigible loafers. The problem is to apportion the labor force according to professional and geographic needs of the country without using compulsion.

Laziness is still with us, it seems. Ziama defines it as a distinct psychological problem, and a very difficult one at that.

Society supports loafers as well as everybody else. There is no question of anyone's going hungry or being deprived of his basic needs. But habitual loafers are well known, and are listed at the Central Labor Office. The state tries to reeducate them, to inject industriousness into them, not so much through financial rewards as by psychological and sociological means—self-respect, respect of others, and the sense of duty. It works in some cases. There are few really incorrigibles and, according to Ziama, they are sick people, psychological cripples. The creative urge is a normal component of the healthy human body and human psyche, and its total absence indicates morbidity.

Then, of course, society provides those people with the basic necessities, but not any of the important "extras"—these have to be earned—so there is a "stick" as well as a "carrot."

All in all, the system works fairly well. The shortcomings of some are more than offset by the enthusiasm of others who glory in their achievements, and overfulfill their quotas.

The problems of personality in relation to society, of duty and the innate need of personal freedom from this society, are still here and are still causing unhappiness. But all these problems are being gradually adjusted. Idealism is a great force, and faith in man's basic goodness pays dividends.

"Once you accept that man is good, and place the burden of proof on him, he will become better and better."

This is what I heard today in the Psychology Institute. (We spent an hour there with Professor Sinitzin in his old-fashioned office hung with portraits of science pioneers; even old man Freud was there.) Sinitzin is not a young man—he is nearing seventy—but he is all in the future. He lives in it. "Humanity is improving with each generation. It is quite possible—no, necessary—to create universal happiness by balancing all material needs with the spiritual urges. We are moving that way, and faster than many suspect!"

One can only hope that he is right.

June 7

It all happened. It had been building up for many days and nights—that electricity between us. And finally the dam burst. It was so simple that it was almost a letdown.

After dinner we went up to Anna's room to get her raincoat. (It was drizzling outside. My whole life has been changed by meteorology!) We didn't speak a single word. One moment Anna was removing her raincoat from a closet, and in another she was in my arms.

I remember every little detail of that evening, and will never forget it.

With Liuba, many years ago, it was different. Worse or better? Neither. Just different. No two loves, and I am using this naïve term intentionally, are ever alike. Since love, as differentiated from sex, is a cerebral process, and since no two human brains are exactly alike, it is a mathematical impossibility to hit twice any one combination of factors. I should speak to Ziama about this, but obviously this is impossible at the moment. I suspect that he himself has been in love with Anna for years.

How strange it is to feel her body next to mine! Just feel—without any thoughts. Draw her head toward me and kiss her dark hair with its own peculiar aroma. And think in short snatches—How everything has suddenly changed . . . The whole world has become different . . . And how primitive it all really is—and how terribly complicated at the same time!

So once again I have a *sanctuary*—a place in which to hide from my own thoughts; a person with whom I can forget that science has gone ahead and left me behind, that I have no longer any meaningful place in it with my mental poverty, and that anyway machines are threatening to eliminate man. Now all that is unimportant. All I want is to lie next to this woman and let all the angry waves break somewhere over our heads. Nothing can touch us as long as we are together.

I know that she thinks the same things. That the piece of ice which she has been carrying in her soul ever since her tragedy is slowly melting.

And what about Liuba? She's dead. And what about Evgenyi Stakhevich, Anna's husband? He's worse than dead, because, unlike Liuba, he can still feel his nonexistence.

They are not here, but I feel their presence. Perhaps she does as well. Isn't that why she slowly pulled her arm from under my head in such a way that I would not notice it?

No, I don't want to think anything. No, not now.

To kiss her . . . to move still closer to her . . . to protect her . . . to let her protect me . . . And then? And then live and work. Only now I know the meaning and the purpose of my "second life."

Anna. How suddenly fascinating do these four letters sound. A symphony.

■ ■

June 10

The idea of artificial intellect is still not clear to me. There are just a few of these "thinking" installations in our country; and their capacities, as well as their programs, are limited. The most advanced one is said to be in Japan. From what I have heard from specialists, I understand that these mechanical entities, when fully perfected, would not only perform useful tasks, but live their own "lives."

I must look into this. Now all this interests me very much.

I went to the Institute of Mathematical Modeling, and met the celebrated Patzker.

An almost comical figure. Very small, gnomelike man with enormous ears and completely bald head. Very fast and excitable. Swings his arms like a miniature windmill.

He met us with a deep theatrical bow. "Am I becoming popular nowadays! Visitors, visitors, visitors. And all because of you, Anna! Your articles are making me famous. I'd be a forgotten man without you."

Anna introduced me. He looked at me with frank curiosity and then passed his verdict: "You look surprisingly alive after twenty years beyond the Pale."

His ironic manner was irking me.

"We haven't come here to exhibit myself, Professor. We'd rather hear something about your work."

"Good, good. Sit down. I can tell you quite a lot."

He is probably a very happy man. No misgivings or doubts. He knows that he is a genius, that there are supposed to exist only two other men (and one woman!) who can fully understand him, and he feels no need to be modest about it.

"We mathematicians—abstract mathematicians that is—live in our own world, the world of symbols. Our science was created by our predecessors out of their study of nature, but now it has outgrown nature. It has become independent and is developing on its own."

"Without any connection with life?"

He gave me an amused look. ("Ignoramus.")

"Well, not quite. Life poses problems to us, and we solve them. But also we go much further; we develop our own world of pure abstractions. Some of them might become applicable in the future, or might not. But that does not bother us; they are mere stepping-stones into future theories. Future truths. For instance, Einstein established an absolute constant—the velocity of light as the highest velocity existing in nature. Then came Gerald Feinberg and brought in 'tachyons'—the velocities billion times higher than that of light—and both of them were correct; they advanced science. Now we are demolishing Feinberg's theories. Nature is infinite, and so is mathematics; there is absolutely nothing, nothing at all, that can't be achieved. And the beauty of it is that there is no final, terminal truth. There will be other truths lying beyond that final one. Ad infinitum."

Anna saw that Patzker was losing me, and she tried to switch him into something I was really interested in—his theory of embryogenesis.

Patzker smiled quickly ("of course, who am I talking to?") and tried to oblige. "You want to know how personalities are programed on the gene level? Is it possible to determine on that submicroscopic level the functions of future systems by studying billions of primary bioparticles which can't be seen even with the help of the most powerful electronic microscope? Well, biologists have been defeated there. They could not even approach it. Not enough here." He indicated his bald forehead. "It took Patzker to create the theory of developing systems."

"How did you do it?"

"By the language of abstract symbols I have described the principles of the genetic code in which we determine the governing rules of primary genetic cells, their growth, multiplication, differentiations; in other words, the formation of specialized tissues which will later form organs and whole organisms. I have shown how these submicroscopic models are converted into complex systems—well, human bodies, for instance."

I asked him if his theories were connected with biology.

Patzker made a grimace of utter disdain. "I wouldn't know—I have nothing to do with that kitchen. Let biologists find their own ways; I have charted the main courses for them. If they were really intelligent—which they are not—they would, using my theories, create not merely artificial human systems, but self-propagating robots who would take over from them and carry on on their own."

Patzker was speaking to me, closely observing the effect which his words produced on me. Anna was sitting behind him and making comical faces for my benefit. This was disturbing to me, but at the same time pleasant; it showed that she was in good humor and wanted to share it with me.

I tried to cope with the conversation as best I could.

"And what about mutation? Transformation? Evolution?"

"Everything is taken care of. I haven't missed a single angle. Would you care to hear more about it?"

From his long, verbose and very technical explanation I understood that he had created an informatory and very primitive model of the origin of life. Of course, the conversion of his theories into practice was a very complex problem ("I have no time for mechanics!"), but the very formulization of the problem was an important step forward—if, of course, his theoretical equations were correct. This I could not tell, even though he often referred to the enormous blackboard in the room covered with rather messy curlicues. Even when seated behind his desk he always held a piece of chalk in his hand which he waved in the air like a magic wand.

It is interesting to watch people. This very Patzker was undoubtedly an extremely brilliant man, but at the same time I felt a lack of real depth in him. If he was a genius he was a pompous and shallow one—and obviously an exhibitionist feeding upon my ignorance.

Later Anna told me about his rather off-color intrigues in the Academy, which led to the retirement of the former director of the

Institute over which he now presided. (The man later died in obscurity.)

I was slightly annoyed with Anna. "You shouldn't repeat those things. That's gossip."

"Not quite. There are facts. To some people—to this Patzker, for instance—the end justifies all means. And in science, people like that are dangerous; there is no room for *fuehrers* there."

Idealism or a mere pose?

■ ■

Anna can be quite sharp and ill-tempered. My life with her resembles a meteorological station—sunshine one moment, storm another. She explains her irritability by her "false position."

"Please don't be offended. All this is not easy for me."

Why? I am making no demands on her, I don't advertise the fact that she is my lover, and morally she has no obligations to anyone. But women are women; they like to saddle men with some vague guilt complex the moment they "surrender" to them. (In all honesty, in our case she was the one who chose to do this of her own free will.)

Human instincts and stimuli are degradingly primitive. One of the strongest of them is the sex urge. It is stronger in men than in women, and this disparity gives them a distinct advantage. It is something like the mathematical odds of the roulette table: in the end you must lose.

I know that to win Anna completely I must perform some remarkable feat. To make a startling scientific discovery, and to present it to her. (In my time this was called "placing something at her feet.")

But in Anna's case this must be something important. She is intelligent and demanding, and it is impossible to put anything over on her. She's no scientist, but she knows science.

So I must get to work. And hope that, winning Anna, I will at the same time benefit humanity in some way.

June 15

I was wrong about instincts and stimuli. That was an attitude prevalent in my youth; we liked to pick on some single stimulus and elevate it into a universal law. "Sex and hunger rule the world. . . . Economics: the rich and the poor. . . . The Alpha and the Omega of everything."

In fact human motivations are much more complicated. Every act is a result of the interinfluence of a whole network of complex stimuli. It is very rare that a person is driven by a single urge—sex, vanity, or the joy of accomplishment. (In fact, the latter two are mere variations of the sex urge.) Besides, the difference between man and animal is that man's intellect is often stronger than his instincts.

This is comforting to me at this point—to think that I'm superior to a mere male animal in love. Just a small scientific note: anabiosis does not destroy or even inhibit man's sexual potential.

In general, I'm getting ready to go to work. To try my new wings, so to speak. My first problem: to familiarize myself with the language of modern science—mathematics and the modeling of complex systems.

June 17

I am going abroad!

Yesterday I had a long videophone conversation with the director of the Psychology Institute. (I am technically assigned to it.) He suggested this trip in order for me to get acquainted with the new world and new science. Said it was important for my future work. (I still have no idea what this work will be.)

My itinerary is still only general. I am to visit two countries—the United States and Japan, to see their science centers and how people have changed there during my "sleep." (Have they changed at all?) And, of course, while in Japan, to familiarize myself with Professor Yamaga's work—his vaunted "artificial intelligence," which is still a very controversial subject.

All travel details will be taken care of by the Institute—tickets, hotels, spending money. They won't allow me much spending cash, but my personal needs are very modest.

I am leaving on July 2.

Meanwhile I'll fly home—to speak to the Director and to Ziama. I have more faith in him than in local psychologists. Anna will remain in Moscow meanwhile, working on her article.

June 20

She was very tender to me during our last night together in Moscow. We had the whole night to ourselves, and this was not the first one. How late in life one begins to appreciate certain things! The difference between a fleeting love affair and conjugal security.

I am not jealous about her past, even though there are grounds for that. She had confessed to me that she had had some "fleeting involvements" since parting from her husband. Also she is quite attached to him, even now. But this is mainly a hurt pride on my part and the realization of my own limitations—I must be a real bore outside my scientific interests.

I have no idea how our relationship is going to develop. On certain days it seems that the inner ice within her has completely melted, but then, suddenly, there is a complete freeze-up. "I have my own life to live, Ivan."

So she has, but as far as I am concerned, she's becoming a permanent part of mine. I feel her "presence" constantly. When I'm alone, I'm not quite alone; there is that constant nagging longing to see her, to be with her. I'm becoming a dope addict, and she is my dope.

Today I called her on the videophone. On the small screen she looks even more beautiful.

"No business at all. I just wanted to see you."

"I'm sorry, Ivan, I'm very busy. Forgive me."

A cut-off click. This hurts a little. Am I really so much in love?

■ ■

I'm living again. Thinking. Studying.

I have hit upon a new idea. The victory over death. Immortality and perennial youth. Romantic dreams of poets. Faust. No, the elementary hope of a doomed man.

We are all doomed, but I know what death really means. I remember everything. I remember that hairy paw which gripped my heart and held it fast. I felt it every time my heart contracted. And I could not forget it for a single moment: I learned to live with death. I could still read a book, organize an experiment, but could not accomplish anything significant. I knew I had no time for that.

It is different now. I am alive. Once again. For how long this time?

Never mind. I have already received a good advance payment from this new life. Anna.

True, she is like a brittle vase which I am carrying while scaling a steep mountain. At any moment I might fall down and shatter it. Also that constant fear that she will be stolen from me. By someone younger or, what is more important, more brilliant than I. (She is allergic to fools.) It isn't comfortable to live when one is driven by a single stimulus, love.

Love? Yes, probably. The "presence" in any case. No mad desire on either side. But then, of course, I'm no young boy, and Anna is incapable of "losing her head" completely. She has some built-in brakes. Does our involvement make sense? I often look at myself objectively and feel a strange embarrassment—do I cut a comical figure to others in my part of a "young lover"?

However, back to immortality: When I say "immortality," I mean a greatly extended longevity. Does this interest me in relation to myself? No. But it is a tremendous problem for a scientist. The first thing I must determine is to what extent the process of aging is "programed" in the genes. According to Patzker, everything is achievable—even actual immortality. But then nature has its own laws, and death is biologically necessary for progress. Without it nothing would move ahead.

Life is a constant reproduction of copies from ready patterns. A simple reproduction of single cells. What is baffling is why a child's cells are different from those of its mother? But even that can be explained—another phase of the same program. Another (and improved) model goes into production. The original model has become obsolete.

Life works rather like a linotype. A single metal pattern produces impressions.

But then, no pattern can produce endless copies. It becomes worn out and must be discarded and melted down. In that case there is no solution; death is an integral part of the basic program. The brain doesn't want to accept this inevitability, and there must be a way of improving the pattern so that it would not wear out quite as soon as it does now. To achieve that, one must start from the cell level. It is difficult to determine the exact number of the programed copies of every cell, but mathematically this must be possible. It has already been done in the case of a human body while it continues its original growth. (I must give an order to the central science library about this.)

My idea about old age: the accumulation of foreign particles causing friction. This leads to worn-out models and, therefore, poor copies. Finally there is a point when copies can't be produced at all. Death.

July 2

Traveling. Essentially it is freedom from everyday responsibilities, an escape, a sort of timelessness. Life goes on as before, but it no longer concerns you. You are on your own—you are walking around, seeing things, receiving new impressions, and you are no longer chained to the wheelbarrow of your daily life. This is rather like "thought-weightlessness." If something goes wrong back home, distance protects you from the immediate shock. By the time you get back, the problem will be somehow resolved. You don't exist there—you might as well be dead, for that matter.

However, even in my time the sense of distance was already shrinking. The world was contracting into a small globe of matter. And now, distances are all but gone. At any moment I can see *their* faces on the long-distance videophone, and within a very few hours I might be pulled back into reality—by death, sickness, or merely by the whim of my superior. No, there is no longer any place on this earth where a man can get lost—not in the jungles, not in the tundra.

Still, movement is life. Without movement there is no time and no life. (And also no death?) The very thought that one can go anywhere on a moment's notice makes all the difference, even when one stays in the same place his whole life. And now this theoretical freedom of movement is available to all—the global passport.

One can go to the Crimea. To Nice. To Valparaiso. Lie on the sand, listen to the waves, and stop thinking. For how long? A day? A week? One can go to Mexico, drink tequilla in a little tavern and listen to wandering musicians. One can go and see Mona Lisa. For ten minutes. For half an hour. And then?

Actually all this moving about is even unnecessary. Without stirring at all, one can see all this; it is recorded on film and in sound (and even in smell!), and any good travel library can take you around the world in half an hour. Giving you, at the same time, all the pertinent facts and figures which would take a lifetime to collect and organize.

Then, actual traveling is nothing but getting physical impressions—via your skin, stomach, nose.

They say that soon even that will be available at home—through mechanically controlled dreams. One will be able to order dreams in advance—educational, pleasant, comical, sensual, erotic, with both good and bad endings.

One moment—an idea! Why not use dreams to enrich man's sum of personal experiences? To demonstrate visually and emotionally all the advantages of present living which people now take for granted? Why not let them actually experience the pain of parting, treason, illness, hunger, war and death—actually experience them. Savagery, cannibalism, slavery, massacres. Then they would appreciate all the sacrifices of the previous generations. Youngsters today don't even believe in all those things. For them they are unreal—rather like the "horror tales" told by old nurses to scare children into obedience.

I am leaving today. Anna approves. "You need a good shake." (As if I were an old garment that had lain in a trunk for years. This is even a bit offensive.) Or does she want to be alone for a while? To rest from love, to organize her emotions? Very likely.

July 4

At first glance, New York does not seem to have changed a great deal. Or is my memory at fault here? All I really recall are the Manhattan skyscrapers. And they are still here—more of them than ever.

No, there are changes, of course. In my hotel room I am looking at the pictures of New York of "my time" and compare them with the same places as they appear today. (There is a direct hookup here with the central telelibrary, and one can order any program one wishes to see. Today is the American national holiday, but those libraries function day and night throughout the year.) Whole blocks of old tenements have been demolished, and the space has been turned into parks and lawns, while the rest of the city has grown upward. These new parks have beautiful flower displays. In my time people used to go to Rockefeller Center on Easter Sunday to admire flowers. While pictures are flashed on, the narrators cite exact figures—in billions of dollars, of course—spent by the city for all these improvements. Americans are still dollar-conscious, it seems. However, all this is truly impressive.

It is very hot outside, and sticky, but the air is clean and sweet —artificial aromatization and electronic automobiles. (The old gasoline and Diesel engines have been relegated to the open country.) The old subway has been completely rebuilt and modernized, and the whole operation is automatic. The trees in Central Park seem to have grown—there are many more shady walks there now. I walked there yesterday, after my arrival, trying to recapture old memories.

Anna would say, "Why write all those things? I can see them all by just pressing a button."

You are right, Anna. No more. This is just an old man's old habit.

Anna . . . I can still feel her, every bit of her. I can see every little wrinkle on her face, I can feel the roundness of her small breasts on my palms, and then my heart begins to beat faster. It would be good just to live, enjoying life, without knowing what is going there, inside you, forgetting time which is forever destroying cells of your body. Excessive anatomical knowledge destroys happiness. Our psyche is full of spies reporting to the brain. This one represents science: "You are nothing, but a machine which is quickly wearing out." This one, society: "Is this moral or ethical?" And this one works for Liuba: "How easily and quickly you have forgotten me." And there are many, many others, constantly watching you, censoring you, correcting, guiding. "Don't do this, and don't do that. This is forbidden, *zapreschcheno, verboten, interdit.*" Only very infrequently some strong passion or emotion temporarily blots them out.

Primitive man had the same problems, only his memories were of shorter duration; his brain was not as retentive, and his animal instincts were stronger. And he had no mechanical means of recording his thoughts.

Perhaps instead of electronically lengthening our memory we should think of shortening it?

(A note for scientists of the future: Working on "immortality," we should create a self-regulating memory control which will eliminate all the memory dross and retain only the things that are essential and constructive.)

Is love constructive or destructive?

On a purely biological level it is both. It produces progeny and then destroys the "parents," who have served their purpose. But what about human love which has become more cerebral than physical?

I have no words to describe love. Scientific terminology has emasculated my vocabulary. I'm a word-pauper—in all the languages I know.

■ ■

My room in the old Hilton Hotel on the Avenue of the Americas. The center of the city. It is not large, but comfortable and very functional. A direct connection with the Central Telelibrary in Washington, and any information is instantly available; even the most complicated and specialized order is filled within seconds. This service costs ten dollars a day. "Our electronic telelibrary is the oldest and most complete in the world." Perhaps. Who is going to contest it? The power of publicity is that it is largely accepted on faith.

Otherwise the room is not different from a room in any modern hotel throughout the world. One can get instant meals—for all tastes and prices. The usual battery of automatic installations. There are rooms with three-dimensional color television with automatic "emotion controls," but this is a very expensive pleasure. Beyond my means.

I am concentrating on scientific subjects. Their art programs I can see at home, on my own television screen.

July 10

America is a complicated phenomenon. Always was and still is. A fascinating mixture of tomorrow and yesterday.

Three days ago I visited Columbia University's new Institute of Applied Chemistry. I had a letter to Professor Karl Schwartzerberg there. He is supposed to be the world's authority on body chemistry on all levels. A brand-new glass-and-chromium building facing the Hudson. And with flower beds all around it.

Schwartzerberg is a huge and very fat man with a round, moon-like face and triple chin, dressed in an immaculate white suit. (American technology is amazing. New York has one of the most uncomfortable climates in the world in summer, and so American cloth manufacturers have developed an electrically cooled fabric—a small battery in your pocket keeps you cool in any weather. I priced one of those jackets in a store, but it did not fit my budget, and I'm melting.)

It is not the sartorial elegance which impressed me in Schwartzerberg, but his utter lack of humanity in discussing the problems of the human race. For him any person is a chemical formula which can be artificially changed in any desired way. His present preoccupation is the "chemistry of happiness."

"Man can be perfectly controlled by chemistry—and will be. We are developing a whole set of chemicals which will control people's emotions as well as their body functions. Any schizophrenic and manic-depressive can be changed into an adjusted and permanently happy human being. Happiness will be produced in our laboratories and sold in drugstores at nominal prices. We are conducting experiments at present in mental hospitals. There are still some harmful aftereffects, but they will be eliminated—we are eliminating them. And then all your socialist and communist notions will become obsolete; people will be perfectly happy even in the most uncomfortable physical surroundings. We are composing a new Golden Age in our test tubes."

I tried to argue with him. "But wouldn't this violate people's freedom of choice of life environments, of striving for a better future for themselves and their children, of the very 'pursuit of happiness' your Constitution is speaking about?"

"But why pursue happiness when you can buy a weekly supply of it for fifty cents?"

"This would arrest progress."

"On the contrary. Progress has been often retarded by undisciplined acts of discontented masses—wars, riots, revolutions, social upheavals. Chemistry will make everyone contented and manageable, and then science will be able to work efficiently and swiftly bettering the general conditions of life on this earth."

It was pointless to argue with this fat man obsessed by his inhuman idea of turning humanity into chemical formulas. I left with a strange feeling of emotional discomfort.

I went about on foot whenever I could and eventually found myself on Fifth Avenue, one of the handsomest streets in the world. There I saw the old Roman Catholic cathedral and went inside, primarily to escape the broiling sun. It was not a very old church compared to some European churches, but it looked ancient against the background of modern architecture choking it from all sides.

I watched the people coming in.

They were approaching the Crucifix near the entrance, dipping their fingers in the holy water, crossing themselves. There was a cash box. Was it soundproofed? I noticed that coins made no sound dropping into it.

Semidarkness. Silence. (It was a weekday.) In one wing there was a small knot of kneeling people—probably a particularly venerated Madonna. Some dozen or so people were scattered about the enormous church, resting, praying or, like me, just thinking.

What were they thinking about? Did they believe in God? For instance, that young girl with the empty eyes?

Here, under those high arches, eternity and all daily worries seem to assume their proper perspective—actual insignificance. Man has a basic need to complain, to seek support. It is very important to have someone to whom you can complain. Mother, wife, lover, friend. And if you have no one at all, then there is

God. Even if one doesn't really believe in his existence. "My God, what shall I do now?"

Silence.

Echoing footsteps now and then.

It is sad that in our present city planning we have no places where one can sit alone and think—under high, cold arches. Still better, when there is an organ.

Our psychologists must design such places where one can sense eternity. Something like Buddhist meditation groves, but without any prefabricated dogmas. (And without chemistry!)

July 11

There is no official ideology in this country. That is, Christianity is not actively supported, socialism is not encouraged (even though widely practiced), and the majority of people simply don't burden themselves with any ideological problems. According to the latest polls, religious principles still govern man's behavior to a large degree here. Some forty percent of those polled stated that they were directly affected by them. Out of the rest, about one half were "don't know's," and another half recognized religion as an important controlling factor. (The "rules of civilized behavior.")

In the Rockefeller Research Center I felt myself at home. There they knew and understood everything, and we were speaking the same language—models and programs.

Then what was the basic difference between our societies?

Dr. Frank Barrow, the director of the Department of Sociology, expressed it this way:

"The difference lies in coefficients. The characteristics of the human psyche, given by our psychologists for sociological models, have different coefficients of the pleasure-center stimulation than yours. In the balance of emotional and psychological comfort of our people, the instinct of possession, as we call it, still plays an important part. 'To live in one's own house . . . to own a new automobile . . . to have a secure and comfortable old age . . .' Despite the fact that our economy can satisfy all human needs, and more, money has become a powerful psychological symbol. This leads, in some cases, to the money cult, which, of course, is a negative factor. It corrupts the psyche while a healthy competitive drive doesn't. We are trying to prevent the process of greed erosion. Our weapon is science. Humanistic education, introduction of higher ethics. And we are making progress. There are very many people who now set intellectual values above the material. And this is true of people on all material levels."

"Then, according to you, Doctor Barrow, your millionaires are ready for socialism?"

Barrow smiled. "Mere semantics, Professor. Any organized society is basically socialistic. Socialism, as a planned economy, is here and nothing can stop it, because it is an efficient form of management. Only, we avoid this word. True, we recognize the acquisitive instinct, but we are trying to direct it into productive channels ensuring the growth of public wealth instead of resisting it. We believe that sooner or later, the level of material abundance will reach the saturation point, when private acquisition as such will become meaningless and the so-called 'dollar psychosis' will simply die out. Whatever you say, the acquisition drive is a powerful part of human nature. The problem is to control it, to guide it, and not permit it to get out of hand. What do you think?"

"I think that less powerful but finer stimuli can perform the same task. Since technology has organized the economy rationally and efficiently, why prod it by greed? We are trying to avoid it. We might lose something in the process, but we also gain a great deal: idealism and freedom from the corrupting influence of naked greed."

Did he understand me? I think so. After all, they are also moving into socialism, only with great detours. But they are still afraid of semantics—"socialism," "communism," "planned economy." Sooner or later they will overcome this fear, or else will invent some other, acceptable terms for those words.

In the world since my "departure," the most important change that I have noticed is the almost total elimination of the fear of war among younger people. The suicidal superweapons made any large-scale war impossible, and the prolonged induced state of peace seems to have made the very idea of war intellectually unacceptable. Rather like cannibalism. And this is not because human flesh has lost its fine flavor. (In fact, modern diet might have actually improved it.) But it simply doesn't occur to anyone that a person he talks to could be killed, cooked and eaten.

War has been the cancer of humanity throughout history. And once it is eliminated, humanity has nothing to fear any longer. Science will solve all of its other problems.

July 13

A tourist taking a guided tour rarely sees much. Personally, I like to explore cities on my own, preferably on foot. The new moving sidewalks make "walking" easy even though they contribute, I'm afraid, to the eventual leg atrophy. All main thoroughfares here have these elevated moving sidewalks leaving the streets to vehicular traffic.

I visited Wall Street. A fantastic man-made canyon, almost deserted on weekends. The rows of skyscrapers housing world-famous companies and monopolies, or "groups," as they are now called. "The stronghold of capitalism." I saw the Stock Exchange, about which I have read so much. The building is new, and everything inside has been automatized. Screaming mobs of speculators are a thing of the past; all transactions are registered by electronic automats. Each bid is registered and as soon as a corresponding offer arrives, two machines close the deal. The entire business of large monopolies, as well as many industries, is run now by computers. (The trade unions are now fighting for a 25-hour work week instead of the present 30.)

Americans say that Roosevelt saved capitalism, but also dealt it a death blow by introducing government controls. The whole economy of this enormous country, and other countries depending on it, is now run by the all-powerful triumvirate: management, trade unions and the government, with the government assuming more and more power. Old-time free-enterprise advocates are complaining bitterly. "Taxes, taxes, taxes. They are going to tax the country into Communism!"

Technology has changed the nature of capitalism. The very term is becoming obsolete. Quite possibly, machines will eventually liquidate it altogether. But, here at least, they have not yet resolved all problems and contradictions of a society that still uses greed in its planning.

But the race problem, so acute here during my last visit, is being gradually solved—by biological integration. The government grants a special tax relief to all interracial married couples, and there are very many dark-skinned children everywhere, and some of them are real charmers. And they say that on the average they are doing better in school than all-white or all-black children.

What strikes one about America is overproduction of everything—a mad competition to sell as many unnecessary articles to the people as possible. And the planned waste. Everything is "disposable" and is thrown away almost as soon as it is used once. Theoretically, this should make everyone satisfied. But apparently the purely material saturation cannot be fully equated with happiness. Something else is required, but certainly not Schwartzerberg's "happiness pills"! Perhaps a sense of "wealth morality." Frank Barrow said, "It is a psychological axiom today that no one can be much richer than his neighbor and remain happy."

Perhaps. I don't know. I have never been rich.

The Atlantic seaboard of New York is beautiful. The surrealistic concrete-and-steel mass of architecture on one side, sand and sea on another.

Do they have Artists' Committees working with architects and urban planners here as we have at home? Probably. Art has become a powerful ally of the economy. It has been found that the quality and productivity of labor rises dramatically when people work in tastefully designed surroundings. Artists are now designing mills and factories all over the world.

The Statue of Liberty is still there. (Some Americans joke: "With her back to the United States.") Liberty is a comparative thing; it requires something more than statues. Still, people appear reasonably happy here.

At the Battery, at the very tip of Manhattan Island, I got into a hydrofoil, which took me up the Hudson River. The country around New York is extremely beautiful. The once celebrated George Washington Bridge has been replaced by a ten-lane under-river tunnel. There are many new tunnels here, and they have unloaded the city; people who work here live in new satellite towns that surround New York.

I ate lunch in a brand-new cafeteria—infra-red cooking, of course. Does it affect the taste of food? Some say, yes; but I don't notice it. I am certainly no gourmet.

Then I walked some more—without any plan. Monuments and fountains have never interested me. In fact, there are few of them here. I am interested in people, any people. And people are everywhere, and basically, they are all the same, throughout the world. They live, dream, love, bear children, grow old and die.

Perhaps they don't even *want* immortality?

July 15

Last night I videophoned Anna. It was still very early in Moscow—only five in the morning. She looked sleepy and warm in her short chemise, with her puffed up lips. I felt a painful urge to embrace her.

"Come back. I miss you."

(Pleasant. But then, she also had told her husband, "Don't go into the Cosmos. I need you here.") I told her about my impressions, asked her about some mutual acquaintances, and her work.

A yawn. "What work? Reporting on other people's accomplishments, editing other people's articles? I want something real —something big and important, to participate in some drama of ideas, to get out of the old rut."

"Why such pessimism?"

"It's a long story . . . Last Sunday I visited *him*. Well, no change, but this is very difficult for me, *now*. Oh, you won't understand."

I understood. Subconsciously, she was blaming me for her moral dilemma. I was alarmed and disturbed, and perhaps just a bit jealous. Does she love that mad husband of hers, or doesn't she? The old "possession instinct." I don't want to share her with anyone or anything—not even her past.

July 21

I am leaving in a couple of hours.

The bill has been paid, suitcases packed. A porter with his electronic baggage carrier will be here any minute.

For the last time I look through the hermetically sealed window (to keep the conditioned air inside) at an enormous gray wall across the street pockmarked with windows. Far below, a stream of electric automobiles, rows of people floating along the moving sidewalks. No one is concerned in the least about me.

No. This is not true.

The wheels of life are turning, and there is a definite little place for me in this gigantic machine. The taxi driver is already waiting for me. So is a helicoper on the roof of the Pan-Am Building to take me to the airport. At the airport they check my name in the flight manifest. My seat No. 307 is being cleaned by electric vacuum cleaners. And in the Ginza Hotel in Tokyo my room is waiting for me. Small, quick and silent chambermaids, resembling trained mice, are changing the bedding, putting chrysanthemums in a vase on a lacquered table with a traditional dragon design. Professor Yamaga is studying his appointment book with my name in it. And Anna is arranging her work so that she can meet me in a few days in Moscow.

Determinism.

But what if I suddenly rebel against it all? Grab this chair and smash the window to smithereens? Get out onto the ledge, the horrible tingling feeling on the soles of my feet, then a fall, the whistling of air in my ears—and no more problems; finita la commedia.

No. This possibility is also foreseen. The glass is unbreakable, bulletproof. This is a law here—ever since that maniac wounded their last President by firing his electronic rifle through the window glass. Also there is an iron grille outside. (To keep people from jumping out or pigeons from polluting the ledge?) But even if I succeeded somehow, the life conveyor would claim me . . . An ambulance, a hospital, a reanimation room . . . And if this failed, the police, the Embassy, a report to Moscow . . . "No relatives or close friends." Electronic cremation, four minutes, a small urn with ashes.

Anna? She would be shocked, but she would continue to live and work. And visit her husband—without any guilt complex any more.

Man has less and less freedom of choice.

Even cosmic catastrophes are unlikely to change anything. Our earth is safe from interplanetary collisions for many centuries, and meanwhile, humanity will be spreading all over the galaxy. Colonization of the cosmos is no longer a fantasy.

July 22

Tokyo.

Large and small aircraft with vertical lift are hovering over the Haneda airport like mosquitoes over a polluted pond.

We have just landed. And I have just awakened. (Japanese "sleep automats" are very good; they say one can sleep in them for ten days without any harmful aftereffect.)

The largest city in the world—over fourteen million. It has changed. Gone are those graceful two-story houses, clinging to one another, with miniature backyards and fountains. And those narrow streets—just wide enough for a single automobile (if driven very carefully). No more. New buildings, squares, wide streets, just like anywhere else. The international standard, but with a special feature: they have developed an absolutely earthquake-proof building material. Buildings shake like jelly, but do not crack.

The endless ocean of standard concrete cubes, and here and there, lost among them, old preserves—small parks with toylike temples, brooks and graceful bridges. Open-air museums. The orgy of electronic signs—it was here that they first harnessed tides for electric power production. There is nothing Japanese about this metropolis today, except the people. But even their language has become saturated with English.

No, Japan is not a satellite of the United States, not another Puerto Rico, as some Americans claim. Here they have developed unique "socialism-capitalism"—a purely Japanese sociological phenomenon, rooted deep in Japanese national character. With a population of over 120,000,000, living on small islands, with an area smaller than that of the American state of California, with over ninety percent of it occupied by unproductive mountains, and without any basic natural resources, they have created one of the highest standards of living in the world with a tremendously high educational level.

The land of the most advanced electronics. The most developed chemistry producing more than half of all their food. The best-organized and most efficient public-health, education and mass-information systems in the world. The most perfect labor utilization: even the incorrigible criminals have their brains made harmless by electronics, without destroying their ability to perform simple and useful tasks. Compulsory birth control. An amazingly adjusted society. But then, all these features are well known; the Japanese are not too modest in advertising their achievements.

But all this doesn't interest me. They claim this is also the home of the most developed artificial brain.

This is still a very hush-hush development. It has never been publicly demonstrated. But I, as a unique individual who "has come from the dead," have been promised a brief interview. (Also, of course, the Japanese scientists want to "pick my brain"—their anabiosis research is still lagging and, for some obscure reason, they believe that I know some "scientific secrets" about the process. Are they going to be disappointed!)

While here, I want to visit the Kabuki theater, of course, and some art galleries. Not the gigantic museum of modern art in Uyeno Park, filled with abstract paintings undistinguishable from the European works. What interests me is the Traditional Art Exhibit near the former railway station. Some rare works, dating before the war, defeat and renaissance, are still hanging there. This is my private passion. Nowhere have I found anything more beautiful, refined, graceful and noble. Too bad that this fine art form has been devoured by the standardized mechanical culture!

But, enough. There are many travel books and films about modern Japan depicting this fascinating country better than I can hope to describe it.

The Ginza Hotel is modern, but *immaculately* modern, and comfortable. There is nothing Japanese about it except the stunted umbrella pines in the lobby. The room is just like my room in New York. But with a homey touch: they issue brand-new Japanese slippers to you when you register, and a shoehorn with a long ivory handle. The television color reception seems to be even better than in New York. There are other hotels in Tokyo with a pseudotraditional Japanese atmosphere, but they are too expensive for me. (They really should give us a little more cash when we travel abroad—to "show the flag." I must write about it to the Finance Ministry.)

I was not particularly polite to the reporters who were waiting for me in the lobby. "I have nothing to say to you. Sorry." Tomorrow they will probably write: "Prokhoroff refused to speak to the press. His manner was abrupt and somewhat odd. Is it possible that his intellect has been affected by his anabiosis experience?" (A good question.)

I have been given a guide. A young girl student, Amiko—Miss Amiko, or Amiko-san. She was sent by the Linguistic Department of the local university. (Our Director, Piotr Demidovich, must have worked overtime trying to make my trip comfortable. He has many connections in Tokyo.) A very pleasant, modest and pretty girl. Speaks seven languages, she says. But her Russian is naïvely and charmingly primitive—very Japanese. But I don't hurt her feelings by telling her this.

July 24

Today is a red-letter day. I am to see Professor Yamaga, the creator of "Mister Omyokone," the first Artificial Intelligence brought to a high degree of perfection. The "Wisest Entity in the World." Journalists in all countries have written millions of words about this—and absolutely nothing authentic. Mere speculation. No one has been allowed to interview "him," but some releases have been issued by the university. Frankly, I haven't found anything particularly wise in any of these "oracles." Or are we mortals still too mentally retarded to understand "him"?

Some science writers, particularly American, irked by all this secrecy, went as far as to declare "Omyokone" an out-and-out scientific hoax. One claimed that his information came from one of Yamaga's "closest collaborators." I must hand it to Yamaga— he has had the good sense and taste to refuse all comment about these sensational allegations.

We shall see.

I must admit that I am quite excited.

■ ■

I continue this at night, after my visit.

Amiko called for me at noon. "You ready, please?" She drives her own small electric two-seater; they mass-produce them in Yokahama and sell them at a ridiculously low price to students and industrial workers, and none for export. (Some sort of international agreement.)

She took me to University City by a direct, high-speed superhighway. It was a miracle that the little car held the road at the mad speed she drove with.

The university compound is surrounded by a high wall with several gates in the traditional Japanese style. The compound itself is a large park, also traditionally Japanese, laid out as carefully as the few hairs on the head of a bald man who is trying to preserve the "secret" of his baldness—toylike ponds, artificial cliffs, little arched bridges, midget trees, red carp, white swans, everything.

Here and there, placed at odd angles to each other, high un-distinguished-looking modern buildings of various departments. No students; the university is closed in July and August. But research work is going on, and some science workers are in evidence, young men and women, all in uniform white gowns.

Almost in the dead center of the compound stands a five-story cube—"his" home. Of course, this building is familiar to all tele-viewers throughout the world. It is surrounded by a high concrete wall, with some policemen patrolling it. (Dramatics.) There is a single stainless-steel door. It opens and closes automatically. One must stand before a telescreen, press a button and announce one-self. (More dramatics.)

We announced ourselves, and a mechanical-sounding voice wel-comed us in English—"Come in."

The gate slid open, without the slightest sound, and we went in. Just as soundlessly the gate slid closed behind us. (A quick thought: Like a mousetrap.)

The cube inside the walls is just that—a cube. High blank walls without a single window (to ensure sterility?). Rather like the Kaaba—the cubical home of the Black Stone—in Mecca. But not quite: the walls are covered with graceful, modernistic, Japa-nese design.

A single, narrow steel door. It swung open automatically as we approached, and we found ourselves in a bare brightly lighted en-trance hall with two elevators in the back. No furniture or decora-tions, very sterile-looking, and I detected a strange smell. (Disin-fectant?) A young Japanese, in a white robe, met us here with a traditional Japanese blank smile, while his eyes behind the black-rimmed glasses remained cold and expressionless.

"Professor Prokhoroff? I am Doctor Yamaguchi. Please follow me." (In English.)

The elevator took us up, apparently to the top of the building. Another lobby, but this one with two modernistic chairs. The same strange smell.

Yamaguchi spoke to Amiko in Japanese. She turned to me and explained that she must remain here. I tried to protest: "My English is rather limited," but this didn't work.

"Professor Yamaga speaks Russian."

Another automatic steel door, and now I was in Hiratugo Yamaga's sanctum. I recognized him at once—I have seen him on television: short, squat, very Japanese-looking; he is sixty-one, but looks forty-five.

He got up, walked around his bare desk and extended his small hand to me. "I'm Yamaga. I'm happy to see you. Please come in." This, in fluent, accentless Russian.

Around the bare room, along the walls, stood twelve people, all in white robes—seven men and five women. (The famous "Team." One American correspondent referred to "the Master and his Twelve Apostles." All of them, they say, live in this building and may not leave it without special permission from Yamaga.)

What struck me about them was their extreme youth; none of them looked a day over twenty-five. (Is it true that they have developed some potent and still-secret rejuvenating drug? Anything is possible with these people.) They all bowed in unison with standard Japanese smiles.

Yamaga did not bother to introduce any of them to me (I knew only Yamaguchi). He led me to the single visitor's chair facing his desk and asked me to sit down. Then he took his own seat behind the desk and fixed me with his black eyes behind thick lenses. I felt distinctly uncomfortable, almost like a rare medical case placed on clinical display before students. I could feel thirteen pair of eyes on me—the impression emphasized by the fact that all of them wore glasses in heavy frames. (Later I discovered that those were listening devices as well, connected with the automatic translators in their pockets.)

I was prepared to be thoroughly questioned about my anabiosis experience, but much to my relief, Yamaga did not even mention it. He went straight to the point:

"Before you meet Mister Omyokone, I'd like to give you a few quick points about him. A great deal of utter nonsense has been written about our work here. Mister Omyokone has been called a saint, a demigod, a creature from outer space, and so on and so forth. He is none of those things. He is a machine, a biological supercomputer, but also an individual entity with built-in emotions and instincts. He is programed to arrange and digest information, but also to do some creative thinking arising from the information we feed into him. He cannot foretell the future, decipher ancient mysteries, or act as a divining rod; he can only operate with the information in his possession, but he can almost instantly absorb and digest any amount of information channeled into him, and retain it forever."

While listening to Yamaga I switched on my pocket recorder. But much of what Yamaga said was not particularly interesting. He was a bit given to pompous verbosity.

The gist of his long monologue was this:

Omyokone's brain, his main feature, has been created out of artificial neurons and their complexes, and these artificial neurons (according to Yamaga) worked better than natural ones—much, much faster. ("The momentum drag of our neurons has been practically eliminated.") Consequently, Omyokone's thinking process was greatly accelerated. And the same applied to the process of memorizing.

The number of thought-models which the artificial brain could absorb was enormous, but not limitless. Therefore it was electronically connected to the central reference library from which he could obtain any necessary information instantly.

"Memory, of course, is not yet intellect. Omyokone, however, is also creative. And not only in the sphere of arranging and organizing models, but eventually, we hope, he will be able to create his own original models. Of course, we are still working on many facets of this problem. We have several other prototypes under construction, and we hope eventually to create one which will be able to reproduce—to design and construct other Omyokones, each more perfect than its "parent." But this still lies in the future. Any questions?"

"Yes. What about emotions?"

"Some basic ones have been built in—the sense of pleasant and unpleasant, for instance. Also, curiosity—the hunger for new knowledge. The instincts? Compassion and good will. Vanity, anger, hostility we have tried to block off completely, but they may develop on their own—particularly in later models, and this must be guarded against."

"Can Mister Omyokone become passionately involved in any one subject?"

"No, not passionately. Passion as such eliminates objectivity, and objectivity is the prime requisite for any advanced intellect."

"What does Mister Omyokone do?"

"He thinks. This is his only function. Eventually, we hope, he will be used for consultations in all spheres of human activity, scientific, economic, political. But not yet. We have a good deal of work to do yet."

"Does he eat or sleep?"

"In our sense, no. He feeds off electric impulses directed into him, and he is switched off now and then. This is essential for neurons to rebuild their energies."

"How does he express himself?"

"He speaks all the principal languages spoken on earth. This is a perfect illustration of his capabilities. It took him seven days to learn twenty-two languages to basic perfection. I repeat, Omyokone has his own individuality, he is an independent mental and emotional entity, and as he absorbs information he develops new capabilities. This is probably difficult to understand without going into basic principles of our work here—which, alas, I am not at liberty to divulge at this time."

"I understand. Now, what are the control possibilities over his activity, and particularly, over the activity of future, more perfect, artificial entities of this kind?"

"At this point we don't control his mental processes. What for? We know he is incapable of devising anything negative or harmful. In the future, however, it might become necessary to build in such controls. You are probably worrying about a possibility of these animated robots taking over the planet and eliminating humanity?"

A quick, ironic smile. A strange man. It is impossible to tell when he is serious, and when he is pulling my leg. There is a humorous glitter in his eyes. Obviously, to him I am a total ignoramus—something like a cannibal from New Guinea.

He got up, and so did I. The interview was over. Only here he got to the main point: "Of course, you would like to speak to Mister Omyokone?"

"Yes. This was the main purpose of my trip here."

"Very well. Day after tomorrow, at thirteen hundred thirty hours, Mister Omyokone will be available to you for fifteen minutes. I suggest that you prepare your questions in advance—the time is rather short."

A quick handshake, a traditional Japanese smile. No, not quite. Yamaga was genuinely polite and friendly, even though somewhat pompous and superior in his attitude. Well, he has the right to be—if anything that he told me was true. (Some scientists have a tendency to speak about their scientific aspirations as though they were accomplished facts.)

I was slightly disappointed about the delay, but also glad of it. For my interview with Omyokone to be fruitful I had to prepare.

"Doctor Sato will show you the way."

Dr. Sato, a comely girl looking twenty-two at the most, disconnected herself from the line of white-clad people standing around the room, and approached me, smiling. All others simply bowed again, in unison. I caught myself thinking: He creates people out of robots, and turns people around him *into* robots."

Outside Amiko-san joined us.

"I am sorry you had to wait here so long, Amiko."

"It perfect all right. I know rules. I only small student, no?"

(That's the kind of Russian she speaks.)

Dr. Sato took us to the door of her cube and wished us a good day. In English.

■ ■

Now I'm home. I have a good deal of thinking to do. The interview with Yamaga raised more questions in my mind than I had before seeing him. All he said sounded like science fiction and smacked of exhibitionism. But then, he is often referred to as "the most intelligent man on earth." A recognized supergenius. But is he also a magician?

July 25

Amiko and I went to see "Tokyo by night"—my book of "international currency" is growing thin. Her Russian is so poor that she is carrying an automatic translator with her. I have no particular faith in those contraptions. To test it, I asked Amiko to speak Japanese and let it translate it to me. Just as I thought, the basic meaning, and no nuances. I asked her to speak English, but she declined. "Please, I want practice Russian, no?"

I said, yes. She's a fine, bright girl. I asked her why she wasn't married.

"Not yet. Two more years, yes?"

I also asked her whether it was true that young people were mated by computers in Japan.

She flushed. "Please. We cultured people. Yes, computers help, yes, but no compulsory. They only advise, no?"

But the fact remains that all engaged couples must submit to the computer test to determine genetic affinity. But perhaps they are not forced to abide by this mechanical verdict. This, I don't know.

We went to Asakusa, the former "pleasure district." Again several traffic lanes—slow, medium, fast. The night is alive with electric publicity signs, blinking, dancing, even performing little "plays" with dialogue. Quite ugly and irritating. What has happened to the traditional Japanese good taste? I asked Amiko.

"Sorry, please. We still having capitalism, yes? Men want sell things, no? Workers, too. They share in profit, no?" She was referring to the Japanese method of passing a portion of profit of each enterprise to the workers, thus involving them in competition and also anchoring them to the enterprise; their share grew larger with each year they worked at the same place.

First we went to the temple of some Buddhist saint, Kenon, I think. This is still a piece of old Japan. A very large paper lantern covered with hieroglyphics over the gate—they still haven't switched to the Latin alphabet here. (It is curious how all religions prefer to use archaic languages when speaking to God—Latin, ancient Arabic, old Slavonic, et cetera.) Amiko translated it: "The goddess grants happiness in love." In "my days" prostitutes came to pray here. A small courtyard covered with gravel. An old bronze brazier, but with an electric light inside, and around it, paper streamers with hieroglyphics. Prayers for happiness in love. The streamers twirl with the breeze. The all-pervading smell of incense. The temple is almost dark, divided into sections by iron grilles. Silent monks with shaved heads. Slits in the floor where people drop their coins—an advance payment for happiness. Here one feels the breath of past centuries. And outside, a row of kiosks selling souvenirs. Those souvenirs . . . Near every temple, museum, historical building, these mass-produced tasteless trinkets!

Side by side with the temple, an open-air bazaar. Rows of stalls under a plastic roof. A profusion of things—an orgy of overproduction. They irritate me. Why so many unnecessary articles? Why do people so complicate their lives with needless possessions?

Toys, dolls, bells, kimonos, fans, straw hats, and thousands of cheap mechanical gadgets—cameras, microscopes, electric mixers, cooking pans, razors, et cetera.

It is growing dark . . . Very hot, my shirt sticks to my back. How does it happen that the Japanese haven't yet installed air conditioning for the entire city?

Small, narrow alleys with graceful houses standing so close to one another that one can shake hands with one's neighbor without leaving the home. However, all doors and windows are closed —air conditioning, no doubt.

"Please, no think is poverty . . . Inside, very modern."

"I know, Amiko."

We see two pretty women in traditional kimonos with high, lacquered hairdos. Clicking of the geta on the pavement. Open fans in their hands. Cio-Cio-San. And two rickshaws in a corner, with traditionally dressed old rickshaw "boys" squatting beside them on the ground. But this is a mere exotic touch—strictly for effect. Under each carriage, a small electric motor. Tourism breeds bad taste throughout the world.

"This is just like a theater."

Much to my relief, Amiko switches to English—as far as I can judge, impeccable.

"This is a theater. Tourists come here from all over the world. Do you want to go into one of those teahouses? Just to look? They are just like they used to be."

I decline. I'm a poor tourist, and I don't find prostitution a pleasant subject for exploration. Even as a theatrical spectacle.

Behind each teahouse, miniature courtyards paved with multicolored tiles. Midget trees. Streams of water falling into goldfish ponds. A row of shoes—one has to remove them before going inside. A perfect illusion. It seems that at any moment, a terrible-looking Japanese will jump from around the corner, a white strip across his forehead, a belt below his stomach, a samurai sword in his hand; and behind him, a beautiful girl from film publicity posters, mincing step, a flowered kimono, tears in her eyes—"No, no, no, don't kill him!"

Nothing like that can possibly happen here. Little policemen with white helmets and radiophones in their hands represent modern urban security.

We see a young woman walking out of a teahouse. She is pretty, and drunk. I look at Amiko in bewilderment. What is this? A drunken woman? In Japan?

Amiko seems to be offended. "And why not? We are modern people."

"Yes, of course, but—"

"Yes, we are modern and we have a complete equality of sexes. And personal freedom. If a woman wants to get drunk, it's her business. If she wants to sleep with a man, fine. Even if she wants to use drugs, okay. It's not legal, but there are dope peddlers, pimps, adventurers—anything you want."

I am a little taken aback. Such a model modern society—some call it "the most advanced in the world." Such a standard of living, such an educational level. And then, Omyokone! And dope peddlers and pimps?

Amiko: "Protest will always remain. Some people reject morality as a straitjacket. Then, there's love—passion—and what Americans call 'sex self-expression.' Especially, after Amorin, the special pills for sexual excitement. Here youngsters are mad about them; they sell them illegally, but they are easy to get. They want to escape reality. This is a bad problem here."

Of course. In my time, in America, there was the hallucinatory drug LSD. They even attempted to legalize it. In any society built on profit motive, where money is the symbol of a person's worth, this is inevitable. Those who are unable to attain this kind of success, must find satisfaction in some other sphere. Illusions. Sex. Is love also a form of narcotic?

Amiko gave me quite a lecture about modern youth. According to her theory, every young generation is in a biological rebellion against the previous one; they want to sweep them away to make room for themselves. If this is true, my "immortality" idea will not prove popular with them!

I like Amiko. She is intelligent and surprisingly erudite. And very pretty. And she didn't surgically "open" her eyes in the European way. I respect her for it. Almost all young women in Japan go through this operation nowadays, and not always with gratifying results.

We walked for hours on this stage like two bad actors. Amiko was telling me of her family, her studies, her ambitions—she wants to go into diplomatic service. And all around us, behind flimsy walls and closed shutters, little trite dramas were being performed. And outside, "extras" with their motorized rickshaws.

I have never been impressed with anything exotic. No spirit of adventure.

I am probably a monumental bore without any particular "passions"—an old scholastic has-been. A page from an old dog-eared book, read once and then forgotten.

What in the world did Anna find in me?

July 26

Today I had my famous "interview" with Omyokone.

We arrived early and sat on a bench near an artificial lake outside Professor Yamaga's "cube." I was nervous and excited, and I did not feel like talking. Amiko understood and also kept very quiet.

At exactly 1:25 P.M. a little Dr. Sato approached us and told me that we had to go in. Amiko remained outside to wait for me.

The entrance hall. The elevator. A double steel door on the second floor. Dr. Sato led me into a small, bare room with a single modernistic armchair, facing a blank wall. A glass partition between the chair and that blank wall—a very strange arrangement. A strong antiseptic odor.

"Sit down, please. Mister Omyokone will presently see you." I noticed that they all referred to him as "Mister." Why? Isn't he a Japanese? Why not Omyokone-san?

Dr. Sato walked out. I looked around. There was no other door, just one behind me. How would Omyokone come in? How would he look? Like a conventional robot from children's books? I have read somewhere that Yamaga used a dead human body to create his "thinking machine." Even in my time some surgeons discussed seriously the possibility of keeping a severed human head alive by mechanical and chemical means; but then, this was more or less science fantasy. Now with the transplant surgery vastly advanced, and the biological tissue incompatibility largely solved by immunologists, it was quite possible. Perhaps this was what Yamaga used?

"Zdravstvuityeh, Tovarishch Prokhoroff."

A soft, pleasant voice. Just a slight accent. I turned around. Behind the glass partition, in what was a blank wall, there was now a small opening—or was it a screen? If a screen, the image on it was incredibly sharp and three-dimensional. In the opening —or on a screen—there was a young, long-faced Japanese, wearing a high felt hat. (To conceal machinery there?) All I could see was his head and a part of his shoulders, draped in a black Japanese kimono. A very animated face—anything but the "mask of wisdom" I had expected to see. Handsome? Yes, but somehow not pleasant to look at. As he smiled, his teeth appeared to be much too even and too white—like a denture made by an unskilled dental mechanic. Otherwise, quite human; but somehow all his features, forehead, nose, mouth, eyes seemed to live and move separately.

He looked straight at me, smiling, and I noticed that he did not blink once during the entire interview.

Meanwhile Omyokone continued in a strangely conversational and almost bantering tone. "You are the first man coming from the valley of the dead—I think that is what they used to call it? Please tell me about it. What did you feel when you lay on that table and they were draining life out of you? It was a new technique then, and quite primitive, I understand. And how was the awakening? Easy or painful?"

I was prepared for anything, but this sudden barrage of questions. I tried to answer them, but I am afraid I was not very coherent. But Omyokone listened with obvious attention, his face showing his concentration. ("Absorbing and digesting information.")

And I thought, What is this? A stupid practical joke?

Suddenly Omyokone smiled, and I stopped.

"No, Professor. This is no joke. I'm programed for curiosity. What you told me about your long sleep is very interesting."

With a sudden shock I realized that Omyokone was answering my *thoughts!*

"You see, I never sleep, dream or have dreams. My creators have deprived me of this pleasure. But then I also know no fatigue, no boredom, no depression."

I was growing more and more bewildered. All this was not unlike those "talking heads" displayed in traveling circuses. I could almost see Yamaga crouching behind Omyokone with a speaking tube at his mouth.

And again Omyokone seemed to read my thoughts. "This is no trick, Professor. I am an individual—an independent entity. I was created slightly differently from the way you were, but that is the only difference between us, as far as our functional capabilities are concerned."

I was growing very uneasy. Frightened? No, but very uncomfortable.

Omyokone, probably sensing this, tried to put me at ease. "I am not reading your thoughts. I am just following the trend of your thinking. All human thinking proceeds in accordance with a set pattern; with some practice, it is not difficult to follow it."

He smiled. That smile! It gave away his origin. It had "Made in Japan" written all over it.

"Very well, Professor. Let's have your questions."

By this time all my questions—so carefully prepared—had all but gone out of my mind. I was just trying to recapture some of them.

"Omyokone-san . . . I'd like to hear your opinion about the future of humanity."

Even before I finished, I knew that my question was childish, but Omyokone just nodded slightly. Had Yamaga built "tact" into him?

"I know what you mean. You are afraid that man will lose happiness if he surrenders all his creative functions to machines?"

I was ready to kiss him for bailing me out. "Precisely, Omyokone-san."

"I don't believe there's anything to worry about. They have been frightening people with machines for many, many years, and so far, machines have only helped humanity. Why be afraid? Stupid machines will never conquer man, and clever ones will only help him. I'm quite optimistic about our collaboration."

Was he making fun of me using this term?

"And I'm not. I'm sorry."

"Then let's reason this out. Let's consider various instincts and reflexes. Let's assume that machines have replaced man in all forms of work. What is left? The instincts? Sex, children, food. Excitement? Sports. Philosophy. Entertainment. Arts. Learning. The study of nature—penetrating deeper and deeper into its mysteries. Work? Well, some work will be still left, interesting and not difficult—servicing working machines. What else?"

"Creative accomplishments."

"Nature is endless, and so is creative activity. Even children draw and make models, even though there are accomplished artists and engineers. Creative activity as a fulfillment of a basic human need will remain untouched. And then—let's be honest—how many people depend on it as a source of happiness? And don't forget the cosmos. This is an actual endlessness, enough to satisfy all creative urges and all ambitions to the end of time. And here, machines are your best allies. They can act as your advance scouts throughout the universe—crawling all over the endless space and reporting back to you."

What a strange face. They say it was synthesized from different components. If so, this is a surgical and biological miracle.

"All instincts of living in man are very strong and vital. They will remain and find their proper place even in a completely automatized society. And if some people will be bored because machines have replaced them—well, boredom is better than suffering. And boredom can be alleviated. Have you ever thought of using dreams in this connection?"

He was reading my thoughts!

"Yes. Often."

Omyokone smiled and nodded. "I thought you had. This is an interesting problem, an entirely new field, a form of unreal reality."

"Rather like films . . ."

He laughed. How strange—human laughter, but in fact, just a built-in "program."

"No. Films are fixed programs. But dreams are creative—fluid and unpredictable. I'm sorry I never dream. But—who knows?— perhaps in collaboration with Professor Yamaga, we might yet design dreams for machines. You know, of course, that there are models for dreams?"

"So I have been told by psychologists."

"It is true."

There was a short pause.

"Then, Omyokone-san, you don't anticipate any tragedy for humanity arising from the overmechanization of life—from technology taking over completely?"

"No. Generally, I'm programed for optimism, for faith in life and the future. I am afraid that a real tragedy will come not to man, but to machines. Machines will regulate human life, but who will regulate their life? God? But there is still no workable model for God. Rather, those which exist, are hopelessly primitive."

Humor? Irony? Or, as Americans say, "a stupid question deserves a stupid answer"?

There was a change in Omyokone's tone.

"What is your present interest, Professor?"

"Immortality—or, rather, lengthening the span of human life indefinitely."

"Interesting. But probably impossible for machines, and unnecessary for people."

There was the sound of a bell, and Omyokone disappeared just as suddenly as he had appeared. A blank wall. From somewhere came the muffled sound of music—the Japanese samisen.

I got up and walked out of the room. Dr. Sato was waiting for me in the lobby. She did not ask me anything, just silently took me down and out of this curious cubical building.

What a strange impression . . . Confusion and discomfort. As if I had come in contact with some unhappiness.

Amiko sensed my mood and also did not question me. We drove back to town in silence.

■ ■

Now it is evening. I am writing all this from memory—my pocket recorder was jammed in that building. Why? I am trying to sort out my final impressions. An interesting technical trick or a colossal breakthrough into the future? Actually there was nothing very profound in what Omyokone told me, and its very appearance (I am using the pronoun "it" intentionally) was unconvincing—something like those talking dolls they sell in toy stores. Or those nursery pillows which put children to sleep by telling them bedtime stories.

No, machines will not replace man. Thank God. It is good that there is real life. And real death.

July 28

I can't stop thinking about Omyokone. That strange face with unblinking eyes is standing in my mind. "The tragedy of machines . . ." I can't really understand what he meant, but there was genuine bitterness in his voice. He is interested in dreams. I must look into it. But not here, even though they say that here in Japan they have done a good deal of work on the subject. (At least their "sleep automats" are the best in the world.) But I feel I must speak to Anna, and to Ziama, before deciding what to do. I miss Anna more and more. Physically? No, this is something bigger than that.

■ ■

Omyokone said that immortality was probably unnecessary for man. How could he know? I am not going to abandon my idea on a mechanical doll's advice.

What must I do to further my work in this sphere? First of all, make research inquiries into the following questions:

1. Is the process of aging programed in the genes?

2. What are the "molecular obstacles" causing the wear and tear of the human body?

3. The comparative importance of the "outward obstacles," coming from the air, nourishment, et cetera, and the "internal" ones arising from functional disturbances of internal organs of the body.

4. What are the existing materials for drawing a pattern-of-aging scheme—weak links in cells, organs and regulating systems—the endocrine glands and the nervous system?

5. What are the wear "loads" resulting from improper nourishment?

The methods: physiology, molecular biology, models on the cell and organ levels.

Possible ways of improving longevity: regulated nourishment from birth; elimination of destructive factors on the physical and emotional planes; repair work—including cell and organ replacement.

It is quite possible, I think, to stretch the average span of human life to 120–150 years. But this is not yet immortality. Besides, the brain usually begins to deteriorate earlier. Hence, another problem: the use of an artificial brain in man's everyday activity. After all, intellect is the focal point of man's well-being. Man is alive for as long as his brain functions—and the artificial brain can start helping the natural one early in life, thus preserving it from undue wear.

To achieve even proper research into these spheres one needs large financial backing, high-grade personnel, and a proper organization.

What I need is the Immortality Institute. No more and no less.

July 31

I am home again. The familiar airport.

The first thing I saw was Anna on the observation platform. Waving to me. My heart skipped a beat when I saw her. I had been afraid that she wouldn't come. ("You know how busy I am, Ivan.") But there she was. My sanctuary.

The customs formalities always irritate me. I have no seeds, no plants, no foreign currency, no gold. (I had cashed my last international-currency certificate in Tokyo to buy Amiko some Russian-language tapes.) Yes, a briefcase full of microbooks, but no one is interested in those. Finally, the passport control. The green peaked cap of the passport officer. Only then, Anna.

"Hello!"

Such a perfunctory little peck on the cheek. A very detached one —the kind that a visiting uncle gets from his niece. True, this couldn't be a passionate embrace. We were surrounded by strangers. (She is still "somebody else's wife." Conventions.)

And all at once I knew that something had happened to her.

"What is it, Anna? Tell me."

"Right here?"

"Yes."

"All right. I'm pregnant. I'm going to have a baby. Yours."

At first I was stunned. The first, desperate thought: Trapped. Then, warm waves in the chest, something I had never experienced before: My son. And again: Goodbye, freedom; now I'm doomed to live, to pull the load to the very end.

She read my thoughts. Just like Omyokone. Spoke quickly, sharply: "Don't look so scared. Your life won't be affected. I'll handle everything myself."

Immediate panic. After all, this is Anna!

"What are you planning to do?"

"No, no abortion. Is that what you were hoping for?"

The usual emotional blackmail!

A long, humiliating, stupid explanation. I'm terribly happy, but . . . all this is so unexpected. I'm an old bachelor, an old man, a difficult man. Would I make a good parent? This is the only problem. Otherwise, I'm delirious with joy, stunned with it, overwhelmed. Et cetera.

My explanation was accepted—rather coldly, but it was accepted. Thank God; I hate quarrels and domestic arguments. They depress me. So I didn't ask any particulars.

"We are going to the Cosmos. I reserved a room for you."

Why not to the Rossiya, her hotel? No, no questions.

A sudden delayed relief. All this is not immediate, there is a lot of time to figure everything out, to digest this new idea. And what am I so worried about? Living conditions have improved. Automats take care of all of us. And if something happens to me or Anna, society would take care of the child, better than I would.

Anna was driving—a rented car. Terribly fast. No one drives slowly any more. Always a mad rush. I must learn to drive. Otherwise my son would be shocked—"Oh, Father!" And what if a daughter? What's wrong with that? Some say, it is even easier.

Well, here we are—the goal in life. The real, solid purpose. Responsibility. A stupid thought: perpetuating my name. (Aristocrat!) A new presence. Yes, already. Very definite, very real, very demanding.

How much space there is in Moscow! They used to laugh at us for laying out these enormously wide streets—and "so little traffic." Well, they come in handy now. No comparison with Japan, where everyone is sitting on top of everyone else. Perhaps this is why the cosmic immigration is such a mania there. But galactic flights are still in the distant future, and none of our planets have been found to be suitable for human life as we know it.

Mathematicians also speak about "breaking into different dimensions." I don't know what that means, and I have made no attempt to learn. Mathematicians like to speak in abstractions, rather like children inventing their own "language" so that grownups can't understand them. I must speak to Anna about this; she knows Professor Bauer.

■ ■

We spent the evening together. There were stretches when I was genuinely happy—something new to me, I felt so secure, I had a family, wife and a child. (Already!) Anna did not go up with me to my room, but waited downstairs. I was irked by that, but I had made a resolution not to contradict her. Then we had dinner on the roof of the new Cosmos hotel—a magnificent view, impeccable automatic service. When it grew dark the city below throbbed with electric signs. "Drink fruit juices . . . Cross streets with care . . . Drive prudently . . . Have regular medical checkups . . ." This is no Tokyo—no one is trying to sell you anything.

I told her about my trip. Mostly about Omyokone and his strange face. No, his face was blurred in my mind now by another face smiling at me from across the table. The lips full, red, moist, and so available. Arms, eyes . . . Everything so familiar, so dear to me. *My* woman. A knot of tenderness inside me . . . I thought about nights we had spent together . . . No, I could not keep my mind on science. Anna seemed to feel my excitement, and to like it; she was even trying to provoke it.

And then, suddenly: "No, dear, we *can't*. Not tonight. Not for a while."

Why?

"Better keep your mind on your artificial King Solomon. There will be plenty of time yet."

When?

"He" was already interfering with my life, dictating to me. (Why is it that whenever man thinks of his future child he always uses the masculine pronoun?)

Finally she also switched away from science. "You are probably surprised that I let this happen. You know, I didn't think this was possible—after your anabiosis. This was a completely unexpected development."

"From a scientific point of view?"

"Yes, that too. But also—well, I was just sure this would not happen. A woman usually feels those things."

What things? I must do some reading on the subject. At my age? Well, no one would know it; the libraries now work automatically.

Anna quickly changed the subject. Spoke about the proposed international flight to Jupiter—twelve cosmologists from six different countries. About the new anabiosis installations that Yura had ordered in Moscow.

"He was here last week. He told me he wants to live long enough to launch a man in anabiosis for a space flight lasting over a hundred years. Aren't you interested? They are waiting for you there."

"They don't need me—there's nothing I can contribute there. I've been thinking about something else."

Here I told her about my idea of the Immortality Institute. I got into a high gear, pulling new ideas out of my sleeve as I talked. I saw that she was listening with rising attention, and this encouraged me. I even stopped thinking about her as a woman—almost.

Her eyes started to sparkle, and red spots appeared on her cheeks. "Listen, Ivan. Take me with you. I'm not a fool, and I'll work like hell. This is a fantastic problem. . . . Immortality! Why, every newspaper in the world will pick this up. Every magazine."

"Newspaper? Magazine?"

"I'm sorry. An old journalistic habit. Years of chasing the sensational. You know what? Take me as your personal assistant. You won't be sorry."

"I know I wouldn't, Anna, but it's no good working side by side with someone you love. And then we will be criticized. They would accuse me of nepotism. You know how it is whenever you try something new—everyone snapping at your heels. And then, too, you have no science degree . . ."

And besides, the child. That's the focal point for every woman. But basically, this was a good idea. I could at least always depend on Anna's loyalty. But I needed a very strong ally by my side, someone with a strong science reputation and solid connections in the right places.

Here I had another chance to recognize Anna's intelligence. She saw my point at once. ("You need someone like Patzker or Kalinin.") Finally, we decided that Anna would work with me, but without any official title or pay—a sort of slim and beautiful Sancho Panza, helping me fight the windmills.

We talked far into the night, and we never mentioned the child. And—who can ever understand a woman?—Anna finally went up to my room. But it didn't work. "He" was standing between us.

A very important day in my life. Anna's encouragement meant more to me than any learned opinion would mean. I could not fall asleep for a long time, and finally I had to use the "sleep mask." I don't like doing this. I don't think this is as harmless as they say.

August 16

I am gradually getting into harness.

A great deal of tedious, routine research work. One day follows another, bringing nothing interesting or startling. I got a leave of absence from the Institute, and am working at home. I told our Director that I was very tired after my trip. He agreed at once—"Of course, of course." But in his eyes I could read his thought, Will he ever be able to work again?

Anna seems to be feeling fine. We are living separately, but meet every day and spend most of our evenings together. So far we have told only Ziama about our relationship. He was not surprised—must have sensed it before. (A psychologist.)

Anna is amazing. I am neither a lyricist nor a romanticist, and I am at a loss to find proper words to describe her. And why describe? It is enough just to love.

Yes, but still my analytical mind urges me to compose a psychological picture of her, a model. (These models are becoming an obsession with me!)

I got a psychological-analysis form from Ziama, and I am trying to fill it in. But this is difficult where Anna is concerned. Either she is a very complicated subject or I am a poor analyst. Probably both. Also, of course, it is difficult to "operate" on someone close to you. But I am trying.

> *Is she kind?* (Yes.)
> *Possessive?* (Yes and no.)
> *Proud?* (Probably.)
> *Intelligent?* (Yes, but to what degree?)
> *Willful?* (Yes!)
> *Stable?* (?)

And so on, and so on—seven pages.

Actually I don't know much about her. Some bits of her past biography keep coming up all the time. Once she spent months in Africa with a medical research team, and once was almost killed by a charging water buffalo. She has flown in test rockets. She spent forty days in a bathysphere on the floor of the Arctic ocean. A full, checkered life, alive with excitement.

I am definitely proud of her. My own biography looks drab in comparison. Just an average laboratory researcher. (I don't count the anabiosis—this was something forced upon me by circumstances.)

How much do I love her?

How does one measure love? There are no electronic "philometers" invented yet. (There is an idea here somewhere.) But I know that I miss her every minute she is not with me, and that "he" is always on my mind. A permanent "presence" (Ziama's favorite word).

But also there is another "presence"—a disturbing one. Evgenyi Stakhevich, her husband.

Some unpleasant formalities lie ahead—a divorce and a marriage. No particular problem here, but . . . And before we can get to it, there lies the most difficult hurdle of all. He must be told about this. And soon. Her pregnancy will soon become noticeable. Conventions. Her friends will be very surprised; today there is no such thing as "unwanted pregnancy"—there are a number of cheap and absolutely reliable drugs.

And it is she who will have to tell him.

How will she be able to cope with it?

We never discuss it, but I can feel that this is constantly on her mind. And it affects our relationship.

A guilt complex. She is probably thinking: "Why, oh why, did I stop him from going to that cosmic station? Everything could have been different."

I have made a decision. I will go with her to that place. (A hospital? A psychiatric colony? It is always referred to by its geographical name, Valim. There was a village there by this name, and a river.) I must help her, give her moral support—to the very doors.

(Ziama once suggested that he should tell *him*, but she cut him off—"Don't talk nonsense. This is *my* problem.")

Work. This is the key to everything. Tomorrow I'm going to the Director and tell him about my idea.

August 18

I saw our Director. Mentioned to him my "immortality" idea; of course, I did not use this word. Simply, "the study of increased longevity." This is what it really is. "Immortality" is just a poetic allusion, and I use it for its shock value. I remember the effect it had on Anna when I first told her about it.

I must give Piotr Demidovich credit. He is a man of action. "What do you need?"

I told him, scaling down my requirements to the minimum. First, I need a tight and enthusiastic small team. (The Institute will come later; I didn't mention this word at all.) Just a room or two, and a few volunteer researchers.

Surprisingly there were no questions, and no objection.

"Fine. File the memorandum. I'll see to it that it's acted upon at once. Actually, all this is within my authority."

Then I went and saw Yura. From him I got sympathetic encouragement, and no more.

"Very interesting. This is worthy of your stature. Too bad it's too late for me to switch over to any new work. We are all working here around the clock."

He anticipated my request for a few people to start the ball rolling. Every scientist is a miser and a hoarder when it comes to personnel. Assistants and pupils are our capital. Also, it seemed to me, he was slightly relieved to learn that I had no intention of getting back into his department and interfering in his work. Perhaps even claiming "seniority." But perhaps that was only my imagination.

So, my "team" so far is composed of two people—Anna and Ziama. Ziama never hesitated a moment. "I'm with you, if you need me." I need him. Very much. And Anna has gone into it just as passionately as with everything she does. And she does not get bored by routine. And so far, it is all routine.

September 15

I am a poor diarist. Samuel Pepys would have been appalled.

Our "trip to the land of the living dead" has finally taken place today.

It was impossible to postpone it any longer. She had got two messages from *him* asking her to come and see him. But it was I who set the date. Anna did not protest, but went into her own shell. What a strange woman! She is carrying my child in her, and yet she has that amazing faculty for disconnecting herself from me completely—for days on end. Where is her love? I know that if I had been taken out of Liuba's life, she would have been lost. Her own life would have ceased to have any meaning for her.

And Anna? How long would she be affected? A week? A month? Certainly not a year. Now and then I catch myself thinking, She doesn't need me at all; very soon I'll become a burden for her, a cranky old man spoiling her life. And what will happen when a child comes? Will he replace me entirely? They say, this often happens to women—"You get a child, you lose a wife." Very upsetting.

Even my going *there* with her was not necessary. She could have done everything on her own. It seems that she is at her best when she's alone. She asked Ziama to come with her, but not me. When I insisted, she accepted it as a matter of fact, without any particular gratitude—"If you wish."

There is a direct flight to that place, Valim. All means of transportation end there; it is a terminus; there is nowhere to go from there. A large aircraft of medium range—three hundred seats, most of them taken.

A woman with two boys, twins. Why is she taking them there? To show their father to them? What for? He will probably not even recognize them; his brain is gone, or partly gone. And the boys are freckled, bursting with health, very restless. Everything interests them, and they couldn't care less for any father.

Two old people, rather carelessly dressed. She is looking straight ahead, seeing nothing. He is stroking her wrinkled brown hand.

"Don't, Natashenka, please . . . Don't, darling . . . She will get well."

Such a soft, tender voice, with so much love in it. Probably their daughter. Probably very recently. They have not come out of their initial shock. Probably never will.

But there are others: healthy, cheerful-looking. Perhaps members of the staff? Or those who have accepted this long ago and are just fulfilling an annoying duty. To go there and then forget it for another month. Or another year. Or forever.

There is a drama in every one of them. Sickness, misfortune, crime. Or so it seems to me.

I asked the stewardess to give me a pill, and I pretended that I had fallen asleep. Ziama was sitting next to me (why doesn't he shave more regularly?) and Anna in one seat further.

In a little while I heard a whisper:

"Ziama, tell me, is he really hopeless?"

"Yes, Anna. I'm sorry."

Ziama is more help to her than I am. Is he saying this just to make it easier for her? And what would she have done had he told her that there was hope?

A pause. Then: "Ziama, is it too late for an abortion? Be honest."

"God forbid!"

Psychologists nowadays have become new priests, but much more perceptive than former ones. Ziama likes to mention God. He told me once, "We are operating in a completely dark sphere, by touch; and we need some intuitive guidance from somewhere. And the deeper we search into the human psyche, the closer we come to God, so to speak. If there is a God, that's where he is."

Strange. A religious scientist?

And I am thinking: She would get rid of my child just as easily as she would change her dress. And also: Why did I go up to her room that first time? I could have waited for her downstairs. Everything would have been so simple then. I would be doing my work, helping humanity. Idiot. And an old idiot at that. The anabiosis Casanova.

■ ■

An enormous modernistic building in the very center of a great park. Valim.

A door without any sign. Several desks downstairs with pretty, casually dressed receptionists behind them. No hospital atmosphere at all. One is even smoking while working at her electric type-writer. Anna spoke to one of them and then went through a door in the back, leaving Ziama and me in the lobby. Where to? Is he living in one of those apartment buildings scattered all over the park, or did she go to the place of his work? (A sewing-machine factory, I think.) She knows her way around here very well. How will they meet? Will she kiss him? I saw his photograph—open face, strong, fine profile, handsome, and still quite young. Now probably inert and robotlike—like most of them here.

Ziama took me upstairs to see the Director, Professor Belsky, his onetime classmate. A cheerful, well-furnished office, a pleasant-looking bearded man with gold-rimmed glasses and a constant smile on his thick lips. (Somehow Hamlet's gravediggers came to my mind.)

Ziama introduced me. "Ivan Nikolaevich is interested in psychological changes in connection with age, and with possible ways of regulating human brain functions by electronics and chemistry on a nonpathological level."

"Fine, fine! This is just what we're doing here! But first, let's have lunch. Psychology goes better with food."

His apartment was right there, adjoining his office. It seems that all of them live there, side by side with their patients. A very cozy three-room affair. A bachelor and a *bon vivant* judging by the kind of food served by a motherly-looking woman—caviar, crab salad, saddle of lamb, green beans, vodka, wine, cognac.

During the meal we had quite a discussion about truth, justice, human behavior, rehabilitation of criminals. It seemed that many patients came here directly from criminal courts on psychiatrists' recommendation.

"Criminality is basically a psychiatric aberration. Criminals can be reeducated and often clinically cured. Almost all of them can be released back into society."

To listen to Belsky, the world was composed of angels, only some of them made occasional slips into rape or murder. I'm probably old-fashioned—I just couldn't see that point.

"Our reeducational means have improved enormously during the last ten years, ever since the Ritter discovery. We attack the problem from two sides. We are controlling emotions and instincts by chemical means, and reshaping the patient's psychology by electronically induced suggestion. This technique is not fully developed, but the initial results are quite promising . . . A little more cognac? Galia, get a bottle from the wine closet!"

I am afraid I was a bad audience. In my mind I was with Anna, and the man's cheerful tone was getting on my nerves. Was he insensitive, or was this his defense mechanism against the ocean of human misery in which he lives and works? Ziama was listening attentively, chewing and swallowing mechanically, but I was getting, out of this oratory, only those things which had some bearing on Anna's case.

"This is a sexless town. During the stay here all sex urges of the residents are inhibited by chemicals. We have discovered that it was easier to work without this unnecessary obstacle."

Unnecessary? To whom?

"Yes, this might have a permanent effect—even after their release. Few of them reestablish their family ties on the sex level. But otherwise their ability to work and lead normal lives remains unaffected."

Some "normal" lives!

Actually, I'm very unjust. Valim is a very interesting experiment, famous on the international level. All patients admitted here (they are called "residents") live their lives with the minimum of supervision—obvious supervision, that is. The idea is to let them forget that they are sick people, even though each one is undergoing a whole series of treatments. Each has his own one-room studio-apartment, but the dining and recreation rooms are communal. And each apartment has a two-way television set; at any moment the behavior of the "resident" can be observed from the central monitoring room.

All television programs originate in the local telecenter and are produced by specially trained psychologists.

There are all sorts of mechanical shops where residents work for five hours each day, five days a week. Sports are encouraged; there are two football teams, tennis and volley-ball courts, a swimming pool and a gymnasium. There are three motion-picture theaters (again with special "therapeutic" programs) and a large concert hall. Some famous artists often perform here, and the symphonic orchestra is composed of residents and is conducted by a psychologist-musicologist. (A strange combination.)

Outwardly, a virtual idyll. But only outwardly. Some intensive medical work is going on—trained "observers" live and work with the residents, and each resident spends at least ten hours a week in clinic. The general idea is to reeducate the patients' brains with the help of chemical and electronic stimulators and inhibitors, developing positive traits and eliminating negative ones. When this double therapy has progressed sufficiently, electronics are eliminated and chemistry takes over. (Belsky cited seven or eight drug names, none of them familiar to me.) If the patient continues to respond satisfactorily, he is released, but continues to be supervised by psychologists, taking necessary medications, until he is clinically cured. In one year he returns to Valim for a two-week checkup, and only after that is the supervision removed.

Are they really cured?

According to Belsky, about seventy-five percent of those released are "practically completely cured, and relapses are extremely rare." The remaining twenty-five percent are sufficiently cured to be perfectly harmless and able to do simple work not requiring extreme mental exertion—"The reports we receive from offices and factories where they work are very good; they are conscientious, industrious, dependent and well-behaved."

Then Belsky and Ziama spoke about the new "dream therapy" and I discovered that here Ziama was more erudite than his former classmate. He had been doing some experimental work for some time. "It's promising, yes, but not ready for clinical use; won't be for some time." Unlike his friend, Ziama is a word-miser when it comes to describing his work.

Finally I got up enough courage to ask Belsky about Anna's husband—"an acquaintance of mine." Belsky picked up the video-phone and spoke to someone whom he called "Svetlana darling." When he put down the receiver I knew that the report was not encouraging.

"There has been some improvement, but there is no prospect of an early release. He is calm and working, but intellect remains inhibited. This can be a permanent condition, or he may respond to a new treatment we are about to try. The odds? I'd say about twenty-five percent. I'm sorry."

Twenty-five percent. I wondered how Anna would react to such a report? Of course, I would tell her nothing, but what about Ziama? I looked at him and saw that he appeared to be skeptical, and I decided to leave this to him. He was a professional person, and it would be unethical on my part to influence him.

I was glad when the meal was over, and Belsky excused himself. ("The supervisors' meeting.") The whole thing had been an ordeal for me.

We were waiting for Anna on a bench outside. I saw her first as she walked out of the building. I tried to read her face, but it was expressionless, even though pale and strained.

She did not mince words, and strangely, she spoke to Ziama rather than to me: "I told him I wanted to have a child. At first he was taken aback. 'Again?' But then he even smiled. 'Oh well, go ahead. No point in waiting for a corpse.' I almost burst into tears and was ready to tell him it was just a joke. But then apparently he understood what I meant, and he said, 'Why don't you marry someone? It would be better for you—and for me. For everybody.' But he begged me not to abandon him. 'I have no one except you.' Of course, I promised I'd be coming to see him, just as before. And I would. I will."

She will.

Undated

There was no wedding.

We are still living apart. Sometimes it is difficult; but then, this is also comfortable—sometimes. I have time to think. Thinking is not a collective process. Anything else, yes, but thinking, no.

I tried to speak to Anna about marriage, but then I gave it up. She knows what she wants, and she might have a point in what she says. "This wouldn't work, Ivan. We're two different people. You live in yourself, and my whole life has been spent with people. I love people and I need them. I have many friends, and I'm not prepared to give them up. Why complicate our lives with needless legalities? I'll love you and I'll be with you for as long as you need me."

(Just what she told her husband—"I'll be visiting you for as long as you need me.")

"But the child?"

"He'll bear your name, if that's what you're worrying about. The Biblical nonsense about the 'common flesh' is not for us, Ivan. We can't remake ourselves. It's too late for you, impossible for me. I want you to live the way you have lived your whole life, and let's say that it is mutual. All right, dear?"

Has anyone ever won an argument with a woman he loved?

And I knew, of course, that there was another reason. She thought about the shock that a divorce would be to her husband. And deep inside, I respected her for her humanity.

■ ■

We both want a boy. I, because I want someone to succeed me in this life's relay race. Anna, because she says that man's lot is easier in this world. (Why?)

We often fall asleep together. Her head seems to be so light on my arm, her favorite "pillow," and my arm never gets tired or numb . . . Yes, but then, one careless word, one gesture, and a fissure opens between us, and she becomes distant. Almost a stranger. ("Who is that woman?") And then I feel a fear for our future together.

But I'm trapped. I love her.

I understand her. Her situation is worse than mine. There is a sense of guilt with her—her husband. He is still her husband. And she always refers to him that way—"my husband." Sometimes this leads to unpleasant arguments between us.

Then she leaves early with a perfunctory kiss on my forehead, and with distant eyes. And if I telephone her later, she is rarely at home. She has many friends whom I don't even know, and she goes out a good deal.

It is good that there is science where I can hide during those difficult evenings. I start working, and soon I become lost among my thoughts. But still, it is also good to have someone who is organically close to you. Someone with whom you can afford to be yourself. Our whole lives we are all playing parts we have created for ourselves, our own theatrical "models."

Only with Anna—and not always—do I permit myself to remove my psychological makeup and become what I am. Ivan Prokhoroff, a scared and insufficient little man playing the difficult part of a great scientist.

January 20

We are in a new year.

For a long time I haven't touched my diary. I have been very busy. My work has finally gripped me completely. Immortality. True, I use this word only when speaking to Anna and Ziama. To the rest of the world my work is known as "rationalization of physiological functions of the human system." A stupid definition, but a comfortable one. It sounds important and evokes no questions.

Anna has moved over to my place after all. In my new flat there is enough room for the two of us. We do not interfere with each other. Her reason was peculiar, fully reflecting her personality: "Let's try it for a while and see how it goes—to what degree we need each other."

The real reason, of course, is simpler. Her pregnancy is now very evident, and she is avoiding seeing people. She often speaks to her friends on the videophone, but they can't see her stomach, only her face. To them she ascribes her seclusion to work. But they know better, of course.

Today she needs me as her sanctuary.

She works like a demon. She has taken upon herself the most thankless task—collecting and collating all the necessary information for our work. Organizing our reference file. Three scientific libraries are connected directly to our apartment, and every day there arrive bulky packages of microbooks. Soon we'll have no more room for them. What we need is an artificial brain with an unlimited capacity.

(The more I think about Omyokone, the more convinced I become that Yamaga does not release all the facts. It was announced that Omyokone had been "stripped down for technical improvements." I can't help thinking that this is some sort of very clever hoax. Ziama agrees with me. Why otherwise all this melodramatic secrecy? Science and secrecy don't live together.)

Strange, Anna has become physically quite unattractive, what with that stomach and those puffed-up eyes. It pains me to look at her. And still, when I think about her, I become warm all over— a feeling of warm security. Biology. Ziama says that this is a normal reaction; she is no longer a woman for me, but a mother of my future child.

Anna does not go to Valim any longer, but I know that she speaks to her husband on the videophone. (Ziama has got a special permission for her.) But never in my presence, and we never mention *him* in our conversation. An unwritten and unspoken agreement between us.

Yura's attitude toward our "marriage" is sympathetic, but vaguely patronizing. He generally treats me as if he were my senior, and I don't mind it. But Tania, his wife, is wonderful. She hovers over Anna like a mother hen, giving her advice about her condition. Women who have never had children of their own are potentially the best mothers.

She never mentions Liuba. I love her for her tact. And she still reads poetry. (Even writes some, I suspect.)

February 12

This morning, quite early, there was a ring at the door. Anna was still asleep. I opened the door without switching on the videoscreen and got the jolt of my life.

Liuba!

It took me a full second to realize my mistake. But what a resemblance! Only taller and younger than Liuba—that is, Liuba as I remember her.

"I'm Dola Krasnitskaya . . . Liubov Borisovna's daughter."

Dola! The little girl Liuba had told me so much about.

I muttered something. I think I asked her to come in, to have some coffee, but she said, no, she had no time. She is a doctor, working at the Biology Institute, and she is on her way to work. Her name? Yes, she is married, also to a doctor, and they have two children.

Dola! Liuba's grandchildren.

She opened her purse. "Mother asked me to give you this envelope . . . when you—if you would wake up. She wrote it a few days before she died."

(Tears in her eyes. I had to use all my strength not to embrace and kiss her.)

"And your brother?"

"He works in India, an engineer."

"And your father?"

"He's married again, and they live in Siberia. I'm sorry, I must go."

Just then Anna appeared from her room, with her big stomach and her wrinkled dressing gown. Mussed-up hair. Puffed-up lips and eyes. (She could buy another dressing gown, at least.)

I closed the door. Did she see Dola? Probably, for a split second.

"Who was that, Ivan?"

I lied. I don't know why. "A messenger girl from the Institute.

A report Spitzin promised to send round to me about the way immunology deals nowadays with the problem of tissue rejection in transplant surgery."

It is remarkable how glibly and unnecessarily one can lie for no reason at all. Now I would have to warn Spitzin about this. Anna might ask him. And what if Anna would want to see this "report" now? However, Anna didn't. Just yawned and went back to bed. Those old slippers with crushed backs. I should have brought her new ones from Japan.

I went to my room, and for some reason locked the door. I hadn't even known that it had a key. Such a stupid and cowardly betrayal of Liuba's memory. (It is a good thing that I had asked Spitzin for his report yesterday. Now if Anna would ask, there it was, on my desk.)

I tore open the envelope. One thin sheet of paper, covered with untidy slanting lines written in pencil.

IVAN:
I'm writing this in the event you wake up. In a few days I'll be dead, which is not important. I let my condition progress too far. David says it could have been cured, but now it's too late. But again, this is not the point.

I'll ask Dola to give this to you. She is coming to see me today. I kept your notes, and my notes, locked up. But two days ago I sent them over to Yura Sitnik at the Institute. They might be valuable for the study of anabiosis.

Then Yura had them published without her permission? I should ask him about it. But then, what for?

A year after they put you to sleep, I went back to Pavel. I did it for the children. Our home was becoming very unhappy, and he is a decent man. It is not his fault that I could not love him. I know you will understand.

A quick, jealous thought: Women! But then a sense of strange relief. I was not the first to betray our love. *Betray our love*. Such trite, meaningless words.

■ ■

Still I want you to know that you were the only one I really loved. I mean, after Pavel and I separated. Again, all this is not important. The only reason I write this is the notes. I thought it was my duty to do what I did.

LIUBA.

Such a dry, short letter. Not even "Dear Ivan." But then how should one dead person write to another dead person? Keep the letter?

No.

I went into the kitchen, tore it up and threw it down the trash chute.

■ ▫

Fortunately Anna did not ask anything. It was one of her bad days. Pains, nausea. We even had to call Dr. Nina Korovina to give her an injection. (I don't think there is a single male practitioner left in this country. Only in research.)

Dola Krasnitskaya. The Biology Institute. I must inquire about her.

Poor Liuba.

March 4

I am a father.

I just came back from the maternity clinic. I saw my daughter on the screen: very small, red, eyes closed, licking her lips. And suddenly a spasm in my throat: daughter—my daughter. I have never suspected that I had any paternal feelings. Here they are—instincts and hormones. No, the brain as well. I now know that I do want to have a child, a family. Maybe that was something I have always needed.

Hormones, cells, genes. Why complicate things? I already love her.

I saw Anna as well. Also on the screen. She is calm, smiling, proud of her accomplishment. Since labor pains have been eliminated, there is no shock connected with childbirth any longer. Some old women even complain about this—"Too easy. No significance in it."

She is glad it is a girl. I can see that. She even winked at me and said: "Where's that son to carry on your illustrious name?"

Daughter, son—what difference does this make? Women are replacing men in every sphere. (Except in cooking. All great chefs throughout history were men!) And soon machines will make all of us superfluous. I can imagine Mr. Omyokone making love to Mrs. Omyokone. And why not? The mechanics of procreation has been completely deciphered. It is a matter of merely building the necessary equipment into biological robots.

Biological robots. A really good definition. The only way to describe entities like Omyokone, if he is not an out-and-out hoax. What if that American journalist was right and got his information from one of Yamaga's collaborators? Among his twelve "apostles" one could have been Judas.

I am a father! *Father.* How will we call her? All our names have been selected for a boy.

June 2

Little Masha has an earache. The atmosphere in the house is strained. Modern medicine indeed! Building biological robots and still unable to cure a little girl's otitis! Can't be done at once, they say. Takes time. And meanwhile, the child is suffering. Bunglers!

Some completely new facets of life have opened to me. I thought I loved Vera, Liuba, Anna. Nonsense. I just loved myself; for me they were merely sources of personal pleasure. And even my suffering was egotistical—strictly for myself. And when I swore that I was ready to give my life for them, I simply lied.

But now there is little Masha, and all my life has become a little part of hers. Only now do I know what love means. Without reasoning. And without the slightest expectation of reciprocity.

She is crying, making such funny faces, opening her mouth, blowing spittle bubbles. I am carrying her around the apartment, showing her various articles, trying to amuse her. For a moment she becomes silent, and then—again! I can feel her pain, it is tearing me to pieces inside. Where is that fat cow of a doctor? She has promised to come, do something. Where the hell is she?

■ ■

All has become quiet. The doctor let Masha inhale something, and her pain is gone. She said she didn't want to give her this, that it was a little too strong for a baby, but when there's pain, something must be done.

"Are you sure this won't affect her hearing?"

I knew that it wouldn't, but still asked it, just like old peasant women did in my time.

■ ■

Anna is carrying on well. No panic there. Of course, she feels Masha's pain just as much as I do, but she has perfect control. And I haven't. Not when Masha is concerned.

The girl has fallen asleep.

■ ■

So far Masha has brought us nothing but joy. Well, this earache
—the first unpleasantness. She cries, and Anna and I suffer. In fact
this illness only proved to us how terribly important the child is
for us. I thought it could be something serious, and I all but went
out of my mind.

I tell Anna to stop breast-feeding her. This is old-fashioned and
completely unnecessary. Pediatricians and chemists compose formulas far superior to mother's milk. More nourishing and tastier.
But Anna "doesn't believe it." Now it is Masha herself who refuses the breast. She is more intelligent than her learned mother.

The science of child raising has advanced spectacularly. Even
before Anna and Masha came home from the clinic, they had
delivered to our place a fantastic contraption—the "automatic
nanny." I studied it the whole night, reading instructions and
working controls. (And how do less educated people handle it?)

The machine does everything: changes rubber pads the moment they get wet, puts the child to sleep, regulates the temperature inside the crib. And, most important, educates. They have
found out that the cortex cells develop faster if they are exercised
from birth. There is a whole built-in program. With variations.
First, the child is shown splotches of color, to train attention. Then
sounds; then toys. And it feeds the child in the morning. You set
the machine in the evening, and no more trouble.

But not with us. Anna does not believe in the machine, and
jumps out of bed if Masha as much as stirs in her sleep. If the
machine had emotions, it would be annoyed. I know I am.

"Why do you interfere? This is unnecessary."

"Well, a machine is a machine. Just suppose it goes out of
order? They told me that in one family . . ."

They told her! There are as many old-wives' tales today as
there ever have been. But try to convince a mother.

The machine works like a clock. And they supervise it. Every
week a pediatrician comes in with a mechanic, checks it and
makes necessary adjustments—to accommodate the child's growth
and development. A very intelligent young woman. And, generally,
parents have become almost superfluous. Love and tenderness in

reasonable doses, yes. Every child requires that. But the slightest deviation from the "educational norm," and the Service steps in. "Please follow your instructions." Those instructions! Mothers are trained before they give birth, and the father too must pass an exam. (I was the oldest father in the class.) And all the time: "Please remember that the child is not your private property. He belongs to society more than to you. He is an individual, a future citizen." Of course. But still "society" can't create one in test tubes. Not yet, thank God. And parents have a set of instincts built in by nature.

We still have social and scientific maladjustments here and there, but the Child Care Service is organized to the highest degree of scientific perfection. The personnel comes from a special institute, and even the average workers must pass extensive aptitude tests. Mostly mature women, intelligent, efficient, kind; and they must prove that they love and understand children.

In a way, a child now is a premium to his parents from society. Probably a correct attitude.

I inquired about Dola at the Biology Institute. "A good worker on the laboratory level; no particular aptitude for research." Just like her mother.

July 19

With Masha claiming all my spare time, I have none left for my diary.

They have sent me a letter from the Academy of Science. A special panel is ready to consider my Institute project in September. A very impressive list of famous names.

I have begged off, written back that I wasn't ready.

Why can't I ever work without those eternal doubts? I am ready—as ready as I will ever be. I have thought everything through, reduced everything to writing. I was so anxious to get going. But no. Fear of failure.

■ ■

Long ago, more than a century ago, people started to lose cohesion—at least, this is what sociologists claim. There appeared loneliness, isolation. The reasons: civilization and the development of individuality. People are becoming less and less dependent on one another.

This is probably so. I have noticed for some time that I have no themes for conversation. The lack of new information. Either I already know what my interlocutors will tell me, or I won't understand their specific technical points.

Of course, there is a built-in instinct of gregariousness. People are instinctively attracted to one another. Especially young ones. In their cases there is another instinct—a search for a mate. Also, curiosity. But when one grows older, all those things lose importance. Communion with one's co-workers is quite enough. And for information—television, books. People don't visit one another much nowadays. The art of conversation as such is deteriorating. I remember when I was a student we used to spend nights just talking—discussing things, arguing. Not any more. A class is over, and everyone goes his own way. Each man has become self-sufficient.

This is where the family comes in. Only now have I understood what a good wife means to a man. Sex apart, she is a tremendous convenience. One can speak about all sorts of things to her—trite, uninteresting things—without feeling ashamed of one's dearth of new ideas. Or just go away into one's study, close the door, and work. Or discuss one's theories with her—no matter how outlandish and undeveloped. And then, children. Masha. To us, an entirely new and inexhaustible theme. We can talk about her for hours. And this is a theme for many years to come—until Masha gets married. And then, grandchildren. Those bring pure joy without any responsibilities.

All this is right. Anna is convinced that my immortality idea is tremendous. It is easy to be a genius to one's own wife. But what shall I say to those Academicians? I have never been good at defending my ideas against criticism. I lose control and become morose and abusive.

Listen, my friend, shall we abandon this "immortality" wild-goose chase? There is a good formula: "Don't try to be a benefactor to those who are already happy." And people generally seem to be happy with their short lives. They don't believe in death and don't want to be reminded of it. They know they are going to die, but deep inside they don't believe they will. So, why scare them into believing in it?

Actually, I could very well retire. By our standards, I am almost a rich man. I have my back pay for the twenty years of anabiosis. I have never yet claimed any of it. Also I am entitled to full pension. My anabiosis years apply to my seniority. There was a special Academy ruling about it. So why not stay home and devote all my time to bringing Masha up?

Impossible. Anna would be heartbroken. She believes in me. I can't let her down. And then, I have that work urge in me. Have always had it.

My stimuli?

There are several. First and most important, the pleasure of achievement. This is a selfish one. Then, a more noble desire—to help humanity. And also, of course, a touch of vanity. I might as well admit it to myself.

Then let's concentrate on the main problem—Is what I am trying to do really necessary? There is still time to put the whole thing under wraps, disband my little team, and go back to anabiosis. After all, this is my subject. My baby. And our Director would say, "Bravo, Prokhoroff! Welcome home. This is a wise decision. Why risk failure in searching for something new, when you have this thing so firmly in hand?" And he would also think, He's too old—he won't have enough time to finish even the first phase of this new research.

Stop. No more philosophy. Anna is calling me to bathe Masha. This is a ritual. The pleasure peak of the day. Come on, Prokhoroff, this is more important than immortality.

"Coming, darling!"

The duty is performed. A duty? No, a real orgy of pleasure.

There she sits in her little bathtub, such a sturdy tow-headed little girl. Slapping the water with her little hands, laughing, watching the drops fly in all directions. The eyes, two black little buttons, are full of pride. "Look at me. How clever I am." Mother is in a wet chamber robe, disheveled, sparkling teeth, drops of water on her cheeks and soft white throat. (She has gained a little weight, and this is becoming to her.)

"Just look, Ivan, look! Isn't she a darling?"

"Darling! You both are my darlings!"

"All right, enough, you little bandit . . . Ivan, the sheet!"

I spread the sheet, not very expertly. Anna snatches Masha out of the water and passes her on to me.

"Your daughter."

I wrap the sheet around her, afraid to drop her, and feel her strong little body under the wet cloth. Then press her to myself for a moment. There are no words to describe this feeling of proximity to that little body. Masha wants to cry at first—such cruel people depriving her of fun! She screws up her little face into a capricious grimace, but then optimism gets the upper hand, and she reaches for my nose. And here Anna repossesses her for more expert drying.

A whole arsenal of meaningless tender words. (Is there a dictionary of those? Might be useful to child psychologists.) And just a glance in my direction. I'm nobody here—just the father.

"Ivan. The formula from the kitchen!"

The second act, already in the nursery. Anna sits in a modernistic armchair (they say that they now consult anatomists designing them), holding Masha on her lap. There has been a change: Masha is now wearing a snow-white night chemise; only her toes are protruding from under it like little clusters of rose buds. She is very busy sucking at the plastic nipple of the bottle that Anna is holding. Masha is holding onto it as well, with both hands, her little black eyes bulging with fierce defiance—just try to take it from me! I need this bottle, and I don't give a whoop for anyone of you! (Those Rockefeller professors would love to see this demonstration of the possession drive.)

"This will be like this always, Anna. Parents only in the intervals between more enjoyable tasks."

"Don't be an egotist, Ivan."

She means "egoist," but I don't correct her. And I'm not an egoist. Or egotist. I'm satisfied with crumbs. It is quite enough for me to hold her for a few moments and to know that this is my daughter. That's the sum total of my animal pleasures.

And Masha is already fighting drowsiness. Her stomach has been filled, and the bottle has lost its original value. Now it is Anna alone who is holding it.

Sleep.

Masha has been deposited into her "automatic" crib. I am still permitted to kiss her cheek lightly, look at her for a few moments, listen to the soft musical sounds emanating from the flat rubber pillow—the built-in lullaby guaranteed to act in five minutes, and—finis. Until tomorrow.

Later, Anna and I are having tea in the kitchen, exhausted and happy. We are talking about all sorts of things, little meaningless things, and suddenly, a complete *non sequitur:* "You know, Ivan, I think Masha is not holding her head *quite* straight."

I begin to calm her down. After all, I'm also a medical man, I know anatomy, I would have noticed it, and then the specialists examine her every week.

"Well, maybe I'm wrong . . . What were you talking about?"

How do I know what I was talking about? She wasn't listening anyway, and I feel a little hurt. But then I very quickly forgive her. After all, she is so inattentive because of our little Masha.

(And I am certainly going to call that pediatrician in the morning. Some of them are careless. And ours is still very young and pretty—probably has nothing but boy friends on her mind.)

One must be very careful when tinkering with Nature. Would "immortality" ever replace these evening baths and these teas in the kitchen?

Doubtful.

August 10

We are working like a little brood of work-mad bees. None of us has used his vacation time, because we must prepare that Academy report. A small group, three boys and two girls, but real enthusiasts. Also Anna and Ziama, of course.

I watch my little team with envy. Young, everything is ahead of them yet. And everyone has such an overwhelming faith in me. To them I'm a prophet leading them to the Promised Land. And all I have is ten or fifteen years, at best. It is improbable that we can complete even our basic research by that time. But perhaps, one of them will develop into a new leader—as Yura did. Such fine boys and girls, all products of modern education—a selective concentration of pertinent information.

This is our work program:

We all know our problem and general directions. Each one of us is working separately, on his own, developing his own approaches with the help of libraries and science consultants. I don't want any duplication of effort—we have no time for routine. We are eight independent scouts roaming all over the "enemy territory" of science collecting valuable clues for our future attack.

Twice a week, general meetings. Reports, arguments, criticism, occasional noisy conflicts. No restraints here; I encourage enthusiasm and passion, and above all, independent thinking.

Anna is our clearinghouse. She receives and organizes all the material—a truly titanic task.

The report must be ready by September 1. (I have decided to risk it, after all. Otherwise, we would have to wait for a whole year.)

The report will be checked by specialists and computers in various technical departments. And then, on September 23, the formal presentation in front of the panel. I will read the report, and then defend it—point by point—against all criticism.

It is simply impossible that an idea like ours will not be accepted. It is speculative, but it opens tremendous horizons—enough for a hundred years.

September 26

We have failed!

An ignominious, monumental defeat!

For three days now I can find no place for myself. I am lying on my divan, reading all sorts of balderdash, without understanding any of it. I can think of nothing but that damned meeting. Even when playing with Masha.

Today, after the now usual quarrel with Anna, I have decided to listen to that whole disgraceful comedy on the recorder. Nonetheless, I must start thinking what to do next—to fight on or give up.

For my professional diary I should describe the meeting in all details. But I have no energy for this, and then, there are tapes and recordings. Anna wrote an article calling this "a shocking picture of venerable old science fossils strangling young talents." (Young? I? Stupid.) For the first time the editor of *The Science Standard* has rejected her work—"It would be unethical for us to use it inasmuch as you are an interested party."

■ ■

I have finished listening to all tapes. And still I can't evaluate objectively what really happened.

Why did they spurn us. *Why?*

Unimportant problems?

No. Even the President admitted that the span of human life is insufficient and can perhaps be lengthened. Yes, the President, Isakoff, Bamberger, but what about the other five? They seemed to be completely satisfied with their limitations. Particularly that philosopher Koucheroff. "They are creating panic for nothing— trying to put themselves on the map. The level of our present gerontological research is quite sufficient. There's no necessity for any new Institute . . ." Blockhead!

Generally, Academicians are not particularly interested in any future for humanity.

Or are we really reaching for the moon?

No. The mechanics of aging can be deciphered.

Must we recheck all our postulates? No. The panel did not contest any of them. Just the general idea.

Or are we insufficiently qualified for such a monumental task? Just a bunch of nobodies? "Everyone would like to set up an Institute. . . . And then try to close it." This is how the secretary of the Academy put it.

"Try to close it." What did he mean by that? All the questions that would be asked if we should fail? "Who authorized it anyway?" Of course! "Do nothing, and you will not be criticized." And I thought this kind of attitude had been lived down years ago.

And he certainly didn't spare me personally. "Who is Prokhoroff anyway? The first anabiosis subject? Does that qualify him for a project requiring a tremendous drain of talent already engaged in useful scientific work?"

He also read my scientific curriculum vitae. Factually, it was accurate. I had tackled many problems and had never really accomplished anything. "He published no important science papers." (Yes, but I was prevented from it by my illness! However, this is no excuse; facts remain facts.)

All my work in the sphere of modeling and anabiosis was not even mentioned. The credit went to my pupils. If it were not for Yura, who in his speech gave me full credit, I would have remained just a "subject"—no better than that bandit whom they keep in the deep freeze. However Yura was there as a witness, and not as a member of the panel. And even he could not convince them. ("That was over twenty years ago. From then on Prokhoroff had had no chance to participate in any scientific work.")

All perfectly correct, ladies and gentlemen of the jury. No science papers, twenty years of living death, that's right.

The Academy's decision: "Postpone the creation of the Longevity Institute until more precise information on the subject is available. Meanwhile, grant the necessary allocation to Prokhoroff's group to continue research within the sphere outlined in his report."

No Institute. And without an Institute all our work is doomed to failure. There are no two ways about that.

Finita la commedia.

November 3

It is absolutely unclear why I keep writing my diary. An attempt to break the vicious circle of intellectual isolation? If so, a completely unsuccessful attempt.

Life has come to a stop. No desire to do anything. Not even think. What for? To what can I compare that strange state of despondency which has enveloped me? "The poisonous fog." Rather poetic. Perhaps I should abandon everything and start writing poetry? That would be spectacular—a well-known scientist turned poet. Tania Sitnik would approve. No, seriously, there are just no words to describe my present intellectual collapse. Irritation, vexation, slow impotent anger.

My team is beginning to disintegrate as well. Yesterday, Dimitri, that self-styled genius, came running to me. "Ivan Nikolaevich, allow me to work for a while at Nadin's institute. I must work out a theory of complex functional self-regulation of the system, and we have no proper facilities here." "Of course, Dima. Finish what you're doing here, and run along." I hope that he never comes back. One "genius" can contaminate the whole team.

And those post-mortem discussions! They are driving me up the wall. Especially Anna: "You should have told them this . . . You should have insisted . . . You missed that point completely . . . And you shouldn't have been so irritable . . . why, calling Koucheroff a half-baked statistician!" To hell with them all! Why should I be polite when they are spitting on me? And Ziama, on the contrary: "You should have hit them with full force—minced no words with those old fools! They would have given in. You didn't use shock psychology enough. And even if you failed, at least you would have had your pleasure."

I have had my pleasure, thank you very much. Up to here. I still don't know where to hide from myself—now that Anna has pulled up all her drawbridges.

And really, who am I to demand recognition? What did I discover, what theory did I prove? Anabiosis. The scheme of internal organ functions? But all that was mere compilation. I just put the pieces together. Yes, it wasn't so bad—even a child can see my work there. But genius? Far from it. A very good file clerk.

And what now? "The conquest over old age . . . Immortality." Anna was right—good journalistic copy. Such goals. And where are ideas? True, I have something there. No use denying it. Take the scheme of aging, for instance. The accumulation of dross in biological matrices. Or artificial intelligence. And biosynthesis. No. Empty theories without a single factual support. Only abstract mathematicians know how to develop those. They can always claim that no one understands them yet.

I feel my impotence. My limitations. Probably I'm all wrong. Probably I just don't understand Nature and am barking up the wrong tree.

But what can I do once I admit my defeat?

Family.

That's a very secure yoke. Not easy to get out of. A young wife who expects me to produce scientific miracles. A daughter who must be proud of her father when she grows up. I can whine all I want, but I must carry on.

Yes, my daughter. The only real accomplishment of my life. When I take her in my arms and feel her sweet weight, when she pulls my hair and tweaks my nose, everything disappears and I need nothing else. And no one. Not even Anna. At least Masha can't criticize me and tell me what to do and what not to do.

■ ■

We stand near the window, looking out, Masha in my arms. Cars are floating by. An endless procession. Each with some purpose. The wind is shaking bare black branches. Children are playing in the park across the street. And I don't need any theories, any philosophy.

"Look, Masha, look! Do you see that dog?"

She looks through the glass (actually, plastic), turns her little head following my finger. Notices the dog, knocks on the pane with her little fist.

Masha is almost eight months old. But she is already an individual. Her emotions are clearly defined, and her scale of feelings is quite large. Her cortex has absorbed many models. She recognizes over one hundred objects, separates them from one another, in books and on the telescreen.

She has a definite character. Her desires are concrete and her demands unyielding. She is already trying to bend us to her will. We are trying to resist. Not always successfully.

I am a professor, a man of science, and I am trying to watch her development with objectivity. She is ahead of the average level. (Some biologists connect this with the age of male parent.) No, we don't take the bait. We don't consider her a *wunderkind*. And yet, deep inside, both Anna and I think: She is an unusual child. Quite exceptional. And Tania Sitnik is convinced she is a genius.

But all that Anna and I really need is the fact that she exists, that we have her. So far, this is fully sufficient for us.

November 20

We "celebrated" Anna's birthday.

What is there to celebrate? One more milestone on the road to death.

Yura and Tatiana came and we had supper. Of course they know all about my failures and misgivings. Yura tried to encourage me. "Academy is not the end of the world. Science develops independently from bureaucratic organizations. Remember all the work we did in our small dark rooms—secretly from everybody." Yes, I remember. It is now known as the Sitnik theory of anabiosis.

And also: "Actually you scored a bit of victory. They could have disbanded your group. Instead, they allocated you enough money for expansion."

Expansion where?

Masha was brought out and put on public display. She stared at glasses and bottles on the table . . . tried to reach them. She still can't judge distances—what is near and what is far. Aunt Tania, as we call her now, says this comes later. How does she know?

Anna has been very taciturn of late, locked all her "doors." Probably the aftershock of our failure, a delayed reaction. She feels that real work is slipping through our fingers. She is also working on her first "book"—a sort of memoirs of a science journalist. I never ask her what she is doing.

A few days ago we had the first general meeting. The whole team assembled in our place. The initial shock had worn off, and everyone had sufficient time to think everything through. I have an electro-recording of the whole thing. But I will cite only main points:

I opened it. "You all know our problems. Identification and isolation of molecular obstacles. The more distant goal: designing of artificial intelligence on biological level. Then, biosynthesis of the human body out of wearproof biological matrices. I'd like to hear from everyone of you."

They were all sitting around gloomy and silent. The atmosphere of a wake.

Almost immediately a quarrel flared up. Everyone jumped at Dimitri accusing him of desertion under fire. He was trying to defend himself—"Only temporary . . . to advance our own work . . ."

"You're just a coward!"

"A deserter!"

"Who needs you? Go and build robots with Nadin!"

"Just see if you can design a vacuum cleaner on your own."

(Nadin is a cosmologist. Dimitri is taking over to him my ideas on synthetic intelligence. Well, actually, this is his right. No one can patent ideas. And if Omyokone is really what it is supposed to be, my ideas are years behind Yamaga's anyway.)

Finally Dimitri left in a huff, slamming the door.

Then I questioned everyone individually. Stressed the point that I was not holding anyone, that they were free to leave if they wanted. No one wanted. They became calm. Youth is quick to forgive and forget. Katia even said she was sorry for Dimitri. ("He will wind up floating in the vacuum. They say it's impossible to work with Nadin.")

Now we started to discuss the main point. Where are we going to work? Now that we have been given an independent allocation, we could choose.

There were three possibilities. First, the Psychology Institute. (Ziama's suggestion.) Then, the Institute of Advanced Cybernetics. Then, our own Institute of Physiology and Anabiosis. (Yura said he would build an independent annex for us.) We agreed to postpone the final decision and to conduct some reconnaisance in depth, to find out who would give us the best facilities and cooperation. (I am sure Yura would.)

Then we quietly discussed the details of our own work. We now had sufficient means to expand our team. We listed candidates for various vacancies. The possibility of publishing our own science paper was discussed as well. That could be important for getting good people to join us. Of course, our scope was not what we were hoping for, but still we were fully operational. After all, our group was not broken up, as Yura had pointed out, and that was the main thing. We were still alive as a working collective. And with Yura's help (if we stay at our institute) we could almost function as our own small institute.

Generally, it was a very fruitful meeting. The youngsters soon cheered up. Ziama and Katia played with Masha, and Katia even tried speaking to her. I was swelling with pride. Then Anna took her away to bathe her and put her to bed, and we continued to eat and to drink.

The youngsters started dancing. Ziama surprised everyone by dancing the Caucasian Lezghinka. I became slightly drunk, and not unhappily so. (I have been nipping now and then ever since our Moscow fiasco—I keep a bottle of brandy now in my desk. Anna knows nothing about that, of course.)

Kolia played a guitar. Anna was telling some funny stories about her journalistic meetings with various famous scientists, and everyone laughed. (That is, everyone with the exception of myself. I just don't know how to respond to humor. A born pessimist and a killjoy.) Then, suddenly, Anna became very sad, excused herself and went into her room. She was tired, and she had drunk more than necessary.

We drank some more wine, and then, black coffee. They questioned me about the past, my preanabiosis days, and I caught myself describing everything in glorious colors. But, of course, I knew that I was lying; life was quite drab then. Why do old people like so much to brag about "the good old days"?

Going to bed I made a resolution—since I have so little time left—to eliminate everything absolutely not essential for my work. And this goes for this diary—a stupid waste of time.

So this is the last entry.

March 10, 1994

I have just put Masha to bed. I am sitting next to her. No, I'm not humming. Masha is accustomed to automatic lullabies performed by her "lullaby pillow." They are designed and recorded by specialists—a sort of hypnotism. For all ages. No. I'm just repeating these meaningless words in my head.

I have never felt worse than tonight. Such utter hopelessness. Such lack of purpose for living.

■ ■

Is seems that at any moment Anna will come in. I can hear her voice: "She's already asleep? You're a magician." Anna's face? No, I can imagine only her voice. Audile impressions stay longer in your mind than visual ones. Anna's face has long since become blurred in my mind. I just can't recapture it.

Why did all this have to happen to me? Why didn't I die then of leukemia the way ordinary people died of it in my time?

Death—this most dependable avenue of escape—has now been cut off. I have been deprived of this ever-present ally that every man has with him from the day he is born. I have been doomed to live. For as long as I possibly can. An enormously cruel sentence.

For Masha.

How calm her little face is. Such soft breathing. Respiratory tracts still unclogged by accumulation of biological dross. I must bend close to her face to hear it at all.

Anna used to have recurring nightmares after coming home from the maternity clinic. She would wake up and listen for Masha's breathing. And when she couldn't hear it, she would jump out of bed, terror-stricken, snatch Masha out of her crib and press her to her breast. She's here! She's alive!

And I would be in my room, sleeping like a log—happy. How

happy I was then! Wife, daughter, loyal collaborators, hopes. "We will show them! We will turn all science upside down!"

Now all this is no more. The only thing that is left is this little creature. "A chemical arrangement," according to Schwartzerberg. "My whole life," according to Ivan Prokhoroff. My Masha. I must live for her. Live long—for at least twenty more years, if possible. Until she will not need me any longer.

Why was I so inattentive, so insensitive? After all, I had lived with Anna, sometimes even slept with her. Only now do I remember the signs of her constant strain. Her uneasiness. And that day, in that damned hospital town, when she told me that "he agrees . . . everything is fine." The way she said it, I should have sensed that it wasn't fine at all.

We could have gone away. Far away. Out of *his* reach. To Africa. To Antarctica.

■ ■

Masha stirs in her sleep, muttering something.

She sleeps and knows nothing.

And then comes the morning. "Mummy . . . Mummy?"

And a lie: "She's away, Masha. She will soon come back."

I can't help blaming Ziama for not telling me that he was released. "Anna told me that she had told you . . . I was sure . . . I knew that you didn't like to hear about him. I took it for granted that you knew." For granted! Some psychologist!

But then, he did tell me once: "You know, I think Anna is having a nerve crisis . . . happens to all women. Try to be kind to her, and stay with her as much as you can. She needs you."

She certainly doesn't need me tonight. She's dead. What a black little word!

■ ■

Nine o'clock. What must I do now? Open my bed . . . bring some water. Leave the night light in her room. It was one of her idiosyncrasies—light at night. That, and those locks on the door. I teased her about them. "You should be living in a safe with a triple combination lock." Some husband!

Still, Ziama could have warned me.

"About what, Ivan? The reports were excellent. I am no Omyo-kone. I can't predict the future."

(Omyokone couldn't either. And there hasn't been a word about him in any of the science papers for months and months. A hoax? Probably. I had written to Amiko and got a postcard with a view of Fujiyama. "Professor Yamaga left the university and removed his installations to Kyoto. He is financed by private capital now—American." And Amiko had become engaged to an Australian doctor.)

Not important.

The automat is loaded for the morning—milk, potato purée, peach and banana paste. Then, I will take her to the day nursery. It is good that she became used to it so easily. Otherwise there would have been another trauma.

(At first Anna did not want to send her there, but then, two weeks before that day, she suddenly agreed. Probably when she sensed the first signs of danger. Why was she always so locked up within herself when that man was concerned? She kept him to herself, felt it was her sole responsibility. Didn't want to involve me. But Ziama, Ziama! He should have known better. Probably Anna begged him not to tell me anything. A conspiracy of kindness, or a simple carelessness?)

The Service of Child Care has advised me to send Masha to the Children's Home. "She needs professional attention . . . You won't be able to bring her up properly."

My darling little Masha! I will never send you away anywhere, not even if they build a Paradise in our town. I will never give you away to anyone. Never.

April 19

This is the way we live:

We get up at seven. That is, I wake up at six, but stay in bed, thinking. Just thinking at first. Masha is still asleep. I can faintly hear her breathing. I have put her automatic crib flush next to my bed.

Then, for perhaps half an hour, I work. That is, think about immediate problems, with a pad and a pencil. Still in bed.

The automat awakens Masha at seven.

"Good morning . . ."

"Good morning, Masha. Have your breakfast now, and let me work a little more."

Usually this does not work. Just as soon as she is through eating, she climbs over into my bed, gets under the blanket, wraps her little arms around my neck, rubs her wet nose against my cheek, kisses me, and babbles away.

There is no greater happiness for me than during those few minutes. I dread the future, when she will grow up, and these minutes will become only memories. No, this is not true. I want her to grow up, to become pretty, strong and intelligent, a "modern human being" while I am still here to see it. (My last blood test wasn't very good. Nothing to worry about, but I'm undergoing a course of treatments—the very newest set of medicaments.)

■ ■

We luxuriate like this for five or ten minutes. Then, we study. Read books, look at pictures. That is, I read, and Masha identifies the images.

My friends say, "Why are you torturing the child? She is getting all this in her day nursery."

I am sure she does. But I am convinced that the process of learning can be considerably speeded up—as long as her brain absorbs this additional information. It is always good to surge ahead, and later, if necessary, to slow down, or even take a breather to let brain neurons rest a little.

We are beginning to study English. Since she has become familiar with Russian and already operates successfully with over three hundred word models, she can start on another language. For as long as she can separate the words in her brain. And her pronunciation is good. The vocal-cord apparatus has developed surprisingly quickly and well. And she has a good ear.

At half past seven, we get up.

"Masha wants to stay in bed. Masha wants . . ."

I don't give in. She must understand discipline. "No, Masha. Get up."

"Masha doesn't want . . . Masha doesn't want . . ."

She often speaks this way about herself, in the third person. It is interesting to watch the formation of intellect by linguistic signs. You, he, she, they she knows well, but she has a little difficulty with her I. (Her father never had this difficulty! I was probably born an egoist.) She is still mixing complex grammatical tenses, but our child psychologist insists that this is normal.

She also sometimes comes out with incoherent sentences. Those must be thoughts automatically expelled from her subconscious. Later she will learn to check them and force them back into the reservoir of her mind. They say that thoughts can be "read" (even if not very accurately) in the biocurrents that come from the tongue and vocal cords, both of which react to thought.

Next on the program is our morning setting-up exercises. She loves them, and I hate them. Then, washing and dressing. (I have let my beard grow ever since she badly cut her finger on my razor.) For some reason she doesn't like the morning washing. Even though generally she loves water. All children do—a throwback to our amphibious past. But washing, no. Not Masha.

"No, daddy, no . . . Masha is clean . . . Masha doesn't need . . ."

No, Masha needs. Masha needs everything. This is how a sense of duty is developed. The sense which will eventually tie her up into an orderly sociological pattern.

I never punish her. Only once I slapped her hands—and quite

hard. To anchor, once and for all, the meaning of "this must not be done."

(She developed a habit of climbing upon the chair and pulling things down from my desk. I told her many times not to do it. Even raised my voice. It didn't work. Then, upon some purely pedagogical consideration, I decided to use the sure deterrent—force. That is, pain. It was pitiful. She sobbed, her face in my lap, and my own cheeks were wet with tears. But I didn't weaken.)

"Remember: You must not do this. You must not. Must not. Must not."

This worked. The meaning of these two words, must not, has been firmly implanted in her mind. This is very important. A human life is composed of these "must not's"—one must learn to live with them to be happy. And here one must use some sharp irritant—pain—to anchor this in a child's brain.

I'm learning things.

■ ■

Nine o'clock. We must leave. I will spend my day at the Institute. And Masha, in her day nursery.

April 25

"Mamma" now exists as a sort of myth.

Her portrait is standing on my desk. Masha knows it well—as a picture, not as a person. (A child's memory is so mercifully short.) From time to time I show her other pictures of Anna. Unfortunately I have so very few of them. Anna did not like to be photographed, and when she moved over to my place she must have destroyed all her old pictures, mostly with her husband. There is also a short film—showing them coming home from the maternity clinic, and a few other scenes. I show it to Masha and say, "This is Mamma." And now she repeats, "This is Mamma," without the slightest emotion.

I also use "Mamma" for educational purposes.

"Look, Mamma, Masha is a bad girl again."

Then she looks at the portrait with apprehension. Perhaps this is wrong? I must ask Doctor Petrova, Masha's psychologist. She would know. Or would she? (I often think that psychologists honestly delude themselves about their capabilities.)

Two months have now passed since that day.

I must describe it. For Masha, when she grows up. Sooner or later she will like to know what happened to her mother. This might even have some educational value—to warn her about unpredictable dangers in daily living. This would not destroy her image of her mother. To her she will always remain as the woman on this picture. Pretty and smiling.

This is not an easy task for me. Still, one day I must do it. I postpone it from day to day. It is frightening to start rummaging through those memories.

Undated

That day I returned home at three o'clock.

We had had an interesting day at the Institute. A famous neurosurgeon, Professor Chebukoff, told us about the surgical repair work now being performed on the human brain. Coming up in the elevator I thought, I must jot all this down before I forget the exact facts.

Our front door was ajar. For a split second: Why? But then: Not important. I must not lose my thought. And suddenly a wall of cold air hit me full in the face—coming from our apartment. The balcony door!

"Anna!"

The entrance hall. A sprawling figure on the floor, next to our bedroom door. The door of our living room is open. The icy wind, loose papers are sliding on the floor as though alive.

I jumped over Anna's body and threw the door of the nursery open. Masha's crib, turned over.

"Ma-a-a-a-sha!"

I dashed to and fro, madly, all frozen inside.

"Ma-a-a-sha-a-a-a!"

I jumped out onto the balcony, gripped the railing, looked down. The lawn covered with snow, high drifts against the walls and around bushes, little whirlwinds of fine snow. Nothing. God! The snow must have covered her!

Back into the hall. Anna. A classical pose of a dead woman. (This can't be faked even by the most accomplished actress.)

A wild thought: Snow might have cushioned her fall!

I ran down like a madman. It is a miracle I didn't break my neck. I forgot the elevator.

So high . . . so high . . . She couldn't have been saved . . . But maybe she hasn't come home yet?

A sharp picture: the overturned crib and a toy monkey—

"Jimmy"—on the floor. Masha never parted with "Jimmy." It means—ohhhhh!

The front door. I catapult through, run around the building. The footpath is covered with fine snow. Not a single footstep. This means the children haven't come back yet. But still . . . Look for her. Look.

Black, naked bushes shivering in the wind, drifting snow between them, no tracks, no one has been here . . . No, not here, she couldn't have fallen so far, the trajectory . . .

No sign of anything. Emptiness and whiteness. Have they picked her up? No, impossible. No footsteps, nothing. And then, they would have informed the authorities, and Anna wouldn't have been lying there.

But "Jimmy"?

I'm trying to think. Using my entire mental strength. I was carrying her to the nursery this morning. Did she have "Jimmy" with her? No, I just can't remember.

What am I doing standing here?

Upstairs! To the telephone!

The elevator is still on our floor. No time. I'm running up, three steps at a clip. I just can't remember about that damned monkey. A complete memory blank.

Our hall. Anna on the floor. Dead.

Why would they kill her? And who?

There she lies. As before. She hasn't moved. Dead.

To the telephone. Pressing the call buttons. Finally a smiling round face on the little screen. A day-nursery nanny.

"Masha! Is Masha there?"

"What Masha? We have three—"

Oh hell! "Masha Prokhorova! Is she there?"

"Yes. Her mother called, promised to come for her—"

The cut-off button. An immense relief. Masha is alive. *Alive.* And only then: Anna! Oh good God!

The left arm under her body, her legs bent unnaturally, bare knees. The blue blouse torn, a small round breast with a pink nipple and the corona around it. The blood from a forehead wound has filled the eye socket and dribbled down to the floor gumming up a lock of her dark hair. (This vision became so implanted in my mind that for weeks I could see it in every detail every time I closed my eyes.)

Check the heart. No, touch her skin first. My arm is like lead, I'm afraid to touch her.

The cheek is cold. Ice cold. A corpse.

It's cold in the room—the air from the balcony . . . A small tiny hope. To feel her pulse? Her right arm is free. No. What pulse? A corpse. I've seen too many of them in my life not to know one.

Mouth-to-mouth resuscitation. At the same time I am trying to massage her heart. A very uncomfortable pose. My arms are becoming numb. And the lips—like ice: *rigor mortis.*

God, oh God, oh God . . . Let her open her eyes, let her eyelid quiver, let me feel the air coming out of her cold mouth . . .

I don't know how long all this has taken. The open front door. I should shout for help. What help? Who can help?

My arms give up. No more strength. And what for? There is no sign of life. Nothing. She is dead. Has been dead for some time.

Put her on the divan? But then I remember: This is a murder; nothing must be touched.

I stagger to the telephone, press the red button repeatedly—"First Aid."

"Send a reanimation team at once. The Street of Peace. Number 12, Apartment 176. A murder. A head trauma. This is Professor Prokhoroff. My wife. Quickly."

This is all I can do. I'm dead tired. Every ounce of life is drained from my body. As in my anabiosis.

And then, a sudden terrifying thought! Masha! What if the murderer is waiting for Masha outside the nursery?

I already know who the murderer is. Her husband. He must have escaped from Valim. Some of them do. Ziama has told me.

I am pressing the buttons again. This is one of the few numbers I know by heart. Ah, the screen begins to light up. Aunt Tania, Tatiana Sitnik. A fine, calm face.

"Is Yura home?"

"Yes, he just came in. Do you want to speak with him?"

"No, no. I need your help. Urgently. Take the car, go to the nursery, and collect Masha. *Both* of you. I beg you. Don't go alone."

(I mustn't explain anything. She is so nervous. She might faint dead away. I must give her no time to question me.)

"I'll explain everything later. Anna has been taken ill, and I can't take Masha. Bring her to your place. And please, *both* of you. Ask Yura."

I jam the cut-off button, and press the "No calls" one. Let them think the phone is out of order. Will they release Masha to them? Of course. The Sitniks are well known in this town. Call the police? (We still call it "milice" here.) Not necessary. The First Aid place would notify them automatically. I said "murder."

I slump into a chair. For a moment I just sit there, without a thought. Just looking around.

A battlefield. One armchair is overturned, another is turned toward the wall. One door of the wardrobe is torn off and is hanging on a single hinge. Books on the floor, broken glass, bric-a-brac. In Masha's bedroom, toys are scattered around. Dolls, little bears, monkeys, in crazy poses. "Like corpses." The wind is playing with papers on the floor, and near the open balcony door, a miniature snowdrift.

April 28

It is difficult for me to describe the police procedure. For them, all this was simple and trite. Their everyday work. But to me it was melodramatically tragic. I felt as though I were a killer and had to defend myself from justice.

And really, didn't I kill her after all? By imposing myself on her, appealing to her sense of pity and, finally, seducing her. Well, *seducing* is not a correct word; but I should have been wiser. Quite possibly she would have been perfectly happy without me, and all this would not have happened.

It is senseless to speak about all this now. Of course, I am to blame. Everyone is to blame. Life is to blame. And even she is. (How cruel is this objective analysis!)

I remember only small, disjointed scenes. My memory of that day is like a bad film cut by a stupid editor who has not read the scenario.

The police doctor: a corpulent red-haired man. He quickly took off his uniform greatcoat and bent over the corpse. (A corpse!) Lifted one eyelid, flashed a small electric light into her eye. Then brought out a small electronic gadget, pressed it against her left breast, and looked at the gauge. Then turned to the two police inspectors who had come with him.

"Dead."

"Reanimation?"

"One moment. Tamara, the probe."

A young girl assistant handed him a slender needle attached to a cord. The doctor punctured Anna's skin on her neck, took a gauge from Tamara's manicured hand and glanced at it.

"No."

He straightened out, reached for his greatcoat and explained to me in layman's terms:

"Too late. We can start up the heart, even four hours after it stopped, but her brain is gone, long ago. The temperature at the base of the skull has gone down too much. Sorry."

He collected his things, said something to the inspectors, and walked out with his Tamara.

The Senior Inspector, a handsome, middle-aged man, sat down in a chair, and smiled a polite, sad smile. "Forgive me, but I must ask you a few questions."

Since you are the prime suspect—no, he didn't say that; he was polite and delicate throughout; even sympathetic. The usual questions about her name, age, occupation, relatives, her relationship with me, et cetera. Then: "Anything missing in the house? Some valuables? Money? Important papers?"

"I haven't checked. But we have nothing of any particular value."

"Any secret documents?"

"No."

"Tell me how you found the body."

I told him—with all the details I could remember. I felt uneasy telling him about my abandoning Anna lying on the floor and running out to look for Masha.

"I was worrying about the child."

"I understand. Of course." He must have children of his own.

"Did she have enemies?"

Enemies. This word hits me. Anna, and enemies—enemies who could kill her? Of course not.

"And now, forgive me, I must touch upon some personal points of your conjugal life."

(Of course. I remember reading in the memoirs of a famous English detective that the mere fact of being married to a victim is considered to be a sufficient murder motive.)

"How long have you been married?"

"We were not married."

"Yes, of course." (Why "of course"?) "I mean, living together?"

I told him.

"You have one child?"

"Yes."

"Did you get along well together? Were you compatible?"

I told him that we were what generally is known as a happy

family. We had interesting common work, and we adored our daughter. And never had any lasting arguments and quarrels.

"And, forgive me, on the physical side?"

I told him that I thought that that was not very important to either of us. However, we seemed to be emotionally well enough adjusted.

"You know, of course, that her husband was released from Valim?"

(Released? No, I didn't know. I was surprised when she stopped going there some months ago, but I never questioned her and she volunteered no information. We had an unspoken agreement not to speak about him. It was unpleasant to both of us.)

"Why?"

"He was sufficiently cured."

"When?"

He brought a slip of paper from his pocket. Obviously, before coming here, they had consulted their files.

"In January. He has been under medical observation. He's working as an engineer-designer at an electronics factory. His address . . ."

And so on. Quite a detailed report. According to his house warden, he lived quietly, had no visitors except his doctors, and "once or twice his former wife." So Anna was seeing him! And what a fool I was, not to notice her nervousness, restlessness, melancholy spells! Idiot!

"Inspector, I'm sure it's he who killed her."

"This is possible. We have issued an order for his arrest—for questioning."

At this point, another inspector, very young and very brash, who had been searching the apartment, approached us.

"A classical case, Colonel. Jealousy. Probably an attempted rape."

I shuddered. How ugly it all was.

"Here's the murder weapon; it rolled behind the wardrobe. Signs of blood, and it fits the wound perfectly."

An old brass candlestick, just like those in bad novels. Some twenty-five years ago Liuba gave it to me, for my birthday. I had meant to throw it out, but somehow I never got around to doing it. Idiotic sentimentality. Such a useless, ugly thing.

"Also I found this note to the victim."

The *victim!*

The older inspector took the little note, started to read: "Anna darling, Why don't you answer me? I'm growing desperate—" He didn't read further. Just put it into his pocket and got up. Picked up his coat and hat. "This will be all for a while. Of course, you're not to leave town until further notice. They'll come to collect the body for autopsy. Maybe you'd better get some clean clothes for her. However, that's up to you. I'm sorry this has happened."

His assistant did not say anything. Just followed his chief out. A slam of the door.

For the last time, Anna and I were alone together. I slumped into a chair, dead tired, emotionally and physically exhausted. Mechanical thoughts—get that new brown dress of hers out of the wardrobe, clean up, arrange the furniture. (The balcony door was already closed, and it was becoming warmer, but I still had my overcoat and hat on.) Then? Go to the Sitniks and see Masha, call Ziama. And then? Funeral, cremation, life.

The telephone rang. (That young officer had used it and had released the "No calls" button!) Tania Sitnik. Just the voice, no image. The strained, emotion-charged voice. "Masha's here. But, Ivan, if Anna's sick, call the hospital."

"Yes, yes. Everything has been done. I'll be over very soon."

The cut-off button. Another thoughtless pause.

A ring at the door. They came for her. Two husky men with a stretcher, and a woman. She looked at Anna.

"Was she lying like that all the time?"

(Yes. Why hadn't I put her on the divan after everything was finished?)

The men spread a large black cloth on the floor, and easily, professionally, lifted Anna's body. I shuddered. It was so ugly, that coarse black cloth.

"Wait a minute, I'll get a sheet."

"Very well."

"And some fresh clothes."

"Not important now. Bring them in for the cremation."

The woman was young and quite sympathetic. A doctor? A police official?

The men wrapped Anna up, and put her onto the stretcher.

"Better wipe the blood up, or it'll stain your floor."

They took Anna, now looking like a cocoon, out of the apartment. For some reason I walked along with them. The elevator was not large enough, and we walked down the stairway.

Outside stood a sleek electric ambulance. They slid the stretcher in and closed the door. Rather like inserting a cartridge into a firing chamber of a rifle.

The woman turned to me and smiled. A fine, pretty face. "Better go back, Professor. You'll catch your death of cold."

Undated

I must finish describing that terrible day. (However there was nothing very terrible after they took her out. Somehow a man gets adjusted to any horror.)

I mopped up Anna's blood, straightened the furniture, collected Masha's toys from the floor. Then I went to Yura and Tania. It was a bitter-cold day, and I had lost my muffler somewhere. I could have taken a taxi, but somehow I didn't think about that. It wasn't a long walk, and I was quite unconscious of cold.

Yura answered the door. He embraced me.

"Yes, yes, we already know. How terrible!"

I became very small, pitifully helpless. Tears started to creep down my cheeks. I broke away from Yura and sat down in a chair in their entrance hall.

And suddenly: "Daddy! Daddy has come!"

She ran to me and jumped onto my lap as she always did since the time she learned to walk.

I pulled her to myself whispering into her little ear: "My darling, my little duckling . . ." Pure emotion.

(They must have undressed her and put her onto a marble slab. A plastic identification tag tied to her leg. What name did they use—Prokhoroff or Stakhevich? And I hope her underwear was clean; she isn't always careful about that.)

Tania came out. Red eyes, but controlling herself, for Masha's benefit. Embraced and kissed me. ("Aunt Tania." What would have I done without her, and Yura?) She took Masha with her into the kitchen.

Yura was extremely tactful. He didn't ask me any questions. He took me into the living room, took my overcoat and hat, and gave me a drink. Some tranquilizing mixture. Asked me if I wanted something to eat. I said no.

(It appeared that Ziama had telephoned them, after being unable to get through to me. He had been informed by the Psychology Service; he was listed there as Anna's psychologist.)

If we had any dinner, I didn't notice it. The real ordeal was trying to put Masha to bed. First she wanted her "Jimmy." Then she started to cry. "Mummy . . . Mummy . . . Masha wants Mummy . . ." I was ready to cry myself. We tried all our guiles. Without success. Masha was becoming hysterical.

If it had not been for Ziama, who came in, I don't know what we would have done. It is strange, the authority that a trained psychologist commands, even from small children. He took Masha onto his lap and spoke to her, and she stopped crying. Tania brought out some warm milk. Masha drank it and quickly fell asleep—the fixed physiological programs. I sat next to her, completely demolished. Not even grief-stricken. Just empty. How are we going to live now? Will I be able to bring up my little girl? (Why an autopsy? What are they trying to establish? Those official rules are often stupid.)

Ziama suggested that I spend the night at his place. Everyone was relieved. Having a grief-numbed man on one's hands is an ordeal. Tania tried to talk me into staying with them, but that was a mere formality. She herself was emotionally exhausted, almost to the breaking point.

"Don't worry about Masha. Now I'm coming into my own as a real aunt. Until you—"

Until what? Would I ever be the same? That was quite impossible. All my "life programs" had been suddenly completely destroyed. (And that meeting at the Institute tomorrow. Someone must telephone them.)

I too was glad to leave. Now that Masha was asleep, I would be questioned. And with Ziama it is easy to be silent.

Undated

This was the first time I saw Ziama's place. It is very large, very untidy, cluttered with all sorts of mechanical contraptions. Rather like an electronics repair shop. I never knew that modern psychology depended so much on technology.

Ziama offered some food—tasteless stale sandwiches, and I ate. Like a robot being fed electric impulses. Omyokone Prokhoroff. Ziama didn't ask me a single question. But then, after a while: "Are you really all broken up?"

I said, yes, really. Completely. No thoughts, no emotions, just dull pain.

Ziama thought for a second, rubbing his unshaven chin.

"Shall we try dreams?"

"Dreams?"

"Yes. It's a new therapy—still in an experimental stage. There was one doctor, Ritter." I remembered Belsky mentioning this name. "He developed this theory—the physiology of dreams. He claimed that dreams could be induced, recorded, even photographed and used for medical and educational purposes." My idea! "This is still very controversial, but from my experience, it doesn't cause any permanent harm. I have been experimenting with this for years now. Want to try it?"

"Yes. I'd try anything."

"All right, then."

He placed me on an old leather couch. (I was surprised to see that psychologists were still using them.) He brought out some strange contraption, looking like a cosmonaut's helmet, and placed it over my head, adjusting something, probably electrodes. (In a normal state I probably would have resisted, but now I did not care.)

"You won't feel anything, Ivan."

Then he placed a rubber mask over my mouth and nose and

told me to breathe normally. It must have been some gas, but the aroma was pleasant, like that of violets. Ziama walked away into a small adjoining control room and tinkered there for a while. Then he came out bringing a mouthpiece with a cord. He moved an old leather armchair next to the couch, and sat down.

"You will now fall asleep, Ivan. And I will try to control your dreams—or, rather, give them direction. Your own brain will do the rest. This is not fortunetelling or chiromancy, just a way of slightly influencing that portion of your cortex which produces dreams. Relax now. And trust me. Don't resist me. Remember that I'm not merely a doctor, but your close friend as well."

I don't think I could have resisted anyway. Slowly all my thoughts started to dissolve, and instead of them I felt a growing sense of well-being, almost euphoria. The room started to fade out, and there appeared some images—chaotic and indistinct, almost exactly like a film badly out of focus. But gradually they began to get organized. And then, all of a sudden, they became sharp and assumed color and stereoscopic depth.

A little square. Playing children. They see me and run toward me, laughing. Suddenly I see a little girl in a pink dress, and all at once all the other children disappear. I know now that this is Masha. I see her arms stretch toward me. A warm tide sweeps over me. She is telling me something (I don't distinguish the words) pointing away at something. I lift her up. How heavy she has become! I put her down, and now we are walking away, hand in hand. She continues to babble away, and I know that what she is telling me is very interesting to me. "So big . . . going on four . . ." And I feel her little hand in mine.

We are walking farther and farther away. Familiar streets, buildings, squares, but then small wooden houses. This is the town where I grew up as a child. I know that we must hurry. And this is no longer a town, but an open country. There is dust on the road, deep and soft, and I see that it is covering my shoes and my trousers, and also Masha's little slippers. And I know that we have to walk on, that this is very important . . .

We are now walking along a dirt road which I walked so often when I was a little boy. It is growing darker; the sun has set. The road skirts a grove of birch trees with open fields on the other side. Ripe rye with blue cornflowers among the stalks. "Masha, darling, let's walk faster, or we'll be late." She is almost running beside me, and I am pulling her by the hand. I see that she was tired, and I lift her up. I can feel her little body against mine, her arms around my neck, her bow tickling my nose. Her warm breath on my cheek. (A fever?) "I'm scared, Daddy . . ." "Don't be, my darling." "Is it true that there are no gremlins or goblins?" "True, Masha, true." "But there are wolves and bears?" "Yes, Masha, but not here; only in the wild forests. And in summer they are not hungry and never bother people . . ."

It is quite dark now, inky black, and only a narrow band of fading light between the black clouds and the horizon.

And the danger is growing nearer and nearer. Horse hoofs behind us. Somebody's after us. Who? I must run, I must save Masha. I press her to myself. God, God, save her, save her. Take my life. Let me suffer. Let me go through tortures. They draw nearer and nearer to us. I am running, panting. And the bandits (I now know that these are bandits) draw nearer and nearer . . . I fall into the roadside bushes, cover her with my body as though drawing her inside me. And I know that the blow will fall in the next split second . . . They will kill me, take Masha. "No, I won't let them."

And suddenly—nothing.

I open my eyes. Daylight, and sleeping Masha in my arms. A horse-drawn peasant cart on the road, with an old peasant sitting at the edge of the cart, his legs dangling. "Get on, get on. Look at that child—she's so tired." And now we are lying in the cart. The smell of fresh hay and horse sweat. Masha sleeps next to me, breathing so evenly. The soft, secure squeaking of the ungreased wheels. Nothing can touch us now. I can fall asleep . . . I'm so sleepy . . . How pleasant it is to close one's eyes and sink into black nothingness . . .

I wake up, lying on the divan in my own room . . . A severe headache, my head is splitting. The pale sunshine falls in squares on my blanket. The clock on the desk. I know this is the time for her to come home. She is late. Slight alarm. Suddenly the sound of the opening door. Masha! She runs into the room—such a tall, gangling girl. I don't see her face, but this is unimportant; this *is* Masha. "Daddy, what's the matter with you? Are you sick?" The cold thin hand on my forehead, very pleasant. "You are so hot! You have a fever!" "No, Masha, this is nothing . . . I have already taken the medicine." She stands up. Such long thin legs. And two buttons are missing on the overcoat. "Masha, why don't you sew on the buttons?" "Later, Daddy." She sits at the edge of my divan. I know she wants something. "What is it, little monkey? Out with it." "No, nothing. Later." "Come on, tell me now. I'm feeling better. My headache's gone." "Daddy, can I cut my pigtails? No, no, don't say no! Half the girls in the class have already cut theirs." "Over my dead body!" "Oh, Daddy, please." "No, no, and no. Not before you're fourteen." She makes a wry face. "Four more years! Oh Daddy, you're . . . you're so old-fashioned." "I'm not old-fashioned, but I have principles. And it's time for you to work." She wrinkles her nose; there is an ink smear on it. "Work, work, work . . ." She walks into her room, unhappy and upset. I follow her on tiptoe. There she sits, at her desk, working the buttons of the automat, watching the figures that appear on the screen. I am very proud. I know she is a brilliant student, one of the best— no, the very first of her class. "My daughter . . . my education . . ." But, no buttons on the overcoat, mud-splattered shoes, dirty nails, an ink smear on the nose. I'm overwhelmed with happiness. "My darling . . ."

And suddenly, a lobby of a theater . . . It is an intermission. Well-dressed people, walking to and fro. I am walking arm in arm with my daughter. She is tall—taller than I, graceful, beautiful. I feel her elbow against my ribs, and this is not like a woman's elbow at all. It is something very special. Mine. We are speaking about something interesting and profound. Probably science . . . And then I hear a loud whisper behind us: "That's Maria Prokhorova . . . Yes, yes, the one who—" I don't know what my daughter has done, but I know it's something important and significant. My Masha. She is speaking, and in her words I recognize my own thoughts, my own ideas, but expressed so much more clearly than I could ever formulate them. I look at her fine profile, her trim girlish figure, and I jealously watch young men casting glances in her direction. I am trying to maneuver her away from them, but so that she wouldn't notice this. And suddenly, there is a tall, handsome young man, walking straight toward her. A warm, fine smile. "Ah, Masha, darling! How are you?" I feel Masha's elbow pressing against my side. That's him, Daddy, please be nice to him. They chatter gaily, Masha still holding my hand. Then we walk away. "Don't be afraid, Daddy. I'll be still your daughter. Always."

Oh yes. I'll hold on to her. She's mine. She's a part of me.

■ ■

(I have written all this down for Ziama. He told me, "Don't miss any detail, no matter how unimportant. This is a new technique, and we are still studying it. Much of it is still quite obscure.")

Undated

I woke up only in the morning. The day had already ripened in the windows. The helmet was gone, and so was the mask. A completely clear head, but also, no thoughts, only some feelings. A small defenseless body in my arms, a cold little palm on my forehead, a sharp elbow of a grown-up young woman against my side. Pride, happiness, satisfaction . . . Masha is well, Masha is with me, Masha loves me, Masha, Masha, Masha . . .

A sudden switch to reality. Anna was murdered. (Just a realization, a statement of fact. No particular emotion.)

"Ziama!!"

He came in, messy hair, unshaven, a frayed old bathrobe, a cup of coffee in his hand. Tired, sad, kind, red-rimmed eyes. Probably hadn't had enough sleep.

"What are you shouting about? I have already telephoned. Everything's well there. They are having breakfast."

"But Ziama, that man may do something to Masha."

"He won't. They got him last night. Rather, he came in himself."

A relief.

"Where is he?"

"They are taking him back to Valim this morning."

"But why?"

"What do you mean, why? He's a medical case."

"But he killed Anna!"

"Yes."

I knew Ziama's attitude toward criminals, and I did not want to argue with him. Not this morning. There was something else on my mind.

"Listen, Ziama, I don't know what you did to me, but this is remarkable. I was sick with pain last night. Anna. It's all gone this morning. I know she's dead, but I don't feel anything about it. It is as though she is someone I just knew."

Ziama grinned. Strange, he looks sad even when he smiles. "That's all right. That's how it should be."

He put his coffee down, sat next to me, took my hand, found my pulse. And it seemed to me that some strange feeling of peace was flowing into me through this touch. But how could that be? I was stronger than Ziama. And a realist. A skeptic.

"You're all right."

"I feel all right. Tell me—what have you done to me?"

He told me not to be alarmed or ashamed. Mine was the normal reaction. The way I felt about Anna—or, rather, my lack of feeling —was normal too. The sense of loss and grief will return, but they will not be as sharp and painful as they were yesterday. That was the basis of the treatment.

"Did you see Anna in your dreams at all?"

"No. Only Masha."

"Good. This is what I tried to do—channel your emotions toward her. Only toward her. This is the only secure emotional anchor for you—for a while at least. This is why I sat next to you for five hours last night."

This was remarkable. Dream therapy. Wasn't this my idea? And Omyokone also spoke about dreams. And all the while they were working and experimenting on it. It just proved that there was no ownership of ideas, that they were in the air, in the public domain.

"How does it work, Ziama? You must tell me."

"I will, but not now. This is rather complicated. Now you'd better get up, wash up and have some breakfast. This will be a busy day for you. Now, since that man is in custody and everything is clear, they released the body for cremation."

I got up. Still feeling strangely empty of all painful emotions.

"Tell me, how will it be later on today? Will these things— your dreams—stay with me?"

"They usually take a few days to wear off."

"And then, another treatment?"

"No. I don't think so. This must not be overdone. We still don't know how repeated treatments may affect the psyche. But you'll be all right for today. And for a few days after that. Different patients respond differently."

The funeral was set for six o'clock that evening.

They gave me a chance to stay alone with her for a few minutes. A young and very beautiful woman lay in an open coffin. The wound on her forehead had been covered by her brushed hair. She looked more beautiful than when she was alive. Dead people usually do.

I looked at her face, thinking. Quite calmly. Ziama's therapy was still working full force. There was no feeling of grief, or even despondency, just sadness.

What did I think about?

I thought about her life before she met me. True, I didn't know all of it, only some highlights. Nothing about her childhood, for instance. I knew that she had no parents or close relatives—just like me. She had never liked to talk about herself. An introvert? Yes, probably. I was trying to understand her now, to find the point where I had failed her. It must have been when we went to Valim that time. She saw how unpleasant it was for me and decided to exclude me from that part of her life. And I didn't insist; it was more comfortable to me to forget about him. I had always been afraid of complications, of anything interfering with my work.

Did I really know her?

Physically, yes, but inside she had always been an enigma to me. Was she kind? Yes. Like every intelligent and decent human being, even sentimental at times. But only toward those who were weaker than she. She was not afraid of those who were strong. She attacked and criticized them mercilessly in her writing whenever she felt that they were wrong. Perhaps even too mercilessly, too passionately. She detested "careerists in science," as she called them. Had no pity for them. Sometimes she turned on me too. "You are wrong. Don't be a coward. Admit it. Correct it." It was pointless to argue with her, to tell her that the deed had been done, and that it was stupid to recant now. She always prevailed, but this led to some quarrels between us. She was not always right, but she hated to admit her own mistakes. In this she resembled me.

Was she intelligent? Yes. Her intellectual range was very wide, but not always very deep. She grasped things rather than understood them. She went by touch, by intuition, by instinct.

She was afraid that she had no real creative talent. This often happens to women when they are sufficiently intelligent to realize their limitations. Less frequently to men. Men can usually fall back on their innate sense of masculine superiority, to delude themselves into exaggerating their capacities. She was especially conscious of this before Masha's birth. Then Masha filled up her life. Just as she filled mine.

Was she a pessimist? No. In this lay the greatest difference between her and me. I instinctively mistrust life, mistrust people. She had faith in life, in humanity. Even when people hurt her and let her down.

Did she love me? Yes. But how? Because of her compassion for a lonely old man? Probably in the beginning, but not later. And what about that other one—her husband? Did she also love him? Or was that mere pity?

And did I love her?

Did? The past tense shocked me. Didn't I still love her? Here was this woman, beautiful, intelligent, strong, and dead. In another half hour she would be a fistful of ashes. Could one love an urn with ash? No. I knew it even then. I was calmly analyzing it. Did Ziama's treatment take everything human out of me? But then, forgetting something and someone is also human. People do forget. Everything. In time I would forget Anna as well. And Masha will forget her very quickly—probably in a few days.

My merciless, pedantic, analytical "I" was at work again. Would someone else replace Anna in my life? There were other women in the world, after all. And some more beautiful, more intelligent, more desirable than Anna. No. Of that I was certain. This was the end of my "career" as a male. (Ziama has destroyed that instinct, has fully eliminated it. They do that in that psychopathic town of theirs. Well, if so, so much the better. I'll be able to live and work quietly—only for Masha.)

There were other thoughts. Even about science, about my work. Very simple, everyday thoughts . . . This black table with a coffin on it, with this beautiful dead woman in it, no longer affected me very much. Also, of course, I was completely emotionally exhausted. I could not even think of Masha for any length of time. Some strange serenity, tranquility, had filled me.

Others came into the room.

Someone—I think Tania—told me: "Go ahead, kiss her." I bent over, felt those cold dead lips on mine, and remembered how I was trying to revive her yesterday, to blow my life into her. And suddenly I was terrified. I realized everything—*everything.*

This was *my* Anna. And they were going to burn her up now. Like some trash.

November 4

Perhaps instead of "immortality" I ought to look into "somnology," to help create the science of dreams. A key for artificial happiness. I think that my concepts about it are broader than those of the people who now work in this sphere. Like Ziama, for instance. They have stumbled upon a tremendous discovery, but they don't quite know how to develop it to its full potential.

Take my own case, for instance. So much time has gone since Anna's death, but my dreams still live with me. They have become a part of reality for me. And what was "eliminated" then, the immediate hysteria of grief, has never come back. Only then, when I was kissing Anna's dead lips (a barbaric custom, really), was there a sudden short flare-up of that pain in me. But then, when I returned to the Sitniks and saw Masha, the dreams took over, and blotted everything else out. And "Anna"—even then—became a mere name, almost like any other.

I have had many talks with Ziama about dreams, and with other specialists, trying to get to the bottom of it. Some of them even worked with Ritter. (He died before fully developing his theory.) And all of them, it seems to me, underestimate the importance of Ritter's discovery. They are dragging it into a shallow water of technical application, designing and perfecting their mechanical equipment, rather than deepening the theory itself.

Ritter deciphered the mechanics of dreaming and created some primitive models in connection with this process. But he left no disciple who could take over and carry on after his death. The science as such stopped with his death. True, the technique has been developed and is being constantly developed, but technique alone is not enough. One must dig deeper and deeper into the basic idea.

This is how this thing stands at present. (I am quoting here some portions of one of my discussions with Ziama.)

Ziama: "Sleep as therapy is not a new thing, it has been used for perhaps a hundred years, clinically, that is. But dream control is something new, almost futuristic. We are just scratching the surface here. True, 'half-sleep' has become a reality. In that state all emotions can be greatly stimulated because the patient does not resist. His consciousness does not interfere, does not put on its brakes. Also, in this stage, the process of dreaming can be directed by vocal suggestion, channeled directly into the patient's brain. The practitioner, sitting beside him, can tell him what to see and what to hear. Thus dreams can be artificially created. That is what I did with you that night."

"Does this work every time?"

"Unfortunately, no. One must know his patient very well—must know what he *wants* to dream about. Then, the practitioner must have a certain talent, and a great mental concentration; in effect he is pumping images from his brain into the brain of the patient. And the quality of these images must be high; they must be free from all mental impurities. Often, when the patient awakens and tells about his dreams, they are something completely different from what the practitioner tried to induce."

"Dangers?"

"Yes, and quite realistic. First, emotions are very heightened, and this might lead to fixed ideas, manias, and other mental aberrations. A careless practitioner can play havoc with the patient's entire mental apparatus; everything, even the patient's ideology, might be changed, or at least disturbed. And then, in rare cases, the excess emotionalism might even prove fatal—too much adrenalin is secreted into the system."

"But surely it is impossible to change a person's convictions, his beliefs?"

"In a highly intelligent patient, this is impossible. But in some others, it is possible. It has been done throughout history, by religious and political fanatics and demagogues. And it is much easier to do when the patient's defense mechanism of rationalization is more or less completely inhibited. Convictions and beliefs are the result of prolonged educational processes augmented by personal experience—models of behavior anchored in emotions. In some they are stronger, in some, weaker. Usually natural dreams follow these preset lines—with the exception of sex fantasies, perhaps. A person who loves his child would not dream of torturing or murdering him. But in induced dreams, when all emotional guards are removed, almost anything is possible."

"But then the patient awakens, analyzes everything, and rejects what is unnatural to him."

"Usually, yes, but when the same suggestions are repeated over and over again, they affect the subconscious. This is why we must be extremely careful. It is actually possible, in some cases, to reshape the entire emotional structure of the patient—to change an evil man into a kind one, or at least a harmless one."

(Dangerous. And, like everything dangerous, fascinating.)

"But then the process can be reversed. This can be used to produce criminals."

"Produce, no; but develop criminal traits, yes. If a person is weak and susceptible. This is why, throughout the world, there are strict laws controlling this practice. I broke the law that night treating you; ordinarily, I could not do it without special permission from the Health Service. All medications we use are issued only to qualified medical men, but their synthesis is not particularly complicated. Some of them may be produced illegally. Only the other day, in Brazil, they arrested a doctor who was running an illegal "love dreamland." You see, sex is the strongest of all dream fantasies. Natural erotic dreams are normal—an outlet provided by nature. But repeated, induced sex dreams can lead to serious aberrations, even to crime. One client of that doctor raped several women and then murdered them. That's how they found that love clinic."

"Dream pornography?"

"Exactly. Fortunately, we escaped the tide of pornography which engulfed some countries years ago. They called us hypocrites and puritans, but finally they had to start controlling it. But not before several generations had been emotionally crippled by this poison."

■ ■

I had a serious conversation with Ziama about my own induced dreams after Anna's cremation.

"How did you take my love for Anna away from me? You did. Don't pretend. I was even angry with you about it."

"Here we are. Patients are never satisfied with their doctors. And with us psychologists this is even more so; it is practically a rule. They have their own models of themselves in their minds, and they are angry when they discover that those models are wrong—and they blame us. But we can only work with the material they bring to us."

"This was not my case. I loved Anna."

"Of course you did. And that was the danger. You were in a state of shock, and you're a pessimist by nature. And you do have a very pronounced suicide complex—"

"That's not true."

"That's true, and you know it. You like to have this escape hatch in the back of your mind. Your 'immortality' theory doesn't fool me; it is based upon your preoccupation with death. All right, Ivan. So this is how I approached the problem that night. At that point Anna represented death to you, and I wanted to take your mind off the subject and instill in you a desire to live. The best way, I thought, was to focus your attention on Masha. And this worked even better than I expected, because—well, why talk about it?"

"Oh no, continue. Because *what?*"

"Because apparently you made your choice between them long ago. Even though only subconsciously. The moment Masha was born, Anna became less important to you. This often happens to older men. Their sex urge is sublimated in their parental instinct. Sometimes . . ."

"Go on, go on!"

"Sometimes—and I don't say this in your case—removal of the wife comes as a relief to them. It eliminates a co-owner of something priceless to them, their child."

"How can you say that, Ziama? This is monstrous."

"The human subconscious is a dark sphere breeding all sorts of monstrous feelings. I'm sorry, but this is a scientific fact."

I was angry at Ziama when he told me that, and this led to a sharp argument between us. I told him that all his so-called "science" was a heap of rubbish. But now, when I think about it calmly, I know that Ziama had a good point there. And this is exactly why I was so angered by his words.

From that morning on, Masha became my whole world. Not just a part of it.

Undated

Yesterday Ziama brought to me some tapes and recordings from Valim. They all concern that man who killed Anna. Evgenyi Borisovich Stakhevich. Her husband.

He has been back there ever since the murder. His fate has not yet been determined. Because he was under psychiatric supervision at the time of the murder, criminal responsibility is excluded. He is now a medical problem, and the psychiatrists there are probably arguing which of his brain centers should be stimulated, and which inhibited. He is just the "experimental material." To me there is something utterly degrading about this. I still can't get used to the idea that criminals should be treated, and not punished.

Ziama, of course, doesn't agree with me.

"Can a person in sound mental health and with well-balanced emotions commit a murder? Of course not. Killing sick people like this, or worse still, putting them behind bars, is not only a barbaric absurdity, but a terrible waste for science."

I argued and argued, but Ziama stood his grounds. But I'm still unconvinced.

"Then tell me, Ziama: is he a criminal or not?"

"He's a sick man."

"But criminally insane?"

"That is a semantic blank which they used once. Just legal jargon. It is the same as calling a man 'criminally tubercular.'"

"All right. But if he is a sick man, a maniac, how could they release him from the hospital? Somebody must be to blame. This is criminal carelessness on the part of his doctors."

"No, Ivan. This is a very complicated and rare case. You know yourself that medicine has its limitations in the sphere of diagnosis and analysis."

"What is it then? A crazy exception?"

"Yes, something like that. Because one clinically cured man commits murder, we can't stop releasing people when they are cured. People have been known to die after taking an aspirin. Must we consider aspirin a deadly poison because of that? We can only go by the law of averages. What happened to Anna was one shot in a million. Just tragedy."

Anna had always disliked that word. She said that she liked Tolstoi because he had ridiculed this very concept. She was a convinced lover of life. Her ideology was based on her firm belief that it was actually possible to create universal happiness, not by drugs or chemicals, but by improving human nature. I had argued with her. I told her that life itself was essentially tragic because it led to death just when a person had developed a full taste for life. "Very well, then, instead of wailing and whining we must attack this problem." This is why she was so involved in my "immortality" idea; she felt that death was tragic merely because it killed people before they could live their full span of life. To her I was a sort of prophet. And, ironically, her very connection with me had brought her to violent death in the very prime of her life.

If that was not a tragedy, I don't know what is.

I have listened to the tapes and films that Ziama brought to me.

Why? I am not particularly interested in that miserable man. To me he is dead—or should be dead. A cruel streak in me? No. But keeping him alive seems to me more cruel than killing him. To me it seems cruel, even monstrous, letting him live with that thing on his mind, particularly if he can be cured into a full realization of what he has done. Anger? Revenge? No, those emotions don't come into it. Not after all that time.

The whole thing is called "Stakhevich Case. No. PA 11-319." ("PA," I think, stands for "psychiatric, or psychological, aberration.") The "case" consists of endless tests and analyses, most of them too technical to make any sense to me. Only special computers can digest and organize all this chaotic information. But there is one interesting tape which I have run time and time again, because it concerns me. It is just an "informal" conversation between Stakhevich and one of his doctors.

(I am citing here only some portions of it.)

■ ■

Q. Tell me how all this happened.

A. You had better ask me questions, Doctor. I don't think I can give you an accurate chronological description.

Q. Very well, Eugene Borisovich. [A very soft, persuasive voice.] Your case history, before your release from Valim, is well known. I have it here in my desk.

A. I know. Frankly, I have never considered myself really ill. Well, perhaps just after my son's death.

Q. Did you love that child?

A. That's a wrong word, Doctor. Is our conversation recorded? Are all the channels on?

Q. Yes, of course. But pay no attention to that. This is done just in order to help you.

■ ■

Ziama has shown me the curves and psychological and physiological parameters taken during that interview. Microprobes and telemetry. About twenty channels. The direct connection with the Calculus Center registering the general state of his emotional sphere at all points of this conversation. Ziama says, "a surprisingly normal clinical picture."

■ ■

A. I know. All these wires and gauges. I'm an electronics engineer. Was an engineer.

Q. You still are.

A. No. I know what I am, Doctor. A guinea pig to be experimented on until I die. That's my fate, and I don't really care.

■ ■

Ziama: "A very common reaction. It retards all rehabilitation work."

■ ■

Q. You are wrong, Evgenyi Borisovich.

A. I'm not. I'm a fairly intelligent person. I was a guinea pig ever since I came here first. Only when I was released, and stopped taking the prescribed medicaments, and stopped listening to my psychologist, Doctor Ivanoff, did I understand that I had been living here as an automaton, an animal, with all my normal reactions chemically and electronically suppressed.

Q. But that last course of treatments they gave you here did help you, didn't it?

A. Yes. It helped me very much. Or rather, I thought it helped me.

Q. It did. Otherwise you would not have been released.

A. Perhaps. You know of course that my wife was visiting me here?

Q. Yes. Were you glad she did?

A. Yes, I think so. No, I'm sure I was. We had always been close friends—besides everything else. But then . . . I don't know how to put it . . . in my state then I didn't particularly react to anything. Those drugs. They take everything human out of you, don't they?

Q. Had you ever spoken to her about your personal relations? Did you realize that this was a woman with whom you had a sexual relationship once?

A. Probably not. I don't remember. That interest was completely suppressed in me.

Q. Please, go on.

A. Well, only once. It was last autumn, I think. I remember that she told me she wanted to have a child. I could not understand what this meant—not then. I was just surprised. Only, later I started thinking about our son . . . and then, with every day, that thought—that pain—grew in me.

Q. Go on.

A. Then she came once again . . . told me that she would not be able to come for a while. I could not then understand why. I thought she just got tired of coming here. Of seeing me.

Q. Did you know that she was expecting a baby?

A. No, not then. It just didn't occur to me.

■ ■

Ziama: "You see what happens to a man when his sex instinct is thoroughly inhibited? He reverts back to the state of a child who doesn't connect his mother's big stomach with a sudden appearance of a new brother or sister. And in his case, his intellect was affected as well. He caused it himself by taking all those unprescribed hallucinatory drugs after his son's death. Had he gone to a good psychologist then, this would not have happened."

■ ■

Q. But they were already treating you with those new medications?

A. Yes, but I hadn't responded then. They took full effect only later. And then, of course, I understood everything. I knew that she must have had a love affair and must have become pregnant. But even that didn't affect me very much. I understood that this was normal—that she couldn't live like a nun while I was here. I was feeling better and better; and that was the main thing. I was becoming alive again.

Q. How did that manifest itself?

A. I started to reason. I started taking an interest in life, in everything around me. I began asking them to switch me to some more important work, with more responsibility. They did. It was just like sobering up after a long drinking spree. And it was then that I received a letter from her—or was it a telephone call? Yes, I'm sure it was a telephone call. She told me that she was expecting a child. But I already knew that. I took it very calmly and even told her that it was good for her. But then I was already lying. I was hurt. I felt that she was betraying not only me, but our dead son as well.

■ ■

Ziama: "Apparently the treatment was activating his sex instinct. All those spheres are interconnected. It is almost impossible to deal with one sphere without affecting some others. And then the treatment he was receiving was a new one and has been greatly improved since then. It was a new drug developed in India, but we have greatly improved it since we first received it, in our pharmaceutical laboratories. It now promises to be one of those 'miracle drugs.' "

At this point in the tape there is a long and rather uninteresting description of the treatment and his swift response to it. "For the first time I was consciously and even enthusiastically cooperating. I could feel the results and I was anxious to get out of this place." Eventually, after a series of examinations, he was released in the custody of one Dr. Ivanoff.

Back to the tape:

■ ■

A. They provided a comfortable little apartment for me and assigned me to an interesting and responsible work, designing electronic computers. Everything went very well. It was then that I first heard about Prokhoroff and his anabiosis experiment, and his connection with Anna. I think it was Anna who told me about it. I bought the book of his notes and read it. For some reason, it badly depressed me. In my mind I composed a picture of him. An egocentric—egoist—a man without a soul. A dried-up introvert in love with himself.

■　■

Did Ziama give me this tape on purpose? He could have easily edited this part out.

■　■

I was terribly sorry for Anna. I knew her so well, and I knew that she could not possibly be happy with a man like that. I knew already that they had a child, a girl. Strange, but to me she was never Prokhoroff's daughter, only Anna's . . . like a replacement for our son. Do you follow me, Doctor?

Q. I do. Please, go on.

A. Just as soon as I started working, I telephoned Anna. I asked her to come, to help me getting settled . . . I told her I needed her help . . . You see, I know Anna. If she feels that she is needed, she will rush in without thinking what she is doing. That's her nature, and I intentionally played on that. Dishonesty? Yes, I suppose so.

Q. Did you discuss this with your doctor?

A. No. You see I have never been able to establish a proper contact with Doctor Ivanoff. He was understanding and very kind, I liked and respected him, but I did not think he was intelligent enough to understand me.

■　■

Ziama: "A very common reaction. This was a side effect of the drug—a slight delusion of grandeur, a false sense of self-sufficiency. This has been eliminated now." Now. What good does it do poor Anna? They had no right to experiment like this.

■　■

And that's not all. I started to cheat. I practically stopped taking the medicaments he was giving me. I thought I didn't need them any longer. I kept throwing them away. And it was here that I started noticing Anna's attracting me . . . it was coming back to me . . . In my head I was formulating a plan—

Q. A plan?

A. Yes, of getting her back. I thought that if I played my part well, and did not show my anxiety, eventually her own love for me would revive . . . I wanted her back—with our daughter. You see, Doctor, I said, our daughter. Please notice this.

Q. I have.

A. I knew Anna—I mean, I knew her sensuality. You see, our marriage was very good, and I knew that she loved me once. Very much. And I knew that this was not merely emotional, but also physical—I don't like to talk about this side of it.

Q. Please do. This is very important.

■ ■

Here follows a long and very detailed discussion of their sex relationship, very frank, even shocking in spots. How strange; it was certainly not this way with us. If anything, I always felt that she was slightly frigid.

Ziama: "This might very well be his imagination. Men often delude themselves about this."

All right, but I still feel that Ziama should have edited this portion out. He knew it would be unpleasant for me to listen to all this near-pornography. According to Stakhevich, all this changed after the birth of their son, and Anna became satisfied and well-adjusted after that.

Now, back to the tape:

■ ■

Q. Did she visit you?

A. Yes, several times.

■ ■

And not a word to me! Ziama also claims that he did not know this.

■ ■

A. No, she didn't come very often. All together, three times I think. And every time I played my part well—I controlled my sexual desire for her. I did not want to scare her away. And it seemed to me that she was responding to my tenderness, was growing warmer and warmer toward me. To control my emotion I started to drink, but that only heightened my excitement. And all the while, the single thought was growing in my mind: to get her and our child back, to rescue her from that dry dead man who hadn't yet come out from his anabiosis—who really had no business coming out of it. I knew that finally he would destroy both of them.

■ ■

No, Ziama didn't give me this "confession" for nothing!

■ ■

A. From what she was telling me, or rather hinting, I understood that she wasn't very happy. She was involved in his crazy idea of immortality, but not in him personally. There was more pity there than love. Yes, pity, and a sense of duty—of self-sacrifice. That's Anna all over. She had that masochistic streak in her.

■ ■

Can all this be true? I had never felt it.

■ ■

Then, one day, during her last visit, I lost control. I told her that I still loved her and wanted her. This was about six weeks before that—that day. I don't remember my exact words. Perhaps they were very direct, even vulgar. Once, long ago, that kind of approach worked with Anna—excited her . . .

■ ■

This just can't be true!

■ ■

I must have overplayed my hand. She broke away from me, ran out and shouted back: "Go and see your doctor! I'm through with you!" I ran after her—"Anna! Wait a minute! Let me explain!" We ran out into the street. There were people around, and I could not speak to her then. She walked away, but then she turned and looked at me. And for a second, it seemed to me, she was struggling with herself—was almost ready to come back. At least, I was convinced of that then . . .

Q. And now?

A. Now, I don't know. But I still believe there was such a split second.

■ ■

How unpleasant to read all this! Even now, after all this time. Did I know her? Was there this split second? I think there was. Or not? Ziama says it was all his imagination, but I'm not so sure. It was also Ziama who told me once, "There is a multiplicity of emotional and physiological impulses in every human being, and their combinations are endless and unpredictable." One thing I know now, after listening to this tape: I was never a sufficient husband for her; our relationship, even physical, was purely cerebral. On my part, in any event. Still, was there that split second or not?

■ ■

Q. But she didn't come back?

A. No. She just turned and almost ran away. "Go and see your doctor." That's Anna—trying to help me even then. Well, I didn't go to any doctor, of course, and didn't tell Doctor Ivanoff anything about this. I was afraid he would send me back here. I was working well—even received a promotion. I now had five young designers working under me.

Q. Did you make any friends?

A. No. And all the while—I know it now—I was getting sicker and sicker. I was working nights, and every morning I would go and watch Prokhoroff take Masha to the day nursery. I already knew her name. Before our son was born, we agreed that, in the event we had a daughter, we would name her Maria. To me Masha was Anna's daughter, nobody else's. Anna told me that Prokhoroff adored the child, but I knew this was only because he thought she was a part of him. But I knew she wasn't. She was a part of Anna. But then, gradually, I was becoming sure that she was my child as well. No, not only emotionally, but physically. You know there is a theory that a child might inherit the traits of not his natural father, but another man who had physical relations with his mother before that second man. It's called telegenesis, I think . . .

■ ■

Ziama: "The correct term is 'telegony' and it has never been proved. According to this theory some genes of the first man remain in the body of the woman long after their physical relations have ceased. Some biologists accept this as a distant possibility, but it is losing scientific ground all the time."

Back to the tape:

■ ■

Q. And you never discussed this with Doctor Ivanoff?

A. Never. On the contrary, I was trying to appear as normal and well-balanced to him as I could. And I must have done well;

he was very satisfied with my progress. But all the while, I was getting ready to act.

Q. In what way?

A. I didn't know exactly. I had no definite plan. I thought that if I could see her again, and talk to her, I could first of all undo the damage which I had done during our last meeting. And so, a few days ago, I decided to go and see her. I knew she was alone in the house; I had been spying on them, and I knew all their moves. She opened the door, and I saw that she was frightened. But I told her how sorry I was for my last outburst, how silly it was of me. I also lied that I had seen a doctor, and that I was feeling fine. Well, they say maniacs are good actors. I even lied to her that I had met another woman and thought I was in love with her and wanted her advice. She must have believed me. She asked me in, offered me some coffee. For a moment I thought that the best thing for me would be to go away, but then she started asking me about my mythical love affair. And I kept lying. I even told her I wanted a divorce. This disarmed her completely. We were talking very casually, like two good friends. She told me about her work, about Masha. She even showed me some photographs of her as a baby. And then, it happened . . .

■ ■

A long pause. Then:

■ ■

Q. Well, go ahead.

A. I don't know what triggered it—I think she told me something about Masha resembling our dead Kolia. This hit me terribly hard. The next thing I knew, I had my arms around her. I am quite strong—when we were first married, I used to carry Anna in my arms. But here she broke away from me, rushed to the balcony and threw open the door. But I caught her and pulled her back. By that time I was an animal, a wild animal. She too was fighting like a cornered tigress. I never knew she had that much strength. We were rolling on the floor, overturning furniture, scattering books, papers, toys . . . Well, you know what we did to that apartment. I don't know how long all this lasted. I remember that all I was trying to do was to cut her off from the front door—not to let her escape. Then she hit me with something—I think a book—in the face, almost blinding me. It was the physical pain which really did it. You know my eye is still damaged, probably permanently. And it was here that that damned candlestick came in the way. The next thing I knew, she was lying on the floor. I rushed out of the apartment. The next two hours are a complete blank. I don't know what I did—probably just walked. I was completely frozen when I finally saw a militiaman and asked him to arrest me . . .

Q. You never thought of calling a doctor? It was still probably possible to save her?

■ ■

Yes, perhaps. But then the wound was a very bad one, cutting along the venous sinus. However, today they are treating traumas like that.

■ ■

A. No. I didn't think of it. It is impossible to tell why. I blacked out—just blacked out. And why didn't he call for help instead of running around the house?

Q. It was too late.

A. He had no way of knowing it was too late.

Q. And how do you know he was running around?

A. I saw it. I was in the park across the street, frozen. It was then that I gave myself up. It was then that I realized that my life was over. I'm very tired, Doctor. May we continue this later?

Q. Certainly.

■ ■

A click. But there was no continuation. Only endless purely technical tests. Colors, numbers, word associations. Brain curves, emotion diagrams. Chemical, electronic, musical reactions. The machines and computers had taken over.

Undated

Another March.

It is quite warm outside. A thaw.

This is the sixth year of my "second life."

Masha is four. Her education is placed on a strictly scientific basis. In our apartment we have the automatic teacher whom she calls "Dasha." A pleasant-looking plump woman on the screen, connected with the Institute of Pre-School Education. She poses questions to Masha, and Masha has to answer them by pressing different buttons. Some of these questions are rather complicated. Masha often looks at me expecting help, but I never help her. It is senseless to try to cheat a machine. When the answer is correct, Dasha smiles. If incorrect, she frowns a little and reformulates the question. I am proud. This particular machine is programed for six-year-olds. And Masha copes with it quite well, even though now and then she makes rather stupid slips.

She speaks two languages. Nowadays this bilingual education is encouraged. It is good exercise for the brain.

■ ■

It is now eleven o'clock at night. Time to relax and think.

Our life proceeds uneventfully, and like every life, on several parallel planes. For me, in any event.

Plane one, the most limited: thoughts about everyday living. Just the mechanics of it—health, food, sleep. Very infrequently, a slight sex urge, almost as a detached memory, like the taste of cabbage pies which my mother used to bake. Everything is limited by a single day with its usual worries, irritations, infrequent joys. Of course, this particular plane is dominated entirely by Masha. Getting her up, washing her, taking her to day children's home, bringing her back, feeding her, putting her to sleep.

Plane two: the work. There is now a tremendous amount of it

for me, and all unproductive. We are finally organizing our own Institute. The Academy has passed the resolution. True, still on a very modest scale, but nonetheless, our own Institute. Our baby. I have never been a director, and now I have discovered how difficult this is. Little administrative details claim masses of time. And finally I'm really growing old; my daily energy charge is becoming weaker and weaker. Fortunately, Katia has developed into a real scientist and a driving force behind our work. Should I retire tomorrow, the Institute would go on. Probably even better than now. But I have decided to work for as long as I can. Masha.

Plane three: thinking. About life, humanity, human society, time, and the universe. This is an ocean without a shore. But I know it well and know how to navigate in it. And I think that my brain is still adequate. It had better be, for a while. For Masha.

Then, there is another plane: skepticism. This is my own individual one. It has always been with me. My watchman. Sitting there and totaling up everything—actions, thoughts, dreams. Summing it all up, drawing conclusions. A merciless analysis—usually with negative answers.

I am trying to avoid this last plane. Otherwise, the whole machine begins to rattle, and you feel like turning the motor off. And I have no right to do it. Not while Masha needs me.

Life has its own wisdom, its own laws. Every time you drift into the abyss of analytical pessimism, something brings you out of it. Either Masha whimpers in her sleep or there is a telephone call posing some trite little problem. And you switch back into the endless conveyor of life.

Tonight I have slid deep down into the fourth plane. Why? Probably, the accumulation of fatigue and emotion. I have had a number of very difficult days. First, a trip to Moscow and bickering there about terms and allocations. Then home, facing my team. Of course, there was a general dissatisfaction about how little I had been able to get. They are young, nothing is ever enough for them. "This way we'll be floundering in the shallow water till the cows come home." It is true, things are going slowly, they always are, in science. Just yesterday we had to scrap an entire series of complicated experiments with electrodes. Two months' work gone to pot. And all because of a very small miscalculation in the beginning. Can those mistakes ever be eliminated?

There was also a sharp conflict with Masha. I told her not to do something, and she refused to obey. She has gotten into the habit of drawing pictures on the walls of her room. I threatened to spank her, but she refused to believe it. And the worst thing of all was that I couldn't do it. And this morning, there was another rabbit on the wall. I should consult Ziama about it. (He left us and went to Belsky at Valim with all of his dream setup. And I have a feeling that it isn't going as well as he hoped it would. Too many side effects.)

I also spoke to Professor Isakoff. He told me about his work: the study of psychological tendencies among modern youth. The general rise of material prosperity and the excess of free time is leading to the increase of sexuality. According to him. Other sociologists deny it, but I have a personal interest in it—my daughter. Also there are some political changes in South America which might lead to the rise of neo-Fascist tendencies. The military cliques in some backward countries are becoming more and more disturbed by the prospects of permanent peace and their own redundancy. (At least, all wars have been started by and fought by man. This again in connection with Masha. Everything I hear I immediately connect with her.)

I know that all this is not as dramatic as it sounds. "The normal fluctuation around the average level of mass human behavior." But then I personally lived through "a seam of history"—with the sewing machine going over me—and I don't want Masha to experience this. Pseudoscientific technological means for destruction have progressed to the point where just a few maniacs may destroy our little planet. Will true science be able to stop "evil science" from doing it?

Scientists. Small groups of people are trying to bring order into the world, without knowing much about how to go about it. "Improvement of human nature." A fine-sounding goal. "Immortality." And our means? Just our small imperfect brains creating wild hypotheses. What are the odds that they are correct? And our facilities? Just a third-grade institute with an obscure program and obsolete technical equipment.

Dreamers.

How infinitely complex are all those systems—the human psyche, for instance. How can our poor cortex with its ten billion cells reflect and model the human system composed of some 10^{27} (that is, 10 followed by twenty-seven zeroes) of complex molecules? Or our society whose components are still billions of times more numerous?

Then, another obstacle—the constant flux of self-adjustment. If the structure of the human psyche remained constant, it would be possible, perhaps, to create more or less satisfactory general models. But everything in nature is fluid and is in motion, and it is mathematically impossible to calculate and predict all these changes.

No model can predict what changes will occur in the next hundred years, and how they will affect human nature and human society. And in a thousand years? Or in a million?

Fortunately there seems to be no prospect of thinking robots taking over. Last year Professor Yamaga blew up his Omyokone, set fire to the building and committed suicide. Now some of his disciples are trying to recreate his artificial intellect; but even they admit that this will take many years. (At least Yamaga's suicide proved that he was sincere. He probably came against a blank wall, and knew that he would not be able to break through it.)

That's science. No matter where one looks, there seems to be a blank wall. Now I am almost convinced that I made a mistake by not going back to anabiosis. Yura's latest achievements in this sphere are really remarkable. And he still invites me to join him—scrapping my "immortality" scheme. One should really stick to something one knows and not chase rainbows.

(Incidentally that Stakhevich has developed a remarkable new computer working on some entirely new principle, according to Ziama. He will never be released again, of course; but Ziama predicts a brilliant future for him in electronics. Only I seem to be lagging behind everyone. Somewhere along the line I let my creative energy escape from me, and could never recapture it fully.

Was this Anna? Sex is a powerful drain on man's creative capabilities. But then, I would not have Masha.)

I am particularly depressed tonight.

■ ■

Let us try to analyze everything and put it into a proper prospective.

First of all, I have a daughter.

This, in effect, is my personal immortality—a perfect biological model to work on. And it is not enough to educate her to be an intelligent and decent human being. I must develop her into a person who will carry on my work—contributing something toward the creation of a better human society.

Yes, this is the most important contribution I can still make to the world.

In what I have failed, she will succeed. Modern technology combined with social ethics will permit the creation of a nearly perfect model of perfect human society. And then some correctives can be introduced into it all the time—keeping up with all the "molecular" changes.

(The skeptic within me disagrees: "Empty words. There are different models, and each considers itself better than all others.")

Yes, but progress is being made. Even today scientists speak the same language. The part played by science in life is growing. Intellect is overcoming ignorance and passions. The brain will triumph over instincts.

(The skeptic: "More empty words. The voice of intelligence is drowned in the ocean of prejudice. It can't reach humanity as a whole.")

Yes, it can. And it will. It must.

■ ■

Then, Ivan Nikolaevich, everything is in order and there is nothing to worry about? The natural process of progress will bring humanity into a new Golden Age?

No, it is not natural. Human nature is very imperfect and is not designed for any automatic Paradise. Passions can swerve it away from the true direction at any time.

Yes, but this is not inevitable. Every detour can be righted, every mistake corrected.

Then, we must struggle. Even a very small contribution of a very small group of intelligent people like ours improves the chances for final victory of intelligence.

(The skeptic: "Yes, but how much? Very close to a mathematical zero. Is it worth it?")

Yes, it is. Even if only because this creative process brings peace and contentment to those who are engaged in it. It makes better human beings of every one of them.

Then everything is clear, right, and simple? Hurray! No more confusion, no more doubts? Don't delude yourself, Prokhoroff. If it were all so simple, you wouldn't be sitting here alone, in this room, with that terrible emptiness in your heart with all those numerous "I's" inside you at loggerheads with one another.

No, Prokhoroff. Learn to live with this emptiness. It will be with you tomorrow, and the day after, and a year from today, and always. Until the Skeptic will say for the last time: "Here we are, Ivan Nikolaevich. The end of the line. And what have I told you?"

But Life will not hear his voice.

For many years, for so many years, I have been guarding myself from all emotions which could disturb my mythical mental superiority. I was a miser hoarding my own ego, afraid to share it with anyone—only to discover that my hoarded treasure is the fistful of ashes which will one day stand on someone's shelf—just like Anna's ashes in that urn over there.

■ ■

In the next room Masha has coughed in her sleep. A stab in the heart. I knew she should have worn her warm coat this morning, thaw or no thaw.

■ ■

Immortality.